THREADING THE LOOM

A NOVEL BY
CAROL CRAIG

Library of Congress Cataloging-in-Publication Data

Craig, Carol, 202e
        Threading The Loom / Carol Craig.
    p. Cm. -- YA Fantasy
        ISBN 978-1-73622227-5-1

Interior Design by Sara Rolat.
Cover design by Darrin Brenner: D. Brenner Art & Design.

Printed in the United States of America
09 10 11 12 13 RRD 7 6 5 4 3

The Tapestry Series:

… is filled with adventure, survival, courage, restoration, and friendship. The author's voice is rhythmical and poetic, making the fantasy much more engaging. Brigid Dunsmore never had a dull moment: bats, insects, plagues, caves with jeweled-looking stalactites and stalagmites, flower gardens, and danger. This book has it all: good versus evil, laughter and tears, and a very satisfying ending.

Award-winning author of *Captured Secrets*, Carmen Peone

I don't want to spoil this wonderfully engaging read for anyone, so I won't give away why this loom is so amazing or why it's so sought-after by both the heroes and villains. Such a well-written, captivating, and original story for all ages!

Evan Howard, Author of *The Galilean Secret*

This author, Carol Craig, brings to our literary world her expertise in word crafting. I read the entire book in one day! It was too hard to put down. Brigid, though downtrodden, is brought through amazing challenges that threaten to change her good spirit. One woman stands alone to face the traditions of an emotionless community, where no one dares stand up to the heartless standards, let alone allow any woman a voice or emotion. Like a fever, the masses follow her, enabled by her bravery to proclaim a joyful existence and denounce the ideology of evil ruling mankind.

Karen Hall, author of *Hasonta, The Lost Tribe,* and *Jennica's Secret*

Other Novels By Carol Craig

From The Tapestry Fantasy Series:

Dancing the Loom
Threading the Loom

Southern Historical Novels:

The Vast In Between
The Great Unraveling

The Mending Warrior Series:

A Thousand Bits of Wonderful
A Walk in the Dark

For Les, Sara, and Kaylee
My three beacons of light

Strange times are these in which we live
When old and young are taught falsehoods
in school. And the person who dares to tell the truth
is called at once a lunatic and a fool.

~Plato

All around the manor, the distant sound of fireworks pop-pop-popped from every corner of the kingdom. I peered through the window of my bedroom in time to see the pyrotechnic displays bursting through the overcast sky in a kaleidoscope of color—every color in the rainbow, in fact. Mouth open in equal parts fear and awe, I rushed out of my room and down the stairs, my blue falcon trailing me with a squawk. The celebrations for the New Year were slated for later in the month.

So why are fireworks going off now?

But before I could posit an answer, Private Tucker burst through the door dressed in his military uniform and let out a blast. "He's dead. Alaric the Third, son of Faineant the Foul, is dead!"

Everyone rushed to see what all the fuss was about. Soon the entire household had joined in the parlor to hear the joyous news. But I, Brigid Anne Dunsmore of the house of Dunsmore, formerly a scullery maid, felt as though a stormcloud were hovering over my head, just waiting to burst. To rain down on each and every one of us. I tried to still my breathing but couldn't.

I watched as my beloved Henry clasped his brother Thomas in a rare display of affection, while Beatrice, Jocelyn, and Gertrude danced circles around the pair. Only Emma, like me, remained quiet. Her reasons for doing so remained unclear, but I had a feeling it had more to do with her love for Thomas and her jealousy of said women than for any sadness at Alaric's departure. Alaric, who had rained terror on us all, sending out armies of ants by the billions to subdue us with their formic acid, coddling moths to tear the very clothes from our body, and wee little beetles that when paired with sun appeared like small jewels, though they were anything but what they appeared. In ancient times, those beetles had been the scourge of Egypt, a plague upon the land.

No, Alaric had tried to thwart us at every turn until I, along with Henry, Thomas, and Emma, had formed an almost entirely female army to subdue him. Though we had failed in our mission, it seemed that nature had done what we could not.

"Wait!" I shouted, throwing up my hands.

The dancing ceased with a little help from Lord and Lady Bookbinder, who begged for quiet in their household. "What is it?" the staid Lord Bookbinder demanded, recognizing that I needed to be heard.

"How did Alaric die?" I asked the messenger.

Everyone stopped, all eyes riveted on Private Tucker.

"Yes, how *did* he die?" Lady Bookbinder's normally well-coiffed cornsilk hair sat askew at this early hour of the morning.

For all his stature, the private merely said, "It's claimed that he was poisoned, but by whom, we have no idea. Not yet, at any rate."

Despite everything that the man represented, I, like the others, breathed in a collective gasp of disbelief. Who? One of ours . . . theirs? Who had done the deed?

As if he could read my thoughts as surely as Alaric had read the thoughts of those closest to him, a trick I had yet to understand, Private Tucker said, "It's too soon to say. But I grant you, we are looking into it, as are Alaric's allies, I'm sure."

Lady Bookbinder paled, her normally hearty complexion sallow. Even Lord Bookbinder seemed nonplussed, his dark visage and equally dark hair a contrast to the vapid color of his face.

For her part, Emma walked over to Lady Bookbinder and clasped her hand in a sign of solidarity, her long red hair curled and appearing as fresh as though it'd been recently styled and groomed, despite the early hour. Light freckles dotted her face against green eyes, and yet she was the picture of a woman in love, as though she wore a constant halo.

Henry must have sensed my distress because he bade the trio of women to let him through so that he could come stand beside me. A little over a year had passed since we'd returned from our foray to Alaric's fortress that bordered Canada, to the northwest of where we lived in upstate New York. Henry wrapped me in his arms, much to the huff of the other three, and pressed my head to his shoulder. His long red hair had been pulled back and tied with a leather thong, but his face was still tanned from our days in the countryside.

"What is it?" He tucked aside my nearly black hair that had grown and filled in over the past six months. "Why aren't you happy?"

How could I tell him? I don't know how I knew, I just *knew*, in my heart of hearts, that something was wrong. What should be a blessed event that would spare many lives, was not.

"I don't know, Henry, but I'm afraid."

"Of what?" he pressed.

Again, I simply shook my head. It must seem silly to him. As I lay my head against his shoulder, I drank in his scent, so like cinnamon and honey. How I had missed that this past year, since we'd returned from our quest to halt the reign of terror bestowed upon us by Alaric. Slowly, Henry had been reabsorbed into daily life, and it was as if our time together had been merely a dream. We had been a team, he and I, and I had felt his love as surely as the first rays of sunshine in spring, the smell of meadowfoam that scented the fields and provided nectar for the bees.

I peered up at him, tears staining my eyes, tears that still must not be shed according to the "traditions" I had come to loathe. Only in the privacy of each others' company had we been able to show real emotion, unlike on our trek, where I had been allowed to lead, to change the rules, to treat others with the kindness not allowed now that we were once again entrenched in the manor, located within the surrounding countryside. Why, oh why, were we powerless to change these loathsome rules?

Henry lifted my chin and kissed me tenderly to the intake of breath from all those around me, for it was the height of poor etiquette to do so in public. Still, he never wavered, merely searched my eyes, those most cerulean blue orbs that had reminded my mother of arctic ice, the bubbles squeezed together so tightly that they radiated sparks of blue light flecked by tiny bits of gold.

"Do you love me, Henry?" I whispered in his ear.

"How can you doubt it after all we've been through together?" he murmured, aware that all eyes were upon us.

I sighed then, relieved to know that although he'd once again been pressed into service, he still remembered me. Still cared for me.

"I don't know." I bowed my head, unwilling to look him in his beautiful brown eyes, he with the swath of red hair that swooped down on one side to meet his ear. He who knew me better than anyone else, possibly even better than Emma. "I'm just feeling insecure, I suppose."

"Well, don't," he reprimanded. Once again, he lifted my chin so that I might face him. "If you're worried about something, perhaps you should query your loom, see what it has to say about all of this . . . with Alaric and the like."

My magical loom foretold the future. I had been so relieved to find it unharmed upon my return, safe in the bosom of the manor, that I had stroked it, spoken to it as if it were a person, telling it about our heroics, about our catastrophes, about everything it had missed since I was gone. In return, it gave me information, warning me that something was afoot. And yet, whenever I asked it directly who or what I should fear, it supplied only a shadowy figure as though shrouded in darkness. But I could feel the evil intent and it frightened me. I hadn't told Henry about it. He already thought me daft at times. Thought me incapable of ever understanding the intricacies of the traditions laid down—more like laws, really, but highly unjust laws, as far as I could see. Laws that made us all unhappy in equal measure, save perhaps for me, who felt it more keenly. For I hadn't grown up with these laws and knew none of them. All I knew was that no one must help me learn them. I must learn them for myself through pain and consequence, which often resulted in rashes, sore feet or knees, cuts, bruises. Fortunately, they were fewer now—now that I had made a pact with my fellow female warriors not to harm them, and they were to harm none of those who had served in our army as well. But that still left a fair number of antagonists to smite me when I had failed to do what was expected.

Henry tweaked my nose and jerked his head toward the staircase where my beloved loom lay waiting for me. He was right. I hugged him tightly, wishing I could go on hugging him forever, but I realized by the clearing of Lord Bookbinder's throat that we were making a spectacle of ourselves. So, I gave a brief curtsey and said a hurried goodbye, then headed upstairs, my blue falcon, Phinney, hopping first on the Big Ben finial at the bottom of the stairs, then up the railing, all the while letting out satisfied chirps. I, on the other hand, ran up on stockinged feet, slamming into the door at the top of the landing where my room resided. The door flung open with a resounding crash, and much to my surprise a woman, one of the downstairs maids, rushed to her feet and let out a cry of alarm.

"What are you doing here?" I realized too late that the woman was carrying a letter opener that she wielded like a knife.

"Stand back!" she declared, her eyes wild and her narrow features appearing suddenly catlike. "I'm here to collect the loom."

"Jesse, is that you?"

But Jesse no longer looked like the scullery maid from the Bookbinder household, for her hazel eyes held something vague and sinister in them. Something she had hidden from me before. And as if to prove it, the loom began tapping out a rhythm, light dancing across it in vivid colors—blue, green, yellow, red. All the colors of the rainbow. And when the loom was done clacking, there stood a young man who looked shockingly similar to Alaric only with a normal widow's peak instead of the reverse widow's peak that Alaric sported. His features were narrower than Alaric's, his lips more full, almost feminine in their appearance. He was shorter, but he bore the same arrogant smirk, as though he alone knew a secret that the rest of us were not privy to. But what frightened me most, he bore the same ring as Alaric. The evil prince would have never given it to someone other than a son.

Yet Alaric had no son, had he?

Few displayed any emotion as they laid Alaric to rest beneath an oversized monument meant to reflect the man himself. Birsha stood before the vast assemblage, his breath

clouding the frigid air, every man, woman, and child in the
village forced to attend, despite the bitter cold of late December.
He clapped his gloved hands together for warmth. Birsha
detested that he'd been named "Son of Wickedness" by his cruel
and demanding caretaker, who had stood in place of his father
and kept him safely hidden in the forest, training him for the
day when he would take over his father's kingdom.

Birsha scanned the men and women before him wondering
who had done the deed. Who had killed his father, Alaric? His
eyes halted at the Kazakh dressed in a red fox fur, felt-brimmed
hat, his large yak-hair vest draping his massive shoulders and
fur-lined knee-high boots gracing his feet. For a brief moment,
Birsha took stock of the man, of the bald eagle attached to
his gloved hand by a leather lead. He had heard through the
grapevine that Alaric was afraid of the Kazakh. It was rumored
the man had set his birds upon an ally who had crossed him, but
poison? He hardly seemed the type.

Birsha's golden eyes, a gift from his mother it was said,
moved next to Generals Cedric and Weathermore. They had
been loyal confidantes of Feinart the Foul, but no love had been
shared for his son, Alaric, according to Birsha's informants. Both
were getting on in age. Weathermore was tall and swarthy, with
a neck as thick as the trunk of a *quercus blanchette* oak whereas
Cedric was short and small. No, Cedric reminded Birsha of an
aging Napoleon . . . without the widow's peak, the lucky man.
Birsha had done everything he could to avoid *that* particular
inheritance of his father's, but to no avail.

As the trumpets began to announce the commencement of
the ceremony, Birsha turned to view Alaric's Council, a strange

mix of men and women with talents so odd as to be almost unbelievable.

First among them was Cricket, the entomologist, a tiny woman with odd brown eyes, no irises whatsoever. And despite the gloom, or perhaps because of it, her clothing shimmered with jewel beetles that flashed aqua blue and purple wings. Today, her cotton candy hair had been tamed with some unnamed oil and braided into a myriad of miniature braids that made her appear as though she had dozens of snakes cascading down the sides of her face. According to Birsha's records, she kept all manner of insects, from potato bugs down to click beetles whose acrobatic abilities were known far and wide. They ate other beetles. Birsha grimaced at the thought.

Next came the goddess of both weather and nature, Tempestous, whose fiery nature was on full display. Today, her flaming moire robe and red hair seemed especially feral amid the new-fallen snow, her pale skin and blood-red lips a blotch against the landscape. Birsha shuddered to think that she controlled nature in its many more abhorrent forms.

Birsha continued down the line, moving next to a pair of reptile wranglers, brother and sister, as it were. Liz Herd's skin was mottled and reptilian. Instinctively, he stepped back, wanting nothing more than to be away from her and her brother Chame Leon who, like his namesake, could change color at will. It was now a frosty white. But it was their wide-set, almond-shaped eyes and golden irises that were most mesmerizing. Birsha forced his eyes away to the next person on the Council.

This one was no better than the last, for his name was

Fishmonger and his skin was scaly and flashed the color of a rainbow trout. It was said he preferred predator fish like the shark and the piranha. Birsha moved quickly on, stopping in front of the Queen of the Mammals. Birsha paused when he saw her and cocked his head, confused, for she was nothing if not ordinary. Human. Birsha had overheard one of the staff saying she was kind to her animals. What on earth was she doing among this misanthropic bunch, he wondered with a frown? But he had no time to ponder her further, because at that moment, the trumpets ceased and all eyes turned to Cedric and Weathermore, who took turns lauding Alaric's many feats, his successful raids. The pair spent a great deal of time speaking about the man before they gave the go ahead to lay Alaric's body to rest beneath a tomb that had been especially designed in onyx with pillars and capset. On it, in bas relief, was the image of Birsha's late father in full military regalia, the cape appearing as if it were truly flowing in the wind. But what unnerved Birsha were the marble eyes, so realistic beneath the heavy fold of Alaric's brows that it appeared as though he were glaring at Birsha wherever he moved within the snowy setting. Birsha stamped his boots in the crusted snow, wishing he could shed himself of the fear those eyes instilled in him as easily as he had the crusted snow beneath his boots.

"Here we lay a great man to rest," he heard Cedric say.

Then slowly, the casket was lowered into the gaping hole, a wound gouged into the earth before the monument. Birsha didn't begin to breathe again until the last of the shovelfuls of soil was strewn, muddying the snow around it. As if to wipe away the stain, another man came with shovelfuls of snow to wash the landscape clean.

"Now we must pray," Weathermore said. They bowed their heads, the villagers shuffling their feet to warm them. Children moaning about the cold were quickly shushed. For what seemed an inordinately lengthy amount of time, even for Birsha, Weathermore prayed. Prayed for the kingdom, prayed for the weather, prayed to win future battles. And finally he prayed that Birsha would bring honor and glory to the kingdom.

Birsha's chest swelled. Even before the old man had died, Birsha had wanted to expand the kingdom. Had seen his time on the stage as the natural progression of things. He didn't realize the praying had stopped until he heard the words, "And now we introduce you to your new ruler and king, Birsha." Birsha opened his eyes only to discover all eyes on him.

"Welcome," he said to one and all. "I am your new leader. I will continue the benevolence of my father before me."

But to his surprise, instead of welcoming him in return, he saw hundreds, if not thousands of eyes light up in fear at this announcement and a brief murmur that rose up like a squadron of army ants.

"Well, well," he muttered. Apparently, his caretaker hadn't told him everything.

2

"I repeat, what are you doing here?" I said to the scullery maid. Clearly, she had sought to avoid detection as she skulked around me, her finely honed letter opener still poised my way.

"You say anything to anyone about me being in your room, and you'll breathe your last," she said, her dark eyes feral in the way they stalked me.

I had been through too much, seen too much, to let her stop me with a simple letter opener. With one swift kick, I arced my leg out and landed her on the floor, all the while praying that she didn't impale herself with her makeshift weapon. As soon as she hit the floor, I knelt down to see that she was okay. Fortunately for me, the letter opener flew across the room, landing beneath my beloved loom. For seconds, I glanced away from her, but that's all it took. Before I could fathom what she was doing, she grabbed the leather thong around my neck and yanked. Then she scrambled to her feet and bolted through the door.

I gave chase, yelling the entire way down the stairs. By the time I reached the landing, everyone was there, all except Jesse.

"Did you see her?" My breathing came in short bursts.

"Who?" Henry balled his fists, as though ready to do battle for me, if need be.

"Jesse . . . the scullery maid," I said when I saw his blank look. "She was one of Alaric's plants here to steal the loom, but I stopped her! She grabbed my necklace instead. Have you seen her?" I repeated breathlessly.

All present shook their heads, confusion written in the puzzled expressions and arch of their brows. My eyes flew wide. If she hadn't come this way, then the only way she could have gone was . . .

I ran back upstairs, checking each room as I went, barging in on poor Gertrude who had returned to her room to preen. It wasn't until I arrived at the final room on the landing that I saw the open doorway and window, the drapery fluttering inward as if on a sultry breeze. But it was anything but sultry on this brisk day. I raced to the window and peered down. The fop had planned well, for a rope hung from the window, no doubt to lower my precious loom to the ground once Jesse had it. To a waiting carriage, if my suspicions were right. As if to prove my point, I noticed fresh tracks wending off into the distance. My heart stilled in my throat, for she had the one thing besides the loom that had tied me to the past—my round locket that when opened with a tiny latch produced a hologram. A hologram in which I could conjure up any time and place in my childhood.

It was all I had left of my family. The family that had been stolen from me. Sorrow swept over me in a wave of grief, so much so that I forgot all about tradition and wailed through the opened window.

Down below, I heard footsteps tromping their way up the stairs. Moments later, Henry appeared at my side and wrapped me in his arms while I wept on his shoulder.

"She has my locket, Henry!" My throat closed tight with despair.

Soon, a whole host of eyes were staring back at me with alarm as I continued to sob, not caring how I looked or what punishment I would receive. I had done the unthinkable. I had defied tradition by crying. I would pay for it later that day or on the morrow, but for now, the only thing that concerned me was that my locket was gone, and with it, my past.

"Henry, may I speak to you?" Lord Bookbinder stood near the door of what turned out to be Jocelyn's room, Lady Bookbinder at his side.

Henry hugged Brigid a final time, but not before he had promised her he would find her locket and return it to her, its memories intact. In the meantime, Jocelyn shooed everyone out of her room, incensed that so many eyes had been cast over her private domain. Henry just hoped that Brigid would be okay until he could set off to capture the thief and the person who had aided and abetted the scullery maid. Then he followed his parents downstairs.

"What is it?" Henry asked, once they were safely ensconced in the study. Scores of books filled the shelves, many with miniature paintings of famous people set into the fine Moroccan goat-skin leather. Shakespeare, who needed no introduction. Anne-Josèphe Terwagne, political activist from the French Revolution. And lastly the Italian, Catherine de Medici, queen consort of France. Those were but a few of the fine collections Henry had cherished, even as a child. Yet now, as he stood before his parents, he couldn't help but feel a twinge of nervousness when he saw the undertones of concern they shared with a single look.

Lord Bookbinder cleared his throat. "See, it's–"

"Just that we need you to do something for us," Lady Bookbinder said, cutting to the chase. She had yet to don her daily outerwear, still dressed in robe and slippers. It was so unlike his mother to be seen by so many in her nightwear, but today's circumstances were unique indeed, as the fireworks had yet to cease, sounding like nothing less than a hundred guns going off at once.

Yet again, the pair flashed nervous glances at each other, the stress of the moment sending shards of fear glancing through Henry.

"Spell it out, already," Henry said in a rare pique of anger.

"Son–" Lord Bookbinder clapped his hands together. "We need to send you on a reconnaissance mission . . . to see what this new king is like. This Birsha person. We would send one of our spies, but we trust you to be discreet."

"You will be leaving by nightfall." Lady Bookbinder clasped Henry's arm, her gray-green eyes filled with apology.

It was not a request.

"But what of Brigid's locket? It was given to her by her parents . . . the parents she hasn't seen in over two years. She doesn't even know if her family is alive, much less where her brothers and sisters reside."

Lord and Lady Bookbinder knew all about Brigid's unhappy break from her family after their fortunes had been lost, each of the family's members scattered to fate's whims, Brigid as a scullery maid in Ma'am's household, her brothers and sisters to parts unknown. The only one whose whereabouts Brigid knew was that of her mother, and she lived in a cramped apartment in a town far from here.

Lady Bookbinder reached down and grasped Henry's hand. "A locket is nothing by comparison to what we are requesting of you. We have a disguise prepared for you. You will be going as Count Augusta from Durham, England. I will send a tutor with you to practice British dialect and to fill you in on the details. Until then, you are to go upstairs and rest. We are preparing your horse."

Henry thought of Windtamer, the horse he'd been given as talisman. Old Red, the horse he'd had for years, had been none too pleased at having been supplanted by the newer thoroughbred. He'd given Henry the cold shoulder more than once, and had even gone so far as to cater to Brigid whenever the two were together, acting as if Henry weren't even present.

"Did you hear what your mother said?" Lord Bookbinder faced Henry, he too in robe and slippers, his pipe laying cold on the gargantuan desk.

"Yes, I heard," Henry said with a sigh.

Now to tell Brigid. He doubted she would take it well. They had been apart so much this past year, since he'd been required to attend his duties. And Brigid . . . well, she had been all but forgotten. He'd seen her floundering while at the manor, having little to bide her time. Just one short year ago she had been leading an army of women. Making decisions. Enduring hardships. She'd become a true leader. Yet here she was once again relegated to the role of "woman," as if that were the only position in life afforded the fairer sex. Nurturer, Mother, Manager of Household. No doubt Brigid had done little in regard to any of these occupations expected of a woman. No wonder she was floundering. There was no place for her here.

"But Mother . . . Father," Henry implored, "I can't leave Brigid behind, alone. She needs me."

"You have no choice, Henry." Lord Bookbinder narrowed his eyes, meaning for Henry to broach no opposition. "You will do as requested, do I make myself clear?"

"I'm sorry," Lady Bookbinder quickly inserted. And he could see that, indeed, she seemed very sorry, for her expression was one of utter contrition, and the light in her eyes had dimmed as she fought back tears, the few that Henry had seen over a lifetime at the manor. For tears were thought to make one appear weak, but Henry knew this not to be true. He'd seen them in Brigid . . . the other women. And he also saw the healing they brought to all, Henry included.

"I will do as asked." But so as not to be totally cowed, Henry turned back one final time before leaving. "But if it was up to me, I would take Brigid. You couldn't find a stronger person than her . . . man *or* woman."

Lady Bookbinder gasped, while Henry's father slammed his fist onto the table. Nobody spoke to him that way, Henry knew. But he was beyond caring. He needed to speak to Brigid, and he needed to speak to her soon.

"What do you mean, Henry is leaving?" I turned on Emma who had risked coming to my room despite knowing that I might react badly. And indeed, she was right, for I couldn't stop pacing and I'd bitten my lip almost to the quick.

"You have to calm down, Brigid," Emma said. "I'm sure Henry plans to tell you."

But anger had supplanted all reason and I turned on my heel, throwing a hand in the air. "And when was he planning on telling me that?"

Emma pressed a finger to her lips, urging my silence, but fire burned in my belly, and no doubt had clouded my features, because I had risked all for this family of his and yet I was still being treated like a child. And perhaps that's what women were to them, children. I forced a deep breath, determined not to let my emotions get the best of me. I knew that many deemed women equals, but many more did not . . . . far from it. We were to be seen but not heard, to cook, to clean, to take care of our families, and if we had none, then other women's families. Never were we allowed to think, to form an opinion other than the prevailing ones heretofore set out by men. No, we were chattel, nothing more. And I couldn't accept that. Not after everything I had been through with women who had shown untold courage in battle and beyond, who had risked life and limb for their compatriots. Who, in the end, had become sisters and friends. I had enormous respect for most of them.

For one brief moment, I closed my eyes before opening them. "When does he leave?"

Emma's expression was heartbreaking, for it was clear that he would be departing sooner rather than later. I fought back tears—tears that could only bring about more misery. As such, my throat tightened instead and an unfathomable weight settled on my chest.

"He leaves tonight," she whispered.

She tried to reach a hand out to me, but I couldn't be consoled, not yet. I needed time to process what she'd said, to come to a decision, for no way would I let him be drawn to the fortress of Alaric's men without me at his side because whether he knew it or not, we were a team. And a good one at that. And I loved him. Just not these accursed traditions.

"Tonight," I finally said through clenched lips.

Emma simply nodded. "Thomas says he won't let Henry go by himself."

A wave of relief washed over me. At least someone was thinking clearly.

"And Brigid," Emma said, her head down and her voice conspiratorial, "I won't let Thomas go without me, either."

"Then it's done." I embraced her suddenly.

She stepped back so that she could look at me fully. "What do you mean?"

"I won't let Henry go alone, either. I'm coming too," I added, to further my point.

Phinney began to chirp, as though putting her two cents in, as if to let me know that she refused to be left behind either.

Emma plopped down onto the chair next to the bed, the loom at her side. "You know Henry's never going to allow all of us to put ourselves in harm's way."

"I know." I sat on the bed. "So how do you propose we go without him knowing that we're coming until it's too late for him to do anything about it?"

"Well…" Emma said, dragging out the word. Then she leaned in and began whispering. "Winnifred has an invention that she's built. She wants us to come see it."

"An invention? What kind of invention?"

Emma just shrugged, her red hair flowing in the breeze, as I had yet to shut the window that I had opened after the harrowing event that had just occurred, needing fresh air to calm my dejected spirit. I hadn't even had time to figure out what to do about my locket before Emma had come barging into the room, rosy red cheeks burnished from the news she'd just collected from Thomas.

"Dunno. Winnifred's always inventing one odd thing or another. Said something about a compass and compressors. I have no idea what she's talking about. But she thinks it will help us next time Alaric—I mean, this new fellow—comes calling, whoever he might be."

"Hmm." I ran a finger across my lips, thinking. "What if we go into town, meet up with Winnifred. Then have Thomas come up with some lame excuse why he needs to stop at Winnifred's house."

And just like that, Emma and I were once again co-

conspirators to save both Henry and Thomas, *and* our kingdom.
We would just have to take our lumps, come what may, and
I knew they would come. I clung to the foot post of my four-
poster bed, or at least the one lent me by the Bookbinders. We
could explain that we wanted to celebrate the news of Alaric's
death with our friend. The Bookbinders would believe that.
But no sooner had I thought of it, my cheeks warmed, for
the Bookbinders had been nothing but kind to me. I hated to
deceive them, but for Henry's sake, I would have to.

"I'm in," Emma said with glee.

Yet when we looked at each other, we could read the
trepidation in each other's eyes. The last time we had risked all,
Emma and Thomas had ended up in the dungeon, and Henry
and I had rescued them. If only we could be so lucky the next
time around.

"What do you mean they're gone?" Henry saddled his horse
and cinched the strap around Windtamer's middle.

Thomas entered his horse's stall and placed the bit into her
mouth, then brought the horse out to stand beside Henry's.

"What are you doing?" Henry groused as he prepared his
horse's saddlebags.

Before Thomas answered, he lifted his saddle onto his
horse's back with a loud "oomph" and pulled the reins up over
her head. "I'm coming with you," he said as though it were the
most natural thing in the world.

"What do you mean?" Henry demanded. "Have you

spoken to Mother and Father?"

"No, and you're not going to, either. I'm not letting you go alone."

Henry stopped what he was doing. He patted his horse, giving himself time to think. So far the day had turned into a nightmare. One of Alaric's spies had broken into Brigid's room and stolen her locket, now his parents were sending him on a very dangerous mission. Worse yet, he hadn't had a chance to speak to Brigid, to explain what had happened and to say his goodbyes. His throat constricted as he began stuffing his saddlebags with all the supplies he would need for the trip. According to his parents, more supplies would be waiting at a nearby stop, in town. And he had yet to locate the person who was to train him in all things British.

"I can't go anywhere until I meet with the linguist who is to fill me in on what I'm to know about this Count Whoever."

Without missing a beat, Thomas said, "Oh, I've taken care of everything. We'll meet up with him in Battersbog."

"Really?" Henry shook his head, certain he was missing a screw or two, what with everything that had occurred on this cold December day. "Are you certain?"

"Dead certain," Thomas said.

Then why did Henry feel like his brother was up to something? Still, he was glad to have him along, if only for the first leg of the journey. Once he met his British contact, he would leave Thomas behind. For his own good.

3

I'd had yet to see Winnifred's place at the outskirts of town, and I wasn't the least bit surprised by the small stone cottage, its front lined with a boxwood hedge, two leafless yellow forsythias at either corner on this cold December morning. But what *did* surprise me was Winnifred's mother who ushered me out back, rather than inside the bright stone cottage. She led both me and Emma to a large red barn that seemed to teeter slightly, as though ready to be unmoored from its rather unstable foundation.

Inside, I heard the pounding of metal upon metal and felt heat emanating from within as though from a blast furnace. To both Emma's and my surprise, when Winnifred's mother cast open the sliding doors, there sat Winnifred on a stool, wearing a leather apron and coveralls, a large hammer in her hand. Her dark hair had been chopped short, and she was wearing a pair of goggles to protect her eyes from any flying debris. And by the look of things not only was there plenty of flying debris, this was a blacksmith's shop and she, the very undersized blacksmith.

"What on earth are you making?" I shouted to be heard over Winnifred's hammer. And I had to admit that the invention she was working on *was* quite impressive.

She stopped hammering long enough to say, "It's a spring-loaded catapult and timer. See you just set the catapult—sort of like a mouse trap. Then there's this timer here, which I filched from an old clock. That way you don't have to be near it when it goes off. I set it and voila! Bob's your uncle."

"What?"

"Oh, sorry, a British expression. Right-O."

I peered around and saw that Emma was as wide-eyed as me. For all around us, in various stages of construction were a whole host of fantabulous creations of dubious origin, cannibalized from any number of things. Some were artistic in nature—a beautiful garden gate wrought with rare Chittenango Ovate Amber Snails paired with two spatterdock darners, a rare form of dragonfly. They were quite thin, and a tantalizing blue and black, while bearing crystalline wings. Somehow she had made them shimmer as though translucent. In fact, they appeared as though they were ready to take flight. To the left of that, she had created a lovely bench with two Canada lynx holding up the body of the bench, complete with black tufts of hair that seemed to waft from their ears while they sported a collared ruff 'round their necks as though regal, like the ones belonging to royals I recognized from drawings I'd once seen. But then again, that's when I'd had a nanny, a family, and an education befitting one of wealth. All that was gone, I realized with sadness. Instead, I now had a new family, one I had come to love through the course of the past winter. Through our trials.

"What's *that* thing?"

Emma pointed to a wagon wheel that had been laid on its side, a large bamboo pole running upwards as though for a boat mast. And indeed, circling skyward was a mast made of some material that reminded me of bat wings.

"That's one of Leonardo Da Vinci's designs. An aerial screw. He couldn't get it to work, but I thought maybe if I used lighter materials . . ."

"What's that material you used for the . . . wing?" I raised a skeptical brow.

"Don't ask."

"But—"

She shook her finger at me, all the while tsking as if I were an errant child.

"But—" I protested again, then understood instinctively that she meant never to answer me. I inspected the mask closer and drew back, my face awash with disgust because maybe they *were* bat wings. After all, I'd seen tiny silk threads sewing them all together. But where had she found so many?

As though she knew what was coming next, Winnifred held up a hand, one brow arched. "I told you, no questions, but I will say this, I need to find something lighter than a wagon wheel. The construction is right, but it's way too heavy." Changing the subject, Winnifred stood and faced us. "So I hear we're on the move again."

"What?" I turned to Emma to see if she knew what

Winnifred was talking about.

Emma merely shrugged then turned her attention to something that looked strangely like a cart with wheels slung low to the ground. On the back was what appeared to be a giant clock that spun 'round when twirled. Emma touched it and jumped back when she discovered it moved with just the slightest touch of her hand.

"Balsa," Winnifred said, before Emma or I could ask. "It's one of the lightest weight woods in the world. I tried it for the first time with this machine, which needed to be light if I'm to time travel."

I laughed until I realized she was serious. "You really think you can build a time machine?"

"Never know 'til you try."

She spoke with such confidence that once again I had to laugh. "Why don't you use balsa for the wheel of that thing?" I nodded to her aerial screw. "By the way, what does it do?"

She blinked, reminding me of the mouse I'd first pictured her as so long ago. "It flies," she said, as though I'd gone daft in the ten minutes we'd been there.

"Oh!" I thought of Phinney, who was at home throwing a royal conniption fit because I wouldn't let her join us. "Does it work?"

"Not yet, but it will." She fussed with some wire that had come loose on the aerial screw.

Emma was the first to speak up. "So, what is this about being on the move? Who's on the move?"

"Why, you and Brigid and Thomas and Henry." She dug a rag from her pocket and began wiping an oily part on her time machine. "And now us."

"Us?" Emma and I said in unison.

"What are you two? Magpies?" Winnifred pulled down her goggles from where they lay on her forehead. She began pounding with her hammer again.

"Winnifred!" I yelled. "WINNIFRE–"

"You don't have to shout." She pulled off the goggles and set the hammer on her lap. "They're on their way here."

"Who?" I demanded, hands on hips.

She shrugged. "Why, everyone, near abouts. They miss you. They're tired of all the traditions. They remember what it was like with those gone, and well, let's face it, most of us would rather face the enemy together than fight tradition alone. It's harder to take, once you've experienced . . . *normalcy*."

I knew exactly what she meant. Ever since we had returned, I had been floundering. I'd lost my sense of purpose, my will to . . . well, live. For wandering about the house didn't feel like living, not really. It felt more like a slow death. And if I died, I'd rather it be quick and in the bosom of the people I loved and who loved me in return. My one great escape each week had been to practice maneuvers with my women to keep us sharp. Then each had returned to their own hamlets for daily target shooting practice, whether by arrow or gun.

How to explain all this to her? But then, when I glanced at her, I saw tears in her eyes and knew that she felt as I did. Life hadn't been the same without each other. But what would Henry think once he learned that an entire army of women were on their way to accompany him to this new emperor's fort?

Just then, tiny Yesimeh poked her head through the door.

"Yoohoo! Anyone home?"

Before anyone had a chance to respond, Winnifred jumped from her seat, knocking her hammer onto the floor with a loud clang, and ran over to scoop Yesimeh up in a bear hug and twirl her around. "You're back!"

"Yes, and I have news," Yesimeh said, her dark owl eyes taking in each of us in turn. "The women have been asking around. The new ruler is indeed Alaric's son."

"I didn't even know he was married, much less had children." Emma pulled up a chair for Yesimeh while the two of us stood, still tired of sitting after our ride into town.

"Yup. Kept 'im hidden, he did. Not that Alaric was ever married. More like he went through a bevy of beauties. But this was the closest he had to a wife. A consort, really."

"What's the son's name?" I asked, hoping to learn anything I could about the man.

"Birsha. Apparently, he looks a lot like his father, only shorter, but we don't know how he is in temperament. We're hoping to learn that soon."

"That's what Henry is being sent to learn." A chill swept over me every time I said it.

Though small and wiry, with long dark hair, Yesimeh had a head on her shoulders and was always thinking, planning. She was our brains. I was the heart. Winnifred was our courage. And Emma . . . well, Emma was simply a friend who loved us almost as much as she loved Thomas. Well, maybe not *quite* that much.

Over the next few hours, more and more women filtered in until the barn was sated and the surrounding countryside was equally filled with women. Each of them were clad in armor, designed by Yesimeh and sewn by the women themselves, or hammered in Winnifred's forge. The upper body was done in a tightly woven gray-green mesh with a lightweight breastplate beneath it, while the arms were clad in the more traditional crenulated armor of a warrior. The same mesh ran down the legs, with knee boots made of leather and lined with lamb's wool. The tooling on them was so exquisite that I bent down to have a look at them.

"We used some of the same motif as the one from our new flag." Here, Yesimeh had one of the women unfurl the flag they had designed for just such a purpose. "What do you think?"

I drew an intake of air, for on it was the Bookbinder's manor house, which appeared imposing on the vivid blue background. The field at its side was lined with sunflowers. And up above the left tower, Phinney hovered. But what touched me most was the large skeleton key in the corner. Only Emma knew about my forays as a child, where I had gathered the keys from a large key ring next to the door of my family's home and tested each lock. My heart overflowed with love for my friends.

As for the boots, they'd sewn a vine with butterflies and keys on it, the manor house on the toe of the boot and Phinney in the corner, resting atop the loom. They were beautifully crafted. I stood, thanking each and every one of them for their hard work and foresight.

While immensely grateful for all the women had done, I wondered what the Bookbinders would think once they learned that our makeshift army was again in the ready. Furthermore, what would Henry think when he discovered that we had gathered out of class, as it were? I shuddered to think.

One by one, we greeted each other with cries of joy, hugs, some tears, and old-fashioned affection. We were all boisterously carrying on, the glade filled with a cacophony of sound, when suddenly silence prevailed and all eyes turned to the one who had caused it.

Beatrice.

Emma paled, as the last time Beatrice had joined our party, she had been sent home in disgrace after she'd brutally attacked one of the other women. Plus, she had vied with Emma for Thomas's attention, an unforgivable sin in Emma's mind.

For a moment, no one spoke. At last everyone moved back as though repelled by her and gave me and her a wide berth from which to speak.

"So, Beatrice," I started, "why are you here?"

Beatrice nervously licked her lips and searched for any allies who might come to her aid, but seeing none, returned her attention to me. "I'm here to ask for my position back."

I heard a collective gasp, but none were more surprised than me for she had made it clear in the past that she thought herself better than the rest of us. But more than that, she held to the traditions that believed in punishment over reward, pain over happiness. And the truth was, I didn't trust her. I heard a rustling from behind and another gasp.

"What are you all doing here?" I heard seconds later.

I would recognize that voice anywhere. For one brief moment I thought to turn and launch into Henry's waiting arms, but when I pivoted on my left foot to go to him, I saw that his expression was forbidding. I froze, mid-flight.

"Henry?" I said tentatively.

"What is all this, Brigid?" he asked. "I tried to find you earlier, to tell you I would be leaving for a while. I never expected . . . this!"

I read the anger in his voice and blanched. Emma, bless her, came forward. "Don't blame Brigid, Henry. It was my fault. I let it slip to Gertrude and Jocelyn that you were leaving on a mission and . . ."

I breathed a sigh of relief. It didn't take a scientist like Winnifred to see that what had started as an innocent sharing of confidence had turned into a circus, if ever there was one. At that moment, Jocelyn and Gertrude stepped forward.

"I'm afraid it was our fault." Jocelyn's shiny blonde hair glistened in the sun.

"Roseland's carrier pigeon had stopped in to deliver a message–"

"And I told everyone else. Well, not everyone, but the word spread," Roseland said. "We just wanted to join you, to help you in any way we could."

Henry threw up his hands as if in surrender. "Okay, okay, I get it." A reluctant lopsided smile formed on his lips.

My shoulders sagged. Here was the Henry I knew and loved. He slid off his mount, Thomas following suit. Emma stepped forward and threw her arms around Thomas, eager no doubt to show Beatrice there was no place for her here.

After a brief moment, Beatrice cleared her throat, and once again we all paused, still uncertain whether we could ever trust her after what she had done the last time we were together.

"So, may I . . . return?"

I flinched as I sought an equitable reply. "Not as a leader, and truthfully, I would have to speak with the others first. It's a decision we must all make."

"Very well," Beatrice said. "I will step away while you speak to each other, but before you do, I want you to know that I've changed. I no longer believe in the . . . traditions."

She had paused so long before adding that last part that I wondered what she was hiding. Or perhaps she found it distasteful to downplay the traditions that held us all captive.

I only knew that we took stock of each other for just a moment more than what might be deemed comfortable, then we women stayed put while Beatrice left the clearing. Once she was out of sight, the women formed a circle 'round me, women from every direction hurling either insults or reasons we should give the very arrogant Beatrice a chance to prove herself.

In the end, it was Henry who grabbed our attention with words that surprised me. He looked directly at me when he said them, causing me to flinch yet again. "Brigid, when you first came, no one wanted you, no one trusted you. They thought *you* were odd because you hated the traditions. And yet you've become a light during our darkest hours. Would you refuse to give her the same chance we gave you?"

My cheeks burned with shame, for Henry was right. Everyone deserves a second chance . . . Beatrice, even this Birsha fellow. Though he was Alaric's son, how did we know what kind of man he was until we saw him for ourselves? Perhaps he was different, more willing to unite in a new direction?

And yet, even as I thought it, a more cynical side thought, *Yeah, right. And the luna moth dances in daylight.*

4

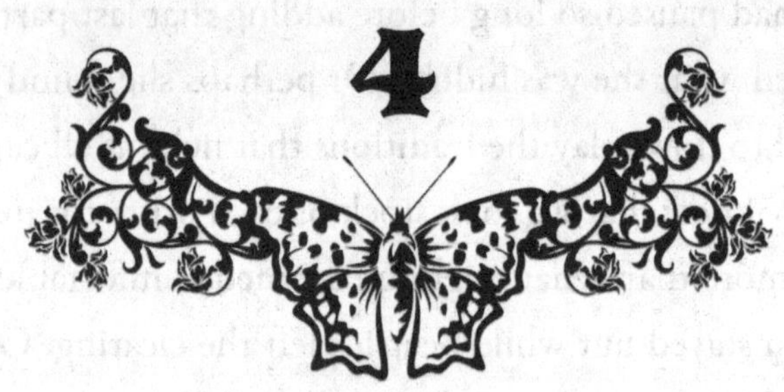

Birsha patted his gloved hands together as he toured the military grounds. But first he had gone through a list of Alaric's belongings. He was surprised at the vast wealth his father had accumulated during his years as ruler. And indeed, he'd discovered a veritable museum of artifacts from every part of the world. From Egyptian gold face masks to the Antikythera Mechanism from Greece that was said to unlock the cosmos, but which simply looked like a door knob with gears to Birsha. He'd discovered marble statues, an ancient copy of The Book of Kells from Ireland. Even an old Viking ship that took up an entire room. The breadth and variety were without end.

Shaking his head, the young ruler regarded the men, now *his* men, perform their daily drills, each outfitted in clothing not fit for the cold. When Birsha had asked the commanders why the clothing was so minimal, he was told that Alaric believed it kept men strong. The commanders had also informed him that rations were kept to a minimum not only to save money, but to keep the men hungry. He pulled at his budding goatee, anger bubbling up inside him. What sort of man did this to the people who were supposed to protect him, support his kingdom? No wonder Alaric's people had reviled him so.

"I will plan a different course."

Birsha hadn't realized he'd spoken aloud until Alaric's adjutant, Siegfried turned to him. "Sir?"

"Sorry, just thinking out loud." Birsha started for the gate to the fort when he turned back suddenly. "Siegfried?"

"Yes, sir?"

"What did you think of my father?"

Birsha must have taken the man by surprise because Siegfried stammered, his eyes peering around as though searching for someone to save him.

"You don't have to be afraid, Siegfried," he said. "I'm not like my father."

But it was clear by the ashen face of the acne-scarred man that he didn't believe it for a single moment.

"I see," Birsha said. "Your expression says it all." He raised a single brow then strode away, determined to strike out on his own. Create a new kingdom that reflected his personality, not his father's. But first he needed more training, for though he didn't want to walk in his father's shadow, he planned to fill his shoes. He peered down at his feet and almost stumbled, as his feet were much smaller than his father's. And if he was to rule the entire kingdom, as his father had hoped to do before him, he had better get busy. With that, he made his way through the massive iron gates and into the maze of warrens that hid a man who wanted to be hidden, even a ruler.

"So, we agree?" I told the women in the clearing who nodded their heads, appearing as reluctant as I felt. "Alright, then call Beatrice to us."

Five minutes later, I watched her return and regarded her carefully. Her dark black hair reminded me of a woman from a fable, only she had a heart of ice. Or at least, until now. Again, I wondered if we could trust her–the green-eyed vixen who had done everything she could to woo young Thomas to her and out of Emma's grasp. Poor Emma, who stood off to one side, fire darting from her eyes even as they glistened.

"We'll give you one final chance to show that you've changed." I wanted to add, *Don't make me regret my decision.*

She nodded in agreement.

"Okay then, you will be part of Gertude's group."

Gertrude was about to protest, but thought better of it. "Come with me," she said, her eyes revealing to anyone who cared to look that she thought this a bad idea.

When everyone had begun gathering into groups to plan the upcoming trek, Henry grabbed my arm and ushered me to the side of the barn where we could speak without hindrance.

Before he said anything, he reached out and yanked me to him. For several minutes, we relished in each other's embrace. He finished by kissing me softly, then more soundly, until he finally pulled away, both of us breathing heavily.

He ran his fingers through my hair, all the while gazing at my odd eyes, the bits of fire and ice that had caused people to stare from the time I was young.

"Brigid." Henry's expression was one of sanguine pity for me. Before I could protest, he put a finger to my lips. "Hush! I need to say this. You know how much I want you to go with me . . . the women too. But I'm supposed to be going to gather information. We march in with an entire contingent of women, and we will be breaching our pact. This is just a fact-finding mission. That's all."

My mind scrolled through the possible dangers he might encounter. The prospect of watching him leave to face the unknown alone sent my heart racing and left me feeling breathless. I had been so lost upon our return from the unnamed war with Alaric. My role as a leader had been diminished to that of handmaiden and it didn't suit me, not one little bit.

"Henry, I can't lose you again." I struggled to keep my voice calm. "There's no place for me back at the manor."

He bent down on his haunches, surveying the land around him, anywhere except to have to face me and what I'd said. Finally, he peered up at me. "I know it hasn't been easy for you."

"It's been nearly impossible!" I blurted out, then immediately regretted it. I was used to the punishment that came my way because of such an outburst, but the "traditions" held no sway here, thankfully. Still, they loomed like a waiting specter. "We women are relegated to jobs that quite frankly bore me to death. I mean, I don't mind some of it, in moderation. But a steady diet of cooking and cleaning with nothing to fill our souls, while you men are out doing important things–" I left the words unfinished.

"Hard work, too, Brigid. Don't forget. We do things that you women wouldn't want to do."

"But some of us would, at least some of the time. Why must we be one thing or another? Why can't we divide jobs more equitably, share in the varied work?"

Henry reached a hand out to me. "Walk with me," he urged.

I took his hand, gladly, eager to walk off my angst. There were so many things I wanted to do, so many things I wanted to be. But the world had created boxes. This box a woman's, that box a man's. We were all trapped inside boxes that society had created to contain us.

He led me to a stream, whose gurgling sound immediately stilled my disquiet. Dappled shadows of leaves played a rhythm on the water and for all the world the shadows looked like little sprites, hopping from rock to rock. I could even hear their giggles, the boys with their conical hats, tights and pointy slippers, the girls in dresses and tights, their hair ringed with miniature daisies like the ones we'd made daisy chains with in school. I reached down to scoop one up in the palm of my hand, but they simply flowed through my hands like water and disappeared into the shadows. I had never seen such things before and turned to Henry in delight. He laughed and shook his head.

"Water sprites," he said. "According to the alchemist, Paracelsus, water sprites can breathe air. Sometimes even fly. They're said to be able to change shape, transmute into other forms. To alter reality, not just for themselves, but for all humanity."

"Really?" I reached out and tried to grab another one, but this one too slipped through my hands like sand through an hourglass.

"See?" he said.

"Well, if they can change the world, why don't they?"

"It's not their world that's being affected," Henry stated matter-of-factly.

"Ooh! Look at that!" I reached for a toad that had emerged from a strand of wet marshy mud land."What is it?"

"A *scaphiopus holbrookii*."

"A what?" I said, turning to him.

"That's an Eastern spadefoot, to you. They have warts."

"What?" I pulled my hand back.

"This one's a male. You can tell by the stripes that run from its eyes to its dorsum. The lines are more visible in the males, and they're shaped like an hourglass."

"Hmm," I mused. But before I could capture the wee beastie, one of the sprites appeared wearing cowboy boots, a ten-gallon hat, and she was carrying a lasso, which she threw over her head in a series of circles, then tossed it over the toad's neck. Within seconds, she had it saddled and off she rode across the shallows of the stream with a hearty "tee-hee" as she disappeared from sight. I merely shook my head and laughed.

Just then, from somewhere downstream, I heard two male voices and the name "Birsha." Henry put a finger to his lips and grasped my hand as we tiptoed nearer so that we could listen in on the men's conversation. We bent down behind a stand of especially tall fern.

"Met 'em, when he was a teen."

I peered between a spot where two fronds converged. Though I could only make out the one man, my heart stilled, for it was the trapper—the one who was supposed to have led us through the Adirondacks on a previous trek, but who had fled part way, never to be seen again. *Until now.*

"And what was he like?" The other man spoke with undisguised yearning, his voice low and gravelly.

"The devil his'self, just like his dad, that one. Not as bad in some things, but he's used to the good life. 'e'll stop at nothing to have it all."

"What do ya think he'll do, now that he's in the driver's seat?" the gravelly-voiced one said.

"Dunno, but one thing's for sure. The boy's got a chip on 'is shoulder. Father sent him away as a young child, never acknowledged him. Pretended he had no son. A boy like that can come to no good. Not only that, but the bugger was raised by a mean howdya do, a Marie Antoinette, 'let them eat cake' sort, who lined her pockets with silver, while barely feeding the boy. As for love? She couldn't be bothered, that one, least that's what *I* heard."

"You hear about this woman war party? What d'ya suppose that's all about?"

The trapper peered around then lowered his voice. "I think they's on the move again, but I haven't found out why yet. But I will. Mark my words."

As I listened, a frond tickled my nose, and try as I might, I couldn't stop the explosive sneeze that rocketed my corner of the forest. Before I'd had a chance to gauge the men's reactions, Henry lifted me to my feet and yelled, "Run!"

My feet fairly flew so that I felt like one of the sprites hopping from one log to another without touching ground. We turned this way and that, every time they neared, twisting out of their grasp. In the hubbub, I threw a shoe, but we couldn't stop despite the pain that rocked me each time we stepped on a sharp stone.

"Quick! This way," Henry hissed. And indeed, he was right, for ahead of us was an open space, and then the barn. We just had to hope they hadn't caught sight of our faces before we rushed into the clearing, which was filled with women campers. Within moments, we had faded into the crowd of women and ducked inside the barn, where Winnifred was once again busily working on one of her inventions, so absorbed, in fact, that she hadn't seen us enter. We ducked down behind her time machine, scarcely daring to breathe, the sound of clanging behind us.

Now that we were truly alone again, I whirled toward Henry. "What will we do about my locket?"

"Actually," he said, "I spoke to the liveryman, and he said that someone fitting Jesse's description rode in with a man. And Brigid–"

"Yes?" All I could see of Henry was the outline of his shadow amidst the gloom.

"He was wearing Alaric's coat of arms on his breastplate."

I gasped, fearing the worst. No doubt Alaric had sent Jesse to spy on those in the manor, to secure the loom, for Alaric had made no bones that he wanted it . . . dearly. But Alaric was dead. Had Jesse even known that when she'd gone to my room?

Or perhaps she had used the distraction to collect what she'd come for, Alaric or no Alaric.

"And Brigid?"

I closed my eyes, not wanting to hear the words I knew he was about to say.

"The liveryman said they were headed north."

Try as I might, I failed to halt the rising tide of angst I felt deep in my chest. I opened my eyes on a sigh. "To the fortress."

In the darkness, I saw him nod. Now I had one more reason to join him on his trek. Come what may, I would retrieve my locket, and with it my family. The Jackals could not have them. Not as long as a single breath lived inside me.

5

Birsha waited for the news, certain it would come any time now. He peered out over the ramparts, every nerve on edge. It was the price he'd paid for power. Despite the cold wind, he refused to leave until he'd heard the news.

"Do you think they'll suspect anything?" asked his longtime ally and half-brother, Pietra Goren. He was a tall, thin, bookish sort of twenty-three winters.

"I doubt it." In his heart, Birsha knew that the generals would be on their guard during these untested months. They'd spent too many years on the knife's edge not to.

Pietra nodded, but Birsha sensed his doubt. For years, Birsha had attended classes with Pietra and his other half-brother, Agnold, who stood on the other side of Pietra. The two had become his constant companions, all sharing similar backgrounds and experiences, but only one slated to become crowned prince of the kingdom. That spot was for Birsha alone.

Birsha tugged at his goatee. For the past couple of days he had taken to braiding it as Alaric had, hoping that the likeness would help to secure his leadership in the peasants' minds. He knew he was playing with fire. Now he just had to hope it didn't come back to burn him. He wanted new leadership–his own people in place, not Faineant the Foul's men. Theirs was another generation entirely. So many changes had taken place in the interim, and the generals had to be in their eighties by now. What did they know of the future? Birsha wanted to modernize his kingdom, bring it into the 19th century. But one thing he knew–Alaric had been right about the loom. He would need it if he was to own the kingdom–all of it. And own it he would. He lifted the collar of his pea coat to cover his ears, which were growing colder by the minute.

"There!" Agnold cried.

Birsha's eyes strayed to where Agnold had pointed. Agnold was a swarthy fellow with a full beard and cap, his round face filled with youthful glee. Whereas Pietra was thin and pale, learned, a deep thinker. Agnold's hair was full and wavy–almost an amber color, whereas Pietra's hair was a mousey brown. Birsha would do well to have both of them at his side, but first he needed the others out of the way.

The minutes ticked by before Birsha's messenger finally made the landing. Birsha quickly whisked him inside, into his inner chambers so that they could speak in private.

"What have you heard?" He offered him a seat nearest the window, which Pietra shut the minute they were inside, closing the plush damask drapes as well so as not to be seen *or* heard.

"They have been taken to their chambers. They should be dead within the hour."

Birsha lay a hand on his writing table to steady himself. The next hour would test every nerve in his entire body, but he had to hold course. Had to appear shocked by the news, remorseful even. And yet he could waste no time in setting his course.

He put up a hand to silence everyone, then stood and strode for the door, opening it and calling for his adjutant who was stationed at the end of the hall.

"Tell the Kazakh to prepare his bird . . . the little one. The devil bird. I need to have a message sent out."

The adjutant bowed and then left. Birsha stepped inside and closed the door, turning back to the three men who were waiting in silence, their faces eager.

"Gentlemen," he said, offering them each a drink. "Prepare for the days ahead. In one week's time, you are to be named my new generals."

"Do you think the other warriors will accept us?" Pietra asked, his expression filled with angst. "We're young, untried, untested."

Birsha narrowed his eyes, turning on his half-brother. "You don't think I know that? But that's what all those years of sitting in class, practicing on the battlefield was for. So that one day the three of us could take over the kingdom, am I right?"

"Of course you're right." Agnold stepped forward, giving Pietra a scowl. "And we are behind you all the way, aren't we, Pietra?" Agnold asked pointedly.

Pietra's chest heaved, but at last he nodded.

"Brothers 'til the end," they said in unison. The motto they had used since childhood. Now, fate would put them to the test, Birsha knew. Hopefully, they would not be found wanting.

"What do you mean he's gone?" I nearly shouted as I tore through my tent and went running toward Henry's.

Thomas was the first to catch up with me, Emma close on his heels. The chill morning air sent clouds of steam climbing upward into the sky. Last night, once we were certain that the trapper had decided against searching our camp for me and Henry, we'd taken refuge in our separate tents, but not before we'd been assigned a guard to be stationed near our tent flaps so that they could monitor anyone trying to enter during the night. So how had Henry eluded the guard?

"His things are all missing and his horse is gone from the stable. The liveryman was asleep when Henry came by to collect Windtamer," Thomas quickly explained.

And indeed, Henry's things *were* all gone. I knelt on my haunches, closing my eyes to steady myself before opening them again.

"What if he was kidnapped, Thomas? Have you thought about that?"

"See reason," Emma said, her green eyes filled with worry.

"Would he have taken his belongings, his horse, if he had been kidnapped?" Thomas countered.

"No, I suppose not." But still, the thought of Henry leaving without me, without telling me, seemed so out of character for the Henry I knew. "We have to go after him." I moved toward the tent flap, but Thomas grabbed my arm to stop me.

"I think what Thomas is trying to say," Emma interjected, "is that if Henry had wanted you to come–wanted *any* of us to come–he would have said so."

Thomas nodded solemnly, consolation written in the downturn of his mouth. "Another thing, Brigid. According to the guard, the tutor who was to train him in all things British arrived last night. Henry met with him after we all went to bed."

"Do you think the tutor brought a message from the Bookbinders?"

Thomas pursed his lips. "Most likely," he said with disdain. "My parents would have thought this gathering of female warriors a quixotic quest, and surely they've heard by now that too many people have gone missing not to have put two and two together."

I plopped down on my bottom, defeated. The thought of Henry having to face this new threat, this Birsha character, alone, didn't sit well. Not one iota. And yet, what could I do to stop him?

Just then, a rider came barreling into camp, his horse lathered. He narrowly missed one of the young women exiting her tent, so intent was he to reach us. We quickly exited the tent to greet the stranger and to find out what had sent him on such a wild chase into our camp. The horse slid to a stop in front of us, tossing its head up and down and snorting its displeasure for having been ridden so hard.

"What is it? Do you have word of Henry?" I demanded, before the stranger even had time to dismount.

"Henry?" His beefy round face went blank. "Can't say as I

know what you're talkin' about, ma'am. I'm here about Birsha, the one who's taken Alaric's spot now that he's gone."

"And?" A small crowd of women gathered around us at the news. I suppose this information, if important, affected us all.

"We think he's done away with his generals. Sometime yesterday. Just got the news by way of carrier pigeon of their deaths."

"How do you know that Birsha was the one responsible?" I frowned at the news.

"Well, we don't know for sure, but who else would want them gone?"

Indeed. I scrubbed fingers through my hair, not caring what I looked like at this point. Things had just gone from bad to worse. And Henry was heading straight into the jaws of the jackal. Now, more than ever, he needed me . . . needed *us*.

"Do they know why Birsha did it?" I asked, hoping to keep the quiver from my voice.

"Rumor has it that he plans to succeed where Alaric failed."

"What do you mean?" Both I and Thomas spoke at once.

The stranger was dressed in a wrinkled vest, breeches, and boots, as well as a long-skirted coat to keep him warm. At this, he tipped his hat.

"He plans to take over the entire kingdom, for all of us to be his subjects."

A brief murmur arose followed by an eerie silence that had us all regarding each others' reactions to the news. I could see by the somber expressions that this news had hit all of us hard. So, Birsha was not to turn a new leaf. No, this younger version of Alaric had even larger ambitions than his father, so much so that he had taken the lives of his generals. What kind of man did that? But I knew. A man who none of us could trust. No, it was time to face our adversary. To save Henry. And to collect my locket that had been stolen from me. My holograph images of my family. My memories.

Henry couldn't get over how different this trip was compared to the previous one. The last foray had started out with butterflies leading the women's army through a meadow, women giggling, frolicking toward their future. This time Henry felt a molten weight against his chest as he and his new traveling companion wended their way up the earthen staircase toward the lakes above. As if the weather had decided to match his mood, it lay in gloomy sullenness, a cloak of misgiving added in for good measure.

He'd been so busy grieving over all the things he'd lost—Brigid, Thomas, Emma, and the women he'd come to view as family—that he hadn't realized his tutor was speaking to him until he heard the words, "Are you listening to me?"

Henry glanced over at the very refined young gentlemen who had dressed completely wrong for the weather. He wore a thin long coat, cravat, and silk waistcoat, along with linen breeches that disappeared inside wellingtons. His hair sported a natural curl that appeared styled, and truth to tell, he looked as if he'd done not a lick of work his entire life as evidenced by the softness of his hands.

"What? Oh yes, of course," Henry said, even as his

thoughts returned to Brigid. What would she think when she arose to discover him gone? Perhaps she already had. Hopefully, she knew that he had done this for her own good. It wouldn't be safe for her to come with him, under the circumstances. And a woman's army would only cause the new leader to suspect that they were using the change in command as a pretext to invade. No, he couldn't have it, he decided with a tug on the reins to spur Windtamer on through the harsh winter weather.

"As I was saying," Sir Robert said, his horse trotting to keep up, "you are Count Augusta Davies, an industrialist from Durham, England, originally from Essex. You want to sell young Prince Birsha on the idea of a railway system."

"A railway system?" Henry bent down to avoid a bigtooth aspen branch that had yet to don its leaves. Though Henry had got wind of such a machine as a train, the idea that it might be so near at hand surprised him and he arched a brow.

"Not to worry," Sir Robert said. "It will be years before such an invention can be put into operation in the Americas, but the very idea of it should be enough to gain the young prince's interest, no?"

"Right," Henry said as they climbed another steep incline that opened to a clearing at the top, a burst of steam accompanying his breath.

He stopped for a moment to let his horse graze. From where he sat, he could see over a wide expanse of terrain. Here, everything seemed normal, no magic whatsoever. All of that had disappeared with the truce between his people and Alaric's. He peered back at the direction from which they'd come. Somewhere, out there, Brigid was discovering his ruse.

The thing that made him saddest was that he wouldn't be there to take her in his arms, to let her cry on his shoulder, since he would be the reason for her tears. His throat tightened at the thought. *I'm sorry, Brigid.* He just had to hope she would forgive him his subterfuge.

6

I had scarcely taken in the news that Henry was missing when Gertrude came running toward us, her golden locks flying in the breeze, her blouse buttoned wrong so that her entire shirt appeared askew. This from a woman who normally had impeccable taste that showed in her clothing.

"What is it?" I demanded as I scoured my head with my hands in frustration.

"Winnifred." She leaned forward, taking a gulp of air before lifting her head to face me. "She's gone. I can't find her anywhere."

"What?" I pushed past her as a line of people followed, Thomas and Emma first, Gertrude close behind, many of the others pressing their way in.

As I entered the barn, my eyes were temporarily blinded, taking moments to adjust to the gloom. Once my eyesight had finally returned, I peered 'round me. Dust settled on the air where light shone through the windows. It appeared gold and glittery, as though some fairy godmother had sprinkled stardust throughout the barn. And indeed, as though I had wished it so, I heard titters of laughter in the corners and turned, first one way, then the next, but I could never quite see what was just beyond my vision.

"Is someone there?" I called into the shadows. "Speak to me. Come out where I can see you."

And for one brief moment, I saw it, almost elfin in appearance. A water sprite. But why were they here, inside a dry barn? They preferred all things liquid.

"They can breathe both water and air, sprites can." Emma bent down and began speaking to them in baby talk.

"Don't you think they're a bit old for that?" I said, churlishly.

"No!" Emma continued to speak to them in her childish Cockney accent. "They are small beings, childlike in their ways. But don't cross them!" she added, lest I dare to do so.

"But why *are* they here?" I sneezed, sending the sprite flying through the air to land on Winnifred's work table. The sprite scolded me in something that sounded acutely like gibberish.

Emma merely laughed as she stood to get a better look at the little hothead. "Now you've gone and done it."

"I couldn't help it." I wiped my nose with a dust rag Winnifred kept on a shelf. "The dust is awful in here. Can you ask her where Winnifred went?" I pinched my nose to hold back another sprite-blowing sneeze.

Emma bent over and spoke in the same gibberish that the

sprite had, only hers was a good deal less heated. When she was done talking to the sprite, she stood up straight, but a puzzled expression graced her pale face.

"The sprite says that she's gone to the Great Beyond."

I gasped, as did numerous others behind me. "Winnifred is dead?"

Emma quickly bent down and translated before once again facing us. "Not dead. Gone."

I rubbed my forehead, feeling a distinctive headache coming on. "Gone where?" I finally managed. "And please don't say to the Great Beyond, because I don't know what that means."

To help me understand, Emma pointed to the spot where the time machine had sat last night, when we were hiding out from the trapper and his friend. My scalp prickled at the sight. Where on earth could Winnifred have taken it to? "I no more believe in time travel than I do little sprites," I told Emma.

"And there's your problem," she said, brows raised over sparkling green eyes that reminded me of the Emerald Isles. She nodded toward the sprite as if to say, "See there?"

"Okay, so the possibility exists." Had you asked me this time last year if I believed in magical looms, rampaging insects and birds, and sprites, I would have said you were off your spindle, but this past year had taught me more than I had ever cared to know.

The sprite spoke once more, Emma translating. But she needed no translation because I could see by the arc of the sprite's arm that she was pointing toward the future, toward a time that had yet to exist. To keep myself from fainting dead away, I fell into the chair that only last night had held Winnifred.

"So, how did she get there?" I demanded.

But before Emma could ask the sprite, I recalled my conversation with Winnifred from the night before, when she had discovered us in hiding. Henry and I had told her about the trapper, about the sprites we had seen. And I had noticed a glimmer in her eye, as though the wheels were turning.

"Emma," I said, snapping my fingers, "you know all about sprites from your home country, yes?"

"Aye, I do. Why?" She frowned, not catching my drift.

"What exactly are sprites good for?"

I hadn't meant it to come out that way, but I could tell by the way the sprite began chittering that I had offended it yet again. "Sorry!" I said, before the sprite did something to me that I would regret—not knowing the capability of such tiny creatures.

"Be careful," Emma chided. "They're the warrior clan of the pixies."

"Yikes!" My head hurt worse.

"They're said to have the powers of elemental transmutation." In explanation, Emma opened her hands like a book.

I stood, hands on hips. "Speak English."

"Supposedly, they can rearrange matter." Seeing by my frustrated expression that I still had no idea what she was talking about, she added, "It's possible that with Winnifred's time machine and their ability to transmute—"

"That they took Winnifred to another dimension?"

"Precisely," she said with a flourish.

All around us, I heard whispers and gasps. Now, not only was my scalp prickling, but I felt almost as if I had heat rash. How? How was such a thing possible? But then I had only to look at my loom to know odder things existed. So, Winnifred had gone somewhere, but where?

"Ask her how we go about getting Winnifred back?" After all, I couldn't very well leave to go in search of Henry until I found Winnifred and made sure she was safe and alive.

The sprite waggled a finger for Emma to come closer. For several minutes they spoke in hushed tones, the sprite's mouth to Emma's ear. All the while Emma's face went from a frown to one of amazement followed by fear and then excitement. When at last they were done speaking, Emma turned to me. "We call her."

I threw my hands up. "Call her? Call her how? Yoo-hoo, Winnifred!" Admittedly, I was being a bit over-dramatic to let Emma know how foolish that sounded.

Emma lifted a single brow. Until now, I'd forgotten that she was a redhead and that redheads had reputations, or at least this one did. Eager to get on her good side, I shrugged and mouthed "Sorry!" to which she simply narrowed her eyes in warning. But good sport that she was, she reached over and grabbed something that looked like a bullhorn. She handed it to me.

"Hello!" I shouted, but heard only an echo that seemed to go on and on forever. "What now?" I asked Emma.

"Call Winnifred. Tell her we need her to return." When I didn't move quickly enough, Emma snapped her fingers, all the while nodding her head.

I felt silly, but I did as told and was rewarded with a series of sniggers from those around me. When I was done calling her, I turned back to Emma, my lips pursed and my hand on one hip, my face as warm as if I'd stood out in the sun for half a day. "So? What now, oh swami? Got any other stupid ideas?"

But I had barely spoken those words when from inside the speaker I heard a faint voice calling from a distance. Thomas held up his hands and urged everyone to be silent.

"It's Winnifred." Excitement welled up inside my chest followed by a clamor from those around me who'd heard the good news.

"Shush!" Thomas shouted, giving them all a final warning.

Sure enough, I heard it again. The voice sounded tinny and far away. I fought down the urge to jump inside the speaker and grab Winnifred, bring her home before anything could happen to her.

"I'll be back soon. Give me a day," she said. "I have big news."

But before I could ask any more questions, her voice faded and she was gone. The people inside the entire building and beyond erupted in a shared groan. Try as I might, I couldn't reach her again. Now I would just have to wait. And pray that we could catch up with Henry before he entered the fortress walls.

I awoke the next morning to a sight I'd never seen before. As I stepped outside my tent, first I blinked, then rubbed my eyes to be sure I was awake. But no, there it was again. It was as though the air had turned to liquid or jelly overnight, so viscous that it felt as though I were underwater instead of on dry land. Furthermore, as I moved through it, ripples appeared in all directions. And the color! The only way I could describe it was like shards of obsidian that, when broken, contained a smoky color, semi-transparent in its view. The farther up one looked, the smokier the color. And yet it broke up into multiple planes, as though layers of shale that had been disturbed by a volcanic eruption, sending the layers scattering every which way.

"Do-you-see-it?" I said to Thomas, who was already up, stoking the fire. Though how he got it going in this oddest of weather was anyone's guess. But my words came out in slow motion, my voice sounding as though it had dropped an octave.

"I-do," he answered, his voice even lower and slower than mine.

As I approached him, my movements reminded me of the Greek word "strobos," a word meaning twisting or whirling, for that's what my limbs were doing, as though the shadows of my arms and legs were visibly following me.

"Call-a-council-meeting. Maybe-someone-will-know-what's-happening-and-why."

I couldn't help but wonder if the two worlds had collided somehow—the future and the present. Perhaps this was something slipping through from the other dimension.

Twenty minutes later, women were seated in a swath as far as the eye could see, though truth be told, I couldn't see that far with this foul weather we were having. I began by standing and shouting to be heard, but I soon discovered it better to have the words relayed to the back of the gathering through a series of couriers.

"Does-anyone-know-why-this-is happening?" I said, holding my hands up to encompass the sky. "Could-this-be-caused-by-Winnifred's-time-travel? Another -dimension-bleeding-into-ours-perhaps?"

Many nodded, as though the thought had occurred to them as well, but Yesimeh stood, still tiny, having grown not an inch since I last saw her. And if anything, her brown hair had grown longer so that she looked like a pixie of sorts.

"Not-at-all!" she declared. "This-is-the-work-of-Tempestous."

"Tempestous?"

"A-sort-of-Mother-Nature," Yesimeh explained.

Somehow I had pictured her as docile and kind-hearted. This was anything but.

"Well-you-have-to-admit, Mother-Nature-can-be-a-bit-intimidating-at-times."

I cocked my head, determined to give her that. Weather could be unpredictable at the best of times, what with tornados, hurricanes, and lightning strikes that caused fire wherever they landed.

"She's-one-of-Alaric . . . I-mean-Birsha's-inner-circle."

I paced, until I realized how long it would take to get from one position to the next. "So-why-would-she-throw-such-a-tantrum?" I asked.

"Isn't-it-as-plain-as-that-freckle-on-your-face?"

My hand darted to the one lone freckle on my cheek. Was it that obvious to everyone?

"She-loved-the-generals. They-were-her-mentors. Birsha-made-a -huge-mistake-when-he-got-rid-of-them."

"How-do-you-know-it-was-him?"

But before I had even finished talking, she pierced me with those expressive eyes of hers that revealed how stupid I was being without ever having to say a word.

"Alright-alright!" I said, hands held out. "Let's-just-say-that-he's-the-most-likely-suspect."

She blinked once and nodded, then stepped back and took a seat, her job clearly done. This just made the whole situation that much more dangerous for Henry. Did he even know what he was walking into?

Oh, Winnifred, where are you?

I needed her back so I could go rescue Henry, though I'm certain he would feel it was the other way around, that he was the one rescuing me!

All I could do now was to go back to my tent and wait. With that, I convened the Council. But it would be hours before I had my answer.

For what seemed eons, Henry trudged through the smoky fractals of light alongside his new companion, Sir Robert from Durham, England. It amazed him that not only could he breathe the odd air, but that it prevented the rain from soaking through the cloud layer and reaching the ground. Instead, it simply rolled off the canopy. Where it went, he had no idea. Furthermore, it created a pocket of protection against the cold, so much so that he had removed his heavy coat for the first time in days. Still, the slog of riding their horses through the thick layers had tired both the men and their horses.

"Let's-pull-over-there." Henry pointed toward a meadow amongst a stand of trees. It would offer them protection should the canopy disperse and the rain return.

Sir Robert offered no protest, but simply guided his horse toward the aforementioned meadow.

"What-do-you-suppose-this-is?" Sir Robert asked in the drawn out sounds Henry had come to expect over the course of the day.

"I-don't-know." And yet Henry had a very uneasy feeling about all of this. Did Birsha know they were headed his way?

Had the odd weather been aimed at him and Sir Robert?

He pastured his horse then set about starting a fire for the evening meal while the horses grazed. As long as the weather held, there would be no learning the English vernacular. As it stood, it was hard enough speaking in his own dialect. He just had to hope that the odd fractals hadn't affected the grass, so they could feed the horses.

8

The weather cleared just after supper and still Winnifred had yet to reappear. The change of weather was a relief for everyone, but most of all for me because now I could make better progress when I went in search of Henry. That is, *if* Winnifred ever returned.

We were almost ready to call it a day. I decided to take one last gander through the barn before retiring for the night. As I did, I wished I could summon her up, make her hurry. But what if she *couldn't* return? As I inspected her many odd inventions, most with a slightly greasy mechanical odor, I fought down the rising panic in my chest. Then and there, I decided that if Winnifred didn't return by morning, I was going in search of Henry, with or without the others. I doubted he knew what was happening with Birsha and his generals, and perhaps Tempestous as well. If indeed she was the one to have caused this awful weather, she had overcome her snit—for the time being at least—and set us free of the foul climate and its many layers.

I was about to turn when something odd appeared out of the corner of my eye. It started as a swirling of miniscule dots that grew in proportion over the course of a few minutes. The dots began to grow, take shape. Then before I could ponder what was happening, Winnifred appeared seated in her time machine, the sprites that surrounded it all chittering at once in their funny little language that sounded akin to bees buzzing over some exotic flower. Everyone around me gasped, as did I. For in her hand she held something that looked like a metallic golden jellyfish. The light shone through it, causing it to give off a warm glow that fairly lit up the room and made it sparkle. Whatever it was, it was surprisingly beautiful.

"Look what I brought back with me!" Winnifred cried with glee as she unstrapped herself from the cockpit. She stepped out with the help of the sprites, who had taken turns pushing with a chittering that sounded like "heave-ho, heave-ho," as far as I could tell. Finally, with much struggling on Winnifred's part, they had her in a standing position. "It's a quantum computer!"

"A quantum what?"

"It calculates things—millions and billions of things. It's still in the experimental phase, but it holds great promise. It can outperform even a super computer. They say that with the help of this computer, they will perform operations one day with mechanical robots. I'm going to try to make it operational."

I shook my head. "I have no idea what you're talking about."

"No worries." She removed her helmet and goggles and

placed them on her workbench as she stood. "Right-o, then. Is everything okay on this side of the universe?" She bent over and shook her hair to rid herself of helmet hair.

I plopped down on a chair opposite her, cupping my chin in my hands. "Hardly."

"What do you mean?" she asked.

The sprites danced all around us, one of them tugging at a lock of my hair until I cried, "Ouch!" and pushed her away. Unfortunately, because of her size and weight, she flew across the room with a high-pitched "whoosh!" and landed against the leg of a sawhorse. She scolded me in a chitter that went on for some time. Great! Once again I had made a sprite mad.

When the sprite had finally recovered from her snit, I quickly brought Winnifred up to speed about what had happened over the past few days, informing her of the generals' deaths, Henry's escape into the night, and the odd weather we'd had that was beyond explanation.

"Phew!" she said when I was finished. "And I thought my past few days have been weird. Did you know they have hovercraft in the future and airplanes that travel at the speed of sound? They tried self-driving cars, but they were a disaster. Accidents everywhere." She shuddered.

"Winney, I have no idea what you're talking about. Would you come down to earth long enough to help me figure out what to do?"

"About what?" she asked.

I closed my eyes, feeling as though I might burst. "I need to find Henry. Your time machine couldn't help me with that, could it?" I said, only half serious.

"No, of course not." Then turning her head, she yelled, "You! Mini-sprite! Leave that catapult alone." She snapped her fingers several times before the errant sprite went on its way, giggling the entire way. Then to me, she whispered, "They can be a bit of a handful." Her eyebrows lifted in a conspiratorial way.

I could just imagine how difficult it had been to keep them in line in a completely different dimension, let alone this one. But back to my earlier question. "Why can't your time machine help me?"

She cocked her head back and forth. "Because I have no control over where or what time period it takes me . . . at least, not yet."

"Oh," I said. "Then how did you get back here?"

"I can put it in reverse. That's not a problem, but where I land in the first place is a bit of a mystery at this point."

"I see," I said, though I couldn't imagine where she had been or what she had seen. "You're back now, thank heavens, so I can go in search of Henry. I need to leave first thing in the morning, if I'm ever to catch up with him."

"We're coming too," she said with a frown. Then she offered me her full attention, now that she realized I meant to leave no matter the cost.

"No, it will take too long to bring an entire army–"

"But, Brigid–" Winnifred walked around the stained and worn workbench to speak to me directly. "All these women have come here . . . because of *you*! Why do you think they left their homes and families?"

I shrugged.

"Because you made them believe in something bigger than themselves. You made them see that things could be different, that we don't have to live by these awful traditions that have made us slaves to a machine with no head. You were the one who gave us hope that we could work together for a cause without tearing each other apart. We need that, Brigid. Especially in today's world where everything is so topsy-turvy."

And I did see it, more than she could ever know. I had been lost back at the manor, the horrible oppression of days spent with some awful pain, rash, or ailment crushing my spirit. Each day I'd spent like that had furthered my resolve that things must change or we would all be doomed. I had seen it in the other women's eyes as well—the suffering, the misery—when it didn't have to be this way.

"But Winnifred, if you all come with me, Birsha will think he's under siege. It will break the pact we've had since our last foray."

For a moment, Winnifred fell silent, but I could tell she was thinking about something. Finally, she said, "If you really believe that Birsha had the generals killed, do you think he'll honor his father's pact with us?"

I sighed, the thought having already occurred to me. "The truth is, I've gone over and over it in my head, but I just don't know. I don't want to cause Henry any more problems than he already has."

Winnifred, who was not the warmest and fuzziest of companions, reached out her hands to me. "You always try to believe the best in people. I think that's why you didn't know about our world until you found the loom. But Brigid, most people aren't like you. They can be petty and mean. And then you take someone like Alaric, someone who is truly evil and . . . well, the world can be a scary place, Brigid."

I knew she was speaking the truth. I wanted to continue to believe that life was fair, that people were inherently good. But I had seen what evil could do. I just hadn't expected it among our *own* people. I suppose that's what had saddened me to the core for I had hoped that we were different. That our rule was one of benevolence only, true justice. Compassion. But it was none of those things. Learning that had somehow changed me, aged me. Made me less trusting, and that was the part that saddened me most. I had seen how it had divided families, friends, society, until we were all at each other's throats. Such strains had caused a rift that would soon unravel our world if we weren't careful. We needed each other—mothers, fathers, sisters, brothers, friends. Without those connections, the tapestry from the very loom that kept society working as one would vanish. Disappear. The consequences of such a loss had weighed heavily on me over the past few weeks, sleep next to impossible.

I thanked Winnifred and told her I would see her tomorrow. But even as I did, I knew that I wouldn't see her. I, like Henry, planned to make my way out alone during the wee hours of the morning, to find him, to help him in any way I could. But like all great plans, in the twilight of the hours before dawn, someone was hatching another plan. A different plan. One that would see my plans go awry.

Birsha called the Council to order, fire simmering in his belly like a hot coal from one of the many ornate brass braziers that littered his personal quarters. Seated around the large oak table were those oddest of characters that made up his council. But the one he was here for, the reason he had called the Council, was not to hash out the loss of the generals, but to proclaim two new generals, his half-brothers. *And* to catch Tempestous at her own game.

"So—" he began, guards stationed at both exits of the room as well as to each side of him, just in case anyone had grandiose ideas of ridding the kingdom of its newest heir. "I'm sure you know why I have called us together."

His eyes bore into Tempestous, whose red hair and fiery nature seemed more so today, for far from being compliant, she appeared recalcitrant, her lips pursed and her eyes giving off sparks that flashed through the room. Even her clothing sparked, as though lit from within. It singed those closest to her, so that both Cricket and Liz Herd got up and moved. Chame Leon followed Liz Herd's lead, so connected were the pair.

"First order of business—" Birsha narrowed his eyes and set his jaw. "Another outburst like the one we had over the past few days, and you, Tempestous, will be confined to the dungeon. Do I make myself clear?"

For several moments, her eyes flickered, flames leaping behind her irises, but finally they dimmed and she sat deeper into her chair, giving only the briefest of nods. Still, she would not look at him.

Birsha fought the urge to reach over and slap her, but he knew it would only create more enmity. And he had yet to solidify his power.

"Does anyone else want to speak?" he demanded, leaning across the table, one brow raised and eyes blazing. He watched as the Council members wilted in their seats, each and every one of them. "Good." He lowered his voice, careful not to gaze too long at any one of them.

"If I may–" the Kazakh said, startling Birsha. "I received word from your adjutant that I am to send the little dragon to your enemies with a message."

The little dragon is what the Kazakh called the Nightjar, a rather grotesque looking bird that was said to possess evil and stalk the night. Merely a superstition, an old wive's tale. And yet it was a quite frightening little bird when it startled one in the darkness. "That's right," Birsha said. "It's better they know now who is in charge."

"I see." The Kazakh turned, as if he were about to leave, but then he stopped, narrowing his eyes into two tiny slits.

"Anything further?" Birsha demanded.

The Kazakh cleared his throat before answering. "It's apparent that you mean to replace your father's generals, am I correct?"

Birsha froze, never once forgetting the image he'd been regaled with over the years of the sheer brutality of this man, if crossed. Birsha knew he could outwit the rest. He'd had a lifetime of learning, in that regard–a real-life game of chess he'd been taught in training for his role as leader someday. People had died in those games. He'd had to learn to outwit them all to stay alive. And he had. Now, if nothing else, he had Alaric's wits, his sensibility. His cunning.

Birsha bowed his head slightly to the Kazakh in acknowledgment. "My half-brothers here will take over where Generals Weathermore and Cedric have left off." He rubbed a finger beneath his nose, a nervous tic when flustered that he'd hoped to overcome. "So sad about their . . . demise."

The Kazakh merely stared unblinking, as though one of his predator falcons or hawks. The man caused Birsha's very bones to shiver as if the Kazakh was even now picking the meat from them.

"Yes," the Kazakh finally said. "I can see that you are quite upset about the news."

For several seconds, they stared at each other until at last the falconer broke the silence between them. He dipped his head slightly, his next words bringing a warning. "You would do well to be *careful* in the upcoming days. Anything can happen when one is new to leadership." Then, before Birsha could say anything further, the Kazakh turned on the heels of his fox-fur lined boots and left. Not even the guards deigned to stop him. And truth to tell, the anxiety Birsha had been feeling with the Kazakh standing so close fell away the moment the man was out the door.

Fishmonger, who had been seated closest to Birsha, flashed his scales, an odd trick of his that Birsha had noticed before. It reminded him of the territorial hummingbirds that were somehow able to bend their feathers, flashing bright, ever-changing colors to intimidate their opponents. Birsha wondered who the Fishmonger saw as his opponent, the Kazakh, one of the many oddities from the Council, or Birsha himself. Birsha ground his teeth together. He would do well to keep his eye on that one.

"Now that we have that matter settled, I want to introduce you to my new generals, Pietra and Agnold. We will have a ceremony in the upcoming days. And then, after the new year, we will march on the Bookbinders."

"But why, sir?" said the Queen of Mammals. "We have a pact."

He turned on her with such ferocity that she winced, and tucked herself as far back as possible to prevent him from hitting her. Slowly, he allowed his anger to ebb.

"That pact was between my father and Sirs Roger and Bookbinder. I am my own man." Then, in his oiliest voice, he added, "As I'm sure you can see."

The Queen of Mammals gulped, then nodded. Yet again, Birsha wondered how such an innocent person had come to be among this pack of wolves. Her hair looked like cornsilk and traced the waistline of her pale blue dress, a plain white cotton blouse beneath it. And she was small, no more than five foot four at best. Add to that the very modest way that she held herself and Birsha would have guessed her a milkmaid, not a queen of mammals. But perhaps that was her allure. Who could say? He only knew that it was time to make his move, to show the entire kingdom what he was made of. That he was manufactured of sturdier stuff than his father. That he would not settle for a portion of the kingdom. No, he wanted it all. But more than that, he wanted his name to go down in history as Birsha the Magnificent. Only then would he know true happiness.

9

The closer they got to the fortress, the more nervous Henry was becoming. Despite Sir Robert's constant attempts to teach him a posh-sounding British dialect, he found himself saying, "Huh? Eh? Could you repeat yourself?" far too often. So much so that Sir Robert had begun to despair that Henry would ever learn.

Just as Henry let loose a low rumble of frustration in his chest, they came to the hillside overlooking Saranac lake, a heart-shaped lake that only served to remind him of Brigid, of how close they had become over the course of their travels. She had been the one constant, the only person he truly trusted besides his brother. Oh, he loved his parents, knew they meant well, but they were of the previous generation and bought into the traditions that kept them all in its thrall, as though a thing rather than a person or persons who were pulling the strings of

their fellow countrymen—like a marionette, up down, up down.
Henry never knew when an arm or a leg would be yanked
in a direction that would send him spiraling to the ground.
And although he was free of that here on this windswept
mountaintop, the smell of fir and pine lending a small measure
of comfort, he couldn't escape the feeling that his time here was
limited, that without Brigid at his side, he had no hope of ever
making it back alive. Though why he thought so, he couldn't
say. He just felt it, inside himself, like a living thing.

"Are you alright, good fellow?" Sir Robert said, concern
causing his mustache to droop.

Henry shook himself free of the feeling, determined to
muster on. He was about to say something deprecating, but
before he could open his mouth, something flew in just over Sir
Robert's shoulder and landed on an overhanging branch.

Henry leaned forward, face pinched as he inspected the odd
creature. Flustered, Sir Robert peered over his shoulder in fright.
"What is it? What do you see?"

"There!" Henry pointed.

And sure enough, a small bird had alighted upon a branch,
a rather sinister look about him. His eyes, decidedly dark, were
framed by two sets of feathers that looked like ears. They stood
sentinel to a rather wide skull, a semicircle of caramel feathers
on the crown above his eyes. For all the world, it looked as
though the bird was scowling at them. Worse, as though it were
a miniature dragon of some sort, come to create havoc.

"What do you suppose it is?" Henry's horse backed away, as
though it too were disconcerted by the tiny creature.

For a moment, Sir Robert simply stared, then placing

his spectacles on his nose, he said, "I do believe, if I'm not mistaken, that it's the great eared nightjar from India, though I've read that they have them in Southeast Asia as well."

"*Asia?*" Henry's mind ran through the possibilities. But then he thought of the Kazakh. He was from Asia–Mongolia, actually. And he raised birds. Perhaps it was one of his, but why was it here? For what purpose?

The odd little creature looked as though it were wearing a black bib. It made a sound like "put-a-wee-o." All of a sudden, it flew towards them making a whistling sound as it went. Without thinking, Henry ducked just as the bird flew over his head.

"These birds are usually seen only at night, which is why so few have been spotted." Sir Robert placed a hand on the scabbard of his rifle. "Just in case he's rabid."

Henry nodded. Why such a small devil bird such as this could frighten him was a mystery, and yet so much of nature had turned on them lately that he had developed a keen sense of watchfulness.

"What is that?" Sir Robert said, pointing.

"What is what?" Henry followed the man's finger. At first, he saw nothing, but then, upon closer inspection, he saw that indeed a small cylinder hung 'round its neck. "Do you suppose it's a message?"

"Only one way to find out." Sir Robert attempted to imitate the bird sound but failed miserably.

"Let me give it a try." Henry recalled that he'd been rather good at bird calls as a young boy growing up with the free run of the manor. "Put-a-wee-ya!" he called.

The bird tilted its head this way and that.

Henry tried again. "Put-a-wee-yo."

The bird ruffled its feathers, as though considering a fly across the meadow.

"Put-a-wee-o," Henry intoned.

Before he knew what was happening, the bird flew right to him and landed on his horse's pommel, spooking Windtamer. Henry clasped the cylinder before the bird could bolt. And he had only seconds to grab the one around the nightjar's neck because Windtamer's front hooves came up in the air, landing with a thump on the ground that sent the bird flying for cover. Too late, he noticed a second cylinder attached to the bird's ankle. By the time Henry had a chance to open the cylinder he'd obtained, the bird was already gone. Henry blinked, wondering if he'd imagined the entire episode.

"Can you read it? What does the message say?"

Henry read it alright, and what it said chilled him to the very core.

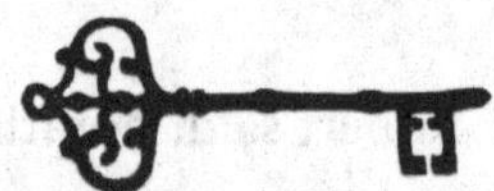

Dawn had yet to show itself amid the blue-gray of nighttime. Though not a morning person by nature, this time of day always fascinated me, the smell of agriculture, of cattle in the near distance, of dew dotting the grass and feeding it with moisture. It was in these hours that I felt at one with nature. Could imagine possibilities not yet born. And in this vision, I now added Henry, my most ardent of supporters. I saw us riding horseback together, me on Old Red, Henry on Windtamer.

Red had yet to forgive Henry for giving him up so readily for a younger horse, one with spirit and drive. Whereas Red was more loyal, more determined and knowledgeable. Those rarest of gifts, so often overlooked.

I filled my saddlebags with as much dried food as possible, adding to that the few articles of clothing I would need besides the ones I was wearing. Next, I added my tent to the necessary items. Lastly, I tied my bedroll behind my saddle and attached an ax and any other tools I might need along the way. I had just finished cinching the last of the straps in place when I heard feet on gravel and pivoted.

I recognized the outline of Winnifred amid the remaining nighttime gloom. "What are you doing here?"

"I could say the same for you. Going somewhere alone?" She crossed her arms as though a schoolmarm speaking to her recalcitrant student.

"So what if I am?" I laid a hand on the horse's pommel as I prepared my leap into the saddle.

No sooner had I spoken, then all around me, as if by magic, women appeared, their upright manner making it clear they were just as incensed as Winnifred that I had chosen to ride without them.

My shoulders sagged. How to explain?

"I didn't want to go without each and every one of you, but Henry's life is at stake. One wrong move and he could end up in the same dungeon as you were in, Emma."

Though I couldn't see her, I knew she was out there among the throng, Thomas too.

Suddenly, a lantern switched on, bathing us all in a

subdued golden light, whose rays cast shadows all around us. From out of the darkness, I could hear the sprites chittering among themselves and my shoulders sagged further. Even they had thought to reprimand me in my hour of need. I dropped the horse's reins to which he whinnied and shook his head, as if in agreement with the rest, though I couldn't help but think it had more to do with his continued snubbing of Henry.

"So talk to me. What would you do, in my case?"

"So now she wants to talk," said Winnifred.

But I could hear the lilt in her voice and knew she wasn't mad at me, not really.

"Brigid—" Thomas stepped forward out of the gloom and brought Emma with him. "We've had news . . . since early this morning."

"News?" I said, frowning. "What kind of news?"

Thomas turned to Emma, who nodded her approval for him to continue. "Word is out that the new heir to the throne plans to attack us. All of us. He wants the kingdom for his own."

"How do you know this?" I demanded. "We haven't sent the carrier pigeon out, and Phinney is at the manor."

Thomas lifted his chin toward a branch. I let out a gasp when I saw it, for it looked like a devil bird, a dragon. Some sort of frightening creature from myth.

"It's a nightjar," Thomas explained. "I have it on good authority. They are a nocturnal bird, but somehow it has made its way from the fortress to here."

"Who sent it?" I asked.

"We believe it was the Kazakh. It was said he had no love

for Alaric, but this new heir may have become untenable. Emma and I think so, anyway."

The pair nodded their heads in unison, as though a single person rather than a couple. It had been that way since Emma first laid eyes on Thomas. She had loved him immediately, as though she could read his very soul and had claimed him, and he her.

So, we possibly had someone in the fortress who was on our side. The thought left me both excited and skeptical, in equal measure. After all, what did we really know about this Kazakh other than the fact that Alaric had kidnapped Phinney as a way to placate the man? Had he reason to placate him? Had there been some enmity between the two? I didn't know, but I planned to find out. Yet the only way I could do that would be to travel to the fortress, to find Henry before he threw himself into the Jackals' den.

"Listen, everyone, I know you mean well, but this is something I must do on my own. I can't risk Birsha's wrath, not until we know for certain that these are his plans. After all, how do we know that someone's not just trying to trick us? So we'll be the first to throw a volley, and then give him cause to attack?"

Murmurs flew all around as the women discussed the pros and cons of what I'd said. Just then, as the first rays of sunshine lifted above the neighboring hills, fireworks went off. And more and more. Probably young teens having a bit of fun in advance of the festivities. We would soon be turning over a new year. In less than a week, the calendar would turn. I wondered if this would be an auspicious year, or a turning point that would throw our world into greater chaos.

For several moments, we all stared up at the sky filled with blooms of color that seemed to come from several directions. The rockets were so loud and shot off with such spirit that none of us recognized the screams until they seemed to be ricocheting through the meadow. Soon, we were screaming too, but why?

Before I could come to a conclusion, I saw deer leaping to the side of us, overhead, all in a state of panic. I crouched, but some were not so fortunate and took a hoof to a shoulder, to a back, to an arm. They seemed to come from everywhere all at once.

"What the . . ." And then I saw it. Flames. But who, or what, had started it?

Birsha strode the ramparts on a rare warm winter's day. He had set his spies in every corner of the kingdom, determined to weed out those who would go against him. More than any other time in his reign, he would be the most vulnerable now. Better to prove himself a strong and powerful leader at the outset, than to risk being seen as the weak son of Alaric the Third, grandson of Faineant the Foul.

"Siegfried–" Birsha gauged the man who had been at his father's side more than any other. "You never told me . . . what did you think of my father?"

"Your father, sir?" Siegfried squeaked, clearly surprised by this line of questioning.

"Did he ever . . . speak of me?" Birsha removed his black, leather gloves one by one to avoid looking directly at his adjutant. "Wonder how I was doing?"

Birsha's mouth twitched. He hated this about himself, that he still sought approval from a man now gone. He'd seen him so rarely in his life, at special functions, mostly, but none of the state functions, for Birsha was a carefully guarded secret. Alaric had kept it so, for many reasons, Birsha assumed. Most notably to prevent him from becoming a target. Yet despite this, Birsha couldn't help but wonder if he'd had other motives. If perhaps he was ashamed of his son in some way. That perhaps Birsha hadn't lived up to the expectations of his father.

"Well?" he said, turning to face Siegfried.

Birsha was surprised when he turned to see Siegfried staring at him, as though pitying him somehow. He had never been so bold as to look at Alaric that way in Birsha's presence, and yet Birsha saw it as a sign that their connection was stronger than that of Siegfried and Alaric.

"If you're asking if your father loved you, sir, I can say unequivocally that—"

But before the man could answer, Birsha's half-brother Agnold came bursting through the door. "It's happening!"

"What's happening?" Birsha strode past Siegfried to grab hold of Agnold's shoulder.

"Pietra and I set Tempestous loose on the village of Battersbog. The whole town is aflame."

"You've *what?*" Birsha sputtered, too angry to know what to do. He had planned for a more subtle approach, to appear as though he were staying true to the treaty without the Bookbinders ever knowing that he was actually sabotaging them. Now there would be open warfare. Birsha covered his face with his hands, feeling a headache coming on. How could his half-brothers have been so foolish?

10

The entire town seemed to be ablaze, people running every which way, a crew forming a human chain from the river to the fireline beyond. Hand over hand, they passed the wooden buckets filled with water, but it was like snuffing out a raging wildfire with a silk water balloon. Still, we had to try.

For their parts, Emma, Thomas, and Winnifred, along with Jocelyn, Gertrude, Yesimeh, and Hannah, were streaming buckets my way in a vain attempt to spare Winnifred's barn and her precious possessions, her experiments. Even her time machine appeared in danger of being licked clean by the fire that voraciously ate up everything in its path. I tossed buckets of water onto the maniacal face in the blaze, a woman whose hair shot out in red, fiery flames amidst an evil smile. Her face appeared warped, like one seen inside a Christmas bulb come holiday time.

Tempestous! For it could be none other. From all that I had heard about her from the men and women I'd come to know while at Alaric's fortress, she wore a demon's crown and acted out of impulse whenever possible. But Alaric had kept her tightly contained. Now, with Birsha in charge, they were clearly less lucky, for Tempestous had put her stamp on the incursion as surely as if she'd placed her wax seal on it.

By now, sweat dripped from my brow, and my hands and clothing were covered in soot. Beatrice stood beside me, throwing bucket upon bucket of water onto the flames, but I could see that we were losing the fight. At last, we stepped back just in time to hear the barn buckle and crack followed by a low wooden groan before the old girl sank to her knees in a clamor of noise, taking her final curtain call before folding in on herself, a dying swan. Even from the distance of the river, I could hear Winnifred's anguished roar. Shards of misery ran through me to hear my friend so distressed at having lost everything she'd ever hoped to achieve, much more than most would accomplish in a lifetime. But I had no time to comfort her or lend her advice about rebuilding. Not so long as the entire town was going up in flames. She would have time ahead of her to design new experiments, create new inventions, even bigger and better than before.

For almost the entire rest of the day, we all fought valiantly, the fire goddess having taken what reserves we'd had left and then laughing as she scampered away on her final dying embers. Though I would have liked to celebrate our victory in turning her away, I couldn't, because in front of me lay a swath of destruction so far and so wide that all I could do was sink wearily onto one of the few spots not covered in inches of ash.

"Are you okay?" Emma asked wearily.

Ordinarily, I might have cried, but the trauma of the day had dried up all my tears, burned them away as cleanly as the fire had the village. Instead, I merely nodded, a lump forming in my throat.

"Here." She offered me a drink from a tin cup that she dipped into a remaining bucket of water from the stream. I accepted it with gratitude and drank it down greedily.

"How is Winnifred?" I asked when I finally came up for air.

Emma blinked rapidly to keep her tears from spilling over. "I gave her a sedative, some valerian root to help calm her. Sleep should do the trick."

But even as she spoke I could hear the quiver in her voice, see her hands shake from all that she had witnessed today. A grayish-white ash lay all around us, making even breathing difficult. I knew that if we were to ever clear our lungs to avoid permanent damage, we would need to vacate the area, but I couldn't bear to leave the others behind, homeless and alone to pick up the pieces.

"The men are already talking of rebuilding." Emma laid her head on my shoulder as we used to do when one or the other of us had suffered at the hands of one of the mistresses of the house.

Though too tired to muster any real enthusiasm, I did manage to say, "That's good."

I didn't know if it was too early to broach the subject, but now, more than ever, I wanted to see Henry, to hold his hand, look him in the eye, tell him what I had longed to tell him since our excursion to the fortress and back. But first, I had to find him.

"I need to leave," I said brusquely.

Emma removed her head from my shoulder and leapt to her knees to face me. "No, Brigid, you can't! As much as you need Henry, we need you. Don't you see?" She captured my gaze to be sure I was paying attention. "We only have each other. Together, we're strong, we can fight any foe. We've proven that today. But alone, we are nothing, Brigid. Nothing!"

Her voice carried such anguish that guilt elbowed me, clocking me squarely in my chest. I rubbed it, as though indeed I had been nudged, then clasped her arm. "If you feel so strongly about it, Emma, then we'll go together. The men can stay here and rebuild, all except Thomas, of course."

"Of course," she added, as though it were a given. "But Brigid—"

"Yes?" I rose to go in search of my horse and my bedroll.

She paused, as though determining how I would react to what she had to say to me. "Other women have asked to join. After this—" She scanned the devastation, her arms held out to encompass the entire region. "Well, let's just say they've had enough. It's time we returned civility and security to the land. But it won't happen so long as there are those who would stop at nothing to destroy us."

I nodded, knowing she was right. It was time to mount a charge. We would all go together, or none of us would go.

Henry was still reeling from the missive that read, "The treaty is up for renegotiation." He knew who had penned the note and why. Still, it rankled. It would mean the end of peace. As he sat atop his horse, he scowled, wondering what he should do about the dispatch. That's when he first smelled the smoke and turned in time to see a great plume of ash headed their way, blocking the sun so that it appeared like a giant red orb. Before he could register a plan, it began to rain gentle ash but that soon turned into a torrent, blanketing the surrounding area in an apocalyptic scene out of *Dante's Inferno*. Fortunately, they were close to a stream, so he jumped down from Windtamer's back and scrambled into the water with two handkerchiefs. He dipped them in water, then wrung them out, Sir Robert doing the same. Henry placed the larger of the two handkerchiefs around Windtamer's muzzle, tying it on as he would a feed bag filled with oats. The other, he tied around his own nose and mouth, hoping to prevent at least some of the ash from entering his lungs.

"We have to go back!" Henry shouted, the ash muffling his words.

"We can't!" Sir Robert yelled back. "We'd never make it through all that ash and soot. We have to keep moving forward and hope that we can outrun it."

"But Brigid is back there, and the women. I can't leave them behind," Henry protested, anguish welling up inside him.

"I'm afraid I will have to pull rank on you, old chap," Sir Robert said. "Your family made me promise that I would do my duty to you, and until we've completed our mission, you are under *my* authority."

To make his point clear, he removed his pistol from its holster and turned it on Henry, causing a tidal wave of fear to wash over him. Only once had he been to sea and had swum in the great wide ocean. But he remembered it well, the swell of the cascading wave as it reached unimaginable heights, only to come crashing down on him, pummeling him into the sandy soil, below. He had been dredged and scoured, turning up on the beach what seemed like hours later, gasping for air, as he was doing now.

His thoughts turned to Brigid. Where was she now? And was she safe? To leave her to this inferno left him feeling just as scoured as if he'd once again tumbled through the thrashing waves of the ocean. He turned away, his throat tight with emotion.

"I'm sorry, Brigid," he whispered.

If only he could get a message to her, find out how she was doing, he might feel better. Perhaps she had returned to the manor, now under the wing of his family. That thought brightened him some. But he knew she could just as easily be in the thick of things or she could be . . . No, he would not think it. Not now, not ever.

As Birsha faced his half-brothers inside the study, he knew they had made a mistake—knew he would need to tread lightly from this point on because of their rash actions. If only he had a card up his sleeve, a pawn to use should the time come.

He'd no sooner thought it than Siegfried took him aside.

"Sir, may I suggest something?" He peered at the two half-brothers, Agnold and Pietra. "Alone," he added.

Birsha released a belabored sigh, but followed his adjutant out onto the balcony of his study. Birsha had been surprised to learn that Alaric was quite the reader. He collected tomes of every kind, from ancient Syriac manuscripts, to Egyptian papyrus scrolls made from reeds found in the marshy Nile river area. Adopted by much of the Roman Empire, the paper was crafted using the ancient technique of peeling the inside of the triangular stalk into long sheets of paper. Alaric even had ancient codices, some dealing with magic and the occult. Birsha had no desire to peer into those. He'd heard of people disappearing into them in a swirl of gold that lit up the night sky, followed by a scream and a whoosh as those unfortunate enough to have been lured in were forever entombed in the tome. He laughed inwardly at his play on words, while secretly delighted by the library that ran floor to ceiling, the leather spines bearing the knowledge of nearly all the world within them, if one were only to look.

"So—" Birsha clapped his hands together, wishing he had thought to bring his Russian sable-lined cape and his fur hat with him onto the balcony. He had yet to grow used to the harsh winters, having been lucky enough to have traveled south for most winters, as his nanny hated the damp and the cold. "What is it you wanted to tell me?" Birsha asked, turning on Siegfried.

To his immense surprise, Siegfried didn't look down, but rather at him, as though he were his equal. *Odd.* The few times Birsha had seen the adjutant with his father, he had seemed rather obsequious, always bowing and scraping. He rather liked this new Siegfried, the one who was unafraid to speak to him openly and honestly. Still, he had best be careful until he knew the true lay of the land. Traitors could be anywhere.

"Well, sir, you might as well know that I have spies throughout the land."

Birsha raised a single brow. "Is that so?"

Siegfried gave one quick nod. "In a position such as mine, it's helpful to be . . . useful."

Ah! So now Birsha understood. The man had hedged his bets against his father's whims. Had seen to it that he was too useful to be set aside. More and more, Birsha was beginning to like the man. He seemed more practical than cunning, almost brotherly. And after the terrible error in judgment of Birsha's own half-brothers, he needed this insider's knowledge to help keep him alive while he adjusted to his new position in the realm.

"I have it on good authority," said his adjutant, "that the son of the Bookbinder manor is on his way here with a British nobleman."

"The son of the manor?"

"Henry Bookbinder, sir. He and the nobleman are nearly halfway here."

Birsha couldn't believe his good fortune. He rocked on his heels, both to stay warm and to give himself time to develop a plan.

"Why have they come all this way?" Birsha asked, puzzled by this strange event.

Siegfried leaned into him. "I have it on good authority,

sir, that Henry plans to come disguised as a British nobleman, to curry favor and to learn what sort of man you are, your strengths and your weaknesses. To take that information back to the manor so that it can be used to halt any future attacks."

"And on what authority did you learn such news, pray tell?"

Birsha could see his adjutant's wheels turning–reveal the source, or keep it to himself for future need? He could also see that it was necessary for the man to reveal at least *something* of value to win Birsha's trust.

"A trapper, sir."

"And can this trapper help capture this Henry fellow?" Birsha asked.

"I could see to it," said his adjutant perfunctorily.

"Then do so, Siegfried." The man was about to turn to step inside when Birsha added, "And Siegfried, thank you. I will repay you handsomely for your aid."

The adjutant paused for so long that Birsha wondered if he'd heard him clearly. But finally, the man nodded, the glimmer of a smile on his lips. Then he entered the sanctuary of the library with Birsha close on his heels.

Henry heard a whoosh and registered pain before he knew what hit him. He peered down at the red liquid flowing down his left arm. Only then did he realize what had caused it. An arrow. Time seemed to stand still, each movement labored even as Sir Robert shouted for him to "Get down!" just as another arrow whizzed by, narrowly missing him. It landed with a thwunk against a large balsam fir. Henry pulled the arrow out of the tree with his good arm and was amazed at the amount of filigree on an object such as this. It was like nothing he'd ever seen. The arrow, instead of being made from ordinary metal, was bright silver and had the scrollwork of a fortress and tower on it. Henry's breathing stilled, for he would know that fortress anywhere. Alaric's fortress, or should he say Birsha's now. The young ruler had been head of his clan for only a short time, and already he had usurped the throne in order to wreak havoc upon the land. Henry had only to look at the ash that drifted down around him to know it was true.

Under his breath, Sir Robert muttered, "Let's get this arrow out of your shoulder and get out of here before—" But he never finished his sentence, because seconds later a trio of men were upon them, rifles at the ready, their masks hiding their identity.

"Help me get this cursed arrow out of my shoulder," Henry pleaded with Sir Robert, who gave a short nod of his head.

With a strength Henry hadn't suspected of the titled man, Sir Robert shoved the shaft in just enough so that he could snap it in two, then he pulled each side out and dug into his pack even as their captors besieged him. Sir Robert kicked with his boot, hitting one man in the stomach, while the other one grabbed Henry and held him tight.

Apparently, realizing that his leader would prefer a live man to a dead one, the man who had captured Henry gave the nod for Sir Robert to continue his ministrations. Deftly, Sir Robert lathered a salve on each side of the wound, then bound the wound with clean cloth.

"That should do, for the time being," Sir Robert said, all

the while scowling at the man he'd kicked. The man rose to
his feet, rubbing his tummy. The two others held tight to their
guns, one trained on Henry, the other on Sir Robert.

Henry quelled the tension in his chest and thanked the
Englishman for his kindness. The future remained uncertain
with this new twist in the tale. All he could do now was to wait
and search for a means of escape. *If* it came.

I bent over the swollen stream and saw myself in the
still water kept free of the eddies by a pile of birch branches,
undoubtedly placed there by beavers building a dam for their
kits. In that still water, I noticed my reflection. How had I gone
from a hearty young woman to an old crone in one short day?
My hair was unkempt and covered in ash so that it appeared
gray and withered. Whereas my face had soot smudges, two
dark ones beneath my eyes. Even my clothing appeared old and
haggard, having taken a beating in all the heat and fire from the
flames. As I dipped my handkerchief in water, wiping away the
smudges, I felt like crying, but the fire seemed to have dried my
tears. I needed to get a message to Henry, but how?

The cool water dripped down my face, staining it with
streaks of soot. I gave a mirthless laugh, looking no better
off than before. Still, I continued to pour water over myself
until my hair and face had gained at least some semblance of
normalcy. When I was done here, I would need to check my
packs to be sure that I had at least a few fresh clothes to sustain
me.

I was about to turn back to camp when I heard a familiar cry and looked up in time to see my beloved Phinney land on a fir branch across the stream.

"Oh, Phinney!" I cried, stumbling across the wet rocks and nearly plunging into a pool of water in my attempt to reach her.

She squawked and flew from her perch, flapping wildly above me in an attempt to keep me from going any further. With her encouragement, I turned back, and no sooner had I fallen to my knees on the moist earth, than she landed beside me, tucking her beak into my wet hair and making small cooing sounds. If I'd been a more imaginative person, I might have believed she was comforting me, and perhaps she was, for she was nothing if not attentive in my hour of need.

"What are you doing here, Phinney?"

It's then that I saw she carried a small metal barrel around her neck with the tiniest of clasps. I opened it carefully. Still, she squawked.

"What have we here?" I unfurled the tiny coded message. It said *We've heard about the fire. Stop. Return to the manor at once. Stop. The mission is too dangerous. Stop.*

It took me a moment to realize that the missive was for Henry and Thomas, not me. The Bookbinders didn't know that Henry was no longer with us. Now, more than ever, I simply had to get a message to Henry, and I had the means to do it.

"Phinney," I said, wobbly as I attempted to stand. "We need to get word to Henry, do you understand? Henry," I repeated, just in case she hadn't been listening. "But first, we need to tell Thomas and Emma the plan!"

I shot up out of the fen, knowing that Phinney would be

one step behind, if not already flying ahead of me. Odd that. Phinney seemed to have a sixth sense about things. Seemed to know what I was thinking before I'd even had the chance to think it, like where I was headed.

"How is my loom?" I asked Phinney, missing it almost as much as I missed Henry. It had been steadfast in helping me survive my many ordeals. Yet, I didn't dare take it into enemy territory. For whoever owned it would own the kingdom, and though we'd been able to protect it up until now, this latest volley didn't bode well. For any of us.

I had been moving so quickly through the forest that I didn't realize someone was ahead of me until I ran smack dab into him with a thud that nearly landed me on my backside. Fortunately, Thomas reached out and grabbed my shoulders before I could fall into the muck and mire.

"Thomas!" I cried. "Thank heavens you're here. We need to send a message to Henry. To tell him to return, at once!"

"Why?" He grasped me by my arms and inspected every square inch of me as though he'd never seen me before, but I suppose I did look a wreck. I swiped at my wet hair that hung limply in my eyes. Though my clothes were soiled, my face, at least, had regained its healthy shine.

"Lord and Lady Bookbinder have ordered Henry to return," I stated triumphantly, handing him the now crumpled piece of paper.

His eyes scanned the words, his eyebrows a shelf to his forehead. He moaned at the back of his throat, reminding me of one of those Tibetan throat singers I'd heard once at a concert given by the Lady's Auxiliary.

"Aren't you happy?" I demanded, bending down to look him in the eye. "Henry can come home!"

Thomas peered up solemnly, his face as ashen as my surroundings. "Don't you see?" He worked his jaw, though whether he meant to cry or to yell, I wasn't sure which. "We can't go back without completing the mission!"

Now he really *was* shouting. Not only that, but he'd crumpled the message and tossed it to the ground where it instantly blended in with the ash. I hustled to retrieve it. What on earth had gotten into Thomas, the most steady of men? His reaction left me feeling uneasy, my fingers trembling as I again opened the message and placed it in my pocket for safekeeping.

"Why, Thomas? What difference will it make if Henry continues?"

"Don't you see?" Thomas said, grinding his teeth together. "He can't go back. Otherwise, we'll always be at the mercy of the Jackals."

Thomas stamped his foot and ran his fingers through his hair, still covered in ash and soot. I'd been so caught up in my own excitement that I hadn't realized how disheveled he looked until now. And I could see it . . . in his eyes. The utter bone weariness after all we'd been through containing the fire. Sparks still smoldered, breaking out in places. A fire watch would be kept for days, if not weeks or months. As the lone remaining man of any stature, it fell to him to do something about all this. And yet, he'd allowed me to reign on our earlier foray to the fortress, had even appreciated that I had taken the helm, leaving him free to do as he wished. But now, with Henry gone, it had broken something inside Thomas and he had become steeled, inured to his role as prince. And yet I could see that he didn't want it–the pressure of it, the sheer weight of such a mantle upon his shoulders.

I reached out and took his hands in mine. "This is not your responsibility, Thomas."

"But Henry's my brother."

His words were so filled with anguish that I nearly melted into him.

"No." I cupped his chin, forcing him to gaze directly into my eyes. "I'll look after Henry." And as I said it, I knew it was true. That I would always take care of him, so long as he would have me, for I loved Henry. I loved the way his shoulders drooped when life grew too hard. How his untamed heart ran wild when he was in nature, the almost childlike way about him that made me want to wrap my arms around him and protect him, hold him close.

"Henry is no longer your worry," I reiterated. "He's mine."

Something fell away from behind Thomas's eyes, as though he had released a huge burden that had weighed him down since childhood. As the oldest, he stood in line as heir. It had been up to him to see Henry grow up smart and strong and capable. The role of teacher, brother, and friend, had been foisted upon Thomas' shoulders. He had carried Henry through life, always making sure that he was safe, secure, loved. Now it was up to me. And I was determined to take on this new role with vigor, if only he would bequeath it to me.

For several moments, Thomas paused. Then finally, he nodded, a flood of relief washing over him. Just then, I heard Emma's voice from over the rise.

"Oh there you are, and Brigid, too. Thank goodness! I've been searching for you everywhere. I've got terrible news! Henry and Sir Robert have been captured."

11

So, it was true. Henry and Sir Robert *had* been captured.
I'd scarcely had time to recover from the fire, and now this news.
I hung my head, not wanting to look up for fear of what Emma
would say . . . do. But she rushed to me and swept me up in her
arms, Thomas doing likewise.

"We'll find Henry," Emma said, "and Sir Robert, too."

How lucky to have two such good friends as Emma and
Thomas, I realized as I relished the warmth of their embrace.
With one final hug, they released me. Now, for the decisions to
come.

"We've already spoken to the women," Thomas said,
peering over at Emma for reassurance. "They're coming too."

He held his hands up, broaching no opposition from me,
but I was beyond that. If Birsha and his men had taken Henry,
then they were no friends of mine, all bets off from the moment

they had abducted him.

"Let's go tell the women to begin packing," I said.

And with that, I began trudging through the ankle high ash, the forest blanketed in it, making it appear ghostlike. Even the sounds were muffled. But oddest of all was the sun, which shone through the layers of smoke. It was huge on the horizon and blood red. Furthermore, it made me shiver, for it looked like a blood moon, an omen so dire that one had only to wait for the evil aftermath.

Both Thomas and Emma's eyes followed mine, they, too, sensing the danger that lurked in the foretelling of the sun.

"Don't look at it," Emma warned, covering her face with her hands. "The sun causes dark shadows when viewing it. People have gone blind."

I knew her words to be true—had been warned from early childhood on. Thomas and I quickly covered our eyes and followed her out of the forest. To my surprise and delight, the women were already packing, preparing for the trek ahead, and not just a few. Women had been seeping in from all across the countryside. Whether they had heard about Henry's capture or merely saw the value of the women's quest because of the fire, I didn't know. I only knew I was grateful for their help. I would need it in the days ahead.

Tiny Yesimeh came forward and bent her knees slightly, as though curtseying. "We've drawn up plans," she said, no longer the ingénue, but a battle weary veteran who knew her worth to the community. She held out a list of supplies we would need for the trek ahead and our plan of attack, should it come to that.

I scanned the two lists quickly, certain she had left out

nothing.

"Perfect," I said.

I was about to step around her to head for my tent, which sagged due to the weight of the ash. In fact, it appeared as though it might topple. It would be hard to rid it of the smell, and yet the entire town had suffered the same fate. As a result, we would all be forced to endure the stench. Still, every last one of us wore a mask to cover our faces. I just hoped we didn't come down with "the sickness" because of the smoke and ash. It started in the lungs with wheezing and coughing, and could sometimes develop into pneumonia. Fortunately, Gertrude was beginning to show the skills of an herbalist and had packed yarrow for stomach cramps, chamomile to help the soldiers sleep and for wounds, white snake root for diarrhea, ague, and fever, and licorice as an antibacterial medicine, among many other herbs. Emma, who had a knack for such things, had taught her all she knew. Said she had learned it at her gran's knee. Those two women, along with several other women, had formed a tight-knit team who helped keep our company up and running.

Yesimeh cleared her throat, refusing to step aside to allow me to depart.

I recognized the sudden discomfort that settled across her fine-boned features. "What is it, Yesimeh?"

"I think you should come with me." She took me by the arm and swiveled me toward what remained of the barn. I looked to Emma and Thomas to see if they knew what she had up her sleeve, but they merely shrugged.

"Alright," I said at last, "but we really need to get going if—"

She had barely maneuvered me into the skeleton of the

barn when out of the gloom, an apparition appeared, then others stepped out of the shadows. For a moment, I thought I was seeing things.

"What is this?" I asked, uncertain what she expected of me.

A small clan of women, children, and two men stepped forward, all of them black, all of them undoubtedly escaped slaves. I drew back in surprise. Though I had witnessed the upper echelons of society with their slaves, my family had never cottoned to it, nor did I. After all, I felt as much a slave as any, due to my more recent circumstances. Only when I was away with these women warriors did I feel as though I was more than just a cog in a machine. Here, I felt known, heard. But it was because I had made it so, by eliminating "the traditions," those most ignoble of rules or laws that kept people in their place, made slaves of both men and women. All of us had become freer, happier, with them gone, as though a foul air had lifted, reminding us that we were human. Equal.

"Ma'am," one of the young women said, two children at her feet and one in her arms, "we'd like to come with y'all. We could cook, clean, anything ya need. Just let us come."

I understood what they were asking and why. Alaric's lair lay just south of the Canadian border. Should they make it across that most invisible of lines, they could live as freed men and women. Though not technically free yet, both England and Canada had been working to abolish slavery. No doubt their best chances for a future lay there.

It took only a moment to ponder the situation. If they were willing to put their lives on the line to earn their freedom, who was I to say otherwise and yet . . .

"If you come with us," I said, "we will supply you with everything you need."

A stir of excitement grew among them, and one of the men, who was clearly the husband of the woman I had spoken with, reached out and grabbed his wife's waist, pulling her to him in a hug that quickly ended with her tugging at the bodice of her ash-covered dress.

I held up my hands until the hubbub died down to a mere rustle of bare feet. "But if you come," I added, followed by an uneasy silence, "you will be treated as equals. You will do your own cooking, your own cleaning. The only thing we ask is that if you have any special skills, tell Yesimeh and she will record them. We all help each other where we can."

For several moments, it's as if the words didn't register. Instead, they frowned, peering at each other as though wondering if they'd heard right.

"Equals?" said the woman, who finally introduced herself as Dele, pronounced Deal-lee.

"Equals," I repeated.

For the next few minutes they all spoke at once in an excited whisper, then Dele turned back to me. "Will the others accept us?"

The truth is, I didn't know, but I couldn't very well advocate for the women and do any less for these women . . . and men. If we were truly to be united, we needed as many hands as possible. Plus we needed to be united behind an ideal, not just a select few individuals.

"Be ready by morning," I said with an encouraging smile. "Until then, stay in here. I will talk to the others." Then I winked, and left them behind to prepare for the day ahead. We had to be ready by morning. All of us.

The next day loomed large. Our ranks had swelled to nearly three thousand women and a handful of men. All around the village, people were sweeping up, washing down, or scrubbing the ash off of everything visible. And still they couldn't hide the devastation of the past two days. In the distance, burned trees stood like sentinels to a dying people. I had to do something, but what? Right now, I had no firm plan, other than to rescue Henry, but that in and of itself was enough. And yet we were always on the defense. We had yet to take the bull by the horns. Go on the offense.

By early morning, just after daybreak, we had eaten, quelled our fires and had loaded up everything we would need. I had spoken to the women about the slaves who had offered to help us, if we would take them to the border. Most agreed to the plan, a few did not. Those women left in the night. I wondered how they would view us down the road, but I couldn't allow their animosity to deter either me or the steadfast group of women who were risking their lives to stop Birsha and his onslaught.

As we prepared for the move ahead, I heard the gratifying sound of the supply wagons gin into action, the squeal of their wheels and the "haws" that accompanied them. I swiveled my horse around and was surprised to see not Emma or Thomas, but one of the new recruits, Elijah Ellis, a black man in his thirties, if I were to guess, and husband to the woman I had met yesterday, Dele. For a reason unknown to me, he had decided to act as my pilot boat, guiding me as we went, pointing out the terrain which he knew well.

"I've trapped in these parts for near all my life." Elijah was tall and lean and sported a vest with a watch fob. "Met my wife when she got shipped up from a plantation down in the Carolinas. Owner was going to sell her away from the estate so she found a conductor who helped her escape. The trapper, who taught me everything I know about the wilderness, found her during a trip to New York. She needed work, so he brought her to meet me, thought she could help me with the cookin' and such. She's been with me ever since."

"You've been on your own for years?"

He laughed. "Not exactly. Trapper got us forged documents and we pretend we're his."

"Why are you telling me all this?" I asked, surprised by his openness.

"Because, from what everyone tells me, you're an outsider like me, ma'am."

I paused for only a moment, then nodded. "I suppose I am."

The miles stretched out before us. From behind I could hear the sprites. Winnifred, who knew them quite well by now, after her excursion into the future, had rigged up a water tank that bounced along behind her horse, in it the sprites. They giggled and yelled "whee!" whenever they went over an especially large bump. We had marched for nearly the entire day when we heard a surprise rumble that lifted the earth beneath our feet, setting it down again, as though the earth were a series of waves rather than solid ground.

"What do you suppose *that* is?" I asked Dele, who had left her children behind with some of the other women to come and join us.

She turned to her husband as though he might have an answer, but he merely shrugged. Again, it rolled through the ground in waves, causing my stomach to lurch. Behind me, I heard the chattering of the sprites.

"Do they know what it is?" I called to Winnifred, who had learned their odd language, at least the rudimentary aspects of it, and could interpret.

"They say it's the Roll-um," she said, bending down to listen further. "A creature that lives beneath the earth and causes the mountains to rise—for the seas to give birth to new territory. They live in silence, unless they are disturbed."

"And what has disturbed them?" I asked, not sure I wanted an answer.

"Oh, well, the Fetters, of course."

I felt as though Winnifred was speaking gobbledygook. What on earth was she talking about? The only kind of Fetters that I knew about were the ones made to enslave mankind.

"And what are the Fetters?" I said on a sigh.

"Why, those are the invisible ties upon the land and its people."

I shook my head at the many cobwebs that seemed to have taken up residence inside my brain. What on earth was the girl talking about?

As if to prove her point, she jutted her chin forward, and sure enough, though not completely invisible, clear tendrils began to spring up out of the ground and wrap around the legs of our horses. The animals' cries immediately filled the air as they fought to escape the cloying grasp of the see-through ivy, or whatever it was that held them trapped.

Yesimeh, who had been riding alongside Winnifred let out a scream as one slithered up her leg and tied her feet together so that she was unable to move. Behind her, Emma and Thomas were slicing at their particular jailers, the tendrils yanking back with a shriek and sucking back into the ground with a tiny puff of pollen that they left in their wake, causing both Emma and Thomas to sneeze violently. But better a sneeze than to be trapped forever in a collection of vines that would eventually choke off any oxygen that we might hope to breathe.

"Quick!" I shouted. "Get your swords."

Together we began chopping. All throughout the miles of women and horses in our wake, we heard shrieks and screams, from the plant or the women, I couldn't tell. I only knew that little by little, we were winning. The clear, jelly-like plants were sinking back into the ground, sending forth puffs of pollen as they disappeared.

When it seemed that nearly all had escaped the wrath of the Fetters, I placed a rag over my mouth to spare me the pollen, then quickly tore it aside just long enough to give the order to march.

As one, the women not only marched, they spurred their poor beasts into action, the animals just as eager as the women to escape the sucking tendrils. Once we were distant enough that I could think back to the odd creatures or plants, whatever they were, it became apparent that they were quite beautiful when caught by the sunlight, giving off an array of colors that reminded me of a rainbow. And yet I had no doubt that they were sent to ensnare us. We would need to be on our guard from now on. But who had sent them? I thought of Mother Nature. But our Mother Nature was kind, compassionate. This seemed like more of the doing of someone like Tempestous, whose role was to hunt and bring down any and all opponents.

I spurred the horses forward because I had no doubt Tempestous was throwing a temper tantrum.

12

Henry's shoulder throbbed and his head ached. Sir Robert had managed to quell the bleeding, but he hadn't the resources to stop the pain. Henry knew that honey was supposed to help protect and heal a wound, if he could only locate some and manage to collect it. He thought back to the last time he had been here, to the bears who had helped them flee the fortress when they escaped, lo those many moons ago. They had returned from foraging with honey on their muzzles. He tried to think back to those locations. The more he thought about it, the more he felt certain that they were nearing one, if only he could find a way to retrieve some of the gooey substance.

Henry leaned over and whispered his plans to Sir Robert. "Tell them you need to relieve yourself," he said, knowing that in his weakened condition he would be in no shape to search through the woods for honey.

"I have just the thing to collect the honey in." Sir Robert produced a jar with a lid and winked.

A half hour later, he stumbled upon a large granite stone beside an open meadow. "There!" Henry urged. "The bears returned from that spot just east of the meadow."

Sir Robert quickly put Henry's plan into action. To be certain that his captors didn't clue into his plan and put a halt to it, Henry let out a loud yelp and began moaning as Sir Robert snuck away into the forest. Henry's captors came over to him to see what all the fuss was about, but Henry merely kept it up until he was sure Sir Robert was out of sight.

"My wound is throbbing." Henry winced. Fortunately, that was no lie, though he'd been trained from childhood never to show pain unless it was absolutely unavoidable.

The three captors looked to each other, before the one who must be the leader of the pack, a large man with a rounded paunch and beady eyes, gave the go ahead with the briefest of nods. In silent agreement, the skinniest of the three men, a rather scruffy looking man with a scraggly beard and wiry graying locks, plunged through his knapsack and pulled out a packet of some indeterminate herb. He kept a canister of hot water, which he now poured into a tin cup, stirring the earthy smelling herb into it, then handed it to Henry.

Henry sniffed at the foul smelling stuff, certain it would do something to quell the pain. For anything that smelled that awful *must* be good for the body. Still, he breathed in the clean scent of the forest before plunging his mouth into the fetid drink and gulping it all down in one quick gulp. Afterward, he shuddered as the three men laughed. Just then, Sir Robert reappeared from the mouth of the forest and gave a short nod. Relief flooded through Henry. Perhaps now he would no longer have to worry about the wound becoming infected.

As the men remounted their steeds, Sir Robert quickly handed off the jar of honey, which Henry hid behind his pommel as he mounted. When he'd finally managed to finagle his way onto the saddle, he turned the lid. Then, in one swift motion, he quickly dunked his hand into the jar, feeling the sticky goo of the liquid amber honey on his hand. He rubbed it onto the wound, then closed the lid and pocketed it in one of his saddlebags just as the skinny man turned.

"Hey you!"

Henry froze.

"You take the lead. That way we can keep an eye on you, make sure you don't fall asleep in the saddle."

The three men laughed. Sir Robert urged him to comply, then spurred his horse to follow Henry's, should indeed Henry fall asleep at the reins.

For the next hour, they trudged through the trails that the Mohawks had forged over centuries of footsteps beating the hard earth to a fine sheen, as well as iron axes used to cut down vines and other growing vegetation along the path. Finally, with the even sway of the horse and the warmth of the day, Henry could no longer stay in his saddle and began to slide. Before he reached the ground, Sir Robert was at his side, helping him down.

"We have to stop, give Henry time to rest," Sir Robert pleaded. "Even you can see that."

Once again, the two men looked to their leader who gave

the nod. "We'll set up camp here. No use bringing him back dead when he will be of more value alive."

Henry was of no use to the others, even though the leader kicked him repeatedly with the toe of his boot to get him moving. Fortunately, Sir Robert managed to get them to back off, preparing the campsite for both Henry and himself.

"Stay put," he whispered. "I'll get us wood for a fire so that we can have a decent meal, at least." He peered at the three drifters with undisguised disdain, then turned to his task.

Meanwhile, Henry slumped down against a log, Sir Robert having brought him a bedroll from which to lay his head while he slept. And indeed, it took only moments before he was asleep, the strain of the day overwhelming him.

When he awoke, he had trouble judging the time. Before he'd fallen asleep, it had been late afternoon, early evening. Now, owls hooted overhead and the fire crackled against the blue-black color of the nighttime. Roasted meat hung on a spit, so perhaps it was not too late. The heaviness of his head had dissipated somewhat, leaving him with a mild lethargy, but at least the throbbing was gone, and when he held his arm up to the firelight, he no longer noticed an angry red welt, so perhaps he would be okay.

"Ah! The boy is among the living again."

The large man—the leader of the bunch—smacked his lips as he chewed on a piece of meat, venison, by the look of it. Henry was about to speak when from behind the man's shoulder first one woman, then another popped out from the darkness that surrounded the fire.

Henry shared a glance with Sir Robert, who seemed just

as surprised as Henry that women were here, but not just any women–beautiful women, one with silky black hair and tawny brown eyes. The other had hair just as silky and long, only red, and instead of tawny eyes, they were an emerald green that glistened against the firelight. They walked sinuously toward Henry and Sir Robert.

"What have we here?" the dark-haired woman said.

But something about them seemed askew, as though Henry were seeing an apparition rather than a real person, and yet he hadn't felt that about the first woman. Instinctively, he knew something wasn't right about this, any of this, and yet, whether it was the medicine or the surprise of seeing such beautiful women in a place such as this, he couldn't take his eyes off of them.

We had been alternately riding and marching for hours in the vain attempt of reaching Henry before he arrived at the fortress. He didn't know all that we knew, didn't have the means to learn what dangers were lurking in the forest, waiting to strike.

Jocelyn and Gertrude rode up beside me and motioned to an odd mounding that seemed to be moving alongside the marching women. As if they too had noticed something strange, Winnifred and Yesimeh came bounding up, their horses in tow. Even Emma rode up in a lather, a surprise since she spent almost all of her time at Thomas' side. Soon, a whole bevy of women had surrounded me, all talking at once.

"Quiet!" I yelled. "One at a time. You speak, Jocelyn, since you and Gertrude were here first."

The normally coquettish Jocelyn appeared downright angry, but it was Emma who spoke up, cutting off any attempt on Jocelyn's part to be the first to speak.

"The Fetters!" Emma cried, as though that should explain everything.

"The Fetters what?" I shrugged my shoulders, all the while wondering how the fauna-like creatures had come by their name.

"Look!" Emma cried, pointing.

I followed her gaze and sure enough, a large waterfall streamed over a rock outcropping, a narrow path beneath it the only way forward. But that was not what had everyone's attention. There stood Dele and Elijah. In front of them, on an outcropping of granite, perched possibly the most beautiful woman that any of us had ever seen and she was pleading for Elijah to help her. She sidled down off the outcropping, then came up beside Elijah's mount, nearly shoving Dele over the narrow ledge in the process. Yet, what was most distressing to all of us was how quickly she had ingratiated herself to Elijah, playing on his sympathies, begging to be allowed on his horse's back, complaining that she'd been walking for days without food or water. But I had only to look at her to know it was a lie.

"Poor Dele," I murmured to unanimous agreement. "But why do you think it's a Fetter? The ones I saw were nearly invisible, with plantlike tendrils."

"That's just what they want you to believe," Winnifred said. And though she had no stake in the game, being as she preferred science to any man, she held a proprietary air for those of us with beaus or husbands.

"It's true," Emma agreed with a fierce nod.

"How do you know?" I asked.

"I've seen one," Emma said.

Only now did I see that her face was pale yet her cheeks flushed, as though she had a fever.

"One of the Fetters has Thomas as well!" Emma cried. "She's back there, around the bend. Quick! Help me."

I thought fast. If what they were saying was true, we would need to stop both women, the one luring Elijah away from Dele, and the one who had already done her best to lure Thomas away from Emma.

"Winnifred, Gertrude, you go help Dele. Emma, Jocelyn, come with me."

And with that, we each went our opposite directions, Winnifred and Gertrude north, Jocelyn, Emma, and I south. It took no more than five minutes at best to locate Thomas, who appeared as if in a trance, the lithesome beauty taking him by the hand toward the forest, all thoughts of his people or Emma gone.

"Thomas!" I called, but he merely looked at me, dazed. "You need to come back to us." I held out my hand, but he only peered at it, as though a large chasm separated us. "Thomas," I said, trying again, "the woman is a Fetter. She's trying to steal your soul. Please, Thomas, look at me, not at her. Right at my eyes."

I could tell it was taking all of his willpower to focus on me, and not the woman whose beauty had wrapped him in a spell so deeply that he was unable to save himself.

"Thomas," I said through gritted teeth, "Emma loves you."

As if to prove it, Emma reached out a hand to him. "Please, Thomas. Don't leave. She's trying to pull you underground, to take you away from us, from me . . ." Emma's voice trailed off in a sound so plaintive as to make the birds above cry down in sympathy.

"Come, Thomas," the waif of a woman said, her voice so smooth and beguiling that it almost had the rest of us bewitched as well. "I will take you home with me."

That was all it took for Emma to let loose a scream so mournful and filled with such loss that whatever spell the woman had cast on him, it was now over and he came to his senses with a shake of his head, as though from a most pleasant dream that he was loath to leave.

"Emma?" He let loose of the Fetter's hand and walked toward us, close enough so that the three of us were able to whisk him away before the woman could do further damage to Thomas's mortal soul. Emma hurried him along, well out of the woman's reach.

With Thomas gone, the Fetter lunged at us, her voice so sickly sweet as to contain a poisonous syrup, it held such venom. "You think you have won," the spirit woman hissed, throwing her long black hair out in an arc. "But we shall have the last laugh. We are beautiful; you are not. We have the breeding and training of the Ages. We know what a man wants. We have only to use our wiles and they are ours." She leaned into me, her eyes sparking fire and ice. "In fact, one of our women has your Henry as we speak."

I gasped. Though usually self-composed in such matters, to know that Henry was being lured away from me through false pretenses, for what purpose I could only gather, made my stomach lurch and my knees buckle. I tried to grab hold of the Fetter but felt only air. She laughed.

"You shall see. It will be easy. Your men—they take one look at us and they no longer see you. You are dead to them. Soon it will be us living in the fine manors, and you shall be our–" She started to say slaves, but amended it to "servants." She stared at me with a sly smile. "And then the kingdom shall be ours. We will supplant you–all of you. And your men will let us, because we are beautiful and we are trained to be everything they want. They won't know what happened to them until it's too late."

And with that, she let out a cackle, her form changing even now to that of a hideous crone. Then she cackled one last time, and sank into the ground, but not before she had turned back to plant form. She reached out one final tendril in an attempt to grab me and pull me under, but I managed to draw my dirk from its scabbard and slice the tendril from around my foot. The Fetter blew a single puff of pollen and then was gone, having left a bruise around my ankle where she had tried to grab me. I was shaking as I made my way back to my horse and to the others.

"Where are they? Shouldn't they be here by now?" Birsha groused.

To keep himself busy, he had taken to cataloging all those oddities his father Alaric had collected, bits of magic from every part of the world, some thought to be long since stolen or destroyed, or simply buried within the tombs of the ancients, but here they were, lining the walls of a room filled with artifacts on full display.

First there was the Cintamani Stone, said to be worn by Buddha himself and able to grant wishes.

"What is this ring?" Birsha asked Siegfried, who was quickly becoming indispensable. Every time Birsha reached out to touch it, words in some ancient script glowed, emitting sparks of light that glanced across the room, making a pinging sound any time it hit against something.

"Oh, that," Siegfried said, shrugging. "That's the Ring of Gyges. Plato wrote about it, I believe."

"What does it do?" Even looking at it caused it to make a funny humming sound, as though it were a living thing instead of pure gold.

"It's supposed to make the wearer invisible, I think. But I also recall Alaric warning that it had a side effect, if you will."

"What sort of side effect?" Birsha said, drawing his hand back in alarm.

Siegfried shook his head. "I wish I could recall. I just know he warned me never to touch it, but he could have just made that up so that anyone with the notion to try it on would leave it alone."

"Hmm." Birsha decided to err on the side of caution, for now.

He peered around the room and noticed an empty glass case in the middle of the wide expanse, as though waiting for something quite special indeed. Beneath it was a gilded mahogany base with lotus blossoms and various beautiful women and finely sculpted men on it. The base was exceedingly large.

"What was the glass case meant for?" Birsha asked, tapping his front teeth with his finger.

"That was meant to house the loom," Siegfried said, halting his cataloging long enough to gaze at Birsha in wonderment. "But if Alaric couldn't get it, you surely won't be able to obtain it." Siegfried gave a small laugh before he seemed to realize his mistake and paused, turning ashen.

A fire started in Birsha's belly and fanned upwards, igniting his face with indignation. He sputtered to speak, but before he could get an intelligible syllable from out of his mouth, Siegfried threw up his hands and at the same time made a quick bow of apology.

"I'm sorry, Birsha," he said, sweat lining his forehead, "it's just that . . . well, you remind me so much of my cousin, and we are nearly the same age. We often teased each other. I overstepped. It won't happen again."

"I see," Birsha said, the heat slowly dissipating. "And you were fond of this cousin?"

"Very fond," Siegfried admitted. "We grew up together, did everything together. He was my best friend."

The admission dampened any anger Birsha had harbored toward the man, to be compared to a favored cousin. Few, if any, of his fellow classmates had spoken such kindness toward him, preferring to view him as competition in the ascension to power. Though he had relished his role as heir to the throne, he had often resented it as well. The lack of privacy, the snarkiness from his peers that went with filling such a role of one so young and yet without the maturity or the experience. No doubt many of his superiors, those in power for years who had not been born an heir but had a greater skill level than Birsha, saw him as a disrupter, an imposter to their greater knowledge and ability. And there was more than a little truth in that. He *did* have much to learn. He knew that, but the only way he could gain the skill level was to simply do the job and call upon the captains of industry and the leaders of the military and political realm to teach him what he did not know. That is *if* they would be willing to teach the man who they would then cede power to as the natural order of things.

Birsha sighed, and placed a hand on Siegfried's shoulder. "Well, then, that is compliment enough. Now, about the loom?"

"Oh, yes," Siegfried said, pulling himself upright. "As you know, whoever owns the loom will wield the power of the kingdom. It was Alaric the Third's wish that we find it and bring it to him."

"And this loom—where is it now?" Birsha walked over to view the large square glass atop the mahogany base. He inspected it carefully, as though by merely looking at it he could make the loom appear somehow.

"The loom is still at the Bookbinder manor."

"And where is that, precisely?" Birsha asked, wishing he were more knowledgeable about the kingdom. Despite his training, much of what he'd learned was completely useless in the real world, he realized now. He needed knowledge, and he needed it fast.

"In Upstate New York, sire. It belongs to a woman named

Brigid Anne Dunsmore."

"And how do I find this Brigid Dunsmore?" Birsha asked.

"Well, she's normally with Henry Bookbinder, the man who the trapper's cohorts are supposed to capture."

Birsha turned on his heel so quickly that he nearly bumped into the glass case. "You say this Henry Bookbinder is friends with Brigid Dunsmore?"

"That's right." Siegfried's expression made it clear that he was surprised by the many things Birsha did not know, despite his training.

"Well, well, will wonders never cease," Birsha said stroking his goatee. "Now I *really* want to meet this Henry Bookbinder."

13

Lips moved behind the screen. An illustrious screen. One of Alaric's commissions before he had died. It was a brilliant turquoise, with all manner of inlays, from a watery blue abalone that shimmered in intensity, to a thin pearl shell veneer mixed with a variety of gems, all designed to display a strutting peacock. Interestingly, the image seemed to move back and forth, as though indeed strutting, depending on where one was standing in the room.

"Birsha is weak," the man said as though in a confessional.

"Not too weak to order the deaths of the Generals," the female council member reminded the man. "One of us could be next."

"You're right, one of us *could* be next," the man agreed. "Have you spoken to the others?"

"I have."

At the sound of footsteps, they waited, listening as the footsteps retreated down the great hallway. Only then did the pair breathe a sigh of relief.

"So then, we are in agreement," the male voice said.

The woman paused, sensing the excitement and fear that those words foreshadowed. "We are in agreement, all save one. But we will deal with that one later, after we've finished the deed."

"Who will you have do it?"

"That is for me to know. Just be sure to feign surprise when it happens." She was about to turn to leave, when she heard the word "Wait!" hissed through the small perforations in the screen, designed for just such a tryst.

"With Birsha gone, which of us will hold power?"

She heard the oiliness behind the question, the raw hunger for the lead position, that of ruler. He was right. One of them would rule, but which one? She had somehow thought that it would be her. After all, she had managed to keep the disparate characters in line all these years. It had never dawned on her that one of the others would desire power as much, if not more than her. This definitely put a new twist in her plans. She folded her hands, rubbing her thumbs together as though they were two opponents, each hoping to gain the upper hand. She would have to plan carefully, from now on. Very carefully.

"We shall see," she said finally. And then she left before the man could further disrupt her plans.

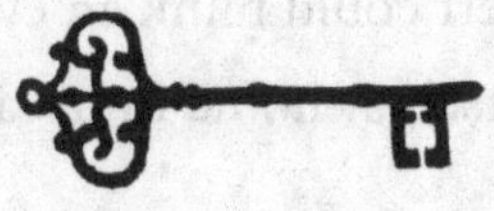

The dark-haired woman eased down beside Henry, her smile coy. He could feel the siren call, as though she bore some invisible string that pulled him toward her against his will. He looked helplessly to Sir Robert, but he was just as besotted by the red-haired woman with the green eyes. And yet Henry could see that Sir Robert was fighting valiantly to pull away.

Henry turned toward the woman beside him. "Who are you?" he finally managed to say.

"I come from far away. My name is Jonquil, after the flower. Do you know of it?"

Indeed, Henry knew what a jonquil was, and yet she was nothing like the sunny flower of his memory. Still, her voice was soft as though trained never to speak in anything but a tinkling melody. It reminded him of windchimes.

"But I was taken away from my homeland by a cruel man," she said and immediately burst into tears.

Before he knew it, she was leaning into him and he was soothing her, running fingers through her silky black hair. She smelled of jasmine and some unnamed spice—cinnamon perhaps. His instinct to protect this small, diminutive creature clamored against the need to be free of her. For nothing about her seemed normal. He peered over at the three grifters and found them secretly jabbing each other. They clearly knew something he didn't.

He then turned his gaze to Sir Robert and was surprised to hear an equal tale of woe from his fellow traveler's red-haired beauty. Before Sir Robert could blink an eye, she too was in tears and had made herself at home in his arms, seeking comfort from a difficult past.

The effects of the herbal drink Henry had taken earlier made him feel weak and lacking control. He had to get a hold of himself before he was mired in something akin to quicksand. Slowly but surely, he pried the girl from him, even as every fiber of him longed to keep her at his side. But what was the saying? Ah, if it seems too good to be true . . .

Brigid, he said to himself. *Keep your thoughts on her.*

And as though she were an antidote to this clinging woman, he began to pull away from Jonquil both physically and emotionally. Again, she tried to wrap her small arms around him, her grip amazingly strong. And again, he pried her loose, her suction like that of an octopus. At last, he managed to separate himself from her and placed his saddlebag between them in case she got the notion to suck him in once more.

When she realized that he was not to be had, her face changed instantly to that of a creature so vile as to toss him over the log onto his back. "Sir Robert!" he yelled, causing the three men to rise.

The sheer volume of his voice stopped the red-haired vixen and gave Sir Robert enough pause that he was able to see the two women for what they were. A ploy by the enemy to steal their souls.

Henry was shaking and he could see that Sir Robert was doing likewise. Fortunately, Sir Robert had the sense to push his shapeshifter away, and she too changed instantly into a monster. The pair started to evaporate into the earth below them, their shadows creating a black funnel of wind. Henry grabbed a hold of the log, and Sir Robert did likewise as the two women reached up one last time with nearly invisible tendrils of a plant to pull the pair with them into a grave of unknowing. For one brief moment, Henry feared that the women would succeed, and then suddenly, with a loud reverberation, they were gone, and the sound receded into the distance until it could be heard no more, a puff of pollen the only thing left in their wake.

Silence followed, then slowly and with greater volume, laughter ensued. Still worn and frightened from the scare of moments before, Henry hissed, "What are you laughing at?"

The three grifters, who had seemed ill-mannered and uncouth mere seconds before, suddenly stood taller, seemed more sure of themselves as though of higher standing.

"Congratulations, men," the leader of the trio said. "You have passed the test."

Henry looked to Sir Robert, who seemed just as confused as Henry. Then he turned back to the trio, the *allegro* of his heartbeat slowing to *adagio*.

"I don't understand," he said. "Who are you?"

As I rode Henry's horse through the narrow passage, the ash still thick despite the distance we had traveled, I could only hope that we would find Henry before Birsha located him and placed him in the dungeon, as he had Emma and Thomas nearly a year ago. Or did worse . . . What if the Fetters were right, that they had only to cast their wiles upon Henry and Sir Robert and all would be lost. I hoped Henry was smarter than that, but stronger men than him had been easily duped. Besides, there was something about the women that I couldn't put my finger on—a highly intoxicating aroma that seemed to render those around them helpless. Perhaps Emma knew what card they might wield over the men, other than their looks. I fell back in the column as I went in search of her.

When at last I found her, she was saddle weary and searching for a place to rest for the night, but none of us wanted to spend another evening amidst the debris of fallen ash if we could help it.

"Do you think we'll ever see the color green again?" she said through the mask. We'd all come to wear them, even the horses who were subject to lung ailments if they breathed the fine dust for too long, according to Elijah.

"We can only hope." I sidled up beside her, our horses snorting a brief greeting as though they too had become friends.

"Look up there." She pointed to a trail that led up the mountain and ended in a round grassy open area. "Maybe we could stay there for the night."

I had to admit, it did look inviting. I motioned to Thomas, who was close by, and pointed toward the open mound, the only green expanse for miles, it would seem. It took him only moments to garner my meaning. He let loose with a loud whistle, and soon the women began heading up the mountain while those who had already passed the cutoff turned back to make the trek skyward.

Fortunately, there was room for my mount as well as Emma's to trudge side by side up the hillside. When we were no longer breathing powdery white dust, should we take off our masks, I pulled mine down, glad to finally breathe clean air, the sweat having condensed into moistened particles around my mouth.

"Those women," I said hesitantly, "the Fetters– they had an unusual aroma like nothing I've ever smelled." I worried that I sounded like a lunatic, bringing up such an odd subject out of the blue. However, when I turned to Emma, I could see that she too had been thinking about them. Wondering. What if? What if the women hadn't arrived in time to stop the men from doing something foolish. Was the Fetters' power really that strong?

"What do you think it was?" Emma turned to me with a frown. My friend, who was nothing if not strong, was suddenly biting her downturned lip.

"I don't know. I thought you might."

"I know the answer," came a voice from behind us, one I hadn't heard for a very long time.

I turned so sharply in the saddle that I nearly came off of my mount. "Kahwihta!" I shouted, immediately handing my reins to Emma and sliding off of my horse in one easy stroke. Though I was wont to admit it, over the course of the past year I had become proficient as a horse woman. Kahwihta slid down just as readily and within moments, we were embracing each other in a welcoming hug.

"How did you find us?" I squealed.

"You make enough noise," she replied, a rare twinkle in her eye.

I had to laugh. "I suppose we do. We'll never make great warriors at this rate."

Over the past year, not only had she aged little, it almost seemed as if she were younger, if at all possible. Her long black hair flowed down her back and her buckskin dress was offset by a slightly darker skinned-skirt and knee-high moccasins. But what drew my attention most was the bump in her midsection.

"Are you with child?" I imitated the act of rocking a baby in my arms.

Her face lit up with the glow of seven suns. "Aye, it is true. I have taken Red Hawk for my husband." She smiled, clearly pleased at this union.

"When are you due?"

She lifted her fingers and counted them off one by one. *One, two.*

"Two months!" I breathed. In two months, I would be an auntie, and yet the very thought was presumptuous of me, filling my face with warmth.

As if she'd read my thoughts, she reached out and touched my arm gently. "I would like you to be my . . . how do you say it in English?"

"Godmother?" I asked, hoping I wasn't overstepping my bounds.

"I do not know this word, but I think it is like our blood sisters. You and I shall be blood sisters and Tahwihta shall be part yours."

"Tahwihta?" I asked, not sure of her meaning.

"My *owira:'a*–my baby girl."

"Baby girl?" I asked, surprised that she already knew the gender of the unborn child when it had yet to come.

"I feel it. She is a girl. And I have asked the shaman and he agrees, so my little Tahwi shall have someone who loves her as I do." She turned to Emma. "And you too. You shall be like a sister to me."

Emma smiled shyly.

"So, about this aroma," Kahwihta reminded us. "We call it the water moon. It is made up of herbs, but which ones, I do not know. They are herbs that draw a man close to ensnare him. Only those with a very dark magic know of their existence and location. But I do not dabble in dark magic, so I do not know which of the herbs are used for such sorcery."

Emma and I shared a glance. At that moment, a chill swept over me. For although Thomas and Elijah were both safe from the Fetters, I couldn't be sure about Henry. Had they entrapped him as they had assured me they would? Even now, had he been pulled to the underworld where all sorts of creepy crawlies lived and went about their days in darkness? I didn't know. Still, my stomach seized up and my limbs felt weak at the thought. I would have to trust that he was safe, for to do otherwise would only pull me down too. And one of us would need to be strong for the days ahead.

"Where is the rest of your tribe?" I asked, eager to change the subject.

"They are on the ridge across the way," Kahwihta said, pointing with her chin to the northeast. "Father said to give you his blessings and to know that we are with you."

A warmth supplanted the worry that had dogged me ever since I'd learned Henry had left in the night to do his duty to his family. To seek out a mission not of his own design, one that could very easily get him killed. No, I could not dwell on it or I wouldn't sleep at night, so instead I focused on what I could do.

"Thank your father for me, when you see him, and tell him that I, too, offer him blessings," I said, happy to know they were so close. Then, turning to our latest concern, I said, "Do you know how much farther the ash has traveled?"

"Not much farther," she said, as we continued to march up the hill on foot, Emma still on horseback. "No more than a quarter day's ride."

Emma and I both sighed with relief, then laughed at how similar we'd become over the course of the past year. We were indeed sisters at heart if not blood. And I knew I could count on her in all things, a rarity considering the traditions that had us all working at opposite ends, or at least it *had* done until we'd committed our fealty to each other never to hurt our sisters in arms. I had been happily surprised to discover that all had remained true to their commitment. The only person I had my doubts about was Beatrice, who still seemed distant and rarely joined in with the others after her attack, one year's hence, against another of our women warriors. If not for Thomas and Henry insisting she be given another chance, I doubted I would have been willing to open a door that might just as easily be slammed in my face. But for now, Beatrice had behaved herself, and for that I was grateful.

We continued to make our way up to the round knoll that had foregone the ash due to its altitude and no doubt wind patterns. I recalled that stiffest of winds from last year with a shudder, the one that had nearly undone my newly formed group of women.

"Have you heard anything of Henry?" I asked on a whim. "He is headed to the fortress with a man by the name of Sir Robert."

A look of alarm clouded her face before she could hide it

behind a ray of sunshine. "Two men?"

I nodded, my breath stilling in my chest.

"We saw not two men, one day's hence, but five such men. Whether one was Henry, I cannot say. They were too far away to see clearly."

I paused and in that moment, a phalanx of women rounded past, as though I were a pebble fighting a stream of rushing water.

"Keep moving," Emma urged, lest we be left behind.

I did as asked, my mind twirling through this latest information. Who were the other men, if this truly was Henry and not some other group of men on the move?

Then it came to me with a snap of my fingers. "His horse, do you recall it? It's unusual."

His spirit horse was unlike any other horse I had ever seen, for it had fine features, as though a thoroughbred among ordinary equines. Its legs seemed almost stylized, like something out of a painting, and its features were bold and unerring. Even the way its black mane blew back behind it as it pranced made it stand out among other horses. I quickly described it to Kahwihta, reminding her of its unique features.

Like the horse, her face grew spirited, as though lit from within. "I *have* seen such a horse as this."

"With a man bearing an accent?" I encouraged, hoping to dislodge a memory.

"Again, they were too far away to tell, but there were five men, not two, I am sure of it."

So where had the other men come from and who were they? Were they Birsha's men?

"Can you take me to them?"

"Tonight?" she asked in surprise.

"No!" Emma hissed. "You can't go out there in the dark without the rest of us. It wouldn't be safe."

"I would have Kahwihta, and perhaps one of your warriors?" I asked.

Emma stopped her horse, causing a near catastrophe as Kahwihta and I almost ran into the back of it, the hundreds of women behind us following suit. Her horse stamped and bit the air, just as upset as Kahwihta and I at her stubbornness.

"You take all of us, or none of us," Emma insisted, her green eyes flashing. "You're always doing this, Brigid. Always taking risks. You have a responsibility to the women now. You've made us *believe* in a different life. In a life where we can be more than just mothers and sisters, helpmates. That we can live a life of value, a life of our own design. You've taught us that we don't have to be cruel to each other to accomplish what we need. We trusted you, Brigid. Now you must trust us, by taking us with you. Allow us to help you."

Despite the restlessness that filled me with angst, I knew she was right. I *did* have a responsibility to the other women. And yet how would bringing them along help them in any way?

Forgive me, Henry.

I would not be able to save him. At least not today. But I would, I promised myself. I just hoped he wasn't already deep within the bowels of the earth, lost to me forever.

14

"Who are you?" Henry scowled at the three rough men who suddenly appeared more cultured, as though they had matured right before his eyes.

"Let me introduce myself," said the man who led the trio. "My name is Nathaniel, and these two men are Levi and Isaac, at your service." He bowed slightly, his diction having taken on a more elite tone.

"At *my* service?" Henry shook his head, not at all sure he understood what was going on. He looked to Sir Robert, to see if he were any the wiser, but Sir Robert merely shrugged and shook his head, digging the toe of his boot into the clay-like soil.

All around them loomed a forest of trees. Henry hadn't taken in his surroundings fully before this, too focused on saving himself from the strange creatures he had just encountered. But as he gathered his wits, he realized that they had happened upon the hunting grounds of a mountain lion, for everywhere he looked, there were bones—bones that made him shudder.

"Perhaps we should take this conversation elsewhere," he said, pointing to the bleached white bones of a stag.

The man who had called himself Nathaniel, merely glanced down, unmoved which only further disconcerted Henry, who wasn't used to ignoring danger signs.

"What do you want from us?" Henry hoped to divert the topic to something that might reveal the reason for the men's change of heart.

"We want nothing—only to help you," Nathaniel said.

Now that Henry took greater stock of the man, he could see his high, aristocratic nose, his prominent brow, his clean and well-trimmed nails. This was no trapper or thief. This was a man of some bearing, so how had he come to be with these other stragglers, Henry wondered?

Nathaniel stuck his hand out. At first, Henry was reluctant to take it, but finally relented and was surprised at the strength of the handshake.

"We're from the neighboring clan, the Macloud's. Alaric has attacked us the same way he attacked your people, and we're here to help you stop him and his men. A trapper hired us to kidnap you and take you to Alaric's fortress, but we hogtied the poor fellow," he said with a laugh.

Henry blanched at the news. So, the trapper *was* working on behalf of Alaric, but Alaric was gone. Henry frowned. "This trapper . . . was he approximately six feet high and spoke with an accent?"

"Aye," Nathaniel said, closing one eye as if to test his veracity.

"I ran into him in a town just outside of the Manor House. I can guarantee, he wasn't hog-tied."

Nathaniel kicked the dirt. "The rotter must've escaped. Fortunate for you that you left there before he captured you and turned you over to Alaric and his jackals."

"Haven't you heard?"

"Heard what?" Nathaniel looked to Isaac and Levi, but the pair merely shrugged.

The horses snuffled in the background.

"Alaric is dead."

Henry noted how quickly Isaac had paled, while a curse rang out from Levi, who clearly found this an unexpected event, to say the least.

"His son Birsha has taken the throne," Henry quickly added. "We're headed there on a mission."

"This is news to me," Nathaniel concurred. "We were called upon to find you and bring you to Alaric."

Before Henry could question Nathaniel further, the man threw up his hands to silence him.

"We were originally placed at the fortress to try to gather information. When I learned that they were searching for you, I offered my services to the trapper, to find you and bring you to the Jackals, but I had no intention of doing so, or at least not in the way expected."

Prickles of heat shot up Henry's back and neck. Could he trust the man? And what did he mean by that last bit? "So, you are a double agent."

"If that's what you want to call it, then yes," Nathaniel agreed, his expression hardening.

"Then why the ruse with those women?" Henry nodded toward the ground where they had last viewed them.

Nathaniel's shoulders relaxed and he wore just the briefest of smirks. "We had to know we could trust you. If you were capable of resisting those two beauties, then we knew you were men of substance."

Henry pulled at his chin, which now sported several days of whiskers. Any longer, and he would be wearing a full-length beard. "So, we meet with your approval then," Henry said, still just as angry as before if not more . . . for being duped in such a cruel manner. What sort of men did such a thing?

He was soon to find out, for Nathaniel said, "Come, we must hurry if we're to arrive at the fortress before this Birsha becomes suspicious of the delay."

"What?" Henry said, balling his fists. "After everything we just spoke about, you plan to turn me in to Birsha?"

Nathaniel spoke as though addressing a child. "We will simply introduce you to Birsha, but let it be known that we will keep you safe from any harm. We have our . . . methods."

"No!" Henry hissed, done with their half-baked plot. He turned toward his horse, eager to be away from these men and their machinations. "I've heard enough. I'll trust my own instincts, not your poorly laid plans."

He had just lifted his foot to Windtamer's stirrup, when he felt a whack on the back of his head and fell to the ground, nearly unconscious.

"You do it our way, or no way at all," said Nathaniel.

Those were the last words Henry heard before succumbing to the blow to his head.

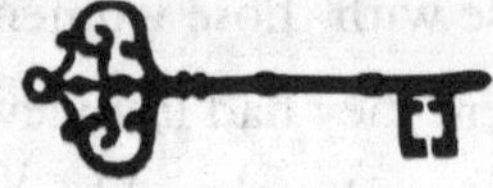

I awoke with alarm, fury coursing through me, for although I had no way of proving it, I knew within my very core that something had happened to Henry. Something that pained him, even now. It was as if, in that year-long search for survival, we had developed an umbilical cord between us that meant if one of us were affected, both of us felt it. And I felt it now, the back of my head aching. I had to tell Emma and Thomas. Despite the darkness, I rolled out of my sleeping bag, lit a candle, and donned my boots. Caring not one whit about the cold, I untied my tent ties and barreled out into the frost-bit night, searching until I found their tent, which had been staked close to mine.

"Psst!" I hissed, and when I heard no answer, repeated the sound. But I could hear the labored breathing inside the tent, so I picked up a pebble and chucked it toward the outline of a person.

I heard an "ouch," followed by Emma whispering, "What's that?" to Thomas.

"It's me!" I cried. "Open up."

"Brigid, what are you doing up at this late hour?" Emma greeted me at the mouth of the tent once she'd untied the strings. Her hair lay askew and her white nightclothes looked out of place in a setting such as ours.

"Henry is hurt."

"Oh, for heaven sakes, Brigid. Go back to bed." A cloud of

steam rose from her lips in the chill mountain air. "You've just had a bad dream."

"I have not." I rubbed my hands together to stay warm. At that moment Thomas popped his head out of the tent.

"Brigid. What's wrong?" He ran his fingers over his bleary eyes.

"It's Henry. Something's happened to him, I just know it," I said, hoping that at least *he* would see reason.

"Henry? We don't even know where Henry is."

"Yes, we do, don't we Emma?"

She rolled her eyes in the flickering torchlight. "Kahwihta says she saw him with three men," Emma explained.

"Why didn't you tell me?" Thomas demanded, fully awake now. "We need to find him, to help him."

"See!" I told Emma.

"There's nothing we can do for him at this late hour," she said to me, then turned to Thomas. "I planned to tell you in the morning, after we got a full night's sleep."

I had never seen Thomas so angry before, his eyes practically aglow with flames. "Would you have waited if it were me who was hurt or trapped by three other men?"

Emma paled, so much so that I truly felt sorry for her in that moment, because she hadn't viewed it in that light. "Of course not," she said hurriedly. "I would travel the ends of the earth for you."

"And I for you, but the same goes for my brother. Do you understand, Emma?"

His expression was so fierce that I grasped Emma's hand to let her know that I supported her, no matter how wrong she might have been in regard to Henry.

"I'm sorry," she said, tears in her voice. "I didn't think of it that way. Of course, we must go help Henry."

Until that moment, I hadn't realized that I wasn't breathing. I took a refreshing breath of air, relieved that someone finally understood and would help me find Henry.

"We'll pack and let the women know that we will be leaving before sunup," Emma said, now fully on board. "Gertrude and Jocelyn have become stalwart companions. They'll keep the women steady until we return."

"Winnifred and Yesimeh, too. They will all help, I'm certain of it," I agreed.

"It's settled then," Thomas said, "we ride in thirty minutes. Be ready."

He didn't have to ask twice. I was already on the run back to my tent, not caring that I stumbled over stones and tree roots to get there.

Birsha and Siegfried had worked into the wee hours of the morning, cataloging all of his father's treasures. Birsha couldn't get over the breadth and depth of his father's collection. He even owned a zoo in the northeastern quadrant of the forest, according to Siegfried.

Birsha rubbed his weary eyes. "I must call it a night, Siegfried, my good man. Could you close up for the night, set things to right? Then we can finish tomorrow, *after* I've had a chance to see this zoo you were speaking of. What sort of animals does it have?"

"Oh, everything you can imagine. It has lions, tigers, crocodiles, and a myriad of apes and monkeys of all species. It even has a Tasmanian tiger or wolf, if you will. It goes by either name. They are almost extinct."

"Is it a cat or a dog then?" Birsha asked, having trouble envisioning such a beast.

"Neither, actually. Though its snout looks like that of a dog or wolf, its back is striped like a tiger, but in fact it's a marsupial."

"A what?"

"They're animals with pouches in their midsection, like a kangaroo or wombat."

"A wom-what?" Birsha shook his head. "Never mind."

"Your father, Alaric, had planned to breed the Tasmanian tiger, but alas, he has never been able to procure another and I fear it may be too late to save the species." Siegfried began packing their latest find into a crate, an illuminated manuscript of the King's Psalms housed in a glass frame.

"Maybe I shall find another Tasmanian tiger and bring it to our zoo," Birsha suggested. But Siegfried gave only a dubious pull of his lips, clearly deciding it better to say nothing than to give his leader false hope.

Birsha was about to stand and call his leave for the night when Siegfried cleared his throat.

"Yes, man? What is it? Spit it out."

"Though I hadn't mentioned this before, what with the lying in state of your father and the—" Here, Siegfried coughed into his hand. "Well, you know."

"Yes, I know," Birsha responded, certain that the adjutant was referring to the generals.

"There is a prisoner, sir, in the dungeon. I think you would be wise to speak with him."

"Speak with him? Why?"

"He was placed there by the Council," Siegfried said, his words measured.

"The Council? For what reason?"

Birsha pushed aside one of the crates with the toe of his boot. The man was talking in riddles.

"The Council claimed he plotted to do away with your father, but I believe he was a scapegoat for more . . . shall I say, *sinister* forces."

"Sinister forces . . . within the kingdom?"

"Aye, you could say that." Siegfried returned to the task at hand, crating everything possible so he could take his leave for the night.

"Who are these forces?"

"It is the prisoner's story to tell, not mine. It's best you speak with him in the morning."

"In the morning?" Birsha bellowed. "In the morning, pah! We shall go now. Finish quickly then take me there."

"But sir—" Siegfried shot back, then immediately went silent when Birsha offered a scowl of warning. "Yes, sir." He quickly finished and shoved the last of the crates in the corner for now.

Then he removed a skeleton key from his vest and said, "Follow me."

15

Henry awoke with a splitting headache. When he tried to move, he discovered that he was tied to his pommel to keep him steady . . . *and* to keep him from escaping. He felt the back of his head, a round goose egg disfiguring its normally spheroid shape. He tried to recall what had happened, but could only focus on the jostling of his horse as it plodded along a trail that must lead to the fortress. They were making much faster progress than they had the last time he'd been through this area, slowed down by a wagon train of novice women fighters. But they had soon learned that women on horseback were much quicker at a forward march than a team laden down with all the luxuries of modern life.

Henry craned his neck to view what was behind him, his shoulders slumping in relief to see Sir Robert put his finger to his lips and mouth the word, "Silence." Henry nodded, then turned back, pretending once more to be asleep. And lucky he was to have done so, because not moments later, he heard the three begin to talk.

"What do you plan to do with the prisoner?" Henry recognized the voice as that of Isaac. He no longer spoke in the gruff voice of a derelict. Rather he sounded as educated as Nathaniel himself.

"We need him if we're to gather the information we need," Nathaniel said, lowering his voice.

"What kind of information?" Isaac persisted.

"And who from?" Levi added.

"You ask too many questions," Nathaniel said. "Just leave it to me. All will be revealed soon."

Dawn was several hours away when Thomas, Emma, Kahwihta, and I left to go find Henry. The year on the road had made me attuned to the sounds of the nighttime. The hoot of the horned owl, that most menacing bird of the Strigiform family, its eyes appearing as if in a perpetual scowl, ears alert for the sounds of humans and other creatures of the night. My favorite was the snowy owl that would disappear into the landscape in winter, only its eyes giving it away. And I loved the smell of balsam fir, eastern red cedar, and pitch pine or Norway spruce. I loved them all, their sweet scent, the smell of terpene from conifer sap meant to keep away bark beetles and invading fungi. They, like me and my clan, fought those out to harm us. The realization that we might be in peril had come to me late, but better late than never, I say. And yet part of me yearned for that time so long ago that I was blind to the machinations of the outer world, sheltered in among a tight-knit family, believing only good in people and the world at large. It saddened me to think that had been taken from me, and yet what choice did I have? I either complied to the world's vagaries and faced it for all of its intricacies, good and bad, or I succumbed to the outside forces and fell beneath the hooves of the conquerors, my spilled blood the only reminder that I had ever existed.

I hadn't realized how long we'd been riding until at last I saw the first rays of sunshine rising from the east in a glorious display of pinks and oranges and blues, awash in a panoply of color. The ash had long since disappeared, replaced by a lush green surrounded by sections of snow where the sun hadn't yet hit. It reminded me how much I loved nature, its exotic scent a refuge in these trying times.

"What will you do when you find Henry?" Emma asked. "Surely he's nearing the fortress by now. We'll never catch up to him in time."

Thomas, who allowed Emma the reins to her life, for the most part, urged her to hush. It was bad enough that Thomas was worrying about Henry, but he knew how fiercely I protected his brother. I could see by his anxious expression that he feared I might fall apart. But I had a mission to accomplish. To find Henry, and to bring him back to the land of the living. I would not fail him.

Suddenly, in the distance, I heard a thunderous noise and could see that the others had heard it as well. Thomas held up a hand to silence either of us should we desire to speak. I had never heard such a noise in my entire life.

"What is it?" I whispered. But I had only seconds before it descended upon us like a horde of locusts and we were swept away.

The prisoner was fast asleep in the underground chamber of the fortress, the conditions appalling even to Birsha, who wasn't yet inured to the ways of his people. The smell alone had him digging for his chatelaine, which he held to his nose. Did they never give these men a bath? Feed them properly? Even the rats seemed to avoid this cesspool of a place, Birsha noted with alarm.

"Which one?" Birsha pointed to the first man whose dark hair was slick with oils from having gone so long without bathing.

"That one, sir." Siegfried nodded toward the third man in chains, whose thin pale arms and face had clearly not seen daylight in some time.

"Unchain him," Birsha ordered, "and bring him to my chambers, but first give him a bath and breakfast. Even a prisoner deserves that!"

One hour later, his hair still wet from his bath and looking a good deal heartier after a decent meal and a fresh pair of clothes, the prisoner stood before Birsha, one of the jailers at his side.

"Give me your name," Birsha ordered. The man's nose sat slightly askew as though once in a fight, the other man clearly getting the better of him.

The man peered first at Siegfried, then at Birsha. "The name's Dexter, sir. Dexter Channing, from New Brunswick."

"New Brunswick?" Birsha said, raising a brow. "And what brings you here?"

"I'm a trapper by trade. My friend and I came south lookin' for pelts."

"And how did you end up in prison?"

The man tilted his head, a nervous tic causing his jaw to seize momentarily. "I was just passing through on my way further south when I was captured by one of your warriors—claimed he'd seen me try to poison the king, but why would I do such a thing?" he said, more animated now and the tic coming faster.

"Why, indeed?"

"They say he was a mercenary hired to take down Alaric," Siegfried offered.

"And what gives them cause to believe such a thing, should it not be true?"

"I may be able to answer that, sire," Siegfried said. "It's rumored that one of the council members was responsible, but which one, I have yet to learn."

Birsha started at the mention of the Council. He had seen the way they watched him when they thought he wasn't looking. The way their eyes met those of the other council members, as though they all held a secret that he wasn't privy to. It had unnerved him the first time it had happened. In this, he was apt to believe Siegfried, but then again, why should he? Who did he really know among this den of thieves? And yet, if he were to follow his heart, he would stand by Siegfried any day over the others. Especially the one with the slits for eyes, the brown pupils elongated and almost reptilian in the way they followed him while at the same time appearing blank, as though no sentient being was behind those eyes, only a prey animal.

"I didn't do it!" the prisoner blurted out. Then he immediately flushed a deep fuschia for having spoken out of turn.

Birsha paced in front of the man. Something about him seemed so pitiful that Birsha had no doubt he was telling the truth. He paused in his pacing and rubbed his black braided goatee.

"If what you say is true, Siegfried, there is no need to detain this man. Go with the jailer, Siegfried. Take Mr. Channing to the outskirts of the village and release him." Then to Dexter he said, "And if I ever see you in these parts again, you shall be hanged, do I make myself clear?"

The man paled, but he bowed his head and said, "Thank you, my lord."

Just as the trio was about to leave, Birsha stopped them with a raised hand. "And Siegfried?"

"Yes, my lord?"

"See to it that the prisoners are fed well and receive a daily bath."

"But, sir—" the jailer protested, a swarthy man with meaty arms and a hulking demeanor.

"No buts, just do as I say."

The jailer had the grace to at least pretend to obey. "Yes, my lord." He bowed, yet his words came out more of a growl.

Birsha knew it would be best to watch the man. One like him had only to say the right word to the wrong person and cause Birsha any number of problems. He had seen his type before. A man like him preferred to stir the pot. He no doubt liked his job as lord and master over those unfortunates sentenced to life in the dungeon. Yes, he would watch him carefully indeed.

"Run!" Thomas yelled to the three of us, Kahwihta, Emma, and me.

We didn't need to be asked twice. Before we'd even had a chance to respond, Red reared up on his hind legs, snorting and pawing the air for mere seconds, then landed on his hooves with a resounding crash. Then he was off, me hanging on for dear life.

From the corner of my eyes, I saw Emma's mouth moving, but her words were lost in the clamor, for above us were bats as far as the eye could see. They moved as a single cloud in our direction. Until today, I had been under the mistaken impression that they traveled in like groups, but as they bounced into Kahwihta and me, my screams resounding against the flap of wings, I saw a number of different species: Eastern red bats, hoary bats, even the tri-colored bats. I strived to stay atop my horse, while Thomas had somehow managed to loop his arm around Emma and pull her onto the back of his stallion so that he could keep her safely behind him. For her part, Emma closed her eyes and clung to Thomas in a grip so tight that it pulled

Thomas back in his saddle, while Kahwihta, the calmest of our group, merely bent down behind my horse to take cover.

Finally, we managed to spot a granite boulder from which to hide until the onslaught was past. We hugged as tightly as possible to a gap between the rocks, pulling our horses in behind us. All except Emma's. Her horse had disappeared in the melee and had yet to be seen.

We huddled, trembling as wings whirred past in a frenzy of sound, some of the bats chittering as they passed or letting loose a high-pitched squeal, all the while pummeling into me and my companions in their fever to escape the sunrise. And to our amazement, just south of us was a giant cavern. In one fell swoop, their numbers narrowed as they entered the yawning mouth of the cave, squealing all the way. The sound seemed to echo for hours, and yet it could have been no more than minutes. Soon, the fluttering had died down altogether and the sky once again opened up to reveal a glorious sunrise.

Still weak from what we'd witnessed, we slowly made our way out of our shelter. Thomas took stock of Emma, checking her for signs of injury, but except for a few scrapes, she seemed okay. Kahwihta seemed the least affected of the bunch, as though able to turn them away through sheer will and determination. Whereas Thomas had taken the brunt of their wings. His brown hair was askew and his face covered in a plethora of red marks from the bat wings. We would need to clean him immediately, just in case. One never knew what disease a bat might carry.

I set to work helping Emma tend to Thomas, whose face was a series of small welts. Fortunately, none were actual bites, but even a scratch could cause hydrophobia, if not careful, a dreaded epidemic in Europe, superstition tying the disease to vampires and werewolves. We helped Thomas down to a small stream and ran water over the many marks, then cleaned them with carbolic acid.

"Ow!" Thomas pulled back his head at the offending sting of the acid.

"Don't be foolish, Thomas," Emma chided, her red hair looking as though it had been through a whirlwind. "You never know what germs the bats carry." Once again, she began dabbing his wounds while I had him sip water and offered up dried pemmican for the journey ahead. We would find Emma's horse later.

"Why are you not more concerned about the bats?" I asked Kahwihta, surprised by how quiet she had been on the subject.

"Because," she said, her eyes drifting to the cave, "we believe bats are divine messengers between God and man."

"Oh." I had learned much from this woman who had given me the name Dancer of Looms on our last foray north.

We were just about finished with the treatment, when Emma leaned over to inspect a spot on my arm. Her face turned as white as the bloomers I'd once worn. "You've been bitten," Emma cried, fighting the tremor in her voice.

For one brief moment, we all stood perfectly still, no one speaking. Then Emma, who was slowly becoming both doctor and herbalist for our band of women, along with a host of other volunteers, quickly dug back into her medical bag, which fortunately she'd given Thomas to carry.

"What should I do?" I said at last.

Emma's crystal green eyes registered fear, and she looked to Thomas, whose eyes told a story of commiseration.

"Emma? Thomas? . . . Kahwihta? Is there any way to treat it?" I demanded.

Emma bit her lip, then nodded her head, but her dour expression wracked me with fear. Reluctantly, she dug through her bag, until she came upon what she was looking for. A knife.

"What is that for?" I asked, my voice inching up an octave.

"It's the only way," Emma said, dipping her head in apology.

"What's the only way?" I demanded, anger and fear vying for a place among my rush of emotions.

"I'm sorry to have to tell you this, Brigid, but we're going to have to cut it out. Either that or you risk coming down with hydrophobia . . . rabies."

We all knew what that meant. The symptoms were too hideous to even consider. Fever, delirium, muscle spasms followed by drooling and eventual death.

It was as if I already had it, for my muscles trembled at the very thought of what Emma was about to do.

"Quick!" Her tone changed so fast that I had no time to argue. She reached into her medical bag and pulled out a small flask. "Drink this," she said. "It has laudanum in it. It will help ease the pain."

I hesitated only a moment before pulling it to my lips and drinking down a long swallow.

"Not too much," she chided, yanking it back before I could drink further.

It hadn't even fully taken hold before she cleaned the

wound, then held the shiny blade to my arm. Kahwihta spoke calmly to me in her language, as though praying over me. As I braced for what was to come, she stared stolidly into my eyes, gave a single nod, then Emma drove the knife blade deep into my arm. Every fiber of my being registered the pain as though it were a thousand knives, not one. Soon, blood oozed between the open lips of the wound. I closed my eyes, fearing I might pass out, though that might be a blessing.

"Take a breath, Brigid. You're turning blue." Emma grasped my face so that I would have to open my eyes and look at her. In a tone that reflected her seriousness, she said, "I'm going to pour silver nitrate onto the wound to cauterize it. Grab Thomas' hand," she urged.

Thomas reached out to me. I looked at his hand as if it were an entity all its own, but in the end I took it. Still, I felt nothing but sympathy for Thomas as Emma poured the lunar caustic onto the open wound, my fingers digging deeply into his flesh. Kahwihta's prayers grew louder, as if to drown out my moans.

"Breathe! Breathe!" Emma coaxed, as I strived to do as requested. "Now I'll sew up the wound."

I didn't think I could take any more. It took every ounce of willpower to keep from passing out, and I have to admit I felt faint, my breaths coming in short pants, my lower lip bleeding from where I had bitten into it. But still she pulled the needle in and out, in and out. It seemed an eternity before she said, "It's done."

For all the pain, it surprised me how quickly the laudanum set in, now that the surgery was over. I said a brief prayer for our safety and Henry's. Then I fell into a deep slumber and didn't awaken until late afternoon.

Henry knew they were nearing the fortress. It was as though the very air had cooled and daylight had turned to nighttime. What better way to bring him in than under the cover of darkness? Every nerve in his body felt on edge. Bad enough to enter this snakepit in daylight alongside the ones you loved, but to enter it at nighttime with strangers who meant to do you harm was too much, even for him. He heard the night owls hooting from somewhere among the forest of trees that surrounded the fortress. The last time he had been here, he and Brigid had entered the underground chambers and had rescued Thomas and Emma from the dungeon. The thought that he might be taken to that hell hole frightened him and he shivered, then held his cloak tighter around him.

"Where are we going?" he managed to say through clenched teeth.

"You don't want to know," Nathaniel said. "Our plans have changed."

"Changed? Changed how?" Henry hissed, every crunch beneath the horses' hooves sounding loud to his ears.

"You'll see."

The air of resignation in Nathaniel's voice sent Henry's heart racing. He feared he was to be the sacrificial lamb, but for what? And why? Were these men bounty hunters? Yesterday, for one brief moment, he'd thought they might actually rescue him, but after he'd been bludgeoned on the head, he no longer held out such hope. Now, he saw only doom ahead. Well, he was a Bookbinder and he planned to wear the name proudly. In ancient times, only monks wrote and tended books for the clergy. Laymen were not allowed to read. Better to keep the masses ignorant so that they could be more easily managed. Controlled. Johannes Gutenberg had changed all that when he'd invented the printing press in 1439. And still society had grown no wiser, had become no less savage.

Just as Henry fought down the lump in his throat, out of the gloom appeared a glowing lamp held by Eleanor and her husband Pierre, along with Master Clyde, the head of the clan. At last, salvation. Henry immediately sat taller on his mount as he signaled to Sir Robert the happy news that he knew these people. They had helped him in untold ways, the last time he was here.

Henry didn't wait for permission. He brought Windtamer to a halt and leapt down to greet them. Master Clyde appeared only marginally older. His hair had grayed at the temples, but he seemed in fine form from a lifetime spent chopping wood and performing manual labor of all sorts.

Eleanor, on the other hand, seemed older, frailer, as though this past year had weighed her down, causing her back to bend slightly. She had borne children late in life. Her daughter, Celestine, and her son, Jean, appeared at either side of her skirt, each taking an arm from which to derive comfort amidst the unending gloom and fog.

"You're back!" Eleanor hugged Henry as though he too were one of her children. "We think of you and Brigid often. How is Brigid?"

"She is well," Henry said in a swell of relief to finally know someone he could trust in these dark woods.

"Why isn't she here, eh?" Eleanor asked, tilting her head.

"Now, Eleanor, don't be bothering Master Henry with a barrage of questions." Master Clyde placed a hand on her shoulder as if to hold her back from any further examination on her part.

"I don't mind," Henry said, and he meant it. For the first time since he'd left camp and set out for the fortress with Sir Robert, he felt on solid ground. No more shifting of the winds. No more danger lurking in every corner. At least for now.

He leaned in closer and whispered, "Do you know these men, Master Clyde, Eleanor?"

"Aye, we do," Master Clyde said with a shrug. "But you won't be happy when you know what they have planned for you." Eleanor nudged him. "What my people have planned for you," he amended apologetically, head down. For the first time since Henry had arrived, the man was unable to look Henry directly in the eye.

"I don't understand." Henry shook his mane. It felt dirty and dusty from days on the road.

"Well, let's take you back to our place, *oui*?" Pierre intercepted. "Then Master Clyde and Eleanor can explain everything."

Henry had the sinking feeling that they would, but that he wouldn't like it. Still, he allowed himself to be led away into the night . . . into his uncharted future.

16

Much to Winnifred's surprise, before Brigid had left camp, she'd put Winnifred in charge of the women warriors. Gertrude and Jocelyn were to be backups as Brigid and the others went in search of Henry and Sir Robert. In the end, Brigid told Winnifred that it came down to her steadfastness and calm in any storm. Not only that, but her ability to think on her feet and make well-thought out decisions.

Now, Winnifred took stock of the women, who were draped all around the open clearing as far as the eye could see, taking a pause from their toil for a mid-afternoon lunch. She could see that they were exhausted, irritable, and at their wits end, and Winnifred couldn't blame them. For the last three days they had helped sweep, scrub, and dispose of the ash and muck from the fire each time they bivouacked. But what had really stuck in everyone's craw was Beatrice. She had been berating and humiliating the women, a means of keeping women in their place in times past. Brigid had changed all that, had insisted that this means of maintaining control would never be a part of her army of women. Winnifred concurred. That was the very reason she had opted to join—to create a new society filled with innately happier people. It had been such a huge success on their first foray out, that they had become a tight-knit group who pulled together to help each other. Yet now, as she saw the weary expression of her filthy, sweaty crew, she decided it was time to relent.

She climbed up onto a tree stump and waved her arms. "Women, go get cleaned up. You have the afternoon off!"

The word spread quickly through the lines of women and a cheer rose up, many jumping to their feet and letting out a joyous cry. One by one, they went to their tents and brought out their ewers to fill by the creek where they would bathe and wash themselves of the gray soot that covered nearly every inch of their bodies. Beatrice was about to join them when Winnifred said, "Beatrice, wait. I need to talk to you."

Beatrice looked around, as though Winnifred had spoken to some other Beatrice. Finally, she pointed at her chest and said, "Me?"

"Yes, you. I want to speak to you in private."

Winnifred marched Beatrice into the large tent. Inside were a table and three folding camp chairs. "Take a seat," she said, nodding toward one of the two chairs opposite hers.

Beatrice did as requested, but her puzzled expression made clear that she had no idea why Winnifred had brought her here. "Have I done something wrong?" she asked, innocently enough.

"You have." Winnifred decided not to beat around the bush but to get straight to the heart of the matter. "I hear you have been berating and belittling the other women."

"They deserved it!" she said without pause.

"No one deserves that," Winnifred countered, leaning in with her hands folded on the table.

"But–"

"No buts, Beatrice. If you have a problem, you come to me and we can talk about it, but we will not humiliate our colleagues, *ever*," she added, in case Beatrice hadn't understood the message clearly. "In this women's army, we treat each other with respect. We have earned it, so there will be no name calling, no putting other women down to show our superiority. You have already had one violation when you attacked one of the other women. This is your second violation. It won't happen again, do I make myself clear?"

Beatrice's eyes became an icy blue and she stiffened as though starched and stuffed like an old pillow case. "I understand." But she refused to look directly at Winnifred, instead keeping her eyes just slightly to the right so as to avoid direct eye contact.

"I want you to understand, Beatrice. We're doing this for all of us. What can happen to one, can happen to another, even you. Do you really want that?"

Beatrice suddenly appeared more contrite, lowering her eyes slightly, her shoulders slumping.

"The thing you have to understand, Beatrice, is that here, we care about each other. The danger alone will test our mettle. We don't need to tear each other down while we're doing it. All of us want a better life. After all, isn't that what we're fighting for?"

Winnifred was amazed to see tears begin to glisten in Beatrice's eyes, and for the first time, she felt as though she may have truly impressed upon Beatrice the importance of what they were doing. The dire need for change.

Winnifred rose and came around the table. As Beatrice stood, she gave her a hug. "Remember, Beatrice, we're all in this together. For this to work, we have to be able to trust each other and we can only do that if we care for each other. And we can't do that if we're tearing each other apart. Agreed?"

Beatrice simply nodded her head and swiped at her tears. "I'll try harder," she said.

"Right-o! See that you do," Winnifred said. "Now scoot! I've got to make some decisions."

"Decisions?" Beatrice asked. "What kind of decisions?"

Winnifred knew she should keep her own counsel, but perhaps by including the girl, Beatrice might feel more a part of things. Change her ways.

"I'm thinking about going after Brigid and Henry and the others. I don't feel comfortable leaving them to fate. We've been a team, and I would like it to stay that way."

"I agree," Beatrice said, to Winnifred's surprise. "No telling what might happen to them and with no one there to help them . . ." She allowed her voice to trail off.

Beatrice's words set off the worry that had been lingering at the back of Winnifred's mind, when Brigid, Thomas, Emma, and Kahwihta had gone in search of Henry. She offered Beatrice a half-hearted smile. "Well, then, I suppose it's settled. I'll let the women know that we are to leave tomorrow. And Beatrice–”

"Yes?"

"Let *me* tell them." Beatrice had already been assuming too large a role in this women's army, and not a positive one. Winnifred didn't want any more back stabbing when it went so much better when the women worked together.

"I understand," she said. Then she ducked through the tent opening and was gone.

And yet, Winnifred couldn't help wondering if she'd heard the last of Beatrice. There was something about her that was hugely unpredictable and she didn't like it. Not one little bit.

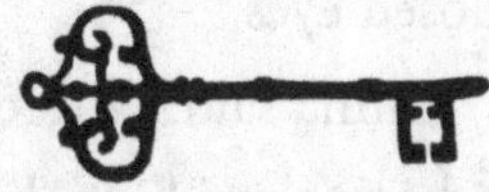

The sun sat solidly in the sky when alas I woke, my eyes fluttering open in an instant. For a moment, I wondered where I was located and found my thoughts drifting back to a time when I was small. I had fallen out of a large oak tree upon a dare by one of my sisters. Then, like now, I lay on my back, facing the sky, stunned. My father was the first to greet me, falling down beside me on bended knee, lifting me up in his huge strong arms and carrying me to the back porch where a line of loungers lay in the ready for a summer of backyard picnics, a perch from which to watch the boat races mid-summer. I had loved the smell of jasmine that floated in on a southerly breeze. The slow lazy pace that marked our days. The smell of newly mown lawn while sucking on icy cold popsicles made with pink lemonade. I loved the feel of the wet grass beneath my bare feet. When had that innocence disappeared, I wondered as I lay there, unready to face the world? But like childhood, it had gone in an instant and the world was a new place, one I had never imagined. A world filled with danger lurking around every corner.

"There you are," Emma said from somewhere to my left. Moments later she was bent over me, her head moving back and forth in her effort to inspect me for signs of disease, I supposed. "You had us worried. I didn't think you would ever wake up. You drank too much laudanum."

As I struggled to sit up, my head felt heavy and the world spun. I laid back down with a thud, moaning as I did. "My head hurts," I said through closed eyes.

"As well it should," Emma said. "I told you to drink a sip of laudanum, not to chug down the whole thing."

I knew she was exaggerating for effect, as she tended to under most instances, but still I was grateful to her for caring. She would make a good doctor, and had proved so many times already.

When the spinning slowed, I once again opened my eyes, my thoughts no longer on me and my immediate problem. "Henry!" I cried. "We've lost a day."

"It couldn't be helped." Emma assisted me to a sitting position.

"Where's Thomas?" I asked, once I could clear my head of the cobwebs.

"He's out fishing for our dinner. He should be back any time now."

I licked my lips, imagining the taste of fresh fish. It would feel good to finally have a meal of fresh meat after so many days of pemmican and dried berries. "Where's your horse?" I said, my thoughts running through what had happened when the bats had appeared.

"We found her, but she's not faring well, I'm afraid." Her pale Celtic skin grew pink as it did whenever Emma was agitated, and her green eyes sparked fire. "Thomas wants to put her down."

I knew that if Emma had any say, Thomas had better leave well enough alone. Although Emma seemed docile enough, taking an almost subservient role at times, she had the mark of a redhead and the fire to match. I had seen her on more than one occasion give someone a good tongue lashing, one of those times to me. I couldn't help but smile at the memory, because although she could be fierce, I knew what drove that fierceness. It was a loyalty and kindness that was matched by few. And I had been fortunate enough to have earned her allegiance, and I would not take it for granted. Ever.

"What will you do with her?" I asked.

"I've wrapped her leg in a poultice to draw out any poisons, should she have been bitten by one of the bats. But I rather think she ran into a sharp boulder in her haste to flee the wee creatures. I've also cleaned her thoroughly and have given her a sedative to keep her calm. Kahwihta has been checking in on her."

As if to concur, I heard a low nicker from somewhere off to the left. I turned my head and saw Kahwihta, along with Emma's horse who was now nodding her head in agreement with everything Emma had said. I had to laugh at the poor horse's antics, as she did look a sight despite Emma and

Kahwihta's best efforts. Her mane was still tangled and her eyes alert, her ears drawn back as if listening for any more bats that might be about.

It was then that the thought occurred to me. "Why do you suppose they were out at dawn? I thought bats returned to their caves to roost before daybreak."

"Usually, they do," Emma said, her expression turning to a scowl. "Something must have frightened them to prevent them from returning before dawn."

"Rabid bats can be seen during the daytime," I noted.

"Yes, but an entire colony of rabid bats? Hardly. No, more likely they tried to return to their roost and something or someone frightened them off."

That thought scared me. Because if it was true, perhaps that someone was still out there, and even now watching us from some unseen location. I shivered at the thought.

"Here, let's make you more comfortable." Emma ushered me toward a fire she had made, where we would be safe from all the animals of the forest. *But not from man.*

"What do you mean you can't tell me your plans?" Henry's throat tightened as Master Clyde, Eleanor, and her husband, Pierre, ushered Henry and the others back to their hut.

The warmth of the fire glowing in the hearth made Henry feel feverish after a week's worth of travel. He tore off his coat and leather gloves, the other men having gone their separate ways. For now. Here, in the home of the people who last year had kept him and the others safe against Alaric and his men, he felt relieved, but for how long? He couldn't bear the thought that Pierre and Eleanor might have turned against him and were planning something that could affect him in a negative way.

Sir Robert, who had lingered behind, also gave his leave saying that he had somewhere to be, someone to meet. How was it that everyone, save him, had a plan of some sort? His plan had flown out the window ages ago. Instead, he had to rely on the hospitality of people who were prepared to throw him under the wheels of a cart in favor of some greater good, which they wouldn't share. Because of all this, he ached for Brigid. Where was she? Was she safe, sound? He had witnessed the ravages of the fire. He prayed that she hadn't been caught up in it, as clearly it had consumed a large swath of land.

"Sit, *oui*?" Eleanor set out a plate of food before him, as though she'd known all along he was coming. "I will explain, as best I can as you eat. Deal?"

"Deal." His stomach grumbled in response to the large duck eggs she placed before him alongside succulent pork. To that, she'd added a side of homemade wheat bread with a slather of butter and honey on it. He hadn't seen food this good in weeks. He tucked in without further ado, not even feeling abashed as he spoke with his mouth full. "So explain. Why am I to be told nothing about this . . . mission of yours?"

"We need you to do something, but it will mean that you need to trust us, no matter how bad it gets." She gave a sideways glance to Pierre who nodded for her to continue. "Something is afoot—"

"Afoot?" he interrupted, wiping his mouth on the coarse

napkin she'd given him.

"Yes." Master Clyde took a seat beside Henry where he was immediately handed a plate just as filled as Henry's, this time by Pierre. "We don't know who, but someone in the Council was behind Alaric's death."

"But I thought you were against Alaric's rule," Henry protested. He swallowed his words down with a large mug of lukewarm tea.

Master Clyde held up his hands, urging Henry to listen to the whole story before he made any judgment. "We are, but I fear that whoever killed Alaric is more power hungry than even Alaric himself. That's why we need you."

"Need me for what?" Henry patted his stomach, his eyelids drooping.

Master Clyde folded his hands on the table as if to relay the seriousness of the quest. "We need you to find information, but we can't tell you where you will have to go to get it. You're only to know that the person you seek is named Kenric. Beyond that, you are to know nothing else."

"At least tell me what I am to ask," Henry pleaded, fear knocking at the door to his heart.

"You are to try to find out who was behind the plot to kill Alaric so that we know who seeks power and why. Anything you can learn about that . . . anything at all–" Master Clyde's voice faded, and the circles around his eyes made evident that he hadn't slept well, either.

"And you refuse to reveal where or how I shall meet this Kenric?" Henry said, voicing his frustration on an angry sigh.

Again Eleanor and Pierre shared a glance that spoke

volumes to the danger he faced.

"But why? Why can't you tell me? Surely the more I know, the better off I will be and the greater help I will be able to supply."

"Not this time," Eleanor said in a mournful tone, as though she too thought it a difficult ask indeed.

Master Clyde stood. "For tonight, you are to get some sleep—rest up for the day ahead. It shall be a long one."

"As if I can sleep now," Henry said with a snort.

Master Clyde nodded to Eleanor who went to her cupboard and pulled out a dark glass bottle with an eyedropper. Even before she set it in front of him, he knew what it contained. Laudanum. He hated laudanum, but if he wasn't to sleep in the upcoming days, he would have to take it if he was to maintain his sanity. He shuddered, then drank it down. What on earth was he walking into?

17

Siegfried barged in just as Birsha was overseeing the stock of animals his father had collected in a menagerie of stalls that barely allowed for the animals to turn around. The smell that greeted him, when he'd first arrived, had been overwhelming. He lifted his chatelaine to his nose, determined to change all of this. These animals deserved space to roam, a clean habitat, fresh water.

"They're here!" Siegfried said, panting, having clearly run the whole way in his search for Birsha.

"Who's here?" Birsha demanded, the animals forgotten, for now.

"Henry and some others. We don't know who the others are, but we know that it's Henry."

"How do you know?" Birsha demanded, turning away from the tiger enclosure.

"He has been here before, a year ago. Henry released his brother Thomas and Lady Emma from the gaols."

Siegfried took short quick steps beside him as Birsha hurried toward the back exit meant only for royalty. He passed a penguin enclosure filled with a slimy green water that reeked with excrement. Already, he had plans in his head that he would lay onto paper before the night was through to see that these animals had better living conditions.

"How did Henry get into the gaol?" Birsha climbed aboard his carriage, his coachman awaiting him, the door opened promptly for his arrival.

"Through underground tunnels, sir." Siegfried's cheeks had turned a bright red from all the running.

"Why do you suppose he's here?"

Siegfried climbed up into the carriage to sit opposite Birsha. "I don't know, sir, but I've heard rumors that it has something to do with Alaric's death."

Birsha fell back in his seat as the coachman yelled a hearty "Haw!" to get the horses moving. He grabbed a hold of the carriage strap to keep from being tossed about as the horses flew across the cobbled streets toward the interior of the fortress wherein lie his courtyards.

Birsha felt his hackles rise. "Alaric's death? What does this Henry have to do with my father's death?"

Birsha must have trained Siegfried with a ruthless stare because the adjutant seemed to shrink in on himself, to grip the seat as though it might fly out the window with him on it. Birsha forced a smile, but it came out a grimace.

"Well, sir, that I don't know."

Birsha thought through what he'd been told. Did he have anything to fear by Henry being here? He didn't know, but he was determined to find out.

"As soon as we arrive at the tower, you are to find this Henry and bring him to me."

Birsha heard a commotion and peered out the window as the carriage came to a grinding halt. "What now?" Birsha growled.

And indeed, all around them were crowds of people, their cries rising up into the air in a cacophony of sound.

"Go out there and find out what's going on, Siegfried."

His adjutant hesitated for only a moment, then quickly stood and made his way out of the carriage.

"But Siegfried–"

"Yes, sir?"

"This had better not be another *surprise*." This time Birsha didn't care that he pierced his underling with eyes like that of an eagle's gaze.

Siegfried froze, as though a mouse searching for refuge. For several seconds, neither of them spoke. Finally, Siegfried said, "Yes, sir." Then he disappeared into the throng of people and was gone.

The flag was nearly ready. Winnifred knew she should be sleeping, but she had been rousted in the night by an owl and hadn't been able to go back to sleep. She couldn't help but feel something was wrong. She didn't know why, but she just knew it. To keep from going 'round and 'round the subject and frightening herself to death, she got up and began sewing the rest of what would be their standard, if Henry and Bridgid would agree to it. It had come to her, as she sat stewing, that a sunflower represented growth, light, nourishment, all the things they would need in the upcoming days. She had placed it on a blue background to represent the sky and set it next to the manor house along with a loom—*the* loom—the blue falcon winging through the sky above. She hoped the women would like it—Henry and Bridgid too. She was pretty sure Thomas and Emma would be okay with it as well, too interested in each other to give much thought to a flag.

She was relieved when sunlight finally poked over the hilltop. Setting all her worries aside, she rallied the individual team leaders to awaken the women and prepare for the day ahead. Yesterday had been spent purchasing any number of supplies in one of the small outposts on the frontier. Despite everything they had been through, the people at the outpost shared what they could with the women, aware that if they were unable to stifle the onslaught from first Alaric, and now Birsha, there would be nothing left for any of them, except slavery, and *that* they would never accept.

For the next two hours, the entourage prepared for the departure ahead. As Winnifred set about her many chores, she couldn't help but wonder in amazement at the coordination it took to man an army of women. To prepare for every contingent, no matter how large or small. She had seen to it that the women had arms, that they were well supplied with food, and had made certain that the coffers were filled with herbs, bandages, and all other medical supplies, should they be needed. And they *would* be needed. After all, they were nothing if not a moving city on horseback. Not only that, the weather could be unpredictable this time of year, and they had to be ready for snow, ice, and any number of surprise elements that might come their way. The frost and cold had already been a bane to their daily existence. Before the two hours were up, as she prepared for the day ahead, she'd gained new respect for Brigid.

"Is everyone ready?" Winnifred asked Jocelyn who had popped up on the other side of Winnifred's horse, Jasper, a small pinto pony loaned her by one of the Oneida women. She liked the male pony because it was short like her, and quick thinking.

"They are," Jocelyn replied.

"Where's Phinney?"

"Gone," Jocelyn said. "I saw her flying south not five minutes ago. I tried to stop her, but she wouldn't respond to my calls. I think she may be heading back to the manor."

"Why the manor?" Winnifred asked with a worried scowl.

Jocelyn shrugged. "She looked like she was on a mission of some sort."

Winnifred fretted over the bird. She had promised Brigid she would look after the falcon. She hadn't counted on Phinney leaving of her own accord, but why had she gone home rather than ahead in search of Brigid? That was the number one question.

Winnifred hadn't realized that Jocelyn was watching her, clearly worried that she might blame her for the bird's disappearance. "Sorry, I was just thinking. Well, Phinney knows her way back. Let's just hope nothing happens to her in the meantime."

Winnifred smiled at Jocelyn to let her know she wasn't mad, while Jocelyn released a sigh of relief. When Winnifred had first met Jocelyn, she had appeared quite prim and proper, but had shown great fortitude over the past year. Her honey-colored hair no longer had quite the sheen it once had, and when not wearing her armor, her clothes were a pair of chaps and a vest over a long-sleeved shirt. If anything, Winnifred thought of her as cowgirl material, like the ones she'd seen on a poster once.

"All right then, saddle up. It's time we were on the move."

With that, Winnifred cast one last longing look toward the world she'd left behind while silently mourning the barn that had once housed her inventions. Everything she loved had been in that building . . . before it had burned. Tears misted her eyes, but she refused to give into them. Now she had Phinney to worry about as well. She set her jaw, then placed her foot into the stirrup and boarded Jasper, feeling once again the joy of freedom and travel. As if Jasper had the same stirrings, he lifted his head and snorted before lowering it twice, and stamping one foot to let Winnifred know that he, too, was ready.

But her horse no sooner took a step forward than she heard a series of shouts from tiny munchkins off to her left. The sprites! She had almost forgotten them. Yet when she turned her horse's head to face the pixie-like creatures, she saw that some of these were not the sprites she had brought with her. And they were gathered in a large group around something that looked suspiciously like–

"My time machine!" Winnifred leapt off her horse in a

single bound, nearly falling to the ground as she rushed to greet them. "Where did you find it? I thought I had lost it in the fire!"

All the sprites spoke at once, each one poking the other to get a word in edgewise. Winnifred rushed to grab the time machine before it toppled onto them, crushing the wee creatures beneath its wheels.

"We rescued it! Hid it down by the river, we did," said a boastful sprite who was more adept at the English language than the others. He rounded his shoulders in a harrumph.

"Yes, but how did you get it all the way here?" Winnifred marveled.

"Heave-ho, heave-ho!" One particularly stout sprite said, sporting a miniature white beard.

But then she saw a friend of the sprite pretending to drive the time machine, all the while making little chipmunk-like noises. Then he tapped his head and nodded, as if to say he had used his noodle.

"You used the time machine to get here?" She was unable to hide her shock and surprise that such wee creatures had figured out how to use it, when she had barely been able to bring herself back to the correct time period.

The stout sprite nodded as all around they shook their heads and giggled. But then the sprites immediately set in pushing and shoving each other until, fed up with their behavior, Winnifred finally put her fingers to her mouth and released a loud whistle to silence them. They quieted only after a fair bit of muttering.

Despite their bad manners, Winnifred couldn't help but laugh. It was just their way, she knew. Still!

When they had finally hushed, she said, "Thank you so much! I can't tell you how happy I am that you saved this for me."

They each made little noises that sounded like a cross between chipmunks and feral pigs, but nonetheless, she had come to appreciate the small people who acted like children in tiny bodies with wings.

Winnifred quickly had several of the women help her load her time machine onto a cart, then once again climbed aboard her spotted pony. She was about to leave when she noticed that the sprites hadn't come empty-handed.

"What have you got there?" She pointed to the sacks that several of the sprites were passing out to each of their members.

"This?" the lead sprite said, in the high-pitched, sing-song voice that she had come to love.

Winnifred nodded. "Yes, that."

"Why, these are our supplies."

"What for?" Winnifred asked, truly puzzled.

"Why, silly woman. We are coming with you and the other sprites, of course."

And with that, they began a whole new round of chatter. Winnifred could only shake her head. "Of course you are," she said with a laugh and watched as they climbed aboard the cart in single file until not an ounce of space was left.

As the women warriors rode away in a phalanx nearly as far as the eye could see, Winnifred heard the first faint pops of fireworks.

"It's New Years," she whispered beneath her breath.

Although the new year was upon them, few had cause for

celebration, not after the fire. Winnifred hoped that the fire wasn't an omen of what lay before them in the upcoming years. She peered over at her time machine, wondering what tales it had yet to tell. It might be weeks, months, or even years before she could put it to use again, but she knew one thing for certain. Someday, she would travel to the future again, or perhaps to the past this time. She had yet to determine time or place. Still, someday she would master it, or it, her. But she was an inventor, and inventors persevered. It was what made them tick. The unknown. The unknowable.

And with that, she tapped the reins and pressed her pony onward.

We had been on the move since I'd come to, now that the laudanum had worn off. Mile after mile we drove forward, but I couldn't shake the feeling we were being watched. Besides that, we had no more than a few hours of daylight left to set up camp. Gratefully, I plopped down onto my bedroll, Thomas being so kind as to help me with my tent. My arm was now an angry welt that throbbed uncontrollably from the surgery done on it earlier. I closed my eyes, wishing away the pain. But Emma, bless her heart, heard from Thomas of my predicament and came to me. Once again, she dressed the wound, first washing it with a mix of honey and grease, something taught to her by Kahwihta and her band. I winced as she poured it over the laceration. Gave a sigh of relief when she slathered it on like a salve and wrapped it in cotton batting, pulling the two ends together with a metal prong.

"Thank you." I lay on my bedroll, appreciating more than ever this small comfort. I desired nothing more than to fall into a deep slumber, my body still reeling from the injury, but that was not to be.

"Brigid," Emma said, tapping my hand to get my attention.

My weary eyes fluttered open. "Yes?"

"We've found something."

"What do you mean you've found something?" I asked, my eyes fluttering closed once more.

Emma cupped my face in her hands to force my eyes open. "What is it?" I demanded, longing desperately for nothing other than to sleep away my pain and discomfort.

"You should come see for yourself."

Emma, who was normally such an empath, seemed unusually dense. Couldn't she see that I needed rest?

"Can't it wait?" My voice sounded churlish, even to my ears.

"No! It's important or I wouldn't ask."

Reluctantly, I sat up, but my eyes felt as though they were being held up with toothpicks, they were so gritty and sore from both the earlier fire and the days of traversing the dusty trails.

Seeing that I would need help standing, she held out a hand to me and heaved me up onto my knees. Slowly, I reached an upright position.

"Okay, then. What is it?"

Maintaining the suspense, she simply took my arm and steered me out of the tent and through the makeshift camp. In the center of the camp, I smelled the cooking fires burning, knowing that I could no more cook a warm meal tonight with my injured arm and sour disposition, than I had been able to set up camp without help. But my stomach had something to say about that because it rumbled as each new wave of aromas greeted us. I stumbled past a spit of roasting venison, my mouth watering instantly.

"Focus, Brigid," Emma said, her sympathy returning as no doubt she too wished to be eating rather than scouring the countryside for some unspecified object to show me.

We walked what seemed miles but could have been no more than a mile or two at best. Exhaustion overcame my willingness to follow her and I paused, refusing to go further.

"It's just around the bend, I promise."

I nearly put my foot down, but I trusted Emma implicitly. Finally, I allowed her to drag me forward, and true to her word, the spot she had wanted me to see lay just around the corner.

"What is it?" I demanded. But the skin on my scalp prickled with an unnamed fear.

"There's been a skirmish. See here?" she said, bending down and pointing to a spot.

"We don't know for certain that it's Henry." And yet even as I said it, I knew I was lying. Somewhere deep inside me, I knew without a shadow of doubt that something had happened here. And as if to prove me right, I wandered further and saw a piece of clothing, but what clinched it for me was the button emblazoned with an HB for Henry Bookbinder. My throat jammed with emotion and my stomach turned, for I had seen that button many times as I had held Henry in my arms, kissed him, loved him.

"Oh my, Emma!" I said, snatching it up in my hands, tears flowing before I could even capture them and tuck them away as I had been forced to do back at the manor.

"Don't think the worst," Emma chided. Yet even as she said it, we both knew that had the roles been reversed, she would be just as agitated as I.

I plopped down amidst the frozen meadow, and as I did, I could see just at the edge of the grasses, which in a few months would sprout wild daisies and the odd blue lupine. There, in the earth, were scratch marks, as though someone had been scratching at the earth, but they didn't belong to an animal. They belonged to a *human*.

Emma and I peered at each other, our mouths agape as we grasped what we had witnessed but were only now processing.

"You don't think–?" Emma said, her green eyes flashing in alarm.

I nodded my head. "The Fetters," we said in unison.

"It's said they lure men in with their beauty, and when they have them firmly in their grasp, they suck them into the Underworld," Emma whispered, as though to speak about them might bring them to the surface for another try at poor Thomas and the others.

Although we had never spoken about what happened between her and Thomas, nor Dele and Elijah, when the Fetters had tried to suck both their men into the Underworld, I knew it weighed heavily on Emma's mind. I had seen Dele staring out into space too, on occasion, as though the experience had scarred her somehow. In the future, we would have to be vigilant, for all our sakes.

"Are you okay?" I asked, despite my own fears for Henry's safety.

"I am. Thomas and I have talked about it. He says it was like being under a spell—that they gave off an aroma that made them hard to resist."

I had done some of my own research about the subject at hand, asking around from the other women, and although no one had experienced the Fetters directly, many a tale had made the village circuit of poor souls lost at their hands.

"I've heard that they are trained to understand the most intimate desires of a man. That they are designed to—"

"*Designed?*" Emma threw up her hands. "You speak as though they were crafted like one of Winnifred's inventions."

Though I had never thought about it before, I suppose that is precisely what I meant. I shivered, eager to leave this place, the meadow so peaceful as to be almost frightening, as though some ogre awaited us in the thicket that surrounded us.

"All I know is that the women say they are bred and trained to capture men."

We both paused, our breathing shallow. It was then I noticed the bleached bones of animals hidden in the brush and realized that we were seated amid a cat's hunting grounds. Emma saw it, too, her mouth opening wide in horror. As if of a single mind, we leapt to our feet, Emma racing to keep up with me. We didn't stop until the meadow was long behind us and the cooking fires before us. I had been so caught up in what Emma had shown me and the bones of animals long dead that I didn't stop until I ran smack dab into Thomas who thrust a plate filled to the brim with succulent foods into both Emma's and my hands. I could have cried, I was so grateful.

"We have to talk," Emma, Thomas, and I spoke as one. We laughed at that. Then we all took a seat by the fire.

"You first," Thomas said.

"Something has happened to Henry," I said, showing him the button.

Thomas' face grew ashen as he reached out to clutch it in his hand, his words to me all but forgotten. "I was afraid of this," he whispered. His eyes went to Emma in apology, for he too had almost succumbed to the wiles of a beast in women's clothing.

"We've got to find him," I implored. "I know Henry. He wouldn't have been pulled under without a fight."

Thomas nodded, but the worry in his golden eyes, so like his brother's, left no doubt that he feared for Henry's welfare. I sucked back the gasp that sought to escape my lips, for no one knew Henry better than Thomas.

I turned inward after that, not sure what to believe. All I had was hope to keep me going in the upcoming days, but hope could be fleeting. I had learned that when I'd lost my family.

Where are you, Henry?

Despite everything, the celebrations for New Year's Eve had begun in earnest. Large caravans moved in and out of the city. Those had been the cover Master Clyde had used to help Henry enter the city in disguise. He had yet to give him any further instructions, which frayed Henry's nerves further. As it was, Henry wore a mask and striped black and white pants with a yellow satin shirt. For the life of him, he felt like a clown, as though he stood out like a lone bard in a town square.

"Hide in plain sight," Master Clyde had told him.

And it was true that no one recognized him in his disguise. If anything, they thought him one of the revelers, for ringing in the new year was nothing if not festive. The mood was one of merriment, people laughing, carrying banners, fireworks exploding in the distance, despite the fact that the sun had yet to greet the night sky. Even the church bells tolled the turning of this page in history. Before Henry, a parade was forming, complete with dogs wearing ruffled collars and men walking on stilts, pants designed to cover their unusually long legs. They threw candy to children as a marching band heralded in the coming new year.

Though unplanned, Henry soon found himself in the thick of it, all around him dancers with tambourines, horns blaring at the edge of the crowd as revelers cheered and waved miniature flags, a testament to the kingdom they resided in. The hurried movement made him feel dizzy, and he was just about to bow out when he felt a hand on his arm. But when he turned, the person he saw did nothing to alleviate his fears. For it was none other than Nathaniel.

"You!" Henry said, failing to hide the distaste in his voice.

"I know what you think of me," Nathaniel said, "but don't. I only want what's best for our kingdom."

"And what about me?" Henry demanded, pulling himself away from the man's grasp.

"All will be revealed soon, but for now you must trust me,"

Nathaniel said, his eyes drooping as though he hadn't slept in a month of Sundays.

"Hah!" Henry said with a laugh that lacked any humor. "And why, pray tell, should I trust *you* of all people?"

Nathaniel's shoulders sagged, and for the first time Henry saw how drastically the man had aged over the course of the past few days. Though clean now and dressed much better than he had been on the trek, his face appeared sunken to match his dark eyes that were framed in a ledged brow that shadowed half his face. His black hair hung limply against his shoulders.

"I know you have no reason to trust me, Henry, but you must, for all our sakes."

Henry didn't know whether to laugh or cry. He only knew he was being asked to do something that didn't sit well with him, something he had yet to learn which only sent his fear rocketing ever skyward with each passing moment.

"Again, what about *me*?" It was the wrong thing to ask and yet he was tired of beating about the bush.

"Just know that we will watch and protect you, always."

Henry blinked, unable to fathom what this man was asking of him, much less why. He was simply to do as told, without any input into the outcome. The only person he trusted enough for that was Brigid, but she was miles away. It was doubtful if she even knew that Henry was here, in the realm of his most hated enemy, only Alaric was no longer here. His son, Birsha, had replaced him. But what did Henry know of Alaric's son anyway? Nothing.

Henry bent his head sideways. "What can you tell me about this Birsha fellow?" he asked, hoping to change the trajectory of their conversation.

Nathaniel sighed. "Unfortunately, very little," he said, steering Henry by the elbow to a more quiet location. He held up a satchel and nodded toward a closed door. "Here are your new clothes," Nathaniel said. "If you want to know who Birsha is, see for yourself."

"What do you mean?" Henry asked, puzzling his brow.

Nathaniel thrust the bag into Henry's open arms. "You want to know about Birsha, then let's take you to meet him. He no doubt wants to meet you."

Henry shook his head, not comprehending, but Nathaniel pressed him toward the opening door, where an elderly woman was waiting to greet him like a long-lost relative. She and a woman just as ancient prodded him through their front room and toward some steps to a back room.

"You can change your clothes in there," the taller of the two white-haired ladies said, pointing. Henry attempted to peer over their heads, but whatever Nathaniel had in mind, it would have to wait, for he was nowhere to be seen.

Henry walked down a descending corridor, entering a low-slung room with only one small bed and a dresser. The door shut quietly behind him. The room was framed in shadows, now that his eyes had adjusted somewhat, but what he hadn't noticed until now was that the room was actually below ground so that the sounds from the alleyway came from above. There, through the dusty curtains, he saw feet going to and fro in a riot of movement. Revelers celebrating the new year that would arrive on the morrow.

His heart raced as he quickly dressed, his fingers stumbling over the silk buttons of the gray silk vest they'd given him. His shirt was emblazoned with his typical monogram: HB. Henry Bookbinder. But wasn't it risky to show his hand in such an overt way? He bent down to place fine leather shoes onto his feet. When he peered in the mirror, adjusting the bowtie that had been afforded him, he had to say, he didn't look half bad, all except for his hair.

Before he could consider it further, he heard a knock at the door. He opened it a tad and peered out. One of the old ladies, the one with the soft green sweater and embroidered collar, leaned forward to inspect him from head to toe.

"You need a haircut, but other than that, you'll do," she said. Then she grasped him by the arm and led him out, leaving his former clothing behind . . . thankfully!

As if in preparation, the other woman, the one in a floral apron, loose socks, and comfy shoes, had a chair waiting for him when he arrived in the main room. The chair had seen better days, its seat worn to a smooth shine, nicks and gouges taken out of it from years of use.

"Sit," the old lady said.

Almost the second he landed upon the seat, she wrapped him in a bib and donned scissors. He heard the confident snip-snips and saw his long red hair fall to the floor beside him. She fluttered over his head like a pearl crescent butterfly until at last she said, "Done," and handed him a mirror.

Fearfully, he held it up to see what disaster lay before him, but instead of despising it, as he had determined he would, he found himself smiling at the masterpiece she had created.

"You're a miracle worker," he said and meant it. He reached

into his pocket to give her a tip, but realized that his wallet was
back in his other pants, the striped ones.

As if she'd planned ahead, the first woman handed him a
satchel with his clothing stuffed inside. She peered at it with
distaste, as though she too thought the clothes garish. Henry
rifled through it until he found his wallet, then brought out four
bits and handed them to her. She shook her head, but he took
her hand and placed the two coins in her opened palm, then
he quickly wrapped her fingers around the two coins before she
could change her mind.

"You're a good boy," she said, patting the back of his hand.
"Now go give 'em what for," she said with a wink.

Though Henry doubted he would be giving Birsha "what
for," he had to say, he liked the two old women. They reminded
him of his grandmother, rest her soul. Often, when his parents
were busy with heads of state and foreign dignitaries, she had
entered his nursery and taken him for a stroll in the gardens,
or down by the pond to hunt for frogs or turtles, forgoing the
events in order to be with him. She, of all people, had nurtured
his curiosity for life and nature. He, in Dutch sailor suit, as
was all the rage then, her in gown and boots. Together they'd
explored the world around them, within a safe and loving place
in which to test his wings.

He bowed ceremoniously, thanking the women. They
cooed like two young doves. Before he could ask anything
further, a knock sounded at the door and the women spoke in
unison, "Duck eggs!" Code, no doubt, for Nathaniel to enter,
which is precisely what he proceeded to do. And true to their
word, the elderly lady with loose socks handed him a basket

of duck eggs that she'd had hidden next to her chair and her knitting.

"Very well," Nathaniel said in reply.

No money ever exchanged hands, which seemed odd to Henry, as it was clear by the look of the shabby interior that they could use it.

"We will keep you ladies no further. Come, Henry!"

Who did Nathaniel think he was, treating Henry as if he were a pet hunting dog rather than an adult who had been making decisions on his own for years now? His dander up, he nevertheless followed Nathaniel out the door. No sooner had they stepped foot outside than an entire crowd of revelers swarmed around them singing "For He's a Jolly Good Fellow." Apparently, it was the cover Nathaniel had requested, for they were enveloped in a swift current of motion only to be deposited in a dark alleyway where a shadowy figure in a monk's hood walked past them. Almost imperceptibly, the man handed Nathaniel a key which he palmed into his hand from beneath the arm of his plain brown vestment. Nathaniel kept walking, Henry at his side. Henry knew better than to ask questions until they were safely inside. But inside where, precisely?

18

When Siegfried finally reappeared in the carriage, he looked as though he'd been through a whirlwind and spit out the other side. His curly hair was mussed and his clothing appeared thrashed, not to mention his feet were coated in mud.

"What say you, Siegfried?" Birsha demanded, anger at the delay sending sparks of fire bursting through his veins.

"Sir, it's the New Year's Eve celebration. Alaric set it up before his death. He was supposed to give a speech at the public square. And you are to sponsor a masked ball to celebrate. A costume ball, actually."

"A costume ball, when?"

"Tomorrow night," Siegfried shrugged apologetically.

"Why was I never told of this?" Birsha demanded, branding him with a glare that could wilt a daylily.

"Sir, begging your pardon, but the Council determined it

best not to bother you with this since you are still in mourning."

The two sat in silence for more minutes than Birsha cared to count. How dare the Council decide what he should or shouldn't be told. *He* was now leader of his kingdom, not the Council. The more he was learning of them the more he was determined to wrest back control before they decided he was no longer needed to head the kingdom. Birsha fought back the bile that rose in his throat at the sheer willfulness of the Council.

"So what did you learn? Do you or don't you know where this Henry Bookbinder can be found?"

"I do, sir, but I doubt you will be pleased."

"Oh?"

Siegfried's mouth quirked slightly, a tell if ever there was one.

"Go on with it then," Birsha said, nudging him with his knee.

"Alright. We had some men watching him. He was in costume and had inserted himself in the parade." As if to buy time, Siegfried licked his lips.

"And?"

Siegfried paled, even though he undoubtedly was not the one responsible. "And he disappeared."

"You say he was dressed in a costume but he . . . disappeared?" Birsha allowed the word to linger between them. "Well, well. Things just keep getting curiouser by the moment, wouldn't you agree?" he asked the adjutant.

The man merely nodded, his Adam's apple bobbing as he squirmed in his seat. No reason to wallow in further discomfort. "Onward!" Birsha told the carriage driver, and with that, the whip cracked and the revelers parted to let them pass down the cobblestoned street.

Thomas, Emma, Kahwihta, and I were preparing for the march northward. It had only dawned on me this morning that today marked New Year's Eve with little fanfare from the three of us. According to legend, this new year coming up represented a major shift in the universe, an awakening of sorts followed by great tumult. And although nothing heralded this shift, I could feel a stirring within as we sat by the fire, warming our hands and feet from a nighttime of cold. It seemed to reach out from the fire, as though each of the sparks contained within it a live entity that danced a jig on its upward flight into the dawn sky and beyond. And as though the very particles inside my body could feel it too, my insides twirled and plied as though a ballerina performing a spirited *pas de basque*. Back forth, forth back, the imaginary feet danced.

As I struggled to calm my inner stirrings, I gulped down a quick breakfast of pemmican and hardtack, a mixture of flour, water, and salt that would keep, over the course of our journey, though it did nothing for our teeth nor our taste buds. Still, I forced myself to bite into it as today promised to be a long day faced with bitter cold and sore rears, but the alternative meant we walked. Better our bottoms than our feet, I decided as I drank down the stiff coffee that lacked milk or sugar. I winced and Kahwihta giggled, as she too found the coffee bitter and unpalatable.

Kahwihta made a motion, pointing at the otter pelt quiver of arrows and pretending to pull back an imaginary bow. She made a "ping" and then a whining noise that sounded amazingly realistic followed by a "thwunk" as it hit its intended target. Then she began hopping around the encampment, her fingers at either side of her ears in imitation of a bunny. Though I was queasy at the idea of her hunting rabbit, fresh food of any sort sounded heavenly so I nodded encouragement.

Soon we pulled up camp and set about on our journey northward. For once, I wished I had Winnifred's time machine to take me to the future so I would know what we were walking into. As we rode our horses through the paths, portions of the hillside covered in snow and our winter coats wrapped tightly around us, I wondered how Winnifred and the other women were faring. Knowing Winnifred, she was running a tight ship. The woman was a dynamo on horseback, always plotting and planning the company's every move. If they had been a true army, Winnifred would have been a general, but alas, women filled only auxiliary roles to the men. And yet the women were an experiment, no different than one of Winnifred's many inventions. They were opening up never before seen paths into the future. Perhaps Winnifred didn't need her time machine after all. She had one and she was it. We all were.

I had been so caught up in my musings that I hadn't seen a tiny sparrow until it landed on my pommel. To my surprise, it carried a note in a capsule tied to its leg. I let the others go on ahead as I quickly stopped to open it. Inside was a note so small that it nearly took a magnifying glass to read it. I could just make out the words, HENRY IS MEETING BIRSHA. COME

QUICK! ELEANOR.

For several moments, I couldn't move. Why on Earth did Henry plan to go through with it, to meet Birsha? What did he hope to gain by meeting with Alaric's son, the son of the man who had hunted nearly all of Henry's people and my own in order to gain control of the entire kingdom, hoping to usurp the Bookbinder kingdom into their own? Despite my many layers of clothing, I clapped my hands to stave off the chill that had settled over me. The sparrow, frightened by my sudden movements, let out a throaty chirrup and flew up a few inches before settling back onto the pommel.

"Sorry, little one." I offered it some of my hardtack which it pecked on only briefly before adding another discontented chirrup to the mix. "Try this," I said, pulling out a piece of pemmican from my leather satchel.

The bird instantly took to the proffered meal. I hoped it would buy me time. I dug into my satchel once more, this time pulling out an ink quill and a tiny bottle of ink. I turned the paper over and wrote, "ON MY WAY. WILL BE THERE IN TWO DAY'S TIME. BRIGID."

Next, I proceeded to fold up the paper and tuck it back into the tiny capsule and shut the lid. For the sparrow's efforts, I gave it another piece of pemmican. When it was finished with its meal, I lifted it onto my finger and rode it to a clearing.

"Off with you!" I said.

For a moment, it merely blinked at me, then finally, it fluttered its wings as though testing them for take-off, moved farther toward the end of my finger, then spread its wings and was off. As the bird reached its zenith, it dipped its wings as if in salute.

I sat there, momentarily, watching it disappear into the frigid skies. Then it dawned on me. I had lost Emma, Thomas, and Kahwihta as I tarried. With that, I gave Old Red a gentle kick and the horse responded as if he were my own. Now, to find the others.

Despite all that had happened over the past few days, what with Alaric's death, Birsha's rise, Henry, Brigid, and the others gone, Winnifred had spurred the women on their way with party favors so that they too could celebrate this most auspicious day. Where the people from the outpost had found such a thing, Winnifred had no idea, but found them they had. As the women warriors drove their horses through a clearing not yet consumed by snow, Gertrude tried to hand Winnifred a noisemaker, one of those insidious roll-out party favors that sounded like a duck quacking. Somehow, Winnifred doubted that men heading for battle did so with party poppers going off at every turn. Still, she couldn't bring herself to deny the woman this one joyous moment of fanfare. After all, it wasn't every day that a new year arrived, much less unheralded.

She was about to tell Gertrude to keep her noisemaker, but hearing the laughter after so much misery over the past few days, Winnifred changed her mind. "Sure," Winnifred said. "And happy New Year's Eve."

"Happy New Year's Eve!" Gertrude shouted, Jocelyn by her side.

Soon an entire chorus of "Happy New Years" rang out as Winnifred took her place in the lead, blowing her noisemaker and yelling, "Onward, ladies!"

As they made their way northward, every bird took flight, flushed out by the raucous sound of the army of women. The women marched like this for at least an hour before the merrymaking ceased. Winnifred wondered what Brigid and the others would have made of their behavior. At the very least, Brigid would have been surprised that Winnifred had allowed it. But perhaps this was how they differed from men. Women weren't afraid to be happy. Weren't hell-bent on making each other miserable, or most of them, at least. Winnifred thought of Beatrice, who was three lengths behind Gertrude and Jocelyn, enjoying a lively exchange with Yesimeh, who, unlike the others, hadn't kept Beatrice at arm's length.

Winnifred patted Jasper's neck. Her horse was fast becoming her faithful companion. Perhaps she'd been wrong about Beatrice. Perhaps she just needed to be given a second chance. And maybe the same was true of men. After all, Henry and Thomas were decent and kind. She considered her own father. She had lost him at an early age. But what she remembered of him had been favorable. Him reading to her, showing Winnifred his many inventions, explaining them all as though she were an adult rather than an eight-year-old with a mind like a loofa sponge. Perhaps that's where she had developed her talent for all things mechanical. But then her mother had remarried and her step-father had insisted she put aside her natural talent for invention, claiming it unlady-like.

Winnifred dipped down to avoid a low-hanging branch.

If it hadn't been for a messy error on her step-father's part, she might have been forced to give up her true calling, the very thing that made her most happy. But he had crossed paths with one of Alaric's council members on his trade missions to the north, before the two kingdoms had squabbled over territory. It had spelled his death. Sadness gripped her at the thought, for although she had hated giving up her talent, she would have never wished such a thing upon her step-father. Or anyone, for that matter.

She had been so lost in thought that she had almost missed it. A treehouse so intricately woven among the trees that if she hadn't looked at it full on, she would have missed it entirely. Had it been here the last time they were here? Or was it more recently built? As a builder and inventor herself, she couldn't help but feel impressed by what she'd witnessed, for it was like something out of a magical kingdom, a fairytale. It rose to the sky in a spiral of architecture, each and every side crooked, no two sides the same. And like the treehouse, the windows were at odd angles that gave the house the impression of a wooden patchwork quilt.

"Gertrude," Winnifred called. "Gertrude?" she shouted when she got no response. But it wasn't because Gertrude wasn't listening. No. Gertrude's mouth hung open as she looked to see what Winnifred was peering at. But the oddest thing happened just then that caused Winnifred's mouth to widen in awe as well. For all around the treehouse, fireflies flashed in a lush display of light.

"What on earth is that?" Gertrude whispered to no one in particular.

"*Photinus Pyralis.*"

"*Photinus* what?" Gertrude said with a frown.

"Fireflies," Winnifred replied in wonder, "but what are they doing out in December? They're usually only out in July."

"I don't know," Gertrude said in a hush, "but I think we're about to find out."

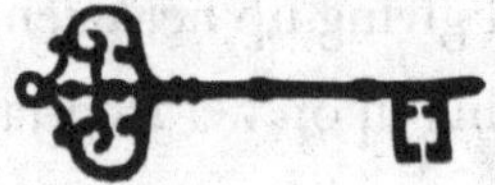

"Where are we?" Henry bent down so that he could fit through the narrow passageway, the dank mustiness making him sneeze. "Whoever used these passages must have been a lot smaller than me."

Nathaniel stopped just long enough to scowl at Henry. "Many people risked their lives to build these underground passages, so think twice before you complain, my boy."

Henry bristled at the word boy, as though he were not yet worthy of the title man. "Where are we?" he finally asked, already winded from scurrying through the warren of passageways beneath the fortress.

Nathaniel stopped and pulled out a map. He held the small torch up to it, his fingers scrawling across the path they had taken. "We're here." He indicated a spot that represented the right flank of the fortress. In Henry's earlier foray into the underground chambers last year he had entered a point just to the left of the inner chambers that represented Alaric's portion of the fortress.

Just then Henry noticed something glowing in the distance. "What's that?" He pointed to a bend in the path.

Nathaniel placed the map back in his satchel and moved cautiously toward it. But as they reached the bend a cavern opened up, the sight within causing Henry's mouth to go slack jawed. Inside were a series of lights hanging from the ceiling, and within that light were thousands of dripping iridescent blue strings that looked like a brilliant chandelier with cascading glow-in-the-dark blue streaks. A thousand bright stars.

"What is it?" Henry asked, his awe evident in his words.

"*Arachnocampa luminosa*," Nathaniel whispered, his eyes alight with glee at the ethereal sight. "Glow worms," Nathaniel explained. "Arachno because of the spider-like silk. Luminosa, well, you can see for yourself why they call it that."

"Are they spiders then?" Henry ducked down at the mention of an insect that could either be good for the environment, or shoot a deadly poison into their unsuspecting prey.

"It's not a spider at all. It's a worm that hatches into a fungus gnat. It's native to New Zealand, of all places. How it got here is anyone's guess, but I have a feeling it has something to do with the entomologist on Alaric's Council."

"Why does it glow?" Henry straightened to get a better look at the mucous strands that reminded him of melting ice.

"The worms release a blue mucus that drips down in silk strings. They use the sticky luminescence to capture prey."

Henry stopped so fast that Nathaniel bumped into him.

Nathaniel laughed. "They're not interested in you, Henry. You're the wrong species, or perhaps the right one, depending on your outlook."

"Why does it look as if it has little blue beads attached to the thread?" Henry leaned in to inspect one especially long strand closely.

"Not to get too detailed, but they regurgitate mucus, which makes up the silk threads. Then humidity does the rest, creating those tiny beads of moisture on the silk."

"Yuck!" Henry said, then realized how ridiculous that sounded. "Well, I, for one, will give them a wide berth."

With that, he stepped to the side and continued through the cavern to the corridor that ran northeast to their current location. Almost instantly, the humidity gave way to warmer climes as they headed slightly upward, the dankness turning to the musty smell of dust.

"We're almost there." Nathaniel pointed to a series of doorways built into the ceiling of the dirt walls. Rickety wooden ladders hung on the wall for the upward climb.

"How will we enter unnoticed?" Henry asked, quite certain that they would immediately be set upon if they walked into a room from out of the floorboards.

"Each trapdoor goes to some hidden part of the fortress," Nathaniel explained, whispering, lest they be heard.

"Where does this one go?" Henry nodded toward the first door.

"That door delivers you to the room of Alaric's current fancy, or at least it did in times past. We don't know enough about Birsha yet to make a determination about what type of man he will be. That's why we need you. We couldn't afford to send a less trustworthy person."

"And my parents wouldn't send their eldest son, Thomas, on such a dangerous mission," Henry grumbled, not that he would have allowed Thomas in harm's way at any rate. Ironically, Thomas was heir apparent to the leader of the next generation of Bookbinders and the territory that entailed. And yet he had no interest in the role. None. Whereas, Henry bore a confidence that his brother never had. Still, he should count himself lucky that it was Thomas who would fulfill the role of heir, should he choose to do so.

"No," Nathaniel replied, in answer to Henry's statement about his brother, "they would not send your brother into the Jackal's lair. Sorry, Henry."

They moved on in silence, each to their own thoughts. Henry had almost forgotten that their mission lay before him, he was so lost in thought, but the reminder came when Nathaniel held up his hand and bent down, peering through a grate above them.

"What is it?" Henry hissed.

"Shh!" Nathaniel placed his index finger over his lips. Then he pointed upward.

Through the grate I could just make out words, but they drifted in from somewhere far off. So many questions rattled around in my head. Where had Nathaniel taken him? To Birsha's quarters? Hardly! No doubt the man would be put off should two strange men show up in his private rooms. And if not, where were they, precisely? Henry strained to listen.

"He's not fit for . . ."

Though the words drifted off, it was clear that they were from a woman.

"Yes, but do we dare . . ."

Henry growled inwardly, wishing he could hear more of

what the two women were saying. Were they speaking about Birsha? If they were in or near his quarters, it would seem likely, as no doubt he was the topic of discussion with so much at stake, and especially after the generals' deaths.

"Shh!" one of the women said. "Someone's coming. Hide."

Hide? Henry looked at Nathaniel in question, but the man merely shrugged.

To Henry's surprise, not only did the women not move farther away, but they seemed to be huddling just above the grate. Henry quickly averted his gaze as he crouched down into the shadows so as not to be seen. But what he had caught a glimpse of was a marvelous display of fiery red.

"Tempestous," Nathaniel mouthed, motioning upward. "From the Council."

Henry peered up in alarm, more alert than ever. Tempestous' breathing seemed labored as she cowered down next to some unnamed woman. Henry spared a quick glance at the woman only to see something that looked surprisingly like . . . snake's skin. His own breathing quickened until it sounded like a bass drum in his chest. He hugged the wall, closing his eyes for fear that if he opened them, he might give away their location by releasing a fear-induced sigh.

For what seemed an overly lengthy amount of time, they all sat there like that until finally he heard one of them say, "He's gone." The pair grabbed hands, then scurried off, but not before something fell through the vent and into his arms.

A key. But a key for what?

19

We pressed on, pushing our horses to their limits as we inched ever closer to the fortress. Without all the heavy cargo of a women's army, we made much better time, despite the winter weather. However, we were so exhausted by the end of the day that we made quick work of dinner and then immediately went to our tents.

By the fourth day on the road, I began to see signs of activity which meant we were nearing the fortress. With any luck, we would arrive by tomorrow morning. But would we be in time to save Henry from himself? I needed to get to him, to help him escape, should Birsha get it in his head to use him as a pawn.

As if reading my mind, Emma sidled over to me, a tin plate in her hand filled with food that should have made my stomach growl but instead made it quiver. I was still recovering from the encounter with the bats, but for now, I had developed no fever or rash. Chances are, with the passage of time, I would be out of the woods, if not now, soon. I patted the log that I'd turned into a makeshift seat and Emma plopped down, setting her plate on her knees even as she moaned and rubbed at her back and neck.

"Oh, Brigid, every muscle in my body aches," she said in a melancholy tone. "You?"

Frankly, I was too keyed up to notice the aches and pains. To be so close and yet so far away made me whirl with emotions. If I could, I would pick up the reins and go in search of Henry myself.

"I'm okay," I finally said. "But I'm worried about Henry. I wish I had my loom, some way to know the future. Do you think I was wrong for leaving the loom behind? After all, it has done so much to help us."

"Perhaps you could get the Bookbinders to send another miniature loom," Emma suggested, tucking a wiry strand of red hair behind her ear as she ate.

"I doubt it," I said glumly. "For one thing, the loom has only ever produced a single miniature loom, and for another, how would I get word to the Bookbinders?" I wished Phinney were here, my lovely blue falcon. I had been foolish to leave her behind with Winnifred and the others. She, of all those around me, could ferry a message back and forth. Though not normally a skill of a falcon, Phinney was no ordinary bird. It often seemed she could read my thoughts. And she had an almost uncanny ability to locate me anywhere, as though she could scent me out, though that was next to impossible. I sometimes believed we shared a common brain, only I had the ability to speak, whereas she merely had the ability to squawk.

As if she, too, could read my thoughts, Emma said, "Why don't you call Phinney? I'm sure she would come."

"Do you think it's possible to just request her and she will appear?" I asked, half in jest.

"You'll never know until you try," Emma said with a shrug.

Just then, Thomas and Kahwihta came over and sat on the ground opposite us. For several moments, they sat in silence.

"A messenger came by," Kahwihta said excitedly. "He was sent by my father."

Kahwihta had an odd way of staring off in the distance as she spoke, as though continually checking the horizon. Thomas had said it was the way of the natives, as though encoded in them from birth. "It has probably kept them alive," Thomas had explained once, "because they always know who's coming . . . what's in their territory."

And yet how could they have foreseen the coming of the white man, smallpox, all the European scourges that had decimated their tribes so that now they were less than half of what they had been prior to the white man's arrival?

"I asked that he send a messenger to your people to tell them where we are."

"Which people? The Bookbinders or Winnifred and the others?"

"Both, though they will find the women first, of course. I asked that they send a return message by way of your bird Po-ni."

"Phinney?" I jumped to my feet, nearly knocking Emma's plate out of her hand in the process. But how would I get

word to the Bookbinders that they needed to get a loom to
the women as quickly as possible? That way, when we met up
I would have some way to learn where Henry was located and
what danger he might be in so I could help. He deserved that,
after all he'd been through these past days. "How soon can you
get Phinney here?" I asked, worried that I might sound rude.

"Three days," she said.

Three days. My heart sank. Three days might be too late.

"Help me," I whispered to the wind, wishing the goddess of
the wind would hear my prayer.

And as if she had, the wind began to swirl, leaves circling
in small eddies, the smell of pines and the odd aroma of rotting
apples scenting the air. In my mind's eye, I could see a shadow
fly upwards into the sky, hear the flapping of wings, and I knew
. . . knew without a shadow of doubt that Phinney had heard
me and was on her way. On her way to help me and my beloved
Henry.

Birsha strode into his inner chambers still unused to the
opulence. His father had spared no expense, employing artisans
of every kind to create a palace within the fortress walls. The
inner chamber was lined with gold, the central candelabra a
golden ship complete with masts and a unicorn figurehead
that, when lit, appeared as though a golden vessel were sailing
across the moon-lit sky. Black and white banded Italian marble
graced the floor, each of his footsteps creating an echo that only
magnified his loneliness. Even his half-brothers seemed more

aloof now, as though they too were plotting against him. How he wished he could throw this all away: the power, the money, the position.

For the umpteenth time since he'd ordered the generals' deaths, he wondered if he had done the right thing. His half-brothers had pushed and prodded until he felt he had no choice. That he'd have a mutiny on his hands if he didn't follow through. The only person he trusted in this god-forsaken place was Siegfried, and even that he questioned. People could change when they felt they had something to gain.

He hefted himself into an ornate gilded chair, listening to the tittering of the women in the outer chambers. Women who wouldn't have looked twice at him now fluttered fans in front of their faces, peering over them with coquettish gazes, all the while flapping unusually long eyelashes at him as though in masquerade. He had no time for it.

He shook his head in an attempt to dispel the horrible images, focusing instead on his time in training. He laughed to think that he actually missed his days in the countryside, tucked away on what appeared to the outside world as little more than a farm. Though he had never warmed to his tutor, he had loved walks outdoors among the wildlife, fishing along the streambeds in search of trout. Taking baths under the waterfalls, diving deep only to come up with a spray of water glancing off his brow. He had answered to no man then. Except for his training, he was free to while away the days as few knew of his connection to Alaric, his father. Only after his father was gone was it revealed to the kingdom that he was the heir apparent. The only people who knew were the two generals, and they were gone.

He rubbed his face with his hands. When he peered up, he was staring at the freestanding globe that filled one entire corner of the room, one of the best libraries in the world as its backdrop. For a moment, he couldn't think what had him so entranced. Granted, the globe was massive and possibly the most beautiful one he'd ever laid eyes on. It was as though it was lit from within casting a glow on everything around it. For some reason, he found himself drawn to it, so he stood, making his way towards it. But before he could come within reaching distance it began to spin, slow at first, gaining speed until Birsha feared it would take flight and launch itself through the huge, stained glass dome above that depicted battles among the neighboring kingdoms.

Birsha swayed at the dizzying speed with which the globe traveled when suddenly it burst open and Birsha let out an embarrassed scream that he quickly subdued. Too fearful to move toward it, yet too mesmerized to look away, he leaned forward and inspected the vast chasm within. To his surprise and amazement, a hologram appeared depicting his father, Alaric, among the nobles of the past, as though having taken his rightful place as heir of the heavens and those who had gone before him. Birsha hadn't realized that his breathing had quickened and his muscles had tensed until he heard the door open and turned.

"Siegfried," he said, with a sigh of relief. "It's you."

"That it is," Siegfried agreed, but his eyes were on the massive globe with its ornately carved mahogany base. "What is it?" he whispered, as though to speak out loud might somehow break the spell cast over it.

"Look," Birsha said, glad to have someone besides him to witness the strange occurrence. "What do you think it wants?" he added, as though the globe were a living entity capable of communicating its desires.

But before Siegfried could speak, the hologram of Alaric rose to the forefront, taking center stage. "Listen to me well, son," the image said in a rich, booming voice that set Birsha back slightly. "I have created this for you." Alaric's hands splayed outward, as if to encompass the entire room and beyond. "Now it is your duty to finish what I could not." His voice had dropped to a mere hum.

With the sound, came an implied "or else." Or else what, Birsha wondered?

"You will unite the kingdom under one rule. *Mine!*" Alaric growled.

"But you are . . . you are . . ." Birsha couldn't bring himself to say dead. Alaric didn't feel dead, at least his image did not. Had Alaric managed to do what no one else could? Rule the kingdom from the afterlife? Once again Birsha felt himself sway, but it would do no good to pass out now, with so much at stake. First he'd had to deal with the generals, then the Council, not to mention his half-brothers, but now his deceased father? A boulder settled on his chest that couldn't be moved. This time he sought a chair nearby and sagged into it, blinking rapidly.

"I don't understand," Birsha said, trying to make sense of it.

"You are to do my bidding. I may no longer be here, but in my world, the human form is a useless feature, no longer necessary." Alaric smiled, but it was a chilling smile that sent shock waves through Birsha. So now he would be expected to do as ordered. He ran anxious fingers through his coal-black hair and realized with astonishment that his normally wavy hair had curled slightly as a result of what he'd just learned.

Though his lips quivered, he said, "And what are the consequences?"

"Consequences?" Alaric frowned, as though confused. "What do you mean by consequences?"

"If I don't do your bidding." Birsha's cheeks warmed, his words breathy with fear.

"Then you shall die, like me," Alaric said with a laugh that sounded more like a growl.

"I see," was all Birsha could think to say. "Very well then. I shall do your bidding."

Alaric laughed, and laughed again, each new howl growing louder all the while, his image fading. As soon as Alaric was gone and the globe had once again closed up, Siegfried dashed over to Birsha to tend to his failing health. For once, Birsha was grateful to have someone, *anyone*, on his side.

Henry was relieved to be away from the sticky glow worms that hung like a blue-lit candelabra from the ceiling of the vast underground cave. The path had narrowed such that they'd had to bend over to keep going. Although Henry didn't normally feel claustrophobic, in such tight quarters with no way to turn around, much less turn back, he suddenly felt as though he couldn't breathe. He forced his feet onward, determined to make it through the bottleneck to the other side . . . if there *was*

another side. He was sweating fifteen minutes later when he was at last able to straighten up and walk normally. The thought of returning the same way he'd come sent cold sweats running rivulets down the sides of his forehead.

"Where are we?" he finally managed to say.

Nathaniel, who had made certain they were dressed to meet the leader of this vast kingdom, must not have thought of what they would look like by the time they traversed the dank and dark pathway. Henry felt certain that his clothes must smell of must and dust in equal measure. More importantly, stains of perspiration and bits of dirt and debris littered his clothing from the ever tightening womb of the passageway.

"If I'm not mistaken, we're near the ballroom. But we need to be in the quarters meant for guests. I have it on good report that two rooms have been kept free for us."

Henry shook the cobwebs from his head. "Why didn't we just enter the normal way, if they are expecting us?"

"Well, not exactly *us*, Henry," he said, pinning him with a raised eyebrow.

"No?"

"No. The pair that were given the two rooms are . . . how shall I say this . . . indisposed."

"Indisposed?"

"Oh, for heaven's sake, are you a parrot? The fact of the matter is, we're taking the place of two businessmen who plan to ask Birsha for prime territory in exchange for their help in subduing the local populace."

"What do they get in return, besides property?"

"Power. It's as simple as that. They get to run the show . . . I mean, *we* get to run the show," he said with a sardonic smile.

In the weeks that they had been traveling, Nathaniel had begun to sport a beard. With his new look came a swashbuckling appearance that made him seem, well . . . oddly debonair. No longer did he seem the evil person that Henry had first encountered on the road.

Still, Henry was tired from the long journey through the underground passageways, his temper slipping, despite his best efforts to do otherwise. "So," he said, unable to hide the sarcasm in his voice, "you've had your friends knock out two poor sods–"

"Sods who deserved it," Nathaniel reminded him with a wink.

"–and we are to replace them."

"Precisely." Nathaniel practically gleamed, and in fact his one gold tooth winked in the light shed by a grate from the city above. But the smile was soon wiped off his face when a bit of dirt from the boot of a passerby fell through the grate and into his open mouth.

"Ptooey!" Nathaniel spit, once, twice, three times to rid himself of the dirt. "This cursed city."

For some reason, Nathaniel's loss of composure lightened Henry's mood and he slapped his companion on the back. "Buck up, old chap," he said, as though in imitation of Sir Robert, a gentleman if ever there was one.

Then Henry nearly ran pell mell, eager to get to wherever they were going–ready to sleep in a comfortable bed for once instead of roughing it on the cold, hard ground. And it wasn't as if it was warm in this subterranean wormhole.

He kept a crisp pace until Nathaniel grabbed the back of

his shirt and hissed, "Stop!" Henry nearly fell backwards in his haste.

"What'd ya do that for?" Henry demanded.

Nathaniel just jerked his head in the direction of a wooden insert that filled one side of the carved-out ceiling.

"What is it?" Henry asked.

"Our ticket out of here," Nathaniel said with one quick bow and a half smile.

Winnifred halted the caravan with a quick slicing motion of her arm. And like dominoes cascading one atop the other, the group of women halted until they were so far back Winnifred could see only a small portion of the warriors. A brief murmur rose like a flutter of butterflies' wings. Winnifred again gave a hand gesture signaling silence. Group by group, the hand signal was conveyed until all were silent. Next, Winnifred gave them the signal to reverse course so that whoever lived in the treehouse would not be shocked to find thousands of women outside their doorstep. When she could no longer see anyone except Gertrude, who had also sighted the treehouse, they began the task of climbing upward.

The stairs to the treehouse were merely wooden steps nailed into the tree itself. They ran in a semi-circle around the central tree, small bridges zigzagging back and forth from tree to tree until at last they'd made the skyward climb. Winnifred's heart gave way as she viewed the sprawling mountains filled with forest as far as the eye could see. Near the base was Heart Lake, so named for its heart-like shape. She marveled at the view as she took in the rich scent of pine and the pungent odor of earth and sunshine. And at the fireflies dancing in delight, not a care in the world. Had it not been for the fact that this was someone's home, Winnifred might have forgotten it altogether, so taken was she with the unending landscape before her.

"Winnifred," Gertrude whispered, taking a hold of her sleeve. "Look."

Winnifred turned to where she was pointing.

And indeed, through the window were a line of elfin eyes, each with different hats. One green and pointy. The other red and sagging, as though the elf had forgotten to starch it. A third wore a blue hat that was like neither of the others. It was a deep blue stovepipe hat made specially for the elf's squatty head. Bushy eyebrows and suspicious green eyes stared out at Winnifred and Gertrude. The oldest of the bunch, the one with the stovepipe hat, was smoking a pipe made from the very wood around them. Large puffs of smoke filled the air. It's then that Winnifred realized by the apron and curly long hair that Green Hat was the mother of the trio, Blue Hat the father, and Red Hat the juvenile, though they were nearly all the same size. Winnifred dipped her head in deference as she turned toward the door and knocked. The door was child sized. As such, when the family of elves opened the door and reluctantly invited them in, Winnifred and Gertrude had to duck to enter.

No sooner had Gertrude and Winnifred stepped inside than they looked up at the vaulted ceiling that seemed to twist in a spiral. A gnarled, hand-hewn piece of timber, a branch, really, held up the loft where a bed lay in the center. On the other side, but much lower, was the child's loft, as evidenced by the many specimens the child had collected: a nest, with beautiful blue and brown eggs; a grouping of feathers of every kind hanging by a strip from the stem of a reed of some sort. It blew in the light breeze that seemed to circle the room. And a branch held a series of clothes for the child to dress in, no doubt made by her elfin mother.

In the center of the room sat a stove that, like the house, had a crooked pipe that ran up to the second story and out of the treehouse. A lamb's wool blanket covered the wooden sofa that was part of the tree itself. And somehow they had managed a pulley system to draw water up to the sink they'd found somewhere deep in the forest and had managed to bring all this way up, no doubt by pulley as well. The entire treehouse was quite ingenious, actually, and Winnifred smiled as she held out her hand and introduced herself to the elves, Gertrude too. But to her surprise all three leaned as one to inspect her hand, apparently believing this was an offering of some sort. Seeing that they expected a gift of friendship, Winnifred quickly reached for the spyglass attached to her belt and held it up for them to see. They each took turns peering out the window at the valley below with their new toy in hand.

"*Gambo!*" the little one said.

"Ah! *Ity gambo!*" the other one agreed, nodding her head. Only Stovepipe Hat stayed silent, arms crossed and his expression stern. Clearly he was having none of this peace offering.

"*Me-si,*" Mama elf said, pointing at her chest.

From what Winnifred could gather, she was asking if it was

a gift for the trio. Winnifried took only a second to reply. Quite a few of the others had spy glasses that she could borrow, and seeing the joy it brought the woman and the girl, she nodded her head and pointed to the trio.

"Yours," she said, enunciating clearly in case they could speak her language.

At that, the trio spoke at once, their odd locution cascading over each other in a waterfall of words.

"Can you speak English?" Gertrude asked, motioning to her mouth.

Mistaking their intentions, Mama elf handed the spyglass back to her daughter and ran on short, stubbly legs to the kitchen, where she produced a beautifully carved hardwood bowl with nuts collected from the forest. She positioned the first one, a shagbark hickory onto a wooden cutting board and hammered it with a rock until the nut meat was visible. Next she broke open a chestnut, followed by several hazelnuts. With this, she added dried fruit that she placed into a small wooden bowl. Then she returned, her movements short and jerky.

"*Ita par vu.*" She held it out to them, nodding her encouragement.

Winnifred took a bite of the nuts as did Gertrude. Then the elf once again began talking in what to Winnifred was no more than gibberish. Winnifred shrugged and shook her head. "Sorry, I don't understand."

She wished there was a way for them to speak. Then as if Stovepipe Elf could see their dilemma, he held up a finger then scurried upstairs, his movements more fluid than his wife's. Minutes later, he returned with an odd contraption that reminded Winnifred of a gramophone she'd seen at the World's Fair, the invention still too new for them to be made available to common people like herself. To her surprise, when the old man spoke into it, his words were instantly translated from Elfish into English.

"Hello, my name is Mikael Anders, this is my wife Eva, and my daughter Karin, ya? We are from the Old World."

Even with the aid of the gramophone, his words bore an accent, Swedish, if she wasn't mistaken. Winnifred quickly introduced herself and Gertrude. "Are there others like you?" Winnifred asked, hoping that she wasn't being too presumptuous.

"Ya!" Mikael and his wife said in unison. "But what are you?" Mikael asked, peering at his wife, their eyebrows knitted in worry. "You don't look like a *Vidunder*."

"A Vidunder?" Winnifred looked to Gertrude to see if she had any idea what Mikael was talking about.

Eva looked at Karin to explain, then they spoke together in quick short tones. When they turned back to face Winnifred and Gertrude, Eva urged Karin, with the nod of her head, to continue. Karin merely shrugged, then puffing herself up to look large and holding out oversized hands made to look like fangs, she growled in her most hideous voice, then stopped, shrugged once more and smiled.

"Do you mean monster?" Winnifred said.

"Monster," Mikael concurred and soon they were all shaking their heads.

"What monster?" Winnifred asked, puzzled by their actions.

"Up north." Mikael spoke into the gramophone.

Winnifred followed suit so that her words could be translated as well. "Up north? Do you mean in the fortress?"

Their serious expressions, and their insistent nodding told her all she needed to know. So, they considered those from the fortress monsters.

"They enslave us," Eva explained. "To perform menial labor. Because we don't speak their language and are small, they think us stupid, easy to control. That's why we make our home in the trees, so that we can easily escape should they find us."

"How do you escape?" I asked.

Mikael bent a finger for the two women to follow and they all marched out onto the outer deck. He made noises for them to continue to follow him around back, where indeed a series of rope netting ran from tree to tree. Winnifred was about to step out onto the netting when Mikael stopped her. He pantomimed that she was too large, that the netting might break, that it was made for smaller people like himself. He also pulled a fire stick from his pocket and lit it to show how he could literally burn his bridges behind him should "the monsters" find him.

Winnifred sighed, and saw that Gertrude appeared stunned by this news. All last year the women had walked amongst these trees, never once suspecting that an entire community lived above them, in the trees' branches.

Winnifred thought she noticed a movement out of the corner of her eye, but when she turned, it was gone. Again she saw movement. She was about to ask the trio what was going on when she caught sight of one especially brave young juvenile, a male, who had come to see the strangers in their midst.

Mikael called to him, and soon, as though the trees were alive, elves of every sort popped their heads out from beneath tree branches. To Winnifred's surprise they had managed to stay camouflaged, an entire community hidden amongst the trees. Before long, the entire clan was clamoring across the bridge to inspect the newcomers. Soon Winnifred and Gertrude were surrounded, the wee folk pulling on their clothing, touching their hair, inspecting every detail of their long, lean bodies.

"Stop that!" she heard Gertrude say when one especially forward elf pinched her to see if she was real. The girl only giggled followed by a smattering of giggles throughout the clan.

Finally getting to what she'd come for, Winnifred said, "Have you seen two men on horseback?"

Mikael shook his head, not understanding. He urged a group of youngsters to bring him the gramophone. When they returned, Winnifred repeated her question into it.

"Ah!" Mikael said with a knowing expression. "One had red hair, yes?"

Winnifred and Gertrude nodded excitedly.

"The other had a *ruley* accent and used the word 'chap', no?" Eva added, not to be outdone.

Though Winnifred didn't know what *ruley* meant, she took it to mean "odd." Excited, she jumped up, Gertrude doing the same. Together they hugged each other, eager to know what had befallen their friends. "Were they safe?" Winnifred managed to add, once they had settled down after the good news.

But instead of providing comfort, Mikael and Eva glanced nervously at each other. Even little Karin seemed more subdued. "They were with several rough men."

"Rough men, what men?" Gertrude asked, beating Winnifred to the punch.

"Scruffy men. No gooders, that's what I think," Eva said, her voice lowering as if to lend credence to their badness. "We hid."

She appeared apologetic at this news, and yet Winnifred knew that their families came first. She would have done the same. "Did you see a woman with three other people?" Winnifred asked. "They were in search of the two men."

Mikael said no, but one of the women from the clan moved forward and said, "I saw them."

A murmur arose. "Why didn't you tell anyone?" Mikael scolded.

"I didn't want to worry you. They seemed harmless enough."

Nevertheless, Mikael scowled, unhappy with the poor woman even though she appeared quite contrite.

"Well," Winnifred said, letting out a breath of air, "at least we know they were well when you saw them last. That's something."

Eva put her hand on Winnifred's forearm, the only part of Winnifred's arm that she could reach. "It will be *adnoff*," she offered in consolation. And yet her eyes spoke of untold sorrow, as though she too had experienced loss at the hands of the Vidunders.

Just then the sound of fluttering wings intruded on Winnifred's dark musings. She looked up to see a blue bird, but not just any blue bird. A falcon.

20

Emma, Thomas, Kahwihta, and I had left the horses behind in a narrow glade next to a stream, protected from the snow so that they would have what grass was available and water until we could retrieve them. As we knelt down in the snow which lay thick upon the forest floor, I shivered. From where we perched, we could see not only the fortress that rose like a behemoth from the snowy depths, but Jackal guards, dressed in furs and hats, leather gloves on their hands, their arms at the ready.

"How will we get past them?" I asked Thomas, to which he had no reply. After a week on the road, his chin was thick with stubble that helped to warm him against the increasing cold.

Somewhere out there was Eleanor and Pierre's home, if only we could find it. We had traveled in fall, the last time we were here. We had followed a simple path that wound its way to their home in the village. But now those lines were blurred, crested by newfallen snow that turned our cheeks candy apple red. My teeth chattered and my feet felt numb. I knew we would soon need shelter if we were to survive another night in the winter of the far north.

"Okay, does anyone know how to get to Eleanor and Pierre's cabin?" I tried once more.

Kahwihta, who seemed to have an uncanny knack for locating what we could not, grunted and pointed due west. We would have to skirt the forest. We didn't dare go out into the open, not with the guards doing watch. They would recognize us instantly for who we were, as our clothing was far different from theirs. They tended toward long gray coats, marmot fur hats, and most wore a red scarf at the neck, their only color. We, on the other hand, tended toward layers in winter. White blouses with dark skirts and vests in a variety of colors, for those without a uniform, that is. And fur-lined capes. The women sported knitted wool caps, also in a variety of greens to mirror the forest. We would need to be careful, indeed.

Kahwihta pointed her chin in the direction we were to follow. She crouched down low, encouraging us to do likewise so that we could hide at a moment's notice. We kept to the south as we headed diligently westward, all the while stopping and starting at the slightest sound. As we neared a snow-filled meadow, we heard voices. Kahwihta urged us to duck into the underbrush with only the downward movement of her hand. Over the course of the past few days, we had learned to read her hand signals, which seemed nearly her sole source of communication when we were on the move. Now, she needn't warn us, for we were all frightened out of our wits.

As we sat huddled in the cold underbrush, I peered through an opening of the few remaining leaves, praying that I would not be seen, but what greeted my eyes nearly sent me sprawling in the snow on my bottom. For it was none other than a woman dressed in a fiery red dress as though she were aflame, her hair the sparks that floated upward in a wiry display of color. Though I couldn't see her eyes, I knew that she was one of the Council, for only they looked like . . . *monsters*.

As if the other three had all come to the same conclusion at exactly the same time, we turned to each other, our mouths opened in horror. For she was not alone. Indeed, two others were with her and both had an oddly reptilian look about them, their skin bearing the hallmarks of a snake, their eyes having the trademark ventricle slits. Despite the cold, or possibly because of it, I shuddered rather than shivered. It was as if the snake people could sense that we were there, for they lifted their heads and an odd three-pronged tongue flicked in and out of their mouths in a few quick motions. As one, we froze, scarcely daring to move, but I knew the male snake, at least, had sensed us. For several seconds, he didn't move, simply stared through unblinking eyes in our direction. How on Earth would we escape?

We hunkered down as low as possible, hoping the wind would change so that they couldn't detect our scent. As though the goddess of the wind had indeed heard our prayer, the wind blew in a southerly direction and slowly the male's head descended, but his beady slits for eyes continued to glance our way from time to time.

"Do you have it?" The woman's red skirt seemed short-circuited by the wintry cold so that it zapped and hummed, sparks zipping this way and that, yet unable to escape into the frigid air.

I covered my face with my cloak, while Thomas used a handkerchief that he tied around his face to prevent the steam from our mouths giving us away, each of us taking measures to ensure our safety.

"It'sss here," Snakewoman said, reluctantly pulling something from her gray coat.

I strained to see what it was in Snakewoman's hand, but the Fire Goddess's back prevented me from seeing what she held. If I moved any nearer I would give our position away. Instead, I willed the Fire Goddess to turn, yet to no avail.

The Fire Goddess reached her hand out to snatch whatever Snakewoman held, but just as she came within reach, Snakewoman snatched it back.

"Not so fassst," she said, her tongue slithering in and out. "Where isss the money you promisssed usss?"

Fire Goddess's dress sparked a fiery red, the sparks defying the cold as her anger swelled. "Give it to me, you little–"

"Or what?" Snakewoman hissed. "You will do to usss what you did to the generalsss?" She laughed, but it came out sounding like hot metal from a blacksmith's forge, dipped in cold water.

"How dare you accuse me." The Fire Goddess' dress fairly glowed now so that it appeared molten, as though lava might drip down its sides at any moment. And indeed waves of heat began melting the snow around her so that soon the Snakewoman wasn't the only thing hissing.

Snakeman had turned the exact color of the newfallen

snow so that all but his eyes were invisible. He tugged on Snakewoman's gown, pulling her toward him. "Our money," he said, his eyes never leaving the Fire Goddess' face. "Or we keep—"

"No!" Fire Goddess cried, the heat from her gown now cooling slightly so that it was a darker, more subdued red. "I have it."

From within her gown was a secret compartment. She pulled out a lovely satchel made of red diamonds that sent shards of light floating every which way. Indeed, they were so lovely that they were almost blinding. I turned away, protecting my eyes with my hand. I heard the sound of coins being exchanged. By the time the satchel was once again returned to its hiding spot within her dress, and I was able to see, the deal had been made. But deal for what?

Emma tugged on my sleeve and tilted her head as if to say, what was it?

I only shrugged, as I had missed it too. Whatever it was, it was worth a tidy sum to the Snakewoman, for she all but glowed as she tucked the coins into her coat pocket.

"We will not ssspeak about the generalsss again," Snakewoman said with a smile.

Then she and Snakeman turned and left for the eastern ramparts of the fortress. My breathing grew shallow, and yet it seemed that it echoed in the silent afternoon for all to hear. I was about to back out slowly when the Fire Goddess turned, and placed what was given her over her head. I froze, my heart skipping in my chest, a cold shiver skipping down my spine. It was a locket. *My* locket.

In that moment, Fire Goddess swiveled it open and there was my family calling for me, but I couldn't answer. Before I could let loose the scream that had settled in my chest, Thomas threw a hand across my mouth and held me tight. Tears formed bright against my cheeks but I could do nothing to win them back. And yet I vowed then and there that one day I would retrieve my locket. And when I did, I would keep it forever, and nothing or no one would ever take it from me again.

Henry finished putting on his taupe silk puff tie, then buttoned up his double-breasted paisley silk vest with pearl buttons. He stood back and inspected himself in the mirror of the armoire. Now, clean shaven and freshly bathed, he had to admit, he hadn't seen himself like this in a very long time. He fell back onto the bed with its full canopy and brushed at his shoes that he had newly polished. He put them on and laced them before heading downstairs for breakfast, a new man.

In the glass atrium, he spotted Nathaniel, who looked just as dapper as Henry himself. He was seated next to the far wall and already had a steaming coffee carafe placed before him. Everything about the room screamed opulence and refinery. Compared to this, his life in the manor had seemed nothing short of ordinary.

"Ah!" Nathaniel said as Henry walked towards him. "I see you found me. How do you like our surroundings?" His arms splayed outward to encompass the whole of the place which revealed potted palms, giant ferns, and even a water feature complete with a waterfall that cascaded into an open koi pond.

"No expense spared, I see."

Though Henry appreciated his beautiful surroundings, he thought of all the people in the village back home who worked so hard to survive. His family often grew extra vegetables and fruit to pass around to those in need. Alaric's constant pillaging had afforded the people inside the fortress a standard of living unheard of in Henry's hometown.

"What will you have?" Nathaniel peered down at the gilt-trimmed menu, the flowery lettering all done in gold.

Henry hadn't realized how famished he was until he scanned the menu and saw eggs benedict with quail eggs along with freshly baked bread, lobster quiche, and scones with sweet butter and guava jelly. His stomach fairly rumbled at the smells wafting from adjacent tables. He ordered the eggs benedict and quail eggs, while Nathaniel chose the lobster quiche. Soon they were tucking into the succulent meal like two half-starved street waifs.

"So," said Nathaniel, when he finally came up for air, "are you ready to meet Birsha?"

The quaking that had started in Henry's stomach earlier in the day and had jangled his nerves, returned. The very idea of meeting with a possible madman turned his insides to a quivering mass of discontent.

Nathaniel pierced Henry with a look that said, "Buck up, man!"

Henry pulled back from the table and freed the linen napkin from his collar, setting it down next to his gilt-edged plate with the initials ASFF in the center and done in royal blue.

Alaric, Son of Faineant the Foul. They had yet to change the plates to reflect the new leadership, apparently.

Henry was so caught up in the opulence of the meal that he had paid little heed to the window that crested outward until suddenly, a huge yellow and brown beast popped its head through the window nearly startling Henry out of his seat. For his part, Nathaniel laughed until he was nearly in tears at the sight.

"I forgot to tell you that the atrium sits opposite the zoo."

As if to prove his point, a large tongue reached out and slurped the plate.

"How unsanitary!" Henry said, not sure at all that he liked having a giraffe lick his plate. He would have thought with this sort of splendor they wouldn't allow giraffes to wander next to paying guests.

"Generally, people keep their windows closed while eating, Henry," Nathaniel teased.

"I suppose they do." But now that the meal was finished, Henry sat back and watched the animal make light work of the remaining bits on the dishes.

"So, how much longer before we meet with Birsha?"

Nathaniel pulled his watch fob out of his pocket and checked his watch. "In one hour. Will you be ready?"

Henry didn't think he would ever be ready, but he didn't tell Nathaniel that. He peered over at the long-necked giraffe, her large brown eyes draped in thick black eyelashes that looked as if they'd been recently curled. Beside her, a baby giraffe poked its head through the window.

"Who have we here?" Nathaniel said, putting a hand out to

the baby.

But the baby giraffe ignored Nathaniel and instead licked a sandpapery tongue across Henry's face. Henry frowned, even as he ran a hand across the giraffe's short stubby mane. It felt like the bristles on the end of a broom. He was anxious to tell Brigid about all the odd things he'd seen so far.

As if to corroborate what he'd witnessed, in walked the strangest mixture of creatures he'd ever seen. He leaned forward and whispered, "Who or *what* are they?"

Nathaniel glanced over to where Henry motioned with his head. "Those are the Council members," he whispered back, careful not to stare. "Rumor has it that they are unhappy with the new leadership. They think Birsha too young to be taking over the reins from his father, too untested. Birsha has few friends among them. If any," Nathaniel added.

Henry tried not to stare, but they were such a unique blend of creatures that he found his eyes wandering in their direction, his ears attuned to every murmur that came his way. The first one in was an entomologist, according to Nathaniel. And as if to corroborate what Nathaniel said, Henry heard live crickets chirping where her braids had been tied off with a bow. It took him several seconds to realize that they weren't bows, but rather crickets used as ornaments.

"Are they real?" Henry's eyes drifted to the woman's dress that glowed with what looked like a thousand shimmering beetles.

"The crickets? That's both her name and her trademark, but get a load of the beetles. Those are glitzy beetles. They use all that sparkle as camouflage."

"Camouflage?" Henry said, thinking the blue, green, and orange beetle the least camouflaged of all insects. If anything, they acted as a magnet, for all eyes were upon Cricket.

Henry's gaze fell to the others wandering in. The most notable among them was a red-headed maven, whose dress fairly sparked with subdued energy. Her name was Tempestous, according to Nathaniel. She was turned away from him so he hadn't got a look at her face. But the other creatures that did face him made his hands tremble, for they were reptilian in nature, their skin no doubt cold to the touch, and their eyes had slits that started out horizontal, but when they became heated, the slits turned in a vertical motion that caused their eyes to widen and their expressions to become more menacing.

Next came a man-fish that Nathaniel called Fishmonger. As he walked, his scales moved, much like the feathers on a hummingbird's chest, changing color at will.

"The colors of his scales match his mood," Nathaniel explained. "If you see magenta, watch out. The fur's gonna fly." He laughed, then quickly coughed in his hand to hide his impudence.

With them was a perfectly ordinary woman. Brown, mousey colored hair, and she was small with delicate features. What was she doing with this motley crew of miscreants, Henry wondered?

Before he could ask, Nathaniel leaned in and said, "That's Mother Nature, Queen of All the Mammals. She is said to be kind, compassionate. She has none of the wiles of the others. I wouldn't be surprised if the rest of them are plotting behind Birsha's back. I wouldn't want that bunch mad at me," he added with one raised brow.

I wondered if the Council would be present when we first met Birsha. I hoped not. Even at this short distance, with them seated just two tables away, Henry could feel a force shield around them, as though the very air was layered with something palpable that breathed. Something malevolent.

As if Nathaniel had read Henry's thoughts, he said, "They're a frightening bunch, are they not? It's said they conjure a force field around them when out in public so that no bad can befall them. It keeps them away from the riff-raff."

Ah, so Henry and Nathaniel were riff-raff now, were they? Henry merely snorted. Birsha was looking the better prospect by far, now that Henry had seen the Council. Well, time to face the new leader. He bid the giraffes *adieu*, then stood, shoving back from the table, Nathaniel following suit.

He tried not to look at the table where, even now, the Council members were eating their food in a most unholy manner, but managed a quick look back as he passed them. What he saw sent a chill running through him. For there, around Tempestous's neck, was none other than a locket. *Brigid's locket.*

Phinney had returned, and with her she brought a miniature loom made of balsa wood and silk, the lightest materials possible. Still, she struggled with the weight and plopped down unceremoniously onto the railing of the elves' home, her feathers ruffled and her breathing labored.

"Poor Phinney." Winnifred scooped her up into her hands and cradled her in the crook of her arm where the falcon cooed pitifully.

Gertrude concurred, both of them sick with worry that they might have lost Brigid's bird.

Stovepipe Hat elf spoke in his curious language to a younger elf who immediately raced into a neighboring hut within the pine canopy of the forest and returned moments later with a pine basket sealed with pine pitch and filled with fresh water for Phinney. He sat it on the railing, then retrieved a leather pouch filled with seeds for the poor beleaguered bird.

Winnifred held the bird up to the water, which she drank down greedily, much to the delight of the elves whose cries sounded like a babbling brook. Then she moved the bird to the seeds. Though she probably would prefer a mouse or some other small rodent, she accepted the gift with relish, eventually hopping on the railing and making quick work of the meal. Afterwards, she nodded off, the loom still attached by a loop around her neck. Winnifred removed it carefully and tucked it into her satchel. At least one worry was off her plate. Now for the others.

"You say the Vidunders have enslaved many of your people?" Winnifred said, speaking through the gramophone.

"Aye, the rotters captured them when they went below," he said, peering over the railing to the valley floor. "Up here, we are safe."

"Safe?" Winnifred frowned, wondering how such short people with squatty legs that wobbled rather than walked could outrun a Vidunder.

To prove his point, Stovepipe gave a whistle followed by a short command. Suddenly, it was as if the trees had come alive, for everywhere elves were on the run, some dislodging the rope walkways so that they swung free, while all throughout the canopy, elves flew from a horizontal pulley system that allowed gravity and body motion to zip them along a series of ropes strung throughout the trees. They stood on a pair of wooden pegs, while above them were wooden handholds that were strung through yet another rope. Then they pulled backward and shoved off with one foot. The weight of their bodies did the rest. In order to reach the adjoining tree they needed enough momentum at push-off. But it was easy to see, they had drilled often on this very maneuver for they were quite skilled, only the youngest having trouble keeping the proper momentum going. It gave Winnifred an idea. It could be their way into the fortress, should they need to rescue Brigid and Henry, Thomas and Emma, or Kahwihta, though she doubted that Kahwihta would follow them into the fortress. Though the Mohawk and Oneida had acted as guides in the backcountry, and had helped with supplies, they had faded into the forest whenever the Jackals neared, preferring to fight another day. Still, they had proved invaluable.

As Winnifred's mind still whirred over the possibility of using such a pulley system to enter the fortress, the noise of flying elves halted completely, only the wind remaining in the eerie silence that ensued.

"Where did the elves go?" Winnifred asked Stovepipe Elf. Only now did she realize that she was whispering, her voice still loud amid such profound silence.

For several moments, nothing moved. She could hear only the sighing of the pine boughs in the suffering wind. Then, she saw eyes blinking here and there and realized that the elves had donned leaf-colored masks that blended perfectly with the forest. And since their clothing was almost entirely a shadowy green, with only a few brown leggings, it made for perfect camouflage.

Winnifred couldn't help but laugh, as did Gertrude. "Well, I must say, you are well prepared."

For the next hour they showed Winnifred their system, which was simple yet ingenious. For that hour she felt as if she were once again in her father's studio, being taught the mechanics behind the many gadgets he had invented, while Stovepipe Elf puffed on a pipe with cherry tobacco as he spoke. It reminded her so much of home that a tear welled in her eye, but she quickly quelled it. It would do no good to become sentimental. Still, she relished the time she spent with the people from this small enclave.

By the time she said goodbye, she felt as though she had really and truly made good friends. She would miss them in the coming days, but for now, she had her people to find. And find them she would.

21

Henry was surprised to learn they would be meeting
Birsha in the library. For some reason, he had thought Alaric
a barbarian, who avoided such things, but he apparently had
more to learn because the library was filled with tomes of every
sort and from every continent. Books lined the walls of the
circular room, a huge stained glass dome sending prisms of light
cascading down onto them so that everywhere he looked, the
glass lit the room in a kaleidoscope of color. He touched one
of the books with gold leaf only to discover a hidden fore-edge
painting of the very fortress and its surroundings along its
edge, when fanned. Books on science, religion, and fauna and
flora littered the walls, all alphabetized and ordered by region.
But what really drew his attention was Ptolemy's *Geographia
Cosmographia* with its colorful maps from 100 AD, all hand-
drawn by the man himself. In it, the sun, moon, and stars

revolved around the Earth, a mistaken belief that had lasted for centuries. Henry placed it carefully back in its cradle.

"Did you get a load of that, Nathaniel?" Henry said, only to find Nathaniel slowly rotating a giant globe in the middle of the room. The globe was equally wrong in its geographical calculations but nonetheless impressive. Henry whistled just as he heard the door open.

"Good Sir. What are you doing with that? Step aside at once!"

Henry pulled his hand back as though seared, Nathaniel doing likewise, only to discover a man no taller than Henry himself, with a braided black goatee and a reverse widow's peak striding toward them at great speed, a riding crop still in his hand. For one brief moment, Henry thought the man might hit him and Nathaniel with it.

Birsha!

Using the alias that he and Robert had planned, Henry introduced both he and Nathaniel. He followed up by bowing deeply, his earlier jitters returning. Nathaniel, who had been the one caught most red-handed, flushed a royal fuschia that made even his ears blush.

"I apologize for my lack of decorum," Nathaniel said, bowing only slightly. "It's just that I have never seen anything so magnificent, your grace."

For one brief moment, Birsha merely blinked, as though caught off guard by the obsequious manner in which Nathaniel spoke. "Aye, it is magnificent, isn't it?" Birsha said at last. "It was my father's, as is everything you see before you."

In the silence that followed, Henry realized that Birsha

was just as taken aback by the sheer opulence of the palace, as though never having experienced it firsthand.

"You didn't grow up here then?" Henry asked, surprised by his own boldness.

"No." Birsha's eyes flicked across the floor, anywhere except on Henry's face, as though embarrassed by this admission.

"Where did you grow up, if I may be so bold as to ask?" Henry watched as Birsha's eyes drifted slowly toward him, a deep pain written in the creases of his forehead. Henry flinched at the sight of such misery.

"In the countryside," the new ruler said. But it was clear there was more to the admission than what appeared at face value, for in the lost expression was a plea . . . to ask no more.

"I'm sorry. I overstepped my bounds. It's just that you seem as amazed as I do by all of . . . this." Henry held out his arms to encompass a room that could have rivaled any in the finest palaces in Europe.

"Yes. It *is* all new to me. Take a seat," Birsha offered. He ushered them to a bank of leather chairs that faced the marble fireplace meant for reading or entertaining guests.

Beside it was a walnut reading chair that one straddled to face the book, hands on wooden pedestals meant for just such a thing. It reminded Henry of a wooden horse.

"I'm sorry I'm late for our meeting. I had another appointment, so I will have to cut this one short, I am afraid. So tell me," Birsha continued, "why are you here?"

Nathaniel took the lead. "Sir, we have come to speak to you about a machine we believe will change the face of industry. A steam engine. A locomotive. We believe it will be the wave of the future. Although it is still in its infancy, and not yet viable, we believe we will have the first prototype available in a few years time."

"Excuse me? What, pray tell, is a locomotive?"

It was easy to see by the bored expression on Birsha's face that he had not the least bit of understanding nor interest in what Nathaniel was selling. But not to be outdone, Nathaniel pulled a blueprint of a prototype out of his leather bag and laid it out on the circular marquetry table inlaid with rosewood.

Henry leaned forward, amazed by what he saw, and noticed with pleasure that Birsha did the same.

"Whoever owns these will own the country. It will allow goods to be transported across the nation in record time. It will also allow soldiers to be transported to any location necessary." Nathaniel allowed the words to filter through Birsha's imagination.

Birsha stroked his goatee, excitement creeping up the edges of his lips. With this, he wouldn't need Brigid's loom. "Soldiers, you say?"

Just then, Siegfried entered the room. "Your next appointment is here."

Birsha sighed, clearly not used to his day being so regimented. "I'm sorry that I was so late for our meeting. We can't discuss this further, today, but speak with Siegfried. We must set up another appointment. Better yet, there is to be a ball tonight. Perhaps you can attend and we can speak later, in private."

The thrill of success had Henry smiling along with Nathaniel, who stood and gave one final lingering glance to the out-sized globe. "Good day, sir. Come, Henry."

Henry shot through with alarm at the mention of his real name, a mistake on Nathaniel's part, but too late to retract it. Hoping to appear nonchalant, despite the error, Henry tilted his eyes downward in deference to the young king. To his surprise, Birsha bent his head slightly as though seeing something in Henry that had him thinking, wondering. But what? What could Birsha have seen in Henry that had him frowning so? Henry was hesitant to find out. He said a hurried farewell, never breathing until the door was shut behind him.

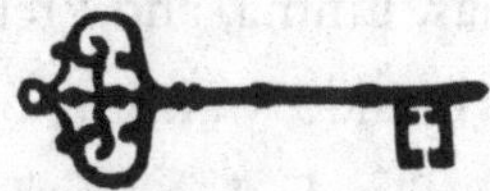

Yesterday, we had remained hidden in the underbrush for nearly an hour, scarcely daring to move until the Lizard People and the Fire Goddess were long gone. Even then, each footfall in the snow had made an unearthly crunching sound that seemed to magnify with each step, so much so that it was near nightfall by the time we finally located Eleanor and Pierre's hut in the woods. I had rapped lightly on her front door, my eyes combing the surroundings for any hint of the Jackals.

The door opened just enough for Eleanor to hold up a lantern and peer out. But upon seeing us, Eleanor threw open the door and ushered us in as quietly as possible. She immediately set about warming our hands, rubbing them in turn while instructing Pierre to put a kettle of water onto the hearth.

"Oh, my heavens, Brigid. You look a fright, all of you," Eleanor added, now tending to our feet which were nearly as frozen.

She urged her son, Jean, to get down the steel trough that was meant for the animals. Jean had grown in the year since I'd been gone, his pants no longer loose as they had once been, and only reaching midway down his calves. I would see to it that he had new clothes in repayment for all his family had done for us.

Moments later, he returned with the trough and set it before us. When the water was warm enough, their daughter, Celestine, poured it into the trough, then, seeing that not all our feet would fit in the metal trough, she brought out a pan for Kahwihta to use. Thomas, Emma, and I removed our stockings and shoes, then sat side by side, warming our feet, the feel of it nothing short of heaven. Slowly, I wiggled my toes, relieved to see that they were still in working order.

Eleanor ordered Pierre to put on yet more water for tea as she searched through her larder for something to feed us. I clapped my hands together for warmth, glad to be so near a warm fire after hours out in the snow, but frowned when I saw that her cupboards were not as full as the last time. Admittedly, it was later in the year, when food was not as plentiful, but they had a long winter ahead before they could once again stock up on supplies.

At the curious expression on my face, she shrugged apologetically at the meager stores. "It has been a harsh year," she explained. "Alaric knew that many of us were involved in your escape, though he couldn't pin it on any one of us, so we were all made to suffer. Food has been . . . well, let's just say it has been less than plentiful this year."

A murmur arose among our entire group. "I'm so sorry." I

knotted my hands together, truly regretting that I had caused so
much trouble for her and her people, who had been so gracious
to us.

Kahwihta, who had been listening, quietly dipped her head
and said, "I will see to it that my people bring you supplies."

"How?" I asked.

"It is not for you to worry, Bri-gid," she said.

And yet I did worry. How could she possibly get enough
supplies behind enemy lines to help these people who numbered
in the thousands? I thought of the surplus that we at the manor
had been able to produce and store this past year with the truce
in place and our stores safe. Perhaps we could also offer up help.
But how the supplies would be delivered, I couldn't fathom.
Maybe I could get word to Winnifred. If anyone knew what to
do it would be her.

I informed Eleanor of my plan and she promised to send
word to Winnifred by carrier pigeon before morning. With
that settled, we spent the second hour tucking into venison
rehydrated in a cast iron kettle set on a tenderhook. That,
mixed with potatoes, yams, and the rare piece of onion and
celery, made for a dinner fit for a king, in my view. When we
were done, I sighed and patted my full stomach, relieved to be
somewhere warm. It didn't take long before all of us were close
to nodding off.

The children gave up their side of the loft, only too happy
to sleep on quilts in front of the open fire. The rest of us
huddled together on a pallet of straw tucked beneath a down
comforter, the shared warmth providing a brief respite from
our weary travels. And yet, as I prepared for the night's sleep,

I couldn't help but wonder where Henry was located and if he was safe. When I had asked Eleanor and Pierre about his whereabouts, they had been illusive, saying only that he was out of harm's way, for the time being. *For the time being?* What did that mean? And yet no amount of prying could produce anything further from the pair. Instead, they warned me to quit asking. As I lay staring up at the vaulted ceiling that evening, I said a small prayer for Henry. Wherever he was.

Gertrude rode off to tell the other women warriors that it was full speed ahead, now that their meeting with the elves was concluded. Winnifred had just saddled up and was waiting for the warriors when she heard a short whistle from inside the shrubbery at the side of the trail. She bent down and, from out of a honeyball plant, came one of the elves.

"Mikael has asked me to go with you—in case you need my expertise, ya?"

Winnifred cocked her head, amazed to learn that this elf knew English. In fact, he was more slender than Stovepipe Hat elf and much taller too, nearly Winnifred's height, which was quite tall for an elf. As if to compensate, his pointed shoes were raised slightly so that when she shimmied down next to him, he was exactly her height. His clothes were different from that of the other elves, too. His vest, although green like his pants, were quite stylish and form-fitted, as was his hand-woven shirt. To hide his pointed ears, he wore a rolled-up bandana around his head that hung down his back in a vee. A rush of heat fueled

Winnifred's cheeks as she realized she had been staring for much too long at the handsome elf.

"My name is Lofgren. Mikael thought it best that I go with you because I am half-elf, half-human. That's why I speak English. My mother was human, my father elf."

Winnifred tried to hide her surprise. And yet when she inspected him more closely, she could see that he had elfin eyes, which were more almond-shaped than most humans, and elfin ears which poked up out of the bandana, but he was built more like a human, his height a compromise between the smaller elves and the larger humans.

When she still didn't speak, he continued. "I am an inventor, by trade. I was the one who came up with the pulley system and the escape route to save us from the Vidunders."

"An inventor?" Winnifred said, unable to hide her excitement to have found a kindred spirit such as herself. "I invented a time machine."

"A time machine. Have you used it?"

"Once." She explained all she'd seen as quickly as possible before the women returned. "I even brought back a quantum computer prototype. It's quite beautiful, actually, but it's nonfunctional, so far."

This time it was his turn to stare, once again causing Winnifred to blush a deep crimson.

"I've never known a female inventor," Lofgren said. "I would love to see your quantum computer, someday. Maybe together, we can figure out how it works, *non*?"

She readily agreed. But before she could talk to him further, he produced a sharp whistle. From out of the underbrush came a half dozen more of the little men, only these men were much smaller. Between them, they pulled a wagon which they harnessed to Winnifred's horse with a breast collar, the sprites now with Jocelyn instead of hooked to Winnifred's horse. The elves' wagon was loaded down with all sorts of supplies. To her raised eyebrows, Lofgren produced a blueprint from his satchel to show her how the pulley and lever system was built and operated. "We may need all this," he said, surveying the mounded contents of the wagon, "if you plan to get inside the fortress."

"Inside?" she said, suddenly at a loss for words. "Why inside?"

For several moments, the elves conferred between each other in their nearly gibberish-type language, Lofgren using the elfin language with his kin. After what seemed a lengthy bout, Lofgren turned back to Winnifred and said in English, "Because, we need to get my people out. And from the sound of it, you may need to get your people out too."

Henry had been only too happy to return to his room until the fated ball that night. Birsha had clearly seen something in Henry that had him puzzled, but what? And the odd thing was, Henry had felt it too, as though he had met this fellow somewhere, years ago. His memory waxed and waned, and yet no matter how hard he tried to winnow the memory out of his brain, he just couldn't do it. In the end, he was relieved when Nathaniel showed up to his room and said, "Let's go see the sights. While we can."

While we can?

Henry grabbed his satchel, Nathaniel having reminded him earlier never to leave anything behind in the room.

"They rifle through our belongings," Nathaniel explained. "Anything you want kept secret, you keep on you."

Henry had learned his lesson well when he'd left earlier and had seen one of the maids go in afterwards. He had made a quick dart for the door and yet already she had knelt down next to his bed and was pawing his satchel that he had placed beneath the bed. It hadn't taken long for her to hear him and scurry to her feet, her cheeks a deep burgundy, an apology on her lips.

"I was just checking that there were no cobwebs," she said, but he knew better.

He plucked the satchel from under the bed, saying, "The room is all yours. Good day, madam." He gave a slight bow while she gave a short curtsey. The experience was a lesson he would heed from that point on.

"Where are we going?" Henry asked, struggling to keep up with Nathaniel, who was on a tear.

"You'll see," Nathaniel said mysteriously, raising a single brow in answer.

Henry followed Nathaniel as they wended down twisting alleyways, the heralders from the past two days appearing hungover and tired. And yet there were still those, especially the young males, who huddled in corners, lighting off fireworks with names like sun spray and rainbow sparklers. Some ran through the streets sending showers of sparks trailing in their wake, all the while laughing and ribbing each other good-naturedly.

This was the first time since Henry had arrived in the city that he was able to take stock of the Jackal Citadel in all its glory. He was surprised to see that it was quite dirty, dust filling every corner. Children in tattered clothes, coats threadbare and worn, the poorer of the street urchins in shoes with thin soles or holes in the toes. And the poorest of the poor donned burlap sacks stuffed with cotton and tied with rope at the ankle. Henry wondered if they knew about the gilded inner palace, the wealth that it contained. Probably not.

As they rushed onto the main road, Henry spied a marketplace filled with what fruits and vegetables could be found so far into the season, potatoes and yams stored in cellars and brought out for market day, children eying the flatbreads cooked over a hot fire and warmed on a large metal cylinder. Henry grabbed Nathaniel's coat to give him pause.

"What are you doing?" Nathaniel demanded.

"One moment." Henry dug through his satchel for the hard-earned coins of the realm. "Here, good man!" Henry nodded toward the half-dozen children as he stood before the vendor.

The merchant took the proffered coin, then set about scooping a giant spoonful of the batter onto the metal cylinder. He made quick work of the flatbread, more like a thin, giant pancake, flipping it once. Then he pulled out a single rolled-up piece of brown paper.

"No need," Henry said. "Could you cut the pancake up for each of these fine ladies and gentlemen?"

The merchant scowled, the apron on his fat belly smeared with grease and batter, but he sliced the flatbread evenly and handed each a piece.

"And there!" Henry pointed at the bottle of jam. "Could you give each child a squirt." Before the merchant could protest, Henry produced another half-penny which he rolled between his thumb and forefinger.

The man rubbed his belly then gave each child a squirt. "Now off with ye, ya lil' devils," the man said, pocketing the coin that Henry handed to him.

The children didn't wait to see what came next. They took off running, all the while giggling and laughing like children everywhere. But before he turned the corner and disappeared back into the alleyways, one little boy, the smallest of the bunch, held his bread aloft and yelled a hearty, "Thank you, sir!" Then he was gone.

Henry laughed. When he turned back he found Nathaniel staring, as though puzzled by Henry's actions.

"You were a kid once, no?" Henry said by way of explanation, but Nathaniel merely nodded, as though mulling that over.

Then, grabbing Henry's arm once more, he urged him on. They didn't stop until they were far from the crowded center of the fortress. Here, life ran at a slower pace.

"So, where are we headed, on this mid-winter's day?" Henry asked, steam puffing from his mouth as he spoke.

Suddenly, Nathaniel pulled him into an alleyway, and urged him up a winding staircase into the tower above. Henry stopped at the top of the turret and turned toward Nathaniel, refusing to go any farther.

"I'm not taking another step until you tell me what's going on," he demanded.

Nathaniel grazed him with a look of utmost seriousness. "See for yourself," he said, stepping aside.

All Henry could see was the turret wall.

"Step closer," Nathaniel urged.

Henry had a feeling that whatever was on the other side of the tower, he wasn't going to like it, and he was right. Because from where he stood, as he inched toward the wall, he could just make out hundreds of people, some his size, some small. They appeared like ants, they were so tiny, but he could see that they were doing something–building a road perhaps.

In this cold?

Henry pulled his spyglass from his satchel to get a better look. And indeed they were a motley crew of people dressed in rags, all dirty, their hair matted and worn. They worked with a furious diligence, but it was clear their hearts weren't into it.

"Who are they?" Henry peered at Nathaniel who had sat down, his back to the thick tower walls.

"The smaller ones are elves," he said, "but you may know some of the larger ones." Nathaniel paused as though giving Henry time to catch up to speed. When Henry said nothing, Nathaniel groused, "They're your *friends and fellow countrymen. Our* people."

Henry turned back quickly and put his spyglass to his eyes. He squinted, wishing he could devine the names and locations of each of the former members of his community and those captured from the surrounding villages. Then he saw it. Men with whips. The realization had him reeling and he plopped down next to Nathaniel, covering his eyes so that the other man wouldn't see the emotions playing in them.

"This is why we're here, Henry. This is why you must help me, even at risk of your own peril. It is for these poor souls who are dying by the hundreds each day that we risk our safety . . . our lives. *Now* do you see, Henry?" he asked, the devastation of his words putting a quaver in his voice.

"Yes, I do," Henry said in a whisper. "And we will save each and every one of them." And he meant it, but how?

That afternoon heralded a flurry of activity. Master Clyde had arrived at Eleanor and Pierre's cottage, along with several of his cohorts, having planned their latest scheme. Master Clyde had aged little in the past year, though others hadn't fared so well. Perhaps it was the glint in his eyes, as though he were hiding a secret, only today I feared that secret would involve me somehow, and unfortunately, I was right.

"See, we want you to wear this, Brigid." From inside a sack, Master Clyde produced a stunning blue taffeta dress with a lace overlay. And on that lace were a myriad of silvery moons and stars that fairly shimmered against the lamplight.

I gasped, for I had never seen anything so beautiful in all my days. It was simply sublime. But wear it where, precisely? I had only seconds to find out.

"There is to be a ball. Tonight. At the palace," Master Clyde explained in micro-sentences that left me confused.

"And you want *me* to go?" I pointed at my chest, all the while peering around me at the others, fearing I had heard wrong.

"Yes. We believe Henry will be there."

"Henry!" I stood, nearly dropping the gown in a pool at my feet.

"Be careful!" Eleanor admonished, stepping in to take the treasured gown from my careless grasp. She hung it carefully on a hook near the door, all the while making tsking sounds as she palmed the dress to be rid of any unwanted wrinkles. Satisfied that it was once again in good stead, she turned to me and produced a lace mask that had been tucked inside her apron pocket. She handed it to me for viewing.

I thanked her and walked over to the oval mirror she kept near the kitchen sink, no doubt for Pierre to use when shaving, every room offering a dual purpose in such tight quarters as these. To my surprise, when I placed it over my face it hid even my odd blue eyes that sent shards of color cascading through the room in ordinary times. Instead, the lace was drawn in such a way that I could see out, but few could see in.

Frowning, I fingered the hair that hung limply at the sides of my rather pale face. In that moment, I felt a bit like a maid rather than a princess, if that is what I was meant to be. I turned to Eleanor, who recognized the problem instantly.

"No worries, Brigid. Your hair will look lovely in time. You'll see."

Master Clyde grunted a hurried echo of what Eleanor had said. "We have it all taken care of, Miss Brigid. You will leave within the hour."

Kahwihta, Emma, and Thomas all stood, as though they too were prepared to exit, but Master Clyde held up his hands to ward them off. "Not the three of you, I am afraid. Just Miss Brigid."

"But she can't go alone," Thomas protested, anger sparking in his eyes. "Surely you wouldn't hand her over to the Jackals without some sort of protection."

Emma gave a fierce nod, but Kahwihta, ever the calm one, stood silently waiting to see where the chips fell before speaking up.

"As I said," Master Clyde reiterated, his mates nodding in agreement, "I have planned everything. I will escort her into the ball where she will go in search of Birsha. Afterwards—" He paused, as though fearing to go on.

Though I had stood quietly by until now, my heart began thudding in my chest for I dreaded what he had to say next.

"I want you to get close to Birsha, to learn as much about him as you can. And Brigid—"

My hackles went up at the sound of my name.

"If you see Henry, you can *not* let him know it is you, do you understand? He is going under the guise of an Englishman. His life depends on his anonymity. Yours too. So stay away from him. Promise me."

Promise him? How could I when I was so close to finding Henry, and hopefully bringing him home with me, safely. Once we located my necklace and retrieved it from that awful woman in red, that is.

But I said what Master Clyde wanted to hear. I would have said anything to get Henry back, to see him safe in my arms once more.

"I promise," I whispered. Then I turned away lest he see the truth hidden in my eyes.

22

Birsha detested gatherings, he was quickly coming to discover as he strapped on gloves and placed the crown upon his head, a cross at its apex and a red fox fur collar at its base. His clothing was equally sumptuous, tailored in the finest silk money could buy. He had opted for a winter jacket done in imperial red and gold, as was befitting his new station. Around the lapels and at the hems of his sleeves was fur to match his hat.

Once finished, he turned to Siegfried who sat on a chair, watching him.

"How do I look?" Birsha knew he was asking a lot of the man, making him both his adjutant and now his personal manservant, but he trusted no one else. "Do I look like the Romanov?"

"Which Romanov is that?" Siegfried asked.

Birsha knew that his adjutant hadn't meant to be insolent,

just that he wasn't quite as worldly as he let on. "Michael the first, the founder of the Romanov empire in Russia."

Michael's grandfather, Nikita, had been the advisor to Ivan the Terrible, whose parents had died young. Then Ivan the Terrible was used as a pawn by the power brokers of the day, left starving and in rags. As Ivan grew, he'd become so ferocious that he'd had the architects of the famous St. Basil's Cathedral's eyes put out, lest they be able to build for anyone save him. Or at least that was the legend, but Birsha knew too well that legends could simply be lies told by powerful people to keep commoners at bay.

"So? Do I look like the Romanov?" Birsha repeated.

"Why, of course," Siegfried said, even as his eyes told a different story.

The poor man clearly had no idea about the vagaries of history, other than that of his own, here inside the fortress. Birsha let loose a low rumble of laughter and slapped Siegfried on the back.

"Come now, we have people to meet."

"Sir?" Siegfried cocked his head as though uncertain of Birsha's meaning.

"Why, you're coming, too. I've set aside an outfit for you. You don't suppose I would go to this event alone?" Birsha dusted off any excess lint from his collar, then took one final look at himself in the mirror. "Your costume is over there. I have made you a pirate. Ahoy, matey!" he cried, brandishing an imaginary sword. But the one he'd given Siegfried was no invisible sword. It was made of the finest silver . . . outside of Birsha's own, of course.

Siegfried paused, frowning as he looked first to the sword, then to Birsha. "But surely you can't mean for me to go—"

"That's precisely what I mean. I refuse to go into that den of vipers alone, Siegfried. You're all I've got."

The moment the words left his mouth, Birsha realized how pathetic that must sound, and yet it was the truth. He no longer trusted even his half-brothers who he'd caught whispering in the hallway, their words coming to a grinding halt the moment he'd come close. Were they plotting against him? His throat tightened at the thought. They had been his grounding in what was an otherwise barren childhood, and now . . . now he wasn't sure he knew them at all. Power and ambition had seen to that. It was a lonely spot at the top. Birsha wasn't like his father, who had learned to move people around as if in a chess match. No, he was more like his mother, the saint of a woman, who hid in the background of a life at court. Who was placed here and there, trotted out only when it was convenient. Then sent to the countryside—out of sight, out of mind—as Alaric ran through a bevy of women, each one more beautiful than the last. Only Birsha's mother was sent far away, from both the castle and Birsha, coming only to see him on the once a year visits allotted. But each time she'd left, she'd cradled his face and cried, telling him she loved him. Until finally, she was allowed to see him no further. Alaric said it was "upsetting the boy." Even so, no one had come to him and asked if he wanted to see his mother. He did. Very much so.

Just then, a loud series of raps jostled the door. For one brief moment, Birsha and Siegfried's eyes locked. But that's all it took for Birsha to convey his unease.

Siegfried said, "I'd best get busy if I am to assist you, sir."

Birsha placed a hand on the adjutant's shoulder. "You're a good man, Siegfried."

"Thank you, sir."

Another loud rap broke the silence, snapping the cord of connection between the pair.

"Open up, Birsha!" Pieter yelled.

The man sounded drunk. So it would begin . . .

A light rapping sounded at the door followed by the words, "Henry, are you nearly ready?"

Henry inspected himself in the mirror one last time before answering Nathaniel. He had donned a costume made of fine silk jacquard in a series of patterns that contained both blue and silver. His sleeves billowed out at the shoulders in an array of fabric, while a blue-gray cape hung lazily over one shoulder. And he wore tights with shoes that reminded him more of an elf or a genie. He picked up his mask and quickly snugged it into place. Though it was made of silver, flashes of blue fanned outward whenever he turned quickly, almost as if by magic. But what made it most fantastical were the broad array of feathers made of the same silver and blue that wrapped around his head as though giving him a hug.

He heard another rapping at the door and yelled, "I'm coming!"

When he opened the door, there stood Nathaniel looking ever the dashing aristocrat.

"Who are you supposed to be?" Henry tilted his head slightly to get a better look at his new friend through the eyeholes of his mask.

"Why, the Count of Dunsmore," he said with a wry twist.

And although there had been a count of Dunsmore, once upon a time, according to Brigid, who had come from wealth before her family had lost it all, Henry highly doubted Nathaniel would have the courage to speak such a name in front of Birsha, his father Alaric being the count's sworn enemy.

"A wee joke," the man acknowledged, "but I figured you, of all people, would appreciate such jest. No, I will claim to be Lord Townsend."

"You are missing the white wig, are you not?" Henry said with a laugh. "Well, you have precisely twenty minutes to come up with a name, my good sir."

Yet even as he spoke the words in humor, the nerves that he had been fending off all day returned with a vengeance. Something about Birsha had given him a sense of *déjà vu*, as though he had seen the man, at some earlier time, while still a lad. He shook off the ridiculous notion, then gave one last look around the room before heading off into the unknown.

Lofgren had been training Winnifred in all manner of warcraft as they narrowed the breach between themselves and the fortress. In order to strategize, they left the horses to a driver, while they holed up in one of the wagons, which moved painfully slow, to Winnifred's dismay. The only bright side was that it gave them time to plot a course – to come up with a way to penetrate Birsha's fortress and to free the enslaved people. As Lofgren had explained, the Jackals held both her people and his.

"This may be our only chance to win them back," Lofgren said, the wagon jostling them around. "Winter without proper food and protection from the elements will be the death of our people, yours and mine. We can't afford to leave them much longer in that God-forsaken wasteland. We must rescue them now."

Winnifred had no doubt he was telling the truth. People had been disappearing. Many, of course, had been killed, but a whole host of villagers had just vanished without a word. It could mean none other than Alaric, before Birsha had taken his place.

The wagon jostled them once more, and Winnifred fell into Lofgren's arms, apologizing profusely as her cheeks glowed a rich warmth of color. But to her surprise, Lofgren didn't let go. Instead, he peered into her golden brown eyes, the expression on his face unfathomable.

Finally, he peered down, as though realizing he had overstepped so soon into their friendship. Still, she could tell that it had left him as unsettled as it had her. She had never known an elf before, and although he was only half elf, there was something different about him, something she discovered she liked. Very much.

His ears were pointed, and he had a slightly green tinge to him that might have repelled others, but to her, that made Lofgren simply unique. *And fascinating.* But it was his eyes that drew her to him, for it was as if she could see into a soul that held an intellect that surpassed her own. And yet, how could that be? Her people had been the ones to create, to build, to grow strong in industry and commercial pursuit. So how was it that his people lived in trees, if elves possessed superior intellect?

Because we choose to live like this.

Winnifred blinked rapidly, hand to her chest as she rode a new wave of ruts and valleys on the road to the fortress. Had he really spoken to her? In thought only, or was this just her imagination?

It's not your imagination. We have no need for words.

Winnifred reeled backwards, crab-like, on the floor of the wagon, needing space, to once again breathe properly, her mind still circling what she had heard. In her thoughts.

This time Lofgren reached out and placed a hand on hers to show that he meant no harm. "What you think you heard, wasn't a fluke. We can mind fuse. In any language."

Winnifred couldn't fathom why she was so angry. Still, she balled her fists and growled. "If that's true, then why the pretense with the flugelhorn or whatever you call that mouthpiece of yours? Why not just speak to me through this 'mind fuse' business, as you call it?"

Lofgren offered a humble grin while shrugging his shoulders in apology. "First off, we didn't want to frighten you, as I see I have now. Secondly–" He held a hand up to keep her from interrupting, as she was about to do. "–we needed to know we could trust you first. "

"And you do?" she said, still in a snit, though she wasn't sure why she found the whole thing so disconcerting.

"Yes," he said simply. "I can feel your goodness."

"Feel it?" She licked her lips, feeling parched, suddenly.

"It's something I alone have as an asset. The ability to feel people's auras." He shook his head. "I'm not explaining it well. Elves aren't good at understanding emotion. Humans are, though you would never know it by the way they treat each other–" He stopped mid-sentence, clearly shocking himself by his unwitting candor.

In the end, it was his honesty that quelled the anger she had been feeling, for it was the one thing she prized above all others. Then she had another thought, a frightening one at that.

"Does this mean you can read my mind?" She reeled back over her thoughts, grimacing at the more candid ones, the ones she had been thinking when he'd held her moments ago.

Lofgren laughed, squeezing her hand to put her at ease. "No. Only your questions directed toward me. Your thoughts are safe from me." He winked, which only enhanced her embarrassment. "Your emotions on the other hand…" He shrugged as if in apology.

Winnifred leaned back against the grain barrel, which she immediately regretted when they hit another bump, leaving her with a bruise on her shoulder blade.

"So, let me get this straight. We can speak with each other through our thoughts and you can read feelings and emotions. Did I get that right?"

"Precisely," he said.

It was Winnifred's turn to laugh because whenever Lofgren tilted his head slightly, as he was doing now, the expression on his face was so . . . so what? So comical. It reminded her of an eager puppy she'd once had that had tilted its head whenever something seemed puzzling to the small pup.

Then Winnifred had another thought. A thought that excited her so much that she jumped to her feet, nearly toppling as the wagon rocked to the left. Lofgren, who was amazingly light on his feet, leapt up to join her, steadying her with a hand to her arm.

"This could be a good thing, Lofgren."

Her words came out so fast that Lofgren actually tilted away from her, frowning.

"No, hear me out. Can this mind fuse thing work at a distance?"

"Of course," he said, as though it were a given.

"I mean a *really* long distance?"

Lofgren clearly didn't get her meaning, as he merely shook his head, never shedding his frown.

"Don't you see?" She paced while holding onto the wooden edges of the berth as she moved, to keep from falling. "We can have your men scattered in different locations. They can send word back through mind meld so that we can coordinate an attack much more quickly than those inside the fortress. We will have a huge advantage. With this knowledge, we can outmaneuver the Jackals because we will possess communication skills they don't."

Finally, Lofgren broke out into a large grin that once again left her breathless. And although Lofgren might not be able to ascertain her thoughts, she felt certain he understood her emotions—emotions that she had best keep to herself, in the future.

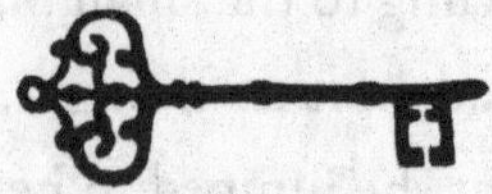

Before I prepared for the ball, Master Clyde said he had something to show me, though he wouldn't tell me where we were going. Instead, he had me dress in the humblest of clothing so that I looked like a carpenter plying my wares. He, too, dressed in disguise so that it appeared we were simply two workmen out to make repairs. He hitched up two mules who looked just as desultory as we did as we made our way along the paths that took us from the forest to the fortress gates. I wore my hat low over my head, a rope belt holding up the overlarge overalls that I had cinched at the straps. Inwardly, I trembled. For if we were caught, we would surely end up in the dungeon or worse, but Master Clyde assured me that he did this on an almost daily basis and that none would be the wiser.

This was the first time I had been inside the fortress proper and I found it a warren of streets, flowing this way and that, all cobblestones, unlike the dirt roads that unfurled like a carpet from beyond the gateway entrance. I had expected opulence but was sorely disabused of any such notion as street urchins ran past us in bare feet and ragged clothing, despite the cold, their feet red and their breath bursting forth in clouds of steam. They would dart into alleyways, disappear into hovels that spit out coal fires that left the streets dirty with grime.

"How can this be?" I grabbed Master Clyde's billowing sleeve as he called the mules to a halt next to one particularly dark alleyway. "I thought Alaric was wealthy beyond anyone's imagination."

Master Clyde offered a mirthless laugh. "Oh, he is rich, Brigid. *Very* rich."

"Then why such poverty?" I nodded toward a hunched old man with a gnarled cane whose ragged coat draped the dusty cobblestone road.

"Because he keeps it for himself," Master Clyde said. "Come, I will show you."

I followed on his heels, fearing in these twists and turns I might lose him and be lost within the bowels of this hellhole forever. Fortunately, just as I thought I might not be able to keep up, he reached out to me and clasped my arm, ushering us up a spiral staircase made of the stone native to this area, a dark gray granite with a bluish tint that gave it an ominous presence that had my teeth chattering.

It seemed that we would spiral upwards forever when suddenly we stopped, giving me time to catch my breath.

"There!" Master Clyde pointed toward the interior of the fortress that hid behind the rather plain exterior structure where the commoner lived.

I gasped at the sight of it. Even in the gloom of this cloudy afternoon, I could see that no expense had been spared, for more gold flanked the dome structure in the middle of the inner sanctum than I had seen in a lifetime. It was a testament to a world of untold wealth. Snow-capped gardens graced the Southern face of the building. Gardens that could rival any of those in Europe and beyond. And to the east of that I could just make out animals, the like of which I had seen only once, when my family had taken us to New York to see animals that had amazed me in their variety and size: monkeys that hooted calls to their mates in loud pants, giraffes with their spots and long necks. Even zebras, which reminded me of nothing more than horse-like umpires at a baseball game. As a child, I had laughed and laughed at the sight of these many creatures. But from here I could see those animals and more on the palatial fortress grounds. There was even a giant chess board with life-sized knights on horseback and bishops with a gold cross emblazoned upon their chests. And sculptures were strewn everywhere, one of Alaric himself atop a horse in a rather grand pose that felt vain in its self-importance.

"I see what you mean," I whispered, as though to speak out loud might send Jackals hurtling our way to attack us with their long teeth and their sharp claws.

"Alaric was a despot," Master Clyde said, he too speaking in a hush. "But that was not why I brought you here, Brigid. There is something you should see. Something that will explain the urgency of our mission and the need for total cooperation on your part. Come."

My nerves were on edge as I traipsed behind him. Tomorrow, I felt certain that every fiber of my being would be worn out from today's foray, but I had no time to ponder that as Master Clyde was on the move, taking the steps of yet another circular staircase two at a time.

I was breathing so heavily by the time I reached the top spire of the staircase that I had to pause to catch my breath. "Why . . . am . . . I . . . here?" I panted, sucking in air like an asthmatic.

But the look on Master Clyde's face held such devastation that it stopped me. I struggled to stand up straight, to see what it was that had Master Clyde looking as if he'd just witnessed a death.

And indeed his eyes were filled with tears, as mine were once I saw what it was that had touched him so.

"Who are they?" I whispered as though by speaking out loud, I would give voice to the horrific things I was witnessing. Beatings. Men, women, and children carrying heavy loads of rock through the worst of conditions, the ground frozen beneath them, wisps of steam a continuous cloud overhead. Most appeared weak, starving, their bodies battered and bruised. "I say again, who are they?" I repeated, this time louder.

He put a finger to his lips. "Quiet," he whispered. "There are spies everywhere."

In this most fearsome of places, I could believe him. I strained to identify those who were clearly slaves. Who were receiving dire punishment indeed.

Master Clyde reached into a pocket of his disguise to retrieve a small spyglass from which to view the scene. "See for yourself."

I quickly put the glass up to my eyes and squinted until the individuals became clearer. What I saw sent my heart cascading to my feet. For there, in front of me, were people. But not just any people. I fought back tears as I saw the mother and daughter who had left our group of women warriors over a year ago. She had been captured along with countless others. And she would die, if she didn't get help soon.

I turned to Master Clyde, my heart stone and my resolve renewed. "How can I help?" I demanded.

"By doing exactly as I say."

23

Winnifred and the army were finally within sight of the fortress. The sun would be setting soon. Lofgren ushered Winnifred to a spot just southwest of the town where he and the other elves had located a hidden glen. Once there, they could practice their archery and magic. Although the women had guns that they had acquired from the townsfolk prior to leaving on their trek, they didn't dare use them and risk alerting the Jackals to their position.

"So, should we begin with the magic lessons?" Lofgren said.

The women archers were practicing riding their steeds at full tilt while hitting the intended target, in this case a hay bale with a bull's eye in the center.

"Magic?" Winnifred peered around the open glade, a small underground stream providing fresh water for the horses and a chance for the women to stock up on their own reserves. "Elves use other magic besides telecommunication?"

Lofgren's eyes held a glint of amusement. "Oh, we have learned a thing or two over the centuries. I, for one, am almost 800 years old."

Winnifred, who had been lifting the bridle over her horse's ears, paused, mouth open and eyes wide with astonishment at this news. "H…how?" she gasped. "I mean is that even possible?"

"Entirely possible…though I may not last as long as the other elves, seeing that I am half human. But then again, we elves don't produce as readily as our human counterparts. That's why there are so few of us."

Winnifred hadn't known any of that when she'd first met the elves. Though she'd heard tales about them, they seemed more the stuff of legend than real flesh and blood creatures. Until now.

Lofgren's lovely green eyes narrowed, his expression more serious. "We could go extinct if we continue to lose our people to the Jackals."

Although Alaric was gone, Winnifred knew that none of them were safe. Birsha was an unknown quantity and the same people who supported Alaric in his quest for territory now served Birsha. But would they accept him as their new leader? Winnifred finished unsaddling her Rocky Mountain horse, known for its ability in the uneven terrain of the backcountry. Her heart resided somewhere near her throat at the danger both Henry and Brigid might be in. And now Lofgren and his people.

"So what sort of magic?" Winnifred asked, not at all sure

she wanted to know.

"Telecommunication, as you know, but also teleportation," Lofgren said.

"Teleportation?" A stirring of excitement grew inside her chest. "You can transport into the future or the past, like I did with my time machine?" She patted her horse on the rump, giving it free rein to roam in search of food and water until she needed him once more.

"Not exactly. Exhibit A."

Suddenly, he began moving at a speed she'd never witnessed before, her eyes scarcely able to keep up with his movements until at last, she lost sight of him altogether. She turned in a circle, calling his name. When he didn't answer, she began to panic, but seeing this, Lofgren leaped from his hiding place among the trees and was standing in front of her in a matter of seconds. She was so astounded at this new ability that she plopped down unceremoniously in the middle of a frozen meadow, still bearing frost in those areas untouched by the sun.

"I take it you don't have this particular magic," he said, shrugging his shoulders in apology.

"And I don't think I can learn that, either," she said with a frown.

"No worries. Surely, you have *some* magical abilities?"

When she shook her head no, he put his index finger to his chin and tapped it, as though pondering this surprising twist.

"Well, that's not entirely true." She began listing the gifts: Brigid's loom, Roseland's carrier pigeon, Peke's snake, and the oddest of them all…Yesimeh's isinglass, a clear cement-like substance made from sturgeon bladders.

"We will find uses for all of these magics," he said with such aplomb that she was apt to believe he would.

"So how is it that these other women have powers and you have none?"

For some reason, she felt as though she were being chastised for her lack of a special power. She had gifts, too. After all, she was an inventor.

"Some magic isn't magic," she said. "Sometimes it's simply who we are that's the *real* magic. It's what we love. For me it's inventing…creating. That's *my* magic."

Lofgren seemed to ponder this. Finally, he nodded his head as though coming to some sort of understanding.

"You are the *inventor* of magic." He nodded firmly, as though he'd just bestowed her with the title.

Once again, she laughed. Before now, no one had ever made her laugh the way Lofgren had. There was something about him that was so genuine. So real. She wanted to rush over and squeeze him, pump his hand for being exactly who he was. Which was what, precisely? She knew little about elves, much less Lofgren, so how is it that he was able to worm his way into her heart so readily?

Surprising her, Lofgren took her hand and said, "Come with me. There's something I want to show you. The other elves and I have been working on it for some time."

His hand was gentle, warm. It gave her a shiver of delight, as though it were the most natural thing for her to be following the orders of an elf. She was beginning to wonder if she had been bewitched somehow, and yet his childlike wonder made her doubt such deception.

As many of the women continued their maneuvers, the others set up camp, as was their custom. They were so busy that none deemed to look their way. As such, Lofgren was able to lead Winnifred up a small path that climbed ever skyward, finally stopping at a curtain of wild cucumber that grew from a ledge beneath a waterfall. The roar of the water pounded in her ears as she reached for one of the remaining cucumbers that looked so much like those she grew at the manor, but as she did, Lofgren smacked it away.

"It's poisonous." He retrieved a linen cloth from inside his pants pocket and wiped her hand gingerly. "Stay close." He tugged her through the curtain of vines and cried, "*Voila!*"

"Oh my–" She found it difficult to speak because what she saw was so beautiful. They were standing just beneath a waterfall that splayed out from a solid granite ledge above them. Maidenhair ferns competed with sword ferns as a canopy that formed a barrier between them and the women below. It was as if she'd entered a magical realm, and she supposed that's precisely what it was.

"Wait until you see what we've done," he said in hushed tones, despite the roaring waterfall.

And yet she had heard him as though the words had been amplified somehow. As if the water were a transmitter of some sort. She shook her head, trying desperately to come to terms with what had just occurred.

"Here," he said, curling a finger for her to follow him.

She couldn't have ignored him if she'd tried, for she was entranced by both him and what he had on offer. For, behind the waterfall was a place she could only describe as extraordinary.

"What is this?" she asked, twirling around in circles to get a better view.

"We've been preparing for the time that we elves would finally come to take our enslaved elves back."

"But it's beautiful! Simply amazing."

And it was, more than she could put down in words. The interior held a small village, complete with streets and elven-sized houses made of all sorts of scavenged dibbles and dabbles, but together, they gave the illusion of high art. The streets were paved in a colorful mosaic of glass. Somehow they had managed to create light that bounced off it in waves. She searched for the source of the light, only to discover a hole three stories up that shot a beam of light across it at midday. Attached to the hole was a series of ladders that seemed precarious at best, but which Lofgren assured her was quite stable, despite its appearance.

Winnifred giggled, for the elves had even managed shops arrayed with all sorts of exciting displays, depending on who might be purchasing at any given time. And yet there were no people here.

"I don't understand. Why have you built an entire village for people who may never see this?"

Lofgren shrugged his shoulders. "You have to understand. Elves love to build, to create. We do it for the sheer joy of it. It's who we are. We start out with an idea—like the one to save our people—and before long we're off on a tangent." Again he shrugged as if in apology. "It's our weakness, I suppose, and perhaps our downfall," he added ruefully. "But there you are."

"Soooo..." Winnifred said, drawing out the word, "you and

I are a lot alike. I can't stop inventing. You can't stop building."

For several seconds they just stared at each other, then the two began to giggle, a bit at first, but soon they were rolling with laughter until tears ran down their face and they both were holding their stomachs to stop the ache.

They sat down next to one of the stalls, this one with handmade toys for children who might never get to hold one of the precious objects, much less play with them.

"I thought you said you don't have many children in your community."

"We don't," he said, followed by more fits of laughter.

"Then why the toys?" she asked, when the gale had finally subsided.

"Because we love children. And I suppose we wish for more of them."

For some reason, that admission caused them both to become more subdued.

Lofgren peered up at the toys wistfully. "It's too bad that there aren't more children to enjoy the toys as much as we enjoy making them. But I suppose that's the way of things. We always want what we can't have."

Winnifred suddenly grew teary eyed. She had yearned for a father, hers long gone. Although her step-father had tried to fill his shoes, he'd never seen her for who she was—an inventor. Independent. Not wanting to be boxed into a position that didn't fulfill her dreams. To be forced to follow the expectations handed down to women. That's why she had felt so comfortable here, where women weren't expected to fulfill roles assigned to them at birth. Never expand beyond home and hearth to a more meaningful role in society. Here, the women saw each other as individuals, with individual needs, not a cookie-cutter image of what a woman should be. And men too.

Winnifred leaned forward so that she could peer at all the shops. One was filled with hand-knitted sweaters, another held a series of knapsacks. Still another contained sheep-wool lined parkas and leather gloves, also wool-lined, or mittens and knitted woolen socks. In one shop, on shelf upon shelf, sat rows of handcrafted boots for the frigid weather.

"It's all for them," Lofgren said, peering up through the hole in the cavern.

"*Them*?" Winnifred followed his eyes, not understanding.

"I think you should see for yourself." He jumped to his feet and ran over to position the ladders.

Winnifred, who was fearless in most things, suddenly trembled because the one thing she feared most was heights. "Oh no," she said, backing away. "You don't expect me to go up there."

"It's the only way you'll truly understand what's at stake." Lofgren held a hand out for her to take hold. "I promise I won't let anything happen to you. Do you trust me?"

She stared at his outstretched arm, eying him speculatively. For several moments, they stood there, each gauging the other's reaction. Finally, she caved. "Okay," she said, taking a cleansing breath before reaching for the ladder.

"Don't look down," Lofgren said. "I've got you."

She nodded once, then tentatively stepped a foot on the ladder.

"Keep going," he encouraged.

Little by little, Winnifred made her way up the ladder, looking only at the next rung, never down, until after what seemed like a half hour or so, she inched toward the hole and the sky above. Someone had thought to put a pole in the center so that it reminded her of a tepee. As she reached the surface, she leaned out and grabbed onto the metal rod then pulled herself up onto the rounded hilltop. Then she scooted over so that Lofgren could come sit beside her. Next to them, a snag of an old conifer clung tightly to a boulder. He reached above him, his hand touching the snag until he found what he was searching for. A rope. He pulled it down and cinched it over the two of them, then clicked it into two C-shaped brackets hammered into the rock to prevent them from falling. From this vantagepoint, they could see across the valley below at what looked like ants, moving.

"What *are* those?" Winnifred asked, not certain what she was seeing.

"Here!" Lofgren pulled a spyglass out of a loop on his belt, designed specifically for such a thing.

Winnifred took the spyglass and held it to one eye then squinted. As she did, images began to take shape.

"Those are people!" she exclaimed, her excitement causing them to sway slightly against the rope.

"Do you recognize any of them?" Lofgren asked, a sudden flash of anger shadowing his normally placid features.

Winnifred put the spyglass to her eye once more and stared as hard as possible, until finally, she thought she might just recognize a few of them. Many were Elfin, though she surmised by the size of one of them that he was part of Lofgren's clan.

And, if her eyesight hadn't deceived her, two of them were a mother and daughter team who had joined their warriors last year. The two had left when Beatrice challenged them. Winnifred and the other women had never thought to see if they had made it home safely. She had just assumed….

But what had her reeling and more fiercely angry than ever before in her life, they were dressed in clothes not meant for the cold. It was easy to see they had lost weight and were mere skeletons. She ground her teeth together, seething that they had been treated so badly. Her teeth started to chatter.

"We had better get down before you catch your death of cold," Lofgren said. "I will need to unstrap you, so hold on tight to the top rung of the ladder."

As he started to loosen the rope, she reached for the ladder rung but missed, twisting around only to catch hold of the pole that ran the vertical length of the cave. Before she could think what to do, she lost her footing. With a whoosh, she felt herself sliding…sliding down the pole, her arms whisking against the metal at a speed that set her hands burning.

"H-help…m-meeee…L-lofgrennn," she yelled, her voice an echo in the cavernous underground room that soon swallowed her whole.

By the time Birsha entered the ballroom, it was already full to the brim with members of the Jackals, their sharp teeth reminding him slightly of wolves, despite their effort to hide them beneath their masks. Though they were the military arm of the kingdom, they held no upper level positions of any real power. Instead, they were merely Alaric's lackeys, according to Siegfried, who filled Birsha in about who stood where and on what rung of society's social strata. Outside of the two generals, who were now dead, only the Council maintained any true power. And the Kazakh. He stood outside the mainframe of society, making his own rules, keeping his own counsel.

Birsha turned in time to see Tempestous striding toward him, hand outstretched, a red mask unable to hide her wiry red hair. Instead of her usual moire outfit that seemed to breathe fire around her, this gown flowed in a colorful display. The brown bodice hugged her so that not a remaining ounce of fabric could be seen outside that which clung to her upper torso, the color and shape reminding him of a caldera. The gown itself flowed from her waist like red-hot lava, small rivulets branching out across a skirt as black as coal. He could swear that he heard a sizzle and popping sound as he leaned in to brush her cheek with a kiss. And though her dress did emit warmth, her hand was as cold as ice, so he quickly dropped it, rubbing his hands together to regain some semblance of heat.

"It's good to see you making the rounds so soon after…" Tempestous paused here, pursing her vibrant red lips coyly and batting her eyelashes. "Well, you know."

Birsha glanced over at Siegfried, then turned back to Tempestous with clenched teeth. He did know. She was speaking not only of Alaric, but of the Generals' deaths, a move he regretted to no end. Undoubtedly, his half-brothers had plotted it so, and he had unwittingly gone along with it. And still he was no closer to learning who had killed his father. He sighed, wishing he understood the inner workings of a kingdom set on the edge of some unknown disaster. He could feel it, see it in Tempestous' eyes that she was planning something, along with the rest of the creatures of the Council who he was coming to see as loathsome indeed.

Just then, Fishmonger came forward to greet them. Though he wore only a collar and tie, his scales flashed reddish orange to match Tempestuous' dress, so that it looked as though he were wearing a suit jacket. A flashy one at that. His gills moved in and out as he spoke.

"So good to see you, sire, and you, Siegfried," he said, his words coming out as though under water. "Have you told him yet?" Fishmonger added, turning toward Tempestous.

Birsha couldn't help but notice the woman's eyes dart around, as if searching for an escape route, but there was no escape. At least not yet.

"Yes, Tempestous. Tell me what?" Birsha said in his most unctuous voice.

For a moment, the lava veins flashed a fiery red and yellow, as though lava was indeed flowing down a mountainside in all its glory. As if to further that assumption, the top of her dress that had hitherto appeared like a caldera, turned coal black followed by an eruption that spewed fiery liquid up the bodice of her dress and into her hair so that it looked as if she were aglow, before once again cascading over the side, only now the rivulets had turned into a molten magma becoming a patchwork of jagged, uneven squares down her dress.

"Now look what you've done!" She peered down at her dress, then turned on her heels and marched away with a fury that sent those around her scattering lest they be singed by the sparks and ash.

Birsha turned to Fishmonger, with only a hint of mirth. "So, sir, again I say, tell me what?"

Fishmonger apparently hadn't expected to be the one put on the spot, as his mouth opened and closed like a fish out of water until, finally, he muttered something about a later time and turned on his oddly shaped tail that had somehow sprouted feet-like appendages that caused him to walk with a mincing step.

"Well," Birsha said, turning to Siegfried, "what do you make of that?"

"It's hard to say, sir. They are an odd bunch, the Council. When Alaric was alive, they seemed a more cohesive group, but without—"

Birsha flinched when he realized Siegfried was about to say "a strong leader."

His adjutant quickly amended it to, "—without the Generals here to keep them in line. Well . . ." His voice drifted off.

"We best keep an eye on them then," Birsha said, and turned to the next person in the line of miscreants who had come to meet their new ruler.

Henry felt as if he'd been walking on hot coals since the moment he'd arrived in the ballroom. It was a sumptuous feast for the senses, no expense spared. It made the outer walls and the people who lived there seem even more mistreated, if possible, to know that such wealth lay only around the corner. And here he was, partaking in it.

He grabbed a toothpick and speared a green olive, appreciating the smooth flavor that reminded him of the manor at holiday time. Next he picked up a plate, which he filled with rare roast beef, sliced thin, the juices running on his plate. He followed it up with fresh asparagus soup, no doubt grown in the lavish greenhouse that sat due east of the inner palace. Butter had been sculpted into designs that foretold both the beneficence of the ruler, and served as warning to those who might cross him, for they were a series of warriors on mounted horses, each more fearsome than the previous one. Henry didn't dare to touch the butter, preferring the small pats of them laid out on a plate chilled in ice. Next, he placed a buttermilk roll on his plate, followed by tropical fruit, unexpected even for a ruler with this level of wealth at his disposal.

Henry took a seat at one of the many round tables, decked with candles and flowers that must have come from the greenhouse as well. Odd flowers in an array of shapes and sizes. One looked like a series of yellow and green birds resting on a stem with green and white leaves. Another looked like a set of pink flamingos all facing center, beaks touching. And still another contained a series of flowers that looked like women dancers, with snow white dresses trimmed in a vibrant, scalloped red velvet.

Henry had been so caught up in inspecting each of the arrangements that he hadn't realized someone was speaking to him until he glanced up to see a very plain looking woman staring at him with a puzzled expression across her brow. She wore no embellishment like the others, except for a few bits of greenery on her dress and a yellow mask that she held with a golden stick in front of her face. Even her hair seemed plain—a mousey brown that couldn't have curled if she'd wanted it to.

"I'm Queen of the Mammals," she said, dropping the mask and taking his hand. "It's so good to see someone new at one of these gatherings."

"Queen of the Mammals?"

"I rule nature—well, at least the animals in nature." She shrugged, as if it were no huge task. "I'm part of the Council." She ended the words in a weary sigh, as if the very mention of the Council tired her.

"Oh," he said, feeling suddenly at a loss for words.

"So where are you from?"

Henry's mind went blank, despite all the preparation he and Sir Robert, along with Nathaniel, had done beforehand to prepare him for this moment. "I . . . I, um . . . am from England." Too late, he realized he'd forgotten the dialect and all Sir Robert had taught him. His face flushed with warmth.

"England? You don't have much of an accent," she proclaimed, clearly confused.

"Uh . . . actually, I just traveled from England. I'm originally from the east coast. Here to sell Birsha on the idea of trains."

"Trains?" Queen of the Mammals said, her lips set in a pout, as though trying to place them.

"They'll revolutionize the kingdom." Henry rushed in without thinking, warming to the idea of this new invention that had yet to make inroads in either kingdom. At the moment, they were merely specs on a piece of paper, and yet it was a wonderful idea. One that Henry planned to tell his parents about the moment he stepped foot on the manor's grounds. *If he stepped foot there again.* After all, until he learned what his parents had sent him to find, he could hardly leave. Then again, what if he wasn't allowed to leave? That thought chilled him. And how could he leave, knowing that so many slaves would be left behind to die in the cold, people who had once belonged to him and his people? Villagers. Neighbors. Friends.

"You were saying?" Queen of the Mammals asked.

He spent the next ten minutes explaining trains and their many usages, the fact that they would carry cargo to the far reaches of the kingdom. He didn't add that they would carry military supplies. Now that he understood their capabilities, he was determined that his family have them first. Whoever mastered technology mastered the world. But what world would that be? And how far would each kingdom go to either preserve and protect their own, or to overrun the other? He swiped at the sweat forming on his brow and was relieved when he saw Nathaniel coming his way to rescue him. But Nathaniel's eyes passed over Henry to a woman who stood behind him, close to an alcove with heavily brocaded drapes. She was stunning in her blue dress with stars and half-moons sewn into the voile, but, more than that, something about her seemed familiar, something that Henry couldn't quite wrap his mind around. Then it came to him as he saw her paw at the place where her necklace should be, the one that had been stolen many weeks ago. His heart leapt in his throat. It couldn't be, could it?

Brigid!

He started towards her but was stopped by a man who seemed intent on meeting him. Rather cheekily, the masked man stood in front of him, refusing to allow him to pass. The man then thrust his hand out before Henry could excuse himself.

"My name is Kenric," he offered. "I believe you have heard of me?"

Henry's voice stalled in his throat as though a dam prevented him from speaking.

"I haven't much time," the man said in a near whisper. "Someone is headed my way. Someone I wish not to see. All I can say is that the person you seek–the one who killed Alaric–is not who you would expect. In fact–"

But before he could finish his thought, he pulled his hood lower around his masked face and turned abruptly to leave. Whoever had the man in his sights would wonder about Henry as well, so he made himself scarce, slipping into the crowd only to deposit himself at the other end of the table, where he filled an empty seat and pretended to partake of the delicacies before him.

Only when the man had passed without spotting him and had exited the main door in search of Kenric did Henry arise from his chair and go in search of Brigid.

24

I knew I was supposed to mingle, but all I wanted to do
was to disappear amid the sumptuous drapes, to pull them
around me, curl up, and go to sleep. Exhaustion at once
overwhelmed me and dragged me into her embrace.

Just a minute of rest, I told myself as I eyed the yellow
satin cushioned seat beneath a pane of leaded glass. With a
sigh, I folded myself onto the seat, wrapped up in a cocoon of
tranquility amidst the gladhanding. And although I had spied
Birsha, I had yet to see Henry with all the costumes the revelers
were wearing.

Where are you, Henry?

I fingered the indentation at the base of my neck where
my necklace had once been . . . my family. Where were they
now? I had cobbled together a family of my own over this past
year and then some, but here even my new family was gone,

the women warriors back at the base, with Winnifred. Dear, sweet Winnifred. She must be frantic, wondering what had happened to us. And now I had a new dilemma. How would I collect Henry, get him to safety, and then save hundreds of men, women, and children who had been captured and enslaved in this forbidding land?

I stared outside through the leaded glass at the streets below. Snow was just now beginning to fall in earnest. I thought of the light wrap I had brought, insufficient for the ride home. Master Clyde had promised that someone would pick me up at precisely 11:00PM, no later. And, supposedly, he had a plan to help the captured escape. But how? And what sort of jeopardy would we be in once I found Henry? *If* I found Henry.

As I brushed away tears, I heard a voice behind me. "Is this seat taken?"

I turned abruptly and would have launched into his arms had I not known people were watching.

"Henry!" I breathed. "It's you. It's really you! I was so afraid." My voice cracked and I peered down, not wanting him to see how much his absence had affected me.

But he lifted my chin so that he could gaze directly into my eyes. Then he pulled out a handkerchief and lifted my mask in order to dry my eyes.

"There, there, miss," he said as though he hadn't kissed me countless times. Hadn't been my closest friend and confidante. "No need to cry. Whatever you've lost, I'll help find it."

Oh, just like Henry to know exactly what to say. "You will?"

"Of course I will," he said, winking.

I laughed then, all the earlier angst swept away in a sea of relief, for if anyone could help me, it was Henry.

"Thank you, Henry," I said, wishing I could reach over and hold him in my arms.

But thank heaven I hadn't, because at that moment, someone came up behind him and tapped him on the shoulder. Henry turned and immediately paled. He snapped to attention and bowed slightly.

"Oh, Henry, at last I've found you," Birsha said, another man with a goatee at his side. "Nathaniel's not with you?"

As I watched, Henry turned to spy what I could only assume was Nathaniel, who stood across the room nervously watching the exchange. When Birsha pivoted to see what held Henry's attention, Nathaniel quickly twirled toward a woman and began speaking with her at length.

"He seems to be a bit . . . preoccupied, at the moment," Henry said with a brief cough into his hand.

"That he does," Birsha agreed with a chuckle. "And who do we have here?" he added, nodding toward me.

"Sire," Henry said, "this is . . . uh, Briga," he ad libbed. Then he turned to me and said, "Briga, this is Birsha."

I caught just a glimmer of fear in Henry's eyes, his words suddenly as tight as his jaw, as though warning me to be careful.

"I hope I'm not interrupting anything," Birsha said, looking between us two as though gauging our connection.

"Not at all," we said in unison followed by a feeble laugh on my part. "How can we be of service?" I asked, hopefully giving Henry time to plan his next words carefully.

"My, my. Aren't you lovely," Birsha said, bending down and

kissing the back of my hand.

I gave over my hand only as long as deemed proper, then pulled it away and tucked it inside a hidden pocket in my dress.

Then Birsha turned to Henry with a predatory smile. "So where have you been keeping this captivating creature?" He stared at Henry for a moment too long. "You are full of surprises, my dear Henry."

I shot Henry a glance and saw that he was not at all pleased to suddenly have a rival. And a dangerous one at that.

Master Clyde watched from across the room. How could he have been so foolish as to think that Henry and Brigid wouldn't find each other–wouldn't risk everything to save each other? And now Birsha had them in his sights.

With a tad more anger and frustration than he should have, he slammed down his glass of mead, nearly shattering it in the process. He had put together a plan, thanks to Kahwihta and the Mohawks, as well as the Oneida. A good plan, if he dared say so himself. But now, all might be at risk. Because if Birsha discovered that Brigid and Henry were within reach, he would use them as hostages and then all his plans would be for naught. He growled beneath his breath.

"Excussse me?"

He turned in time to see Liz Herd, her tongue flicking in and out of a protruding green jaw. His heart sank, realizing they were in true jeopardy now. In the future, he would have to keep his counsel in check.

"Oh, sorry. I just love this mead, don't you?" Master Clyde offered up a lusty growl again to cover his true intentions.

"Oh, aye," Liz Herd said, peering down at her cup. "If you like thisss, you ssshould try the Cobra wine. It's sssimply lusciousss."

Master Clyde peered down at the minuscule red ruby glass with platinum filigree made from the finest silversmith. In it was a vile green liquid that made him cringe, but he merely smiled and politely declined.

"My doctor has forbidden me to drink, but a little mead is mostly harmless," he said, offering a weak smile.

Liz Herd seemed to have noticed that Master Clyde had been watching the pair as they were introduced to Birsha, the new ruler of the Jackals and all that entailed.

"Look at the way Birsssha is ssstaring at that man, as though he knowsss him, and yet he isss new to the kingdom, they both are, are they not?"

Master Clyde's breathing stilled inside his chest, his heart beating double time. "What makes you say so?"

Liz Herd turned yellow slits on Master Clyde. "Why, becaussse, I can alwaysss tell a hunter and itsss prey." The slits that were sideways moments before turned vertically and narrowed, as though Master Clyde were now the hunted, the prey.

"Oh, I see," Master Clyde said, but it came out a squeak. "You are clearly more discerning than am I." Fighting down the burble of fear that rushed up from his chest, he offered a weak smile. Then with a brief bow, he excused himself and made for the exit.

Not until he was outside the fortress gates and nearly to the cave by the waterfall did he begin to breathe again. As the coach whipped through the newly fallen snow, he checked myriad times to see if he were being followed, but fortunately most were taken up with the business of the ball.

After seeing Birsha together with Henry and Brigid, he knew he had to have a contingent plan, and he also knew just who to seek. He had it on good faith from a man he trusted with his life that the elf was seen with an entire contingent of women near the cave. That could mean only one thing. The women warriors were back. And if so, that meant that they had come to make sure Henry and Brigid made it safely out of the fortress.

Winnifred whizzed through the air on the pole that shot through the ceiling of the cave, landing with a plop on a mounded pile of hay that had been strewn at the bottom for those making a quick exit. And though she hadn't planned it, that's precisely what she'd done when she'd let loose of the ladder and grabbed hold of the pole. This must be what a fireman felt like, whizzing down a fire pole when the bells clanged, sounding an emergency.

"Oomph," she said, attempting to stand.

She rubbed her sore backside and had just moved out of the way in time to see Lofgren sliding down, though he seemed to be enjoying it much better than she, for he let loose a loud "Whee!" that continued all the way down, a smile on his face as he landed, on his feet, unlike her, whose rear was still aching from the unceremonious fall.

"Well, well, who have we here?"

To Winnifred's amazement, Master Clyde held out a hand to Lofgren, who he clearly knew.

Behind him was Beatrice, who quickly explained that Master Clyde had been searching for them. "I saw you enter the path beneath the waterfall. I figured you must still be here."

"Right-o!" Winnifred rubbed her hands together to rid herself of the excess straw. Then she held her hand out to Master Clyde. "I've heard so much about you."

"Likewise," Master Clyde assured her. "But I'm not here on a pleasure call, though I *am* glad to see you all."

"Oh?" Lofgren came to stand beside Winnifred, his normally comical eyebrows hovering above steely green eyes.

"You know about the captives?" Master Clyde said, pointing to the ceiling.

"Indeed," Lofgren said. "I was just showing Winnifred."

"Then I suppose you also know that Henry was sent to the palace to seek information."

"We do," Winnifred said. "That's why we're here."

"I thought as much," Master Clyde said, the seriousness of the situation apparent by the set of his jaws. He quickly explained what had become of both Henry and Brigid. "I warned Brigid to stay away from Henry," he added, "only to watch him from a distance–to keep us apprised of his situation. Try to meet with Birsha and to pick his brain, but the cursed girl went and did it anyway–"

"Wait, what?" Winnifred held up her hands. "You're not

making sense. Start at the beginning."

Lofgren ushered the four over to a table and chairs set out for the future dwellers of this subterranean region. The food stand had a decidedly Nordic feel about it which fit Lofgren well.

Once seated, Master Clyde leaned in. "A masquerade party is taking place inside the palace walls. I had sent Brigid to locate Henry, and to learn what she can about Birsha. I don't know how it happened. I was turned one minute, drinking my mead and having a bite to eat. When I looked up, they were together and it was clear by their actions that Henry and Brigid recognized each other despite their masks. But then Birsha found them and the way he looked . . . ."

Master Clyde's voice trailed off and all he could do was "tsk" as Winnifred tried to process what he had told her. How could everything have gone so wrong so quickly? Now she had the two of them to rescue, plus an entire contingent of slaves. Though she and Lofgren had been going over plans since nearly the moment they had met, she hadn't figured this into the equation.

"Maybe you're worried for nothing," she suggested. "Maybe they were merely introducing themselves . . . ohhh! Now that would be bad. But surely both Henry and Brigid had a cover story, no? They wouldn't go in blind."

But it was clear by Master Clyde's expression that although he had forewarned of such an event, it hadn't gone to plan.

"I can't tell you how I know, but I just know that Birsha recognized Henry. He *knows* him! And if he knows who Henry is, he will surely figure out who Brigid is before long. And if he uses them as hostages, then our plan is ruined!" He moaned, running nervous fingers through his hair.

Beatrice stepped forward, dressed now in a coat of armor instead of the more flamboyant dress she'd worn hitherto. And indeed, she did appear transformed in almost every way. Winnifred had been so busy that she hadn't noticed until now how lean Beatrice had become, her muscles rock solid. She'd undoubtedly been practicing maneuvers with the other woman since rejoining them, but to have gained such muscle in so short a time had Winnifred puzzled. It made no sense.

"Please, let me go to the palace." Beatrice turned to Winnifred to make her plea. "You, of all people, know that I have a knack with men."

Winnifred nearly laughed until she realized Beatrice was serious. Certainly men found her attractive, but to have admitted as much surprised even Winnifred at Beatrice's brazenness. It meant the other woman had known what she was doing all along. Had been using her wiles to get what she wanted at court. The thought was both stunning and sobering.

"What will you do?" Winnifred asked, her jaw turned to stone.

"I'll win over Birsha in whatever way I can. If it gives Henry and Brigid time to escape, so be it."

"And what about you?" Winnifred demanded. "What will you get out of all this?"

The truth is, Winnifred still didn't trust the girl fully, and who could blame her? The girl's record was spotty at best.

"I will earn redemption."

Winnifred offered a nervous glance to Master Clyde who

seemed just as uncertain as Winnifred herself. Was this the new and improved Beatrice? Winnifred couldn't help but reflect on the old adage that it was "nigh to impossible for a jackal to give up hunting." But why was Beatrice on the chase, and on the chase for what, precisely?

"We have no better options," Master Clyde said. "Henry and Brigid need our help, and I dare not risk sending any more of our own into that viper's den."

Winnifred rubbed her sore neck as she took stock of the woman.

What are you up to, Beatrice?

Finally, because she could think of no clear reason for her not to go, she gave the okay with a short nod.

"Good!" said Master Clyde, rubbing his hands together. "That's settled."

Seeing that the tide had shifted, Lofgren stepped forward. "To the tunnels it is, then."

"The what?" Winnifred said.

But Lofgren wasn't listening. Instead, he shoved the straw aside and lifted up a trap door with another ladder. "Winnifred?" he said, turning to her. "You will need to put one of the other women in charge."

"Why?" she demanded.

"Because you're coming with me, ya? We need to set up everything for the time that the women arrive. We have much work to do, you and I."

Since when had Lofgren taken over in such a way? But Winnifred knew he was right. They *did* have a lot of work to do if they were to rescue the slaves.

"I'm coming," Winnifred assured him. "Let me speak to Jocelyn first."

Twenty minutes later, after she had spoken with Jocelyn and had everything settled here, she prepared to enter the catacombs. But Winnifred had a fear that she had yet to admit. Just as she was afraid of heights, she didn't like enclosed spaces. And yet if she was to be a true leader, how could she possibly say no?

She took a calming breath, then said, "Give me one second, and then you can lead the way."

He knew! It was as if a wall had suddenly opened up to him and there stood a young boy of about eight, a red-headed boy with bushy hair who was keen on sports of all kinds. Birsha reeled at the realization, and pulled away from the young woman, nearly knocking over a tray of patès in his haste.

"Henry . . . You're Henry *Bookbinder*?" Birsha demanded, taking a step back. "Then you must be Brigid! You were right, Siegfried. Where Henry goes, Brigid goes."

Henry had changed so much since a child that Birsha scarcely recognized him. No longer a boy with a boy's face. Instead, a man. But it was the small scar running just beneath his right ear that cinched the deal. A scar he'd obtained when thrown from his pony. Why had Birsha's nanny taken him to the Bookbinder's manor? To spy on them?

Winded, he whispered, "What are you doing *here*?"

It was as if he had seen a ghost, only this one was very much alive and in *his* kingdom, *his* palace, *his* ballroom. The realization sent shock waves pivoting through the room so that people began screeching and ducking. Birsha had been born with this strange affliction, but had learned to tame it early on. Yet, when the rare event stunned him, before he could get his emotions under control, the results were disastrous, as they were now.

Birsha grimaced as some of the unfortunate women who had been in the way, let out "oomphs" or "ahs," their bodies contorting until the shock wave had passed, only to glance against some other poor, unsuspecting soul. In fact the whole room was now so filled with these waves that it appeared as though the entire group were all in some sort of macabre underater dance.

"Henry and Brigid, come with me!" Birsha hissed. Then to Seigfried he snapped, "You, too."

He shoved his way through the mélèe of people who were bouncing off each other like balls from a bagatelle board.

Not until he reached the library did Birsha stop and turn toward the two interlopers.

"So, it's true. You are the famous Henry Bookbinder, and *you*–!" He pointed an accusatory finger toward the woman with Henry. "–must be Brigid Anne Dunsmore, the woman who owns the loom."

And with that, he plopped into the seat next to the massive eight-foot globe, which instantly began whirring as it swirled faster and faster, until finally it opened with a loud "pop!" only to have a hologram appear of his father, Alaric the Third.

I froze, unable to speak, the thoughts swirling through me as thick and as furious as the shock waves we'd just witnessed in the ballroom. It was as if all my fears were being brought to life, and now, Alaric's ghost had popped up to chastise us as well. Like a soldier, he marched around the enormous circumference of the interior of the globe, his eyes following us around the room, hands behind his back.

"Well, well, well, so we finally meet."

Though in my heart, I knew Alaric was gone and couldn't hurt me or Henry, who had paled to a shade of white I had yet to see before, I couldn't help but worry that some great sorcery was about to occur that would set new gears into motion.

Steady yourself, Brigid.

My hands shook so badly that I grabbed one with the other to try to quell the trembling. But what surprised me most was that Birsha seemed just as cowed as I by the hologram figure marching inside the globe, as though Alaric were still strutting around his kingdom. And in fact, Birsha's hands were shaking nearly as badly as mine.

"How?" I whispered. "Alaric is supposed to be dead!"

Birsha shook his head. "I don't know."

"As you can see for yourself," Alaric said, halting his march, "I am very much alive . . . in a manner of speaking. Tell them, Siegfried!"

"Your father gathered a collection of books from lands far and wide so that he could study the dark arts," Siegfried explained. "He told me that we must never open any of them for fear of what might happen."

"Why did he have them if he couldn't use them?" I asked, Henry nodding in agreement.

"Oh, but he did," Siegfried said, pacing. "Isn't that right, Alaric?"

Alaric nodded.

"He scoured the libraries across the globe," Siegfried added, "to learn what he could about the books in his possession."

"Of course I did, you nincompoop!" Alaric shouted, becoming increasingly belligerent.

The adjutant paused in front of the globe, then took a few steps back, as though fearing the man's reach, even from the afterlife. "Once he had enough knowledge to safely open the books, he did. Still, they were dangerous. He has scars left by some of them."

Alaric merely scowled. "The books are vicious! Stay away from them at all costs," the former ruler admonished. "If it weren't for them, I might still be alive."

All heads swiveled in unison at this news. What did Alaric mean that he might still be alive, if not for the books?

"I thought you were poisoned," Birsha said, confusion causing him to leap to his feet.

"I had heard the same," I concurred.

Alaric surprised us with a laugh. "Oh, I was. But the poison spell came from one of the books." He marched over to the side of the globe closest to the library and bent forward, squinting. After several moments, he said, "There! That one! It was opened on the desk when I came into the room. It's the first time I knew that the globe held a secret. You see, in the book it showed a lever."

Birsha marched over and was about to reach for the red, alligator-skinned book that Alaric had pointed out when his father yelled, "No, stop! You're not to touch it."

"Why?" both Henry and I asked in unison.

"Have you learned nothing?" the previous ruler scolded, his eyes brandishing red warning flashes as though he were a red sector lens in a lighthouse.

Warning. Warning. Warning.

"Why did you open the book, if it posed such a danger?" I asked, still not understanding his logic.

Alaric paused his pacing to glare at me, his hooded eyes bearing the same malevolence that he was so noted for while in life. "I . . . didn't . . . open it," he said, speaking slowly as though I were a child.

And that's all it took because I didn't like being treated as though I were stupid, though I had heard it often enough while at the manor. *"Stupid girl wouldn't know her way around a maze if she'd been born to it. Stupid girl thinks she's somebody, all because she's besotted our poor Henry. Stupid girl will never understand our traditions. Really!"* None of it from the Bookbinders, who were anything if not gracious. Rather from the staff. But I apparently was smart enough to understand their taunts. Not enough to avoid the daily pain that I received. Not that anyone would go out of their way to explain these traditions to me. What I *did* understand, and what I alone had the audacity to speak, is how *wrong* they were. How ultimately cruel and evil the people who would do such things to others when kindness worked so much better. But as long as the people who perpetrated such violence hid behind a wall of secrecy, there would be no making the world better—the people of the manor's lives better. Instead, the anonymity had helped them to become petty and unkind, if not downright cruel.

"For your information, Sir Alaric," I said through gritted teeth, "I am alive, and you are not, so in the future, if you wish to speak to me, you'll do so with respect. And wipe that smirk off your face!" I added, for good measure. "In the meantime, the four of us would like to know exactly how you came to be in contact with the book."

"How dare you, you insolent creature!" Alaric hissed and fumed, reaching for the sword that stood silent at his side until now. "Someone left it there to let me know what they had done to me," he growled, his cheeks glowing hot and his sword swishing the air dangerously close to me.

"Don't let him near you," Siegfried warned. "We don't know what magic he possesses as a result of everything that has happened to him."

"Don't help her, you fool!" Alaric shouted, the globe beginning to tremble and rumble as though ready to topple off its stand from the sheer anger of the hologram ruler alone. "You just wait until I am out of here. I will see to it that you—"

I don't know what came over me. I just knew that I wanted away from those hateful eyes and that hateful man. Without thinking, I slammed the globe shut and for a moment, we all stood staring at each other, uncertain of the ramifications of such an action. Then it happened and we all gasped. The globe began to shudder while glowing a deep red, the shuddering growing longer and louder as we all looked at each other in shock and awe. Suddenly, the globe began to twirl. Slow at first. Then much faster, a whirring sound filling the room. Eyes grew wide and my heart stilled.

"Oh dear–" But before I could get the final word out, the globe took flight and crashed through the stained-glass ceiling. The last we saw of it, the globe was spinning away into the snowy night.

25

Winnifred should have known. She popped her head through the opening that appeared to be in a large barn of some sort and saw Thomas, Emma, and Kahwihta, who had come to help.

The moment Emma saw who had accompanied Winnifred and Master Clyde, she turned an ashen gray and hissed at Beatrice. "You! I should have known you'd never stay away." She gave a mirthless laugh.

Thomas, on the other hand, stood silent, as though a move of any sort might land him in more hot water than he'd seen in a long time.

"It's not what you think." Beatrice clambered through the opening and raised her hands midair. "I'm here to help Henry and Brigid, not to bother you or Thomas, I swear."

"And we all know how good your promises are, don't we?"

Emma moved closer to Thomas and took his hand both in comfort and to protect him from the woman who'd had her designs on him from the beginning.

"Look–" Winnifred jumped in before things got out of hand. "Henry and Brigid are in danger. We have to help them, and as hard as this is for you to digest, Emma, Beatrice has offered her help. Lofgren and I–" She peered around, looking for him. Just then, he poked his head up out of the tunnel passageway.

"Oh, there you are," Winnifred said.

Both Thomas and Emma turned to each other, their faces registering shock.

"Who . . . or rather, *what*, is he?" Emma asked. Then she had the decency to turn a healthy shade of pink at the rather rude question.

"I am an elf," Lofgren said, his head tilted sideways in that puppy dog expression that Winnifred had come to love, his actions often child-like. "Rather, half-elf, that is. Meaning I'm half human too. Lofgren's the name. At your service." He jumped up out of the tunnel and bowed deeply, causing Winnifred to giggle.

Emma shook her head and whispered to Winnifred, as though Lofgren couldn't hear her words. "I thought elves were just a story out of a fairytale."

Winnifred shrugged. "Until a few days ago, I did too, but I can assure you they are every bit real. And he's here to help us. We're going to install a pulley system through the forest canopy, then create a diversion to keep both the guards at the camp busy, and the guards back at the fortress preoccupied. Then, we'll help the prisoners escape."

Emma flopped down on a bale of hay, looking exhausted from weeks of travel.

Kahwihta, who had stood in the background until now, came forward.

"And I have a plan as well. Perhaps we can work out our plan together?" she said. "But first, we have to get back to Eleanor's farm. We've elicited some help."

Before anyone could speak, a creature unlike any Winnifred had ever seen before slithered through the crack in the doorway. Winnifred let out a scream, then fainted dead away.

"Hurry!" Birsha growled, running hands through his widow's peak. "Everything's gone wrong. Guards!" he shouted.

Seconds later, the Jackals, who were always on hand for such things, entered the room in their red uniforms and immediately surrounded Henry and Brigid, their muskets with bayonets attached at the ready should the need arise.

"Place these two under house arrest. They are not to leave their rooms. In the meantime, I must find out what happened to the globe *and* . . . my father."

The pair of Jackals looked at each other and frowned as though wondering whether Birsha had gone mad, and right now, Birsha wondered that himself. After all, though he'd been raised to one day inherit the kingdom, he hadn't learned black magic, nor did he want to, seeing what evil it had caused already. If it were up to him, he would take those books and burn them, or toss them into the ocean. But without first knowing the repercussions of such actions, he didn't dare risk touching them, much less doing them harm. No, he must bide his time. He had much to learn, but at least for now, he had captured the infamous Henry and Brigid, and that was enough. Hostages, and especially hostages as high-profile as Henry and Brigid, could offer up any number of opportunities. He just had to figure out what those were.

"And Siegfried," he said, his words coming out like cannon fire.

"Yes, m'lord?"

"See to it that these two are guarded."

"Yes, m'lord."

"In the meantime, I must return to the ballroom so that no one suspects anything amiss. You, on the other hand," Birsha said, pinning Siegfried with a look, "shall go in search of the globe, *n'est pas?*"

"*Oui, oui, mon liege,*" Siegfried said with a bow, his mouth curving into a smile.

Birsha frowned. "You speak French? Well, well, Siegfried." Birsha shook his head, unable to hide a grin despite the residual anger. "You *are* full of surprises. Someday you shall have to regale me with how you learned the romance language."

"You as well," Siegfried replied.

"*Touché!*"

Birsha pulled a glove from his pocket, tapped it on his hand before placing his fingers in the black silk and wiggling them. Then, with a nod, he set the Jackals upon Henry and Brigid, their shouts and screams muffled by the Jackals, who placed a cloth filled with ether over their mouths to silence them.

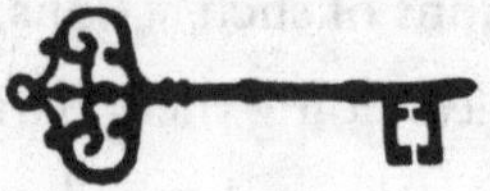

I awoke some time later, relieved to find Henry lying next to me. Although rumpled from being unceremoniously shoved into the room and thrown onto the carpeted floor, he appeared almost beatific, his expression so child-like and free from care while asleep that I felt an almost maternal love for him. I reached out and ran a hand across his face, marveled at its smoothness juxtaposed by the rough texture of his chin.

"I love you, Henry," I whispered to his still form.

Just then, he stirred, his eyes fluttering open.

"Where are we, Brigid?" He jerked his head up only to slump back onto the carpet, not yet fully awake.

For several moments, he lay immobile, his lips moving as though trying to speak but unable to get his mouth to do any more than it had already. Finally, his eyes seemed to focus and he shook his head.

He licked his lips before speaking. "What are you doing in the fortress, Brigid? You were supposed to stay back at camp until I returned!"

"I came in search of you, you big baboon! Why did you go off and leave me like that without a word? And in the middle of the night? Do you know how frightened I was?" Once I got going, I couldn't seem to stop. "And then there was the fire that destroyed nearly the entire village."

Suddenly, all the angst that I had been bottling up in these weeks of searching for him came bubbling over like the contents of a cauldron set on a roaring fire. Henry sat up as best he could and pulled me to his chest, nestling his face in my hair.

"I'm so sorry to make you worry, Brigid. I never meant to hurt you. But I knew that it wasn't safe to come here, and now you can see why." He motioned to the locked door with his chin.

But I would have none of it. "Don't you know, Henry Bookbinder, that wherever you go, I go, danger or no danger?"

He chuckled, then leaned over so that we could touch heads as we always did when comforting each other.

"And by the way, Brigid Anne Dunsmore, I love you, too."

For far too brief a moment, we stayed like that, head to head, Henry's eyes appearing owlish, this close. But it made that moment all the more precious, to feel his eyelashes against mine, his breath sweet, despite what we had endured and would no doubt have left to endure. He gave me one brief kiss, but it held all the promise of a tomorrow, should we find a way of extricating ourselves from this current dilemma.

Henry was the first to pull away. He stood, tugging me toward him. Then he walked over to the door, checking it to be certain that we were indeed locked in, though we both knew it. Furthermore, we heard a clearing of the throat, as though the person on the other side of the door was pondering an answer.

Henry put his finger to his lips, warning me not to speak without saying a word. Then he curled a finger to draw me deeper into the room.

"Where are we?" I asked, once we were as far from the hallway door as possible.

"My room at the palace."

"You have your own room?" And indeed I peered around and saw the vestiges of clothing from his wardrobe, as though he'd left in a hurry.

"It's a long story." He held up his hands, clearly having something to say. "We need to plan our escape."

I eyed the window doubtfully. It was a long way down without so much as a bush to break our fall. Furthermore, people bustled to and fro despite both the falling temperature and snow outside, as well as the lateness of the hour. For the ball was in full swing and everybody who was anybody was there, as I knew only full well.

"I doubt very much that we can plan that as our escape route," I said, nodding toward the street below.

"Hmm." Henry held a finger to his lips and tapped, his mind clearly elsewhere. "So, our only hope is to create a diversion."

At that exact moment, a man stood outside the room and began asking directions from the guard stationed at the door.

"Nathaniel!" Henry whispered excitedly.

"Who?"

"I'll tell you later." He grabbed my hand and nearly dragged me to the door which he began pounding on with vigor.

"Just one moment," we heard the guard tell the other man. "Got us a captive—one of the Bookbinders," he added in an excited whisper.

Still in uniform, the Jackal unlocked the door and peered around the doorway. "What do you want?" he growled.

But before he could ask anything further, Nathaniel slammed him from behind with the butt of a pistol that he'd hidden in an inside pocket while Henry made quick work of the Jackal with a gut punch to the stomach. The two men turned him face up and dragged the supine figure into the room.

"We need to tie him up," Henry said, then looked at me, as though I should have a rope hidden in the room somewhere.

I scanned the room for anything that might be used to subdue the guard, but in the end, the only thing I could see was Nathaniel's ascot. I reached over and said, "Allow me."

"Wha–?" He peered down at my hands, but I was already undoing the loose knots of the silken tie.

This would do for the hands, but what of the feet? Once again, I did a quick perusal of the room. *What? What? What?* Then, with a snap of my fingers, I saw what just might work, if we were lucky.

"Take off your leggings, Henry."

"What? Are you joking? Why I–"

But I couldn't wait to explain. I began pawing at his leggings to which he held tight with a single hand.

"Wait, no!" He backed away and headed for the water closet. On the way, he rummaged through his small steamer trunk, grabbing a pair of pants. "Give me a moment." He scowled at me for my earlier attempt to unseat him, as it were.

For what seemed like far too long, Henry changed in the other room.

"Is he always this fussy?" Nathaniel asked, keeping a keen eye on our prisoner.

"Afraid so," I admitted. "I'd thought with our urgent need that he would forgo the usual niceties, but apparently not." I shrugged and offered him a weak smile.

Finally, Henry reappeared, short one pair of leggings, which he handed to me, his earlier snit having yet to be replaced. I hurriedly tied them around the guard's ankles, using a clove hitch knot taught to me as a child.

"Now what?" I demanded, hands on hips.

Henry scratched his chin, searching for something to keep the man from shouting for help. He snapped his fingers and once again began rummaging through his trunk.

"Aha!" he said, holding up a pair of rolled socks. "Just the thing."

At that exact moment, the Jackal began to stir.

"Hurry!" Nathaniel grabbed the socks from Henry and stuffed them in the guard's mouth. His jaws were like that of a dog, so we would need to wrap something around the snout to keep the Jackal from spitting out the socks with his long tongue.

"Shoelaces!" I cried, peering down at Henry's feet.

"Surely you don't expect me to give up my shoelaces, Brigid."

But I merely snapped my fingers. And although he gave a belabored sigh, he bent over and pulled them out of the metal eyelets. We barely got them cinched in time before the beast came fully alive and began to thrash, his strength well above that of a human.

"Quick!" Nathaniel said. "Grab your things and let's get out of this wasteland."

"But I haven't learned anything of value to take home to my family," Henry protested.

"Henry Bookbinder," I chided, "you will be bringing home the most valuable thing of all."

"Oh, and what is that, pray tell?" Henry said with a bit of an arrogant streak, if I do say so myself.

"You, Henry. You'll be bringing back you." And with that, I flung open the hallway door, peered around to make sure we weren't being watched, then headed for the stairs, the two men close behind.

26

Winnifred awoke to a barn full of people gathered 'round her. She blinked, then peered one by one until she came to confront the creature who had caused her to faint in the first place. She let loose another scream, but a reptilian hand reached out to cover her mouth. Though she fought back the rising panic in her chest, no one else seemed nearly as alarmed as she was at this moment.

"Winnifred," Thomas said in his most calming voice. "This is Chame-leon. He's on our side."

He paused until the wheels clicked in her head and she nodded, her eyes wide despite Thomas' assurances. Slowly, Chame-leon released Winnifred from his grasp, though that was easier said than done, what with his zygodactylous feet that acted like mini suction cups.

Once she'd been released, she crab-walked backwards to put

distance between the reptile and her, her breathing still labored. "Wh-who are you? And why do you look like that?"

"He's from the Council," Master Clyde said. "He has been embedded for some time. We put him there so we could get information. Unfortunately, he is not privy to all that goes on in the Council, apparently, because he didn't know of the assassination attempt on Alaric."

"Attempt?" Winnifred shook her head, which still felt muddled from the fall. "I don't understand. Alaric is dead, isn't he?"

Here, Emma stepped forward. "Not exactly."

Lofgren, who had been nervously watching from afar and clearly hating to intervene as the outsider among the bunch, walked over and kneeled next to Winnifred. He took her hand, as though what he was about to say was of monumental importance.

"We believe Alaric may not be dead in the truest of senses."

"What does that mean?" she demanded, not comprehending.

"Well, let's just say he's taken another form and hasn't yet been released from his chambers."

Winnifred sat up. "You're all talking nonsense. I don't understand."

The members of the group looked to each other for support. Thomas was the next to speak. "You see, Winnifred, in the strictest sense, he's dead, but there is black magic involved, unholy magic that makes his leaving transitional."

"Transitional?" she felt as though her head might explode.

"He may never return. It's sort of like limbo."

Limbo, she understood from Catholic theology. It was when a person's fate had yet to be determined, so the penitent hung in some sort of middle ground, suspended between two worlds, this one and the afterlife. Until their fate was decided, they could neither return nor go forward. In effect, they were stuck.

"Where, exactly, is he stuck *at*?" she asked, not caring one whit that her English had gone to heck in a handbasket.

Chame-leon sighed as he sat on his haunches. "We believe he has been imprisoned in an ancient globe inside the library." He pierced Master Clyde with a look that meant nothing to Winnifred, but she could see by Master Clyde's reaction that whatever the look meant, it had frightened him.

"Tell me. What's going on?"

Chame-leon stood frozen and suddenly blended into the background so that he was all but invisible.

"You can't hide from us," Master Clyde hissed. "We *must* know what has happened."

Chame-leon suddenly came into focus, changing back into colors that were easily visible to the rest, a series of light greens, yellows, and a vibrant orange.

"Sorry, it happens whenever I am upset or fearful."

"Then explain yourself. Now!" Master Clyde urged.

"Before I left the ballroom, I heard that Birsha had taken Brigid and Henry to the library."

"The library where Alaric is said to reside?" Master Clyde said, blanching at this untimely news.

"Precisely. And Master Clyde, Winnifred–" He nodded to include her and the rest. "He knows who they are. My guess is that he'll use them as hostages."

Winnifred gasped, then heard the collective sigh at this unwelcome news. "We must get them out of there."

Although everyone concurred with a nod of each head, no one seemed to know precisely how to do that.

"Where is Birsha?" asked Beatrice.

Until now, she had stood off to one side due to Emma and Thomas' rejection of her and her supposedly altruistic reasons for being here.

"He's back in the ballroom," Chame-leon said. Each eye moved in different directions, his tongue reaching out to snag a fly that was buzzing lazily around the room.

Winnifred groaned at the sight, but said nothing.

"Let me meet with Birsha," she pleaded, first turning to Chame-leon and then to Master Clyde. "Maybe I can negotiate a release."

Master Clyde crossed his arms, as though warding off such a foolish risk without a clear plan in place. "What will we give Birsha in return? He won't simply hand the pair over without something of value."

For a moment, all were silent. Then an idea came to Winnifred, one she wasn't certain would work. Unless . . . .

"What if we offered him a train and a hundred miles of tracks?"

Master Clyde frowned. "No one has even built a train yet. How can you promise him that?"

"I've been reading about them," Winnifred said, her excitement growing. "You're right, no one has ever built one yet, but in England, they're in the design phase. It will be no time at all before one is actually built. It will give us enough time to stall until everyone is out and safe."

"And if he doesn't go for it without collateral?" Master Clyde insisted.

Winnifred deflated as if her silk balloon had popped. Everyone stood in abject silence.

Suddenly, Beatrice spoke up, her voice small but determined. "Then I will offer myself up as hostage."

"No!" Winnifred cried. For as much as she didn't trust Beatrice completely, the girl was one of them. Besides, her family was friends with the Bookbinder clan.

"It's settled." Master Clyde glared, allowing no dissenters among them. "We will take you back to the farm and ready you for the ball, Beatrice. We must hurry!"

Birsha had been mingling throughout the ballroom for over an hour now, tiring of the small talk while always on guard for those who would oppose him. Since taking the crown, he had found himself becoming increasingly paranoid to the point that he was beginning to trust no one.

"When will this cursed ball be over so I can go back to my chambers and rest?" Birsha whispered to Siegfried, who had returned upon giving instructions to one of his subordinates to be on the lookout for the globe and Alaric.

For some reason Birsha trusted Siegfried. He wore no airs, nor did he seem entirely comfortable with his role as advisor, though he was performing his duties with a great deal of alacrity.

Birsha was about to excuse himself to his antechambers to decompress before settling in for the night, but then he saw *her*. A dream wearing a butterfly dress, her sleeves wings, the body of her dress chitinous layers of color. Sapphire blue pooled between the black thoracic segments, with bits of white and a lighter blue and orange scattered here and there. In strategic spots were a series of yellow dots on both sets of wings. The woman's hair fell in creamy black waves that glistened against the hanging candelabras that sent prisms of light flashing throughout the room. Her mask was one giant butterfly that appeared real as its wings fluttered to and fro. For one brief moment, he drew back, fearing that it was Cricket with one of her studies in entomology. But no, as he looked further, he saw that Cricket was across the room and still wearing that incessant dress made of jewel beetles that made funny clicking sounds.

"Sir? You were in the middle of asking me something?" Siegfried reminded him.

Birsha shook off any thought of leaving, instead turning to Siegfried and saying, "Never mind. I can rest later."

Then without further ado, he made his way toward the woman who had so captivated his imagination, intercepting a galant young man who had just offered her a drink.

"No need for that," Birsha said, bowing deeply to the disguised woman. "I will take care of her needs."

"But—" the man started to say. Then seeing that it was Birsha, he bowed deeply as well and said, "Yes, m'lord."

Birsha took hold of the woman's silk-gloved fingers, so delicate against his palm, her hand fitting perfectly in his, as though it were meant to be.

"And who might you be?" Birsha said, wanting to know everything about her.

"The name's Beatrice." The word rolled off her tongue like Pitcairn honey, the rarest of all honeys, its flavors derived from mango, rose, guava, and passionflower, not to mention lata, a vine grown from India to the Philippines.

"Ah, Beatrice and Birsha. The names have a lovely ring, do they not?"

For one brief moment, he thought he'd seen her quiver, but then she quickly recovered, her smile tentative. From the other end of the room, he saw Siegfried peering over a taller man's head to keep an eye on Birsha.

"Quick, if I am to have any time with you alone, we will have to go to the greenhouse. No one should be there at this time of night."

He hurriedly whisked her out a side door and down a series of stairs and passageways until they reached a covered walkway that would lead them directly to the greenhouses. As a child, he had enjoyed the greenhouses on the rare event that he was brought to the palace. Even then, he had been kept in the background, always introduced as one of the many children brought to the palace for educational purposes, never as Alaric's son. He peered to the right and left, down the snowy grass walkway, searching for the globe that had catapulted through the library dome. But he saw nothing that would indicate the sphere containing his father. Nor had he heard from any of his men.

Once inside the greenhouse, whose lights cast an eerie, golden glow over the newfallen snow, he felt the immediate warmth, the pure fecund odor of rotting leaves and rich soil producing an instant calming effect.

"What is that?" Beatrice pointed to one especially unusual plant.

"That's a rare white heron orchid. See, it looks as though it's flying."

And indeed, its lacy outstretched wings looked like a bird in flight with long white tail feathers trailing in its wake. Each room held different types of flowers, here tropicals, in a separate room those from the desert, and still others meant for colder climes.

"But this is my favorite part of the garden." He led her to where a large pond had been built, and in it, lily pads that looked large enough for a man to walk on. Huge pink flowers offset the lily pads and small frogs dotted the pond while koi dashed out from under the lily pads only to disappear just as quickly.

"It's exquisite." Beatrice appeared to relax for the first time since he'd met her.

"I used to come here as a child. Play hide and seek, only no one came to find me." He held his head down–hadn't meant his words to sound so melancholy. But when he peered up, he could see that she was studying him, as though seeing him in a new light.

"You are Alaric's son, no?"

"Well, yes, sort of, I guess." Suddenly, he felt flustered, having never been allowed to admit his parentage as a child lest someone overhear and punish him. He had never been flustered around anyone, ever. "It's just that I was raised as his heir, but I seldom saw him."

"Oh, I'm sorry," she said. "That must have been horrible."

Birsha shrugged. It was just the way things were, yet if he were being entirely truthful, he had longed for the intimacy that he'd seen shown to other sons of men without the responsibility his father had carried on his mantle.

"My family was just the opposite. We were very close. Only . . . ." She paused, as if unwilling to continue.

"Only?"

She shook her head. "Well, I just supposed most families in the world would be the same. That I would find someone who loved me as I did him." Then realizing she'd said too much, she bowed her head and wiped at a stray tear.

"If someone didn't love you, then it was because they weren't looking close enough, Beatrice," he said, shocked that he'd said something so bold. But far from being taken aback by it, she giggled, a sound that was at once like the tinkling of a bell, and watery.

"You think?"

This time she stared directly into his eyes. Tentatively, he reached for her mask and lowered it in segments, the tenderness of that act more potent than a love tonic, for his heart beat rapidly and his hands shook. When she was finally unmasked, he gasped, for she was more beautiful than he could have ever imagined.

For one brief moment, they stood there, the only sound the burbling of the pond. Then he reached over and kissed her full round lips. The taste of her was more intoxicating than a passion flower in full bloom. For several seconds, their lips lingered, as though she too were savoring the taste of them.

When they parted, he had expected her to appear shy or embarrassed. Instead, she stared fully at him and ran her fingers down the side of his face, her eyes exploring every inch of him.

Who are you, Beatrice? I want to know everything about you.

"Here it is." Nathaniel pointed toward the entrance to the tunnel.

"Hurry!" Hearing the sound of footsteps down the hall, Henry grabbed Brigid's hand while Nathaniel wedged open the trapdoor beneath the richly woven Axminster carpet inside the room he'd been given while in the palace.

"Wait!" Brigid hissed. "We can't leave yet."

Nathaniel and Henry exchanged a look of shock and surprise.

"What do you mean we can't leave?" Henry whispered. "It won't be long before they discover us missing." Henry yanked on Brigid's hand, but she stood firm.

"My locket," she explained, trembling. "I saw it . . . on Tempestous. She has it . . . has my family!"

Henry paused, collapsing in relief when the sound of the person's footsteps passed by Nathaniel's door without anyone entering. Henry licked his lips.

"Look, Brigid." Henry snatched up both of her hands in his. "We'll get your locket, I promise. But not here, not now. We've gotta get out of here while we can. We've met Birsha, and from what I've seen, he's not as bad as his father. We might actually be able to negotiate with this man, but we can't do it if we're hostages. Surely you must understand that."

Certain that Brigid would see reason, Henry gave a nod to Nathaniel, who shimmied down the narrow ladder, Henry on his heels. When Henry reached the bottom of the narrow passageway, he held a hand out to Brigid to help her down. For one brief moment, she knelt on the hard floor, peering down at her own hand as though it had a will all its own.

Then finally, she said, "No! You go ahead." Her breathing was shallow and her hand was shaking. "I'll find the locket and then join you. Wait for me inside the tunnel." She reached down to give Henry's hand a final squeeze.

She pulled the hood up on her dress to hide her face, stood, and shut the trapdoor behind her, thrusting them into darkness. Henry could hear the carpet being replaced and listened as Brigid took off at a run out the door and down the hallway.

"Brigid!" he cried. His voice echoed in the chamber. "Brigid!" He scaled the ladder to go after her.

But before he could reach the top, he felt a hand pulling at his leg, wrestling him from the ladder until he landed "plop!" on the earthen floor of the tunnel. Then something landed on the back of his head and everything went black.

27

Lofgren had been moving at such a breathtaking pace that Winnifred's eyes were growing exhausted from watching him as he strung up one zip line after another among the trees. To keep the guards attention diverted, one of the women, who had a special knack for raising insects of all kinds, let loose a swarm of fireflies that normally winked in and out only during the summer months. Somehow, over the course of the past summer, she had managed to breed fireflies that were adapted to the cold. Watching them now, as they danced across the frozen tundra, little blue lights that lit up the night sky, Winnifred could see the magic in them. It sent shivers of delight racing through her. Even the enslaved women and children, who had appeared like nothing more than walking rags, looked up from their work and giggled at the pure joy of watching them dance. But they were soon sent back to their tasks with the crack of a whip that reminded each of the slaves that their fate was not their own. Their happiness belonged to another who was bent on seeing them destroyed, both in health and spirit.

Winnifred clamped her jaw together as she stood atop the high platform inside the treetops. Though she rarely cried, she fought back the aching swell in her throat.

To think that the new year was just unfolding, and this is what it had to offer her people and Lofgren's as well. Brutality. Suffering. Cruelty. Well, with any luck, that would be over. Tonight. But still, it was a fool's quest to think they could overtake such a large army with a ragtag band of women and a lone elf–though they'd had much help from some of the people in and around the fortress walls. The Resistance, as it was now being called.

Lofgren scooted in front of Winnifred and stopped as though a racer at the finish line. She handed him another zip line along with the carabiner clip and a trolley. Eleanor had come to take Master Clyde's place as he worked out more of the details for tonight's attack, while Elijah and Dele were manning another large fir from which to launch the rescue.

Winnifred handed Lofgren the pulley and lanyard that would act as a harness for those flying back and forth through the forest canopy. Lofgren had even managed to put up several staging platforms and a rope and pulley system so that the slaves could be ferreted out of the fir trees quickly. While hand hewn steps, nothing more than strong twigs really, were pegged into the trees themselves, so that the slaves who were timid of the rope and pulley could climb down to the valley floor with the help of aides, if necessary.

"Have you heard anything from Henry and Brigid?" Winnifred asked the frazzled woman.

Eleanor's dark hair had come out of its bun in stray wisps and her face had lines where there had been none a year ago.

"*Non*! The last anyone saw of them, they were headed for the palace library, *oui*?" She bent forward, lowering her voice. "It is said that an orb of some kind was seen blasting off through the skylight at about the time that Henry and Brigid were in there. You don't suppose they were in it?"

Winnifred frowned, giving Lofgren a harried nod as he raced back to add more zip lines and more platforms, taking only brief moments for food or water throughout the night. She was amazed at how silent he could be when focused like this, for security reasons choosing to mind meld with either her or the other elves who had been chosen as scouts rather than risk speaking aloud.

Normally, Lofgren could be a bit clumsy, and occasionally loud. But tonight he was merely a passing shadow, no more than a hummingbird in flight so that even when one looked, they saw not an elf but a movement out of the corner of one eye.

"I doubt very much that Henry and Brigid were launched from the library in an . . . orb," Winnifred said, pursing her lips. Yet with everything she'd witnessed this past year, she was unsure of anything anymore. Maybe Henry and Brigid *had* been launched into the night sky, for all she knew.

"I had hoped you would say that," Eleanor commiserated, tossing Winnifred a gentle smile. "But what *has* happened to them? We've received no word. Not even a hint."

Winnifred had thought of nothing else. They simply had

to get Henry and Brigid out of the fortress before they launched the rescue or they might never get them back. Worse, the pair would probably bear the brunt of the ruler's disfavor at the realization that he had been bested by an army of women.

"Well, we can't do anything about that now, right-o? They'll turn up. I just know it. If there's any way possible."

For the next half hour, Winnifred and Eleanor finished up their tasks. Now all that was left was to wait until midnight. Then, Brigid or no Brigid, the women would launch their attack and just pray that Henry and Brigid found safety.

When I returned to the ballroom, Birsha and Beatrice were nowhere in sight. Fortunately, no one seemed to notice me in my blue sun and moon gown and my matching mask. I skimmed the table of edible delights as I sought my target, Tempestous, but she, too, was nowhere to be seen.

Where are you, Tempestous?

It would be a long night—longer still, should I land in the gaol. So I grazed, savoring the sumptuous feast. Finger sandwiches with fruit flowers gracing the edges. All manner of breads from which to dip the mutton stew. Pheasant and quail eggs in a variety of mottled colors. Then came the desserts. Minced meat pies filled with fresh venison. Plum puddings and pastries of every kind, one looking amazingly swan-like. I stood, gorging for the night ahead.

Finally, seeing that I was getting nowhere when it came to Tempestous, I asked the woman next to me if she had seen her.

"Oh, aye, M'lady, she's in the hall." She pointed toward an open doorway nearly ten feet in height. "I believe she's speaking with one of the Council members."

"Thank you." I curtseyed slightly. As I passed, I grabbed some of the finger foods for Henry and Nathaniel, wrapped them in napkins, then placed them in a purse that dangled from a chain that wrapped around my narrow waist.

I made my way through the throng of people who had become louder and more boisterous with each passing drink, bumping into several along the way and just missing spilled absinthe or vermouth on my gown. When I finally reached the door, I heard voices on the other side echoing through the marbled hallway. For a moment, I paused and stood closest to the drapes so as not to disturb their discussion.

"Where is that blasted man?"

Tempestous' voice!

A man's deeper bass followed. "He's in the greenhouse with a woman by the name of Beatrice, according to my spies."

My heart stilled. Surely it couldn't be *our* Beatrice in the greenhouse with Birsha. No, it must be someone else with the same name.

"Where is she from?" Tempestous demanded.

"No one knows," the man said. "But she's beautiful. Curly raven hair, skin the color of porcelain. Quite lovely. No wonder Birsha is taken with her. I'll have my people check into her origins."

"See that they do."

I fought down the rising panic in my chest, for they could be describing none other than the woman who had been the bane of Emma's existence since she'd first met Thomas.

"We can't let just anyone near our new ruler," Tempestous chastised.

"I agree," the other man said.

Now I had a new worry, rather than just my locket. Beatrice. But what was she doing here? Sensing that the conversation was coming to a close and time running out, I set thoughts of Beatrice aside as I quickly pulled off a single earring to use as a ruse. Then I marched in and ran smack dab into Tempestous with a harrumph.

"See here, what's the meaning of this?" The woman scowled.

Seeing her so close, her bright fiery red hair looking every bit like a flare against the golden interior of the hallway, her skin so pale as to be almost translucent, I froze.

"Pardon me," I said, my words breathy from fright. "But I seem to have lost an earring. I believe it may have fallen off somewhere around here." While all were inspecting me, I quickly gave my earring a toss onto the edge of her molten hot gown that gave off heat in waves.

Tempestuous leaned forward to inspect my lobes and saw that indeed one earring was missing. Then, as each of them bent to the search, I bumped into her, deftly undoing the clasp at her neck. I slipped my necklace from around her neck, heart pounding in my chest, and slid it into the sleeve of my dress, praying that she hadn't seen me do it.

"What's the meaning of this, you oaf?" Tempestous glared up at me and for a moment I thought she was onto me.

I quickly diverted her attention. "Oh, there's my earring!"

I pointed to the earring at the foot of her dress, then curtseyed politely as I backed toward the outer door. "I'm so sorry to have taken your time."

Then to the words "heathen" and "fop," I scooted off toward the greenhouse, for although I had told Henry I would come straight back, I couldn't leave without trying to bring Beatrice with me.

As Beatrice and Birsha entered the third and final section of the greenhouse, it was like walking through a jungle, the humid loam giving off an intoxicating fragrance that reminded Birsha of his greenhouse back home, only this one was four times the size. Palm trees acted as the canopy, while every nook and cranny dripped with staghorn ferns, rare orchids, some that looked like miniature ballerinas, while others bore a monkey face, some sad, some laughing. And here, cherubs danced around a pot made of the finest marble, their giggles giving them away.

"Sorry about that." Birsha nodded toward the dancing cherubs who were clearly delighted to find a couple roaming through their domain.

Just then, he heard the towering greenhouse doors open and watched as one of the gardeners entered with a metal watering can. He grabbed Beatrice's hand and pulled her toward him.

"I want you all to myself," he said, his thoughts of Alaric and the globe that ascended the night sky receding further and further in his thoughts. "And I know just the place. Come with me. I want to show you my nana's drawing room."

He whisked her past the workman, opening the large doors with a whoosh. Instantly, the warmth of the greenhouse was gone, replaced by a brisk wind that tugged at his shirt as though it had fingers and was trying to draw him back indoors. But he refused to be deterred. Instead, he entered the palace through a side door then rushed through a series of mazes inside the palace, the hallways and rooms so convoluted as to easily become lost, if not familiar with its treachery. Yet, at will, he could recall the location of his grandmother's wing of the palace, for she had been his only real friend inside the fortress walls. Like all other women, she had been tucked away in the farthest reaches of the castle, out of sight and out of mind, as was the custom in such patriarchal societies as his.

"Here!" he said.

They entered a large drawing room that had changed little since he'd last been there. Even his grandmother's smell remained—the odor of jasmine that she bathed in daily. Her lap quilt lay across her well-worn leather chair, a reminder of an earlier time when she'd sat by the fire, crocheting. Beside the chair was a marquetry basket filled with every color of embroidery and thread. The corner of the room was where her loom once sat. She'd purchased only the finest of silk for the loom. The loom that Brigid now owned. His throat suddenly tightened at the thought.

He bent down and opened the basket, lifted out the shimmery threads in too many colors to name: ceylon blue, ochre yellow, peacock red, and many, many more.

"They're beautiful!" Beatrice leaned forward to take a closer look. "Were those your grandmother's?"

"Yes." He bit his lip. "She died before I was able to see her one last time."

He hadn't planned to allow his emotions to shine through, but he couldn't hide the catch in his voice, nor the tremor in his chest.

"You loved her?" Beatrice placed a hand on his shoulder.

He nodded briefly and turned his head to hide the tears that threatened to fall. Tears were never allowed among the nobility, and especially not the newly appointed king. Still, he'd yet to master that particular feat.

"Do you sew?" He hoped to win Beatrice to him, to meld her in some way so as to always be part of his life.

"I do." She trained her eyes on his, as though inspecting them for meaning.

"Aye, then I would like you to have her silk thread." He reached into the basket and chose only the most beautiful strands. Then he searched around for something to place them in.

Seeing his dilemma, Beatrice offered up her reticule, a silk bag with a beaded butterfly motif to match her dress. She opened the clasp to show him the interior, empty except for a small brush made of tortoise shell and porcupine quills.

Carefully, he laid the precious threads into her reticule and closed the clasp, her face so near to his that he could smell the sweet scent of lavender in her hair, imagine the moistness of her full lips. He reached forward and kissed her fervently, never wanting this moment to end, to keep her by his side at any cost.

To forget his years of loneliness, the forgotten child of a man of great standing. A mere wisp of a memory in the eyes of a man who sought power above all else. No, this was the result of years spent waiting. Waiting to be noticed. Remembered. Waiting for his time to shine. That time was now, here, with the woman of his dreams. And in one moment of inspiration, he saw her—saw *them,* side by side, leading the nation. He would have her. He knew that now. A surety came over him—one that couldn't be quelled. She was his. Now and forever more. He pulled away to look at her thoroughly—her lovely black ringlets so like raven's wings, her skin as smooth and creamy as that of a porcelain doll. Yes, she would be his. The thought made him laugh until tears bubbled up and he feared she might think him mad.

"What?" she demanded. "What is it? Why do you laugh?"

But he couldn't put his feelings into words. Yet then, with a snap of his fingers, it came to him fully formed. The way he felt about her in that instant.

"I love you, Beatrice. And I want you to be with me, always."

28

When I opened the massive greenhouse door, the humidity washed over me like a blanket, enfolding me in warmth and comfort. The air was rich with possibility, and yet I was placing myself in great danger by coming here. Had I been thinking clearly, I would be down that tunnel now with Henry and Nathaniel, for it wasn't only my life I was putting in danger by attempting to find Beatrice and bring her with me; I was risking theirs as well. And, yet, I would be remiss if I thought only of my own skin, when Beatrice might be in mortal danger.

I slipped as silently as I could into the greenhouse, the pungent smells reminding me of childhood and all things good in the world. The greenhouse had been a haven for me, a place where I could wander, unencumbered by the cares of adults. A world I now understood could often be cruel. Perhaps even as a child, I had understood that in some reptilian part of my brain.

Yet as I moved through the greenhouses, I found no one, least of all Beatrice, until at last I came upon the caretaker of this place.

"Have you seen a woman, black hair, pale skin?" I asked in as quiet a voice as possible, though if they'd been anywhere in the greenhouse, surely I would have found them by now.

"Aye, I have." The man set down his watering can on the moist gravel. "They were headed for the king's mother's drawing room."

"Can you give me directions?" I gulped in air, fearful lest I become lost in the many hallways that ran off at crazy angles that would be daunting for the most intrepid explorer.

The caretaker paused for a moment. Then, as though coming to a decision, he nodded. "Perhaps I should take you there. So you don't get lost." He offered her a wan smile.

"Thank you so much."

I curtseyed slightly, appreciating all that he was doing for me by taking time out of his busy schedule to help even as I worried that I might be naive. That perhaps he had other motives.

Soon we were winding our way through one palace hallway after another. And though I tried to commit to memory every twist and turn, I feared I was becoming lost. How would I ever find my way back to Nathaniel's room and the hidden trapdoor just beneath the rug? I fought down a whirlwind of panic. I would just have to hope I could find it.

"This is the north wing?" I asked in as small a voice as possible, for here the rooms were quiet, as though guarding against silent intruders.

"Yes," the laconic man said, with a slight bow.

"So the rooms where guests stay . . . they would be where?" I paused to catch my breath and to orient myself to north-south, east-west.

"That way." The small man pointed southwest.

I closed my eyes in relief. So long as I followed the southwest axis, I should be okay. Now, to extricate Beatrice from whatever machination she had found herself in.

We once again set off at a trot, the elderly man surprisingly agile for one his age. At last we arrived at a room, and even before we came alongside the door, I could hear voices, one of them Beatrice's, for I would recognize her voice anywhere.

"I will be on my way then, ma'am." The man gave a slight bow. Then he was off, leaving me to figure out a way to make my presence known to Beatrice, but not to Birsha.

But before I could come to a decision about how to accomplish said task, my decision was made for me when my locket rolled out of my sleeve and onto the floor with a metal clang.

"Halt! Who goes there?" Birsha shouted.

Heart thrumming in my chest, I bent down to pick it up where it had landed at the door's opening. When I stood, I was looking straight into two pairs of eyes, one of them questioning, the other fiercely angry.

"Brigid!" Birsha's eyes narrowed. "Why are you here, and what happened to the guards?"

"The guard was indisposed," I admitted with more than my fair share of nerves. "And I have come for Beatrice."

They could wait no longer before proceeding with the rescue. The closer it got to midnight, the more Winnifred knew they had to act before someone discovered their presence. Already they had many close calls that had sent her blood racing, her nerves taut. Lofgren rushed in and paused next to her, mind melding with her to avoid detection.

"It's time, Winnifred. I'm sorry about Henry and Brigid."

Winnifred could only nod, her heart in her throat, squeezing off any ability to speak.

"Should I give the signal to begin?" He encouraged her with soulful eyes that glistened in the moonlight.

Winnifred had already received the news that the women warriors were tucked away in the forest just outside the front gate of the Jackal's fortress. The masked gala had been fortuitous, keeping most busy, while many were said to have imbibed. It hadn't hurt that Master Clyde had someone spike the punch—a mix of spices, citrus fruits, and rum or brandy—with valerian root, a known sedative. The women warriors, with Jocelyn and Gertrude at the lead, would hold the main gate, preventing most from escaping, while Kahwihta had been true to her word and had not only called the Mohawk and Oneida nations together, but had brought the bears with them. They would be responsible for drawing the attention of the captors so that Lofgren and a select group of people could swoop in on the zip lines, while Hannah, Yesimeh, Elijah, and Dele, would man the stations and help usher the slaves down to waiting arms below. Then, the bears would circle around while the Native warriors kept the slave keepers busy. Winnifred and the others would then collect the rescued captives while a team of women warriors would take them to the cave to stock up on clothing and food before returning them to their homeland. Winnifred had given explicit orders to take those enslaved home, while those at the manor had already been informed, thanks to Phinney, who had been quickly dispatched. The Bookbinders would be prepared for the influx. In the meantime, Phinney had left the miniature loom behind.

Before the assault, Winnifred had queried the loom and was both puzzled and amazed by what she saw, for it was black–black as pitch. Black as coal, with only a hazy aura around it that didn't bode well. What could it possibly mean, she wondered? Brigid might know, but Brigid wasn't here to decipher the loom. Winnifred had no time to ponder its meaning because time was slipping away and the last of the ziplines had been attached.

"Well?" Lofgren asked upon his return, his urgency evident despite his amazing calm.

"Let's go," Winnifred said.

And with that, the campaign began.

"Look, Beatrice, I need to get you out of here. I'm not leaving without you." I slipped my locket once again into my sleeve.

The drawing room was large, filled with an overstuffed

chair and a fireplace with two andirons that looked like dragons, their golden eyes shining off and on like a lighthouse beacon. I gulped back my fear. They appeared as though they might come to life at any moment and begin flying around the room.

"How do you know Beatrice?" Birsha turned suspicious eyes to her. "Do you know this woman?"

Beatrice's pale skin had faded to an ashy gray and she licked her lips as though searching for an answer. In the end, all she could do was nod, but I read the terror in her eyes.

"Come on, Beatrice." I held my hand out to her to urge her to come to me, but Birsha grabbed her hand before she could make a move.

"She's not going anywhere!" He tightened his grip. "And neither are you."

"Guards!" he yelled. Too late, he seemed to realize that there were none at hand despite the customary protocol.

Fear gripped me as I reached for Beatrice, who finally came to life. But Birsha held fast to her, the braid on his jaw swinging like a pendulum, tick-tock, tick-tock.

I knew I had but a moment to rescue her, but before I could set loose my plan, Beatrice threw up a hand. "Wait! I have a proposition."

Her chest heaved up and down as she spoke and I feared the poor girl would pass out, not that I was in any better shape to confront our nemesis.

"Here!"

Beatrice withdrew what looked like a map, but which was actually a schematic of . . . . I bent over to look. Of a railway and a design for a train, a new mode of transportation that had yet to be built, but which Winnifred had assured me was just on the horizon.

"Such a thing doesn't exist." Birsha puzzled his brow. "And why give it to me? There's a trap here, surely."

"No trap." But Beatrice's shaking hand told a different story as the schematic rattled like a dusty old corn stalk set upon by the wind. "See here, whoever owns this will own the kingdom."

I scarcely breathed as she spoke, but I could see that she had his attention.

"I give it to you in exchange for our lives. Our freedom."

He paused, as though considering. "And what's to say this can even work? That the two of you won't be long gone and I will be left with a useless scrap of paper. And why are you here, anyway?"

The volume of his voice increased with each successive question, his eyes dancing with anger that he had been so deceived.

"To find out more about you," I admitted, for we'd come this far. "We wanted to know if you were like your father or someone we could negotiate with. Someone who would see the virtue of two kingdoms, ours and yours."

He began stroking his braid, done in an infinity knot, his eyes narrowing. "Two kingdoms." The words rolled around on his tongue like a bad taste and he grimaced at the very idea.

Taking a quick gasp of air, I determined to press on. "We've learned all we need. Now let us go and you will have your schematic. Surely a man of your caliber will be able to find men to build your railway."

"How do I know that everything is here?" He shook his

head. "No! I shall have your schematic and the two of you as well." He laughed at how easily the problem had been solved for him. "Guards!" he yelled once more. "Where are those blasted men?"

Beatrice, whose breathing caused me to fear she might faint dead away, held out a hand. "No! Wait!"

Both Birsha and I paused to listen to what Beatrice had to say.

"Keep me, but let Brigid go. I will be your collateral." Her voice shook. "And I wasn't lying about the things I said earlier, though I may not have told you everything."

"Oh?" Birsha appeared more interested in what she had to say now.

"I . . . I was raised with a family, but most of my life was spent in a boarding school. I was lonely, growing up." Here, her face cascaded as though drawn down by gravity. "So, we are a lot alike, you and I. For years I've searched for a way to feel relevant, to feel loved, I suppose."

The vulnerability in her eyes was so palpable that even I could see that it was true, that indeed she had been locked away and lonely.

Birsha didn't seem to know what to do with this new information, but I could see that Beatrice had struck a chord with the man who peered deeply into her eyes. For several moments, we all stood in silence as Birsha decided what to do next. Finally, he came to a decision with a short jerk of his head.

"You can go, Brigid of the manor. But you will leave Beatrice here . . . *as my wife*."

I gasped. "No!" I lunged toward her, but she backed away

and closed her eyes as if coming to a decision, too.

When at last she opened them, she said, "It's okay, Brigid. I'll be fine, won't I, Birsha?"

He studied her eyes and I could see that despite the horror he represented for our people, that there had been a connection between the two, a deep and profound one. But how? How could this have happened? I felt a knot forming in my stomach.

"It's okay, Brigid. Go! While you still can."

I paused, not wanting to leave her but not knowing what to do.

"Go, Brigid!" Beatrice repeated, her pleading more urgent now.

I took one last look at her and nodded, then I turned on my heels and exited the room, only to discover two guards running down the hall shouting. For one brief moment I thought I was to be arrested, but they passed me by and entered the drawing room. I paused to hear what they had to say before continuing at a run. But the words I heard sent a chill racing through my very loins, for something was clearly afoot. Time was running out.

"Birsha! You must hurry. We have found your father and he has released the Chessmen. And there are warrior women at the front gate. We are at war!"

29

The wait was over. It was as if the very earth had erupted at the same moment. Lofgren and Elijah, along with two other women, zip-lined across the darkened sky, the only light coming from the moon that appeared bluish and bruised. Winnifred stood on one of the platforms high into the treetops, ready to take her turn in the next wave. From her perch, she could see everything. The front gates were overrun with women on horseback. Her and Brigid's warriors. While the Oneida and Mohawk war whoops, coming from the direction of the work camp, kept the attention away from the incoming bears, who were scattering the guards in every direction as they ran for their lives. Most of the bears stopped just long enough to pick up women and children, then lumber off into the forest toward the cave where the rescued slaves would be cleaned up, fed, and then whisked off toward home. In the meantime, Lofgren and his crew whizzed through the canopy out into the opening, gathering other children and female slaves, while at the same time arming those men left behind.

Before Winnifred could react, Lofgren had returned with his cargo, an elderly woman who appeared stooped and frail after the backbreaking labor in temperatures no one should have to endure, much less a woman in her state. Winnifred undid the woman's harness, while Lofgren did the same, then shoved herself into the empty harness, taking with her the other empty harness to be filled with yet another survivor. Speaking not a word, she pushed off with her feet and was soon racing through the night sky. The feeling she experienced as the wind rushed by her was both exhilarating and terrifying. Before she had time to think too much about it, her feet touched ground and she began loading a middle-aged man who was as light as a child. The gravity of what had happened to him set her emotions plummeting, but she would dwell on that later. For now, she had to get him to safety.

Everywhere, arrows whizzed over her, one landing just short of her, another causing her to duck to keep from being hit.

"Hurry!" she whispered. But the man was too frail to cinch his own harness. She set his trembling hands aside and fumbled with the harness until at last she heard a click. With a raise of her hand, the zipline went in reverse, a clever process that Lofgren had yet to explain.

All around her, men and Jackals alike, who had been mustered out into the night and who were in various stages of dress, picked up either musket or arrow and fought savagely to secure the freed slaves from their rescuers. But both the natives and the women's army, along with every other person who had joined the Resistance, fought just as hard to hold them off.

With relief, Winnifred made it to the platform and released her harness, while Lofgren freed the prisoner who was weak with hunger, exhaustion, and cold. Just then, she heard a loud thumping noise and the ground shook, nearly knocking them out of the tree.

"What is it?" Winnifred quailed.

"I don't know," Lofgren answered, in mind meld.

They couldn't wait to find out. They needed to get the last of the men and women to freedom.

"Wait!" Beatrice ran after me even as Birsha came roaring past me to see what all the commotion was about. But not before he'd set a man to guard his newly beloved Beatrice.

When Birsha was out of earshot, Beatrice handed me her purse. "Take this."

"I don't understand." I searched her eyes for some hint of meaning.

"To remember me by. Open it. Please, hurry!"

I did as asked, peering inside the beaded butterfly purse only to discover the most precious of silk threads. But still I didn't understand.

"For your loom." She placed my hands around the gift and cupped them with hers.

Then she hugged me with a fierceness that surprised me. When she pulled back, her eyes were glistening.

"Don't ever forget me, Brigid, promise?"

"I promise," I said, realizing how far we'd both come from that first meeting over a year ago.

For several seconds, we stood staring at each other with compassion and caring. But then the palace rocked with a thunderous roar. *What on earth is that?*

"Go!" she cried. The guard pulled her away from me, pushing her toward the open room. "Go!" she yelled, louder still.

It took no more convincing. I turned on my heels and began running down first one hallway, then another, the sounds growing louder with each step until an especially loud roar and stamping sent me skidding to the floor in a swirl of motion. I knocked into a wall, my ego more bruised than my body. Everywhere around me, men and women came running through doors, shouting, each hoping to make an escape.

I have to find Henry.

In all the ruckus, I had become turned around and no longer knew which way was north, which way south. I attempted to stand, and grabbed the sleeve of a passing reveler, her bird mask askew so that one blue eye showed above her mask.

"How do I find the guest quarters?" I pleaded.

Though she attempted to flee, I held her sleeve, refusing to let go until she told me.

"That way!" She pointed with her chin.

"Thank you," I said. But she was already gone, disappearing into a crowd of people that muscled their way in every direction, no one clear which way was safe, which represented danger.

Though I skirted the gilded hallway walls, more than once I was dragged to my knees by the fleeing throng of people. At last I saw what appeared to be Henry's chambers. Now, if I could just locate Nathaniel's. I kept up the search.

There!

I ran toward it, but the press of the crowd left me no doubt I would be crushed if I didn't escape soon. I reached up and twisted the knob, my hand shaking from the effort. It seemed as though it took forever before it finally gave way and I was able to roll into the room. Unfortunately, several others had as well.

"Get off me," I said to one portly gentleman whose fall had nearly taken the breath out of me. "Please," I added, remembering my manners.

The other person on her knees must have been his wife for she crawled to him and cooed over him, despite my predicament. After several moments of struggle, I was finally clear and sat up, gasping for air.

"This is my room, please leave."

The woman looked at her husband, while the other woman who had fallen, finally opened her eyes with a blink and peered around as though wondering where on earth she had landed and why she was lying on her back.

"Is it safe to go out?" the wife asked. Her delicately coiffed hair had fallen into shambles, her lipstick askew.

But before she and her husband could come to a decision, the thunderous movements that had set everyone afloat like some great dam breaking after a tsunami began again, making the decision for them.

"Get up!" the wife cried.

Both her husband and the other woman rose first to a
sitting position, then to their knees, and finally to their feet.
In the hallway, the melee had subsided while people struggled
to stand. It gave me just enough time to open the door and
send all three packing. By the time I was able to shut the door,
the thunderous movement was once again afoot and I had to
shove with all my might to close the door before some other
unsuspecting soul landed in Nathaniel's room.

As soon as I had the door shut and locked, I paused to
catch my breath. I eyed the red Aubergine rug. It represented
safety, if only Henry had waited for me.

Quickly, I scrambled to the rug and shoved it aside, my
hands fumbling with the trapdoor. Finally, I was able to wedge
it open, just enough light cascading below to see that Henry
had indeed waited for me. He and Nathaniel both. But then I
saw what I hadn't seen before. Somehow, Nathaniel had hog-
tied Henry's wrists and legs. No wonder he hadn't attempted to
rescue me.

Just then, I heard a crack as people were shoved against
the door in a loud exodus. And another. Soon, they would be
flooding into the room and our escape would be for naught.

"Grab a hold of the rug as you climb down!" Henry said,
for although his hands and feet were tied, his mouth had been
left free to berate the gentleman who had stymied him from
coming after me. "Now shut the door."

I watched as the trapdoor fell with a thud, entombing
us in a dark underground cavern. But at least the rug was
still covering our exit. Then the dam burst and the floodgates
opened, the sound of screams and cries echoing in the chamber

above. It was time to make our escape. But how, in such abject darkness?

First Beatrice's deception, and now this! Birsha's feet flew as he chased after the Jackal guard who made haste through the hallways, taking the back ways not open to the general public. Still, he could hear the screams and movements of the throngs of people who must be fleeing the ballroom.

Just then, the Chessmen began another series of moves that shook the building.

Birsha felt the jolts in each of his joints as the giant Chessmen made their moves across the fortress, each footfall so loud and so heavy that it was as if an earthquake had befallen them and these were the aftershocks. As he passed each room, he could hear things falling, glass breaking, trinkets shattering, some of them priceless.

From behind him, the dragon andirons had come to life and were now flying through the hallways, their wings touching either side, their screeches forcing Birsha to cover his ears. As they neared, he ducked to the floor, praying they wouldn't choose that moment to breathe fire, scorching both the guard and him to a crisp.

What on earth?

When the dragons had passed, the guard scrambled to his feet and began to run, Birsha following suit. Before the Jackal guard could turn a corner that would lead to an outside door, Birsha grabbed the man's shoulder to force him to halt.

"Why have the Chessmen been released?" Birsha demanded.

The man looked at him as if he were daft. "Haven't you heard? The Bookbinders and their ilk have come to release the prisoners."

"From the gaol?" When the guard didn't answer right away, Birsha shook him.

"The gaol? No, of course not, from the labor camp."

Despite the rumbles, followed by screams and shouts that seemed to be coming from everywhere all at once, Birsha was cocooned in a bubble of silence.

"Labor camp?" he said at last. "What labor camp?"

The guard cocked his head. "Why, *your* labor camp, sir." He spoke slowly, as though speaking to a simpleton.

Birsha growled.

"Why wasn't I informed of the labor camp?" Birsha demanded, shoving the man against the wall.

"I . . . I don't know." The guard cowered, appearing repentant even though he'd had no responsibility in the matter. "I suppose because they wanted you to settle into your position first."

"Who?" Birsha realized he was shouting, but he couldn't hide the fury settling over him like a moist fog.

"Why, the Council."

Birsha let the man go, spent.

"How could I have been so stupid?" he murmured. He had much to learn, apparently. "And where are these prisoners from?" Birsha ground his teeth together in disgust at the current predicament he found himself in.

"Everywhere . . . all of the villages surrounding the Bookbinder's manor. Your father ordered them captured to use to build our roads and our munitions storehouse."

"In these freezing temperatures? Have they been well kept?"

The Jackal looked at him as though he were a cyclops who had grown two heads. "Of course not, sire. They are hungry and in rags."

Birsha ran his fingers through his hair, something he rarely did unless extremely agitated. "And now the Bookbinders have come to collect them?"

"In a manner of speaking, sire."

Before Birsha could get another word out, he felt a tremor beneath him and heard a crash of yet another priceless heirloom falling off a mantel or a wall in a room down the hallway.

"Is there any way of stopping the Chessmen?" Birsha knew that he couldn't afford to stall much longer.

"Not unless you can call your father off," the Jackal said. "But that's highly unlikely. It's rumored he has been cursed to live out his life inside a globe. As long as the globe is open, he can still act within it."

Birsha growled.

"In the meantime, the women warriors are storming the gate while the Mohawks and the Oneidas have been creating a diversion so that the bears will have time to free the slaves with the help of an elf and other women warriors."

Birsha's head began to throb. He ducked as one of the dragons returned, searching for an exit. Birsha decided to humor the beast before it set the building on fire.

He took off at a run and yelled, "Follow me."

The side door was only a few yards away, its opening big enough for a beast such as this one. No sooner had he opened the medieval-looking door than the dragon flew out, releasing a flame that set the night on fire. Within moments, the second one followed suit and was gone to wherever dragons went to when a world leapt off its axis.

"Hurry! We must find Alaric," Birsha said. "In the meantime, give the order to release the prisoners. This is not our fight."

"Wh–? But sire, you will be seen as weak."

"It is *my* kingdom!" he shouted. "Mine and mine alone." And yet he knew it wasn't true. Not yet, anyway. But if he fought, he wanted to fight on a fair playing field.

"Just do it!" he screamed. Then he set off to find his father. But before he even made it to the corner of the garden walkway, he saw his first chess piece, a giant knight with a sword that whizzed close to his ear.

He threw himself to the ground and rolled before the knight speared him through like a boar on a skewer. Then he ran, the sabaton of the knight's boots threatening to crush him should he fall beneath its shadow.

But as he ran, he discovered that the order he'd just given would never meet its intended target, for there lay the Jackal, his body twisted against the frozen snow, his eyes facing the night sky as though sightlessly witnessing the end of an era.

What in God's name has Alaric unleashed?

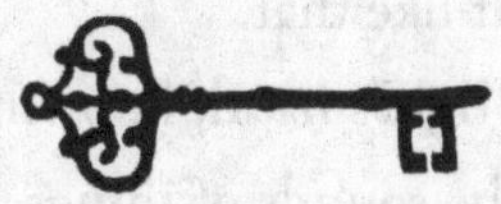

Once Nathaniel had freed him, Henry launched himself at Brigid, relieved to see her alive. He kissed her face, her eyes, her lips, feeling the full moistness of them. Then he drew her into his arms, determined to never let her go again. He should have made it official long ago, made her his forever and ever. He would not make that mistake again.

Nathaniel tugged at Henry's sleeve. He had created a lantern of sorts using the glow worms from the cavern just beyond this leg of the tunnel and an actual lantern, whose wick had long since been eaten up by bugs and time.

"We've got to get going through the tunnel. Now!" Nathaniel added for emphasis.

Before he could speak further, the whole tunnel rumbled and bits of debris fell from the underground walls hewn out of rock and dirt. Henry grabbed Brigid's hand and the three began running. All around them he heard the sounds of mortar, followed by chunks of dirt rolling off the ceilings and sides of the tunnel, covering them in dust and debris.

"We've got to get to the outside before the women are gone," Nathaniel said, his voice echoing off the walls.

"What women?" Brigid demanded. "My warriors?"

"They're freeing the slaves," Nathaniel explained. "But we must keep moving or we'll miss the women."

"They're here?" she cried excitedly.

"They *were* here," Nathaniel corrected. "They may be gone by now, which is why we need to move quickly. And why you shouldn't have taken off like that."

Henry squeezed Brigid's hand, knowing that her heart was in the right place. By the sounds of things, all above them was chaos. He could hear her teeth begin to chatter at the cold, so he stopped long enough to remove an outer coat that he'd grabbed at the last minute before heading to Nathaniel's room and the tunnel below.

"Here, put this on."

She took only a moment to think about it, then shrugged into it, thanking him profusely.

They continued on, coming round the corner into the cavern that housed the worms. Brigid paused to peer up in wonder at the slimy blue gobs of goo that hung from the cavern's ceiling, glowing like one gigantic cabalabra.

"What are they?" she breathed in wonder.

"*Arachnocampa luminosa*," Henry explained. "A fungus gnat. Or, more aptly, glowworms."

"They look like melted candle wax, only lit up . . . and blue." Brigid stood, mouth open as one began to drop.

Henry grabbed her to him before it could land on her with a plop.

"They're bioluminescent . . . and poisonous to small creatures," he explained. "So keep your mouth closed and let's get moving."

Brigid hunched down and followed him closely, when all of a sudden one glowworm began to edge toward her. She shoved herself up against the interior of the cave to keep it from landing on her, when without warning, the cave wall gave way with a loud metallic grinding noise.

"Look out!" Nathaniel said, but it was too late.

Brigid fell backwards and felt the wall give, slightly.

"What is it?" Henry demanded.

Brigid turned and felt around the edges. "A door, I think."

"A door to what?" Nathaniel asked.

Behind a bit of moss growing on the wall, Brigid found a keyhole. "I think it's a hidden door to a hidden room."

At first, Henry didn't connect what she was telling them, then a thought occurred to him. The key that had fallen through the grates near the entrance to their chambers above when they had first arrived! Surely, it couldn't be for this room. Yet he had to try. He put the key in the lock. At first, it wouldn't turn, having rusted a bit. He searched around for something to loosen it, but all he had was his own saliva. To both Nathaniel and Brigid's horror, he spit on the key and thrust it into the lock once more. For a second, it stuck in the lock, but with added pressure, the key finally turned with a loud click, the door opening into a large underground room that was brightly lit . . . by more glowworms. Not only did a giant candelabra of them hang from the ceiling over a floating table, the walls were lined with them so that the whole room had an eerie blue glow.

"What is this place?" She reached out a hand to Henry who hoisted her up.

"I don't know," Henry said, his voice echoing off the walls.

They stood there staring, Henry wondering at the magic that surely created what they were witnessing. Brigid was the first to speak.

"It looks like a boardroom of some sort."

"With a floating table," Henry said.

"And floating chairs." Brigid marveled at them, then walked over to inspect them more closely. She waved a hand beneath and above both the table and chairs. "There are no strings attached that I can see."

"Who do you suppose the room belongs to?" Nathaniel took a seat in one of the glass chairs.

"I don't know." Brigid peered down at herself in the glass table, then drew back with a gasp.

"What is it?" Henry came to stand next to her only to pull away in shock.

Nathaniel leaned forward and he, too, let out a cry of surprise. "What are they?"

"Creatures of some sort," Brigid said in a trembling voice. "I can't even describe them, they are so hideous, but I think one may be Tempestous, the woman who stole my locket. Do you think they can see us?" She ventured a quick look back.

"I don't think so." Henry leaned over to stare at the portion of the table closest to him. "My creature looks the same as before, except it was green and now it has turned a vivid blue. Maybe the images are like place cards for the monsters who sit here."

"Maybe," Brigid agreed. "I don't know about you, but this place gives me the creeps."

"Right," Nathaniel said. "Let's get out of here before whoever was here returns."

They hurried out the way they'd come, each of them no doubt wondering what the room was used for and whether those above ground knew of its existence. The creatures reminded Henry of the Council members he'd seen, and yet most of the ones mirrored in the tabletop were not part of the Council, or at least not that he was aware.

Up above, the screams and rumbling had died down, the

lack of movement more ominous to Henry than the sounds that had preceded it.

"What do you think has happened up above?" Brigid said, as they raced down the corridor, the smell of dirt and decay all around them.

"I don't know," Henry admitted, his breathing shallow despite the exertion. "But I have a bad feeling we're about to find out."

Winnifred felt as though her arms might give out, she was so tired from the exertion of ziplining frightened men, women, and children out of the line of fire. To the north, the Mohawks and Oneidas whooped and hollered, their faces done up in war paint, the feathers from their war bonnets encasing their foreheads and trailing down behind their backs, flailing in the wind as they drove their horses forward. Some threw tomahawks, while others shot arrows. Still others had guns. Winnifred just prayed that they hit their intended targets, rather than the few healthier slaves who had remained behind to help the others.

The battle taking place toward the main gate had died down, but whether as a result of the women retreating or the Jackals, she didn't know. All she could be sure of was that the bears had ferried most of the women and children out of the fire zone, and were escaping to the south through a centuries old path known only to the bears and the tribes. The first path would take them to the caves for provisions. Then, the former slaves would divide into groups that would each go their own way. The elves who had been taken were mostly adults, though their slightly reduced size made them appear more like teenagers than men. They had been given horses, riding in pairs so that the horses still available could carry the remaining few to the south.

All across the valley, bodies lay strewn against the moonlight. For those of the slaves who moved, native women ran forward with travoises and loaded them onto the hides, then horses carried them away, presumably to be attended to by their healers.

At last, Winnifred reached the landing with the last of the remaining slaves, a young man in his early twenties, but for all of that, he looked like little more than a scarecrow, his forehead large and his cheeks concave from an ongoing lack of food. Winnifred's throat tightened. Reaching into her pouch for the pemmican she kept close at hand, she handed it to him. He took it gratefully.

"Thank you," he said through tears that went unshed.

"No need for thanks. Just leave here while you can." She hugged him tightly, then lowered the platform for those too weak to climb down the tree. But before she could get him safely to the ground, the loud rumbling began again in earnest.

"What the—" She didn't finish her sentence because just then, from behind the fortress walls came an army of . . . *Chessmen.* Pawns arrived in the first wave. Then rooks and bishops and knights, the king and queen presumably left behind for safety. The Mohawk and Oneida scattered, grabbing up the last of the fallen and racing away in all directions as one brave warrior taunted the Chessmen to give the others time to escape.

"Lofgren," she murmured beneath her breath. He was still out there. In danger.

At long last, Lofgren returned, his charge less emaciated than the rest, having arrived at the camp only recently. When they had him safely on his way by horseback along with the other survivor, Lofgren turned to Winnifred.

"We did it," he cried, snapping her up in his arms.

"We did at that," she said. But they had no time to celebrate, as the Chessmen were even now headed their way, the earth rumbling beneath them.

"Master Clyde is down below. We'd better hurry!"

Winnifred forced a smile even as her heart felt as though it might give way. "Right-o, let's go."

And with that, they rappelled down the last remaining rope kept for just such a purpose—a quick escape. Within seconds they were on the forest floor, the former exhilaration of speeding through the air gone, replaced by the ominous footfalls of the Chessmen, who were now so close they appeared like skyscrapers amid the canopy of fir trees.

Master Clyde was waiting for them at the bottom along with the time machine, which had been dragged into the open. According to Master Clyde, the sprites, who had been left behind at the cavern for fear of making too much noise, had been called into action when it was clear that time was slipping away for a quick exit.

He wrapped them up in a giant bearhug for no more than a second.

"The horses are all gone," he said, steam rising from his

mouth due to the bitter cold. "Your only hope is the time machine. You'd better go."

And indeed, the sprites had already climbed aboard her invention and were chattering excitedly amongst themselves and making an unholy racket that had the Chessmen looking their way.

Winnifred had no time to think. She grabbed Lofgren's hand and jumped in. Immediately, the wheel began to turn and the time machine began to spin. Slower at first, then faster and faster until the Chessmen and Master Clyde had gone from a simple blur to an inky void. Then stars. Thousands of them. Their movements so fast that Winnifred could see their arc in the night sky.

"What of Brigid and Henry, and Master Clyde?" Winnifred sniffled to hold back tears as time flew by them in a shower of sparks.

"Don't worry, Winnifred. We'll return soon and we'll find them. And when we do, we will free them." Lofgren wrapped his arms around Winnifred, holding her tight, the warmth emanating from him a balm to her battered soul. She prayed that Master Clyde, Eleanor, and the others would be okay with them gone.

"Thank you, Lofgren." Her heart hammered in her throat as they braved the cold. The unknown.

"For what?" he asked, bending forward to view the side of her face.

"For everything," she said. Then suddenly time seemed to slow, the time machine sputtering as though coming to a halt. "For absolutely everything."

30

They were gone. I could feel it in my heart of hearts. The women had left, leaving us to fend for ourselves. Nonetheless, I raced through the tunnel, urging both Henry and Nathaniel on. I was in such a hurry that I hadn't noticed the others had stopped until I heard a whistle and turned around in time to see Henry nod toward a hidden opening. I threw on the brakes and skidded to a halt, nearly twisting my ankle as I turned to race back toward them.

"We're here," Henry explained.

"Where?" I asked.

"You'll see," Nathaniel said.

He walked towards what appeared to be no more than a slight recess in the wall of the tunnel. Confused, I followed, but when I moved forward I could see that the wall was merely an optical illusion that was replaced by a stairway. Steps ran upward to what could only be another trapdoor that led inside yet another house or barn.

And indeed, we lifted the door, a rug above it just as there had been in the previous location, but this opening led to a small room even by ordinary standards.

"Where are we?" I whispered.

Nathaniel pushed past me up the stairs to freedom. Carefully, I tiptoed upward, peering into the room before taking the leap onto the cold wooden floor. The noise must have drawn someone's interest because the door cracked open, and in popped an elderly woman, a second woman about the same age trailing her.

"You made it!" The first woman clapped with delight. "We were hoping you had escaped that horrible place!"

"We certainly did," the other woman said, her voice crackling with age.

Henry, who was just now plopping onto the floor of the room, shook his head. "Wait! I don't understand. If the women had this trapdoor all along, why did you have me enter the tunnel another way?"

Nathaniel merely smiled. "Think about it, Henry. If anyone had been in the tunnel, they would have seen us exit the stairway and the women would have been in danger. But there was no one save us in the tunnel when we returned. Their safety is paramount."

"You're a good man, Nathaniel," the first woman said, patting his back. "Now come!" She ushered us into the next room with a sweep of her hand.

We dutifully followed orders. Inside the main drawing

room were two comfy chairs strewn with knitted blankets and a fire that felt inviting after such a long time in the frigid tunnel. I immediately stood in front of it, as did the others, each of us warming our hands with relish.

But whatever comfort we'd hoped to maintain would be sorely lacking, because the first woman grabbed my hand, and with a throaty laugh, said, "Your chariot awaits!"

The other woman giggled. "It's really just a traveling carriage," she said. "But you'd best hurry. All of the women warriors are gone, as are the bears. A band of the Oneida and the Mohawks are keeping the wounded safe. All the rest have fled from the giant Chessmen."

"Chessmen?" I cupped my hands over my mouth to blow warmth into them.

She spent the next few minutes explaining that Alaric had unleashed them on the warriors, including Winnifred and a half elf, half human.

I tried to wrap my head around everything I had learned.

"Now," the second old woman said, "you must be going, mustn't she, sister?"

"Yes, you must," the other woman agreed.

"Wait! Won't we be sitting ducks?" I felt certain we would be cannon fodder should we go out without any protection.

"Not to worry." The oldest of the two winked, her pink sweater sagging over her slim shoulders. "We have our secrets, too."

Before I could ask any more questions, she opened the door into the frigid night air, snow beginning to fall again in earnest. Oil street lamps lit up the night, and lanterns from those few people left walking the streets. The snow provided an eerie blue brightness that made it feel like a cross between day and night.

We climbed into the carriage and said a hurried goodbye, thanking the two women for everything. Then we drove off into the blue light of moonlight, the freshly fallen snow crunching beneath the carriage wheels. Would the Jackals open the gates for us? I didn't know. I just had to trust the people who had prepared the way, and hope that nothing went awry.

Birsha rolled to one side, the knight slamming his sword into the snow where he'd lain just moments before. Fortunately, he rammed it so deeply into the ground that it gave Birsha the few seconds he would need to escape, but to where? He saw the greenhouse just yards away. The door was large—big enough for the knight to get through. Birsha would need something to jam against the doorway, something heavy. His feet flew. Never had he been so swift on his feet. But as he neared the door, he heard the massive knight let out a huge metallic groan, then set out after him, his footsteps slow and clumsy. And yet the beast was so large that he was on Birsha in a matter of moments. Birsha tugged at the door, praying that it would open.

Time stood still and it was as if everything, including sound, had slowed so that the knight's groans sounded like a water wheel coming loose from its rotating shaft, the noise spinning toward him in a cacophony of sound.

He gripped the door and pulled with all his might. Tonight, the door felt extraordinarily heavy, and still he pulled.

At long last, the door gave way with a whoosh. He welcomed the gardener, who had seen his plight and rushed over to help, scarcely slamming the door behind him before the knight's foot was in sight. Birsha wasted no time finding something to hold it shut.

A palm! The holy tree of goddess Ishtar, in Babylon. *The tree of Paradise.*

These most ludicrous of thoughts came to him as he pushed and shoved the giant planter into place along with the help of the gardener. Together, they shoved yet another palm—this time, a Phoenix palm—in place by the door. For good measure, they wedged a Chamaerops alongside the others.

Birsha didn't dare to breathe when he heard the knight rattle and lunge at the door again and again until at last he gave up and moved on.

"I must get to my father, get him to call off the Chessmen," Birsha told the gardener, a man in his early fifties who had been in his father's employ throughout all of Birsha's life.

"I know a back way," the gardener said with a knowing smile. "Come."

Birsha followed the man. He was a good man, both loyal and hardworking. And indeed, he did know a back way out. Why had Birsha never noticed before? A stairwell, hidden behind a hedge of fronds, led to an underground walkway that reached well into the garden, coming up in an equally unsuspecting location very near the large marble chess board, which had earlier housed the Chessmen, until they had been released by some strange magic that Birsha was unfamiliar with before today.

The marble board stood well above the snow, the four sides each containing stairs leading up to the marble slab so that visitors could look in awe at the majestic creatures who had seemed so lifelike before. Now they *were* alive by some odd sorcery. But they must be made to return to their rightful places, not running amok to play havoc with the fortress and all its inhabitants.

There, in the middle of a maze of topiaries that had always reminded Birsha of living green stones, sat the giant globe, Alaric waving a baton as though conducting an orchestra, the Chessmen his musicians. Each moved according to his orders.

A chill ran down Birsha's back, causing sweat to form on his upper lip and brow despite the wintry conditions. Had his father sent the knight to impale him? And if so, what could Birsha do to stop the man who wielded power from the afterlife, inside the globe which had so gamely encapsulated him?

"Send for the Order of the Jackals immediately!" Birsha ordered the gardener, who paused long enough to dip his head in acquiescence.

The man left at a fast clip as Birsha faced his father, who seemed only vaguely aware of his presence.

"Father!" Birsha moved to stand in front of Alaric so that he had nowhere to look but in Birsha's eyes. "Why are you doing this? Why did the knight just attack me?"

Alaric seemed to notice his son for the first time because he paused. In that moment, the thundering footfalls of the Chessmen paused too, as if waiting for the conductor to begin his orchestration anew. Alaric shook his head, as though waking from a trance.

"That was not my doing, son. Someone other than me was responsible for that magic, I'm afraid."

And yet the man who Birsha knew only from a distance seemed less than repentant, instead focused on the battle that he played out in his head inside the core of the globe.

"I repeat again, why are you doing this? Why are you keeping slaves, and in this weather?"

Alaric's eyebrows furrowed into an exact replica of his reverse widow's peak. "To wield power, you cannot allow your feelings to muddle your thinking. There is no place for emotion if you intend to win at all costs, and we must."

Birsha stood perfectly still, scarcely daring to breathe.

"But why? Why must you win at all costs?" Birsha asked, for the first time in his life, openly questioning the reasoning behind his father's decisions. "The Bookbinders have done nothing to you until today. They only came to rescue their people and to return them to their rightful homes. They were not the first to attack."

Alaric leaned forward, eyes blazing, laser beams of light causing the ground around Birsha to sizzle as the snow and ice melted, leaving him in a puddle of water several inches high. But he refused to back down.

"Because a strong leader believes in conquest! A strong leader leads by fear! A strong leader never backs down." He spoke this last part with a hiss.

Birsha knew then that he would never be safe as long as he stayed here. The Bookbinders were fighting to save their people, to be free from tyranny. To live in safety and security for their families. Alaric and the Jackals possessed none of those qualities.

They simply wanted power, land, and wealth, at any cost.

From the right flank, Birsha heard a commotion. The Order of the Jackals and their many guards had arrived, but appeared confused when they saw Alaric inside the globe.

"I want you to close the globe," Birsha commanded.

The Jackals looked from one to the others, the leader of the pack stepping forward to face the pair, both Birsha and his father.

"Whose order am I to take?" he asked, fear causing him to bare his teeth.

"Mine!" both Alaric and Birsha cried in unison.

"I have been named the ruler," Birsha growled, determined to win this round. The alternative was too frightening to contemplate.

The Jackal growled in turn, only his was low and menacing.

"I will do as you say," he said finally, "for now. But make no mistake about it, I will go to the Council and demand a decision from them. So be sure that you know what you are doing."

Birsha had no doubt that should he run afoul of the Council, his head would be on a spike, and yet he had to take the chance, before the kingdom was destroyed by Alaric's avarice and greed.

"Do as I have commanded. I will take the consequences, come what may." Then he turned to the gardener, who had returned with the Jackals and guards. "Please find the priest and meet me in the ballroom. I am to be wed in half an hour's time. It will be a private ceremony."

"Yes, m'lord." He bowed slightly. Then he was off to locate the priest.

"Now! Close up the globe," Birsha told the Jackals.

"No!" Alaric roared from inside the womb of his globe. "You can't do this to me. I'm your father and I command that you leave me to—"

Birsha gave the nod and before Alaric could continue with his tirade, the Jackals closed the globe to much screaming and blasphemy.

"If anyone needs me," Birsha said, "I will be with Beatrice in the ballroom." Then he turned on his heel and left.

To my surprise, we weren't headed for the front gate at all. Instead, the carriage bounded down one cobblestoned street after another, jostling us so much that Henry had to hang onto me so that I wouldn't go flying out the carriage door on an especially harrowing turn. Everywhere the coachman yelled a warning at the people darting to and fro to escape the Chessmen. The Jackals had also joined the fight at both the front gate and the western edge of the fortress where the slaves were kept working day and night. That left the east section unguarded, for the most part, our best chance of escape, by Nathaniel's reckoning.

"What's in the east?" I asked Nathaniel, who seemed to know more about the planning than either Henry or I.

Nathaniel offered a mirthless laugh. "The zoo."

"The zoo?" Henry and I cried in unison.

My heart sank at the idea. Would we be made to pass large creatures in order to escape? To my utter dismay, that's precisely what Nathaniel intended.

"Don't you think we'd have a better chance fighting our way out the front gate than facing lions and tigers, and heaven knows what else?" I asked.

Nathaniel smiled and sat back deeper into the cushioned seat.

Henry took my hand. "It will be okay. I'm sure he wouldn't take us somewhere dangerous."

And yet, by the looks of things, that's precisely what Nathaniel intended. I peered out the quarter glass and saw the ornate wrought iron gates with the word "Zoo" looming across the top of the gate in huge, flowery letters.

The clip-clop of the horses announced our entry into the zoo, large luminous cages on either side of our carriage bathed in the moonlight's blue glow, the snow on the ground making it appear more like the time just before dusk than well after midnight. Both Henry and I leaned as far as we could to see the animals that Alaric had procured for his zoo.

"What is that?" The eeriness set loose by this most unusual of nights caused me to shiver. For we weren't out of the woods just yet. Far from it.

"It's a quagga mare," Nathaniel explained, "one of the last of its kind. From Africa. It's said to be related to zebras, only it's missing its stripes on the back end."

"Hmm," I said, intrigued despite our difficult circumstances. "And what is that?" I asked, pointing to another cage with yet another oddity.

"Oh! That's a Tasmanian tiger." Nathaniel laughed. "Note the stripes on its back end, just opposite that of the quagga mare."

"But it has a dog's head." I narrowed my eyes to be certain I wasn't seeing things.

"That it does," Nathaniel agreed.

Just then, an ostrich poked its head through the metal fencing, so close to the carriage that I had to lean away to keep it from popping its head through our window and taking a nick out of me.

"They're just curious," Nathaniel explained. "But that's not why we're here."

"Why *are* we here?" Henry demanded, just as uncertain as I about Nathaniel's plan.

"*Be-cause*," Nathaniel said, drawing out the word, "your ride awaits."

"What ride?" I challenged, not at all certain I approved of what he had in store for Henry and me.

As if on cue, the carriage halted with a "whoa" from the driver and a shuffle of hooves from the horses. I peered out the quarter glass and saw a huge male bear standing upright, its paws on the bars as if preparing to make a jail break.

"You don't expect us to ride *that* bear." To his silence I added, "That's a *wild* bear."

"The other bears you rode were wild."

My heart hammered a rhythm in my chest because this bear, a grizzly by the look of it, was much larger than most of the bears we had worked with, and he seemed none too pleased to have been locked away behind bars by humans.

"Trust me, I wouldn't have brought you here if I didn't think it could be done. This bear was stolen from its mother at a young age, but it smelled the other bears. It will follow their scent."

"If it doesn't eat us first," Henry said, suddenly surly at the proposition.

"My thoughts exactly!" I agreed wholeheartedly.

"Well, it's this or the gaol, your choice."

I recalled the dark, dank interior of the gaol, the stench of that place, though the smell here was nearly as bad. Reluctantly, I took another look at the bear, who snarled and snorted, letting out one long bellow as if begging to be freed. I closed my eyes to gather my courage, then opened them. Then I turned to Henry.

"Ready, Henry?"

He paused, his nostrils flaring, then finally nodded. "Ready as I'll ever be. Let's do it."

From that point on, it was as if my mind had gone numb, from both the cold and abject fear, yet our choices were slim. I would take the only choice left open to me.

"Let's go."

Within ten minutes, the bear was free, though we had to do some clear bartering first. Unbeknownst to us, Nathaniel had brought with him a side of bacon, which the bear claimed happily before allowing us on its back. A saddle had been prepared ahead of time by some unknown hero behind the scenes. I hoped one day I could thank whoever had acted as our angel that day. Undoubtedly, many such angels.

I grabbed Henry's hand as he hoisted me onto the bear's back. Nathaniel gave Henry a foot up.

"God's speed!" Nathaniel said, giving the animal a pat on the rump.

To our amazement, the animal seemed to know instinctively which way to go to avoid detection and, within minutes, we were on the other side of the compound walls of the zoo. We fled through a back gate that Nathaniel had assured us was normally kept locked and heavily fortified. But this was not a normal night and most everyone was swarming the front gates and the western flank, where the attacks had begun. And though Nathaniel hadn't said, I guessed that he had paid a few people off or plied them with enough drink to keep them incapacitated while we made our escape.

Within moments, the bear was loping into the night, the moon and stars his only guide; that, and a nose made for tracking wild animals. Yet, here it was tracking its own kind, and I was grateful for it and for the freedom to be beyond the stifling walls of the fortress.

I leaned back, happy to feel Henry's warm embrace. He held me tight, his head on my shoulder, his eyes heavy from a day spent trying to survive.

"I love you, Henry Bookbinder," I said.

"I love you too, Brigid Anne Dunsmore," he replied. He kissed me softly on my cheek until we were safely away and could spare a moment for each other.

From my sleeve, I slipped out the round locket and felt a rush of love and loss to know that my family was so near and yet so far. With reverence, I placed the locket over my head in its rightful spot. Then I held it in the notch at the cleft of my neck. Though I desperately wanted to open it, to see my family after such a long absence, I waited. This was something I wanted to do when I was alone. Safe. Until then, it would have to wait.

31

We arrived at Battersbog to a hero's welcome. All around
us, throngs of people exited their homes to pay tribute to what
we had accomplished. Cries rang out as we passed, children
danced around their mothers' skirts. Fireworks were quickly set,
going off at intervals along with "oohs!" and "aahs!" Everywhere
those who had escaped were welcomed into the folds of the
community, arms open wide to enclose those who had been
without food and warmth for so long.

Within moments, the former slaves were being ushered
into house after house to gather their strength before the final
journey home, whereas the Oneida and Mohawk had headed
toward their winter camp, taking the most wounded with them
to heal before returning to their former lives. As for the elves,
the bears had taken them to their home in the trees. All others
had been brought here. Delaying not a moment longer, the

bears bid a hasty ado with a short motion of their heads and one paw up before departing to their home territories.

Among those who had arrived ahead of us, Winnifred was waiting for me and rushed out to greet me and Henry, as did Jocelyn and Gertrude, along with Yesimeh, Hannah, and the others. Emma and Thomas had already returned to the manor. Ma'am, whom I hadn't seen in ages, had taken time away from her busy schedule to bid us God's speed. She reached out to me as well, giving my hand a squeeze.

"I have to return to my own manor before my husband thinks I've gone missing," she said with a sardonic smile. "But I have just one thing to say—Brigid, Henry, Winnifred, and the rest of you—" She paused, taking us all in with what could only be identified as a mother's love. "A job well done." She winked. Then she climbed back onto the horse that stood at her side, gave one final nod to me and Henry, then spurred her horse on.

A clamor arose as we all reconnected and soon, Henry and I were pulled off the giant grizzly into the waiting arms of my brethren, the female warriors. Though their armor no longer shined like a newly minted half-penny, and they hadn't had a bath in days, they didn't complain. Instead, we did a dance, a *Valse à Deux Temps*, then switched to a circle dance, kicking up our heels for joy. By the time we were done, we were all laughing and crying and hugging each other.

It was then I saw Elijah and Dele off to one side, smiling. I quickly excused myself.

"What are you two doing here?" I asked, surprise an understatement. "I thought you would have escaped to Canada by now. That was your plan, wasn't it?"

The pair looked to each other with a combination of love and tenderness, then back at me.

"We thought about it," Dele said. "And we almost went through with it. But after witnessing such love and devotion to each other and the slaves, we just couldn't. It would have been like turning our backs on our ancestors and we couldn't do it. If you'll have us, we would like to stay. To fight. To prevent this from happening to other people like ourselves and our families."

I couldn't have said it better. I scooped them up into my arms, realizing how lucky I was to have such people in my life. Each and every one of them. These people and the slaves were why I had decided to fight. We didn't deserve this treatment. None of us did. And someday I would work to rid us of the traditions as well. Until those were gone, none of us would be safe. Healthy. Happy. Even in our own land.

They hugged me one more time, then took their leave, headed for their homes, eager to return to their own beds, as was I. That and a warm bath would just about complete things for me.

But as I returned to the merriment, I soon learned of those who hadn't been so fortunate to make it back alive. I personally blamed myself, though in war, I knew life was a luxury for the living. Still, it hit me hard and I allowed myself a few moments to grieve, as did the others.

We spent the night in town, people far and wide taking us in. Henry and I, as well as most of the women, stayed at The Langois' barn, as we had over a year ago. Ingrid ran out to greet me, determined that Henry and I should come to the farmhouse for dinner, along with Winnifred and Lofgren, where she and

Bernard fed us mutton stew and biscuits slathered in freshly churned butter. I would have felt guilty, had I not known the former slaves were just as well treated in town.

We talked and laughed and cried well into the night, until neither Henry nor I could keep our eyes open a second longer.

"Will you be leaving in the morning then?" Ingrid asked.

I told her that we would.

"Bless you, Henry and Brigid," she said, tears in her eyes. For everyone had lost someone to Alaric and his Jackals.

"It's the women you should be blessing," I said. "They made this happen. Winnifred and Lofgren too."

At that, Winnifred beamed. Then we all bid a hasty retreat to the barn, the stars shining through the loft window. Somewhere, out there, was my family. I might never see them again. I knew that now, but I would always remember them.

As everyone settled in for the night, I lay awake thinking back to that odd room beneath the fortress with its even stranger creatures. Who were they and what had they been doing in the bowels of the kingdom? I hoped that I would one day have my answer. Until then, I could only pause and wonder. In the meantime, I waited until the soft sound of snoring blanketed the loft.

With everyone fast asleep, I finally took out my locket as I had promised myself I would when I first escaped the fortress. I pushed the button and watched as it clicked open. Usually, I had chosen a time to return to, but this time I allowed my past to choose. What appeared was a warm night in July. The Fourth. We sisters and brothers were all strewn out on the back of a cart, blankets spread out for warmth. My parents sat on two hay bales holding hands, and together we watched the fireworks over Lake George. The water was awash in vibrant colors that skipped along the waves. Perhaps the earlier fireworks are what had brought this moment to mind. Tears formed as I recalled that night long ago, how happy we all were at that moment, never knowing that we would be torn apart by unsuspecting circumstances. I didn't care that the tears fell unheeded. Let them. How else was I to stamp out the darkness?

Few remained in the ballroom by the time Birsha had fetched Beatrice and brought her to the center of the room, but those who remained, gawked. All over the fortress, the sounds of screams had been replaced by an almost eerie silence that left Birsha feeling unfettered. But he was determined to be married tonight, no matter the circumstance.

"Where is the priest?" Birsha barked, looking to Siegfried for an answer.

From the far side of the room he heard the feeble cry, "Here!" The man came rushing toward them in robes, one arm raised, clearly roused from a night of tending the wounded and dead.

By the time the priest reached Birsha and Beatrice, he was panting and his long scraggly beard hung over his left shoulder. From inside the globe, Alaric had shouted and cursed until Birsha agreed to allow him at the wedding, but he only permitted the globe to be open if Alaric promised to remain silent throughout the ceremony. Alaric had reluctantly agreed.

And so, Birsha had ordered the Jackals to cart the globe into the ballroom. If not for the double-wide carriage doors, the globe might never have fit, but as luck would have it, they were able to squeeze it in. They turned a mahogany table on its back, its legs holding up the world, as it were.

"Is it true you plan to wed?" the priest asked.

His liturgical vestment was of the richest gold, an embroidered cross circumventing the back of the robe. He had worn the vestments to the ball to offer his blessings to Birsha and his reign prior to the festivities. Now, dirt and mud stained the hem, but it could not be helped. He would have to do, as Birsha was determined to marry Beatrice tonight. He turned to her.

In the soft glow of lamplight, he could see that she trembled. And yet her beauty was more apparent now than it had been upon first meeting her—her pale smooth skin, the black ringlets, the brilliant blue of her eyes like the finest blue diamonds. Her throat glistened with just a sheen of moisture, as though inviting him to that space, to kiss her neck, her lips, her . . . .

Birsha drew in a breath. Better not to go there yet. He would have all night with her. A lifetime, the gods permitting.

"Indeed, I need you to perform a wedding ceremony," Birsha told the priest.

"Tonight?" the priest demanded, clearly caught off guard.

"Do you have a problem with that?" Birsha asked, pinning him with a glare.

"N-no, sire. Not at all. It's just that with everything that's happened . . . I would have thought. Never mind," he said at last. "It's no bother."

He looked around as though searching for something to read out of, but in the end decided to go by memory. Yet, as he stood in front of the pair, Siegfried at Birsha's right, the old man said, "You sure you don't want to wait until the ceremony can be more . . . public?"

Though his words were measured, Birsha read in his expression the shock of such a breach of protocol. Still, Birsha refused to be swayed.

"If it pleases you," Birsha said, "we shall have a formal ceremony at a later date in which we will announce the official marriage, but for now, Do…As…I…Say!" Then he turned to the few remaining in the room and shouted, "And none of you shall reveal what has happened here tonight. Do I make myself clear?"

All nodded, fear evident in their eyes.

"Good, then you shall continue," he told the priest.

For the next ten minutes, the priest recited a rendition of the actual wedding ceremony, ending with: "and you shall give generously one to the other, help one another, until death do you part."

"We shall," Beatrice and Birsha said in unison.

Though the room encompassed one globe, Siegfried, several Jackal guards, and the stragglers left over from the earlier ball, Birsha only had eyes for Beatrice. He read the emotion playing in her almond shaped orbs and wondered at her thoughts. Had she come willingly to his home, to his hearth? Or was she simply doing whatever it would take to survive? He hoped it was the former.

"The ring."

Siegfried held out a ring he had found among the many artifacts he'd cataloged since Alaric's death, though death was a misnomer, in this particular case, Birsha realized with a wry glance toward the globe.

For his part, Alaric merely stroked his braided black goatee, his eyes never leaving the new woman in Birsha's life. Birsha wondered what his father thought of her…of him. Did he have any fatherly feelings at all toward him? It's a question he had often asked of himself, both as a child and as an adult. He hoped that he would break the chain of indifference. But could he, never having had family life modeled for him? He just knew that he wanted Beatrice by his side, wanted her to love him as no one had, during his lonely childhood spent in the orphanage and the rare snippets of time spent in his father's presence. He turned toward her, a catch in his throat.

"The ring?" Siegfried reminded him.

"Right." He inhaled deeply of her lovely fragrance, a cross between lilacs and frangipani.

Birsha lifted the ring from the velvet cushion Siegfried had thought to bring. It was beyond stunning and even Beatrice gasped at the sight of it. For, although it was blue in appearance, when the light caught it, it refracted into a myriad of jeweled colors that glanced off the walls.

As he placed it onto her ring finger, he repeated the priest's words: "With this ring, I thee wed."

Beatrice repeated it back to him, her eyes filling with tears. And for a moment, it was as if he could see into her soul and knew, *really knew*, that she was the one. And he could see that she knew it too. He didn't wait for the priest to say, "You may kiss the bride." Instead, he drew her into his arms and kissed her resoundingly, their tears commingling as one. When he pulled away, all the butterflies that graced her dress flew up and circled the pair, as if sanctioning the union. Then they settled back down, a few resting on her hair and his. They laughed. Together forever, at last. Birsha would remember this evening for a lifetime.

In the morning, we headed out to the manor. According to accounts, Emma and Thomas had left the day prior, eager to let the family know that they had survived and that soon all would be put to right. Henry and I said a hasty farewell to the women, who were just as eager as we to return to their rightful homes. Phinney had found us and was now flapping happily ahead of us, chirping all the while.

As we rode, I felt love in my heart for all the women who had so willingly sacrificed their time and their souls for such a worthy cause, some losing their lives in order to save others. A lump formed in my throat at the thought. Though I longed for peace, I hated to leave the women behind. They had become a true source of sisterhood and friendship, and they had eased the loneliness of abandonment in these harshest of times.

I peered at Henry, who rode beside me. "Do you suppose Beatrice will be alright?"

I had hated leaving her with Birsha and his ilk, and yet, Beatrice and the new ruler had an obvious connection. But what sort of man was he? Would he end up like his father, filled with hatred and the desire for conquest? I shivered at the thought.

"Somehow, I have the feeling that Beatrice will land on her feet," Henry said, taking my hand in his as we rode side by side.

"Hmm. Maybe you're right."

Up ahead was the manor. It filled me with equal parts excitement and dread, for I would never be an equal there. I would always be a woman with clearly defined roles . . . none of my choosing. And then there were the traditions. A cloud of sadness enveloped me, and I squeezed Henry's hand, wanting these last few moments together to never end.

Henry halted the horses with a pull on his reins and the word "Whoa." Then, he turned to me.

"There's something I've wanted to say to you for a while," he said, taking me in with hooded eyes.

"What?" I asked, wondering where this was leading.

"I don't want us to be apart anymore. Where you go, I go, and where I go, you go. Things will be different from now on."

"Oh, Henry!" I cried, nearly falling from my horse as I leaned over to kiss him.

He returned the kiss, just as eager as I to be one at last. We stayed like that for some time, neither wanting to be the first to part, but it couldn't be helped. Reluctantly, he pried me loose so that he could look at me again.

"I'll speak to my parents as soon as we return. Agreed?"

"Agreed!" I said through tears.

Just then, we saw people waving and soon the entire family and staff came out to greet us. One of the staff helped us down from our mounts, while Henry's father rushed to wrap him in a bearhug. Lady Bookbinder did the same with me. Soon we were all talking, awash in laughter at the many harrowing tales. Emma and Thomas took their turns hugging each of us. At last, Lady Bookbinder urged us to go upstairs and wash for dinner. I was only too eager to oblige.

Once inside, I took the stairs two by two, Phinney staying behind for the treats Emma offered. When I opened the door to my room, there stood my precious loom, the loom that had started me on my journey. I bent down to greet it like an old friend. It was then I remembered the precious thread Beatrice had bestowed on me. A reminder that she would be with us in memory.

I smiled, recalling her sacrifice. Maybe she had changed after all. I pulled the sparkling threads from the purse she'd sent with me. The threads were beautiful, made of the finest silk, and in rich jewel tones that, when caught by the light, shifted color.

"Here goes," I told the loom, having never before tried my hand at weaving, at least not since I was a child.

I wondered what a magical loom would do with such finery, what it would show me. I had only moments to learn the answer. For when I began to weave, pulling out the weft so that I could thread the shuttle through it, my feet dancing the loom as they had when I was a child, a lovely pattern appeared. My heart leaped with joy at the sight of it, as though indeed I was once again a small girl.

But then, something happened. Something that I could never have foreseen. Something that made my heart leap with fear.

"W-what is going on?" I whispered.

The tapestry on the loom had darkened to nearly a coal black, and sparks began to play across the weave, a few at first, then more and more, until it was fairly dancing with sparks, the sound of them filling the room.

My breath came in short bursts, my eyes wide with confusion.

"I don't understand," I murmured. "How can this be happening?"

But the loom gave a large crackle, as though set on fire, and then came the first of the *TH-WUMPS!*, like the footlights on a stage being extinguished. The light in my room cast lower, along with the daylight outdoors. From outside my window, I heard cries of fright, as though an eclipse had garnished the sun's rays. Another *TH-WUMP!* Again, it was as though stage lights had been lowered, only it was happening all around the countryside. Confused cries heralded from downstairs, causing my knees to quiver.

More sparks shot out of the loom, sending a shower of them cascading onto the carpet. And then came the final *TH-WUMP!* and the lights of my world were extinguished for good as though by a total eclipse of the sun. My whole body began to shake and I could hear an outpouring of cries from every corner of the manor and beyond.

"Oh, Dear God, what have I done?" I cried.

But the world had fallen into darkness.

"I have to find a way to undo this!" I whispered. "To bring back the light."

If only I had the power. I balled my fists. Hate had caused this, I thought bitterly. The same hate that had given us Alaric and the Jackals. But the only *real* power was love. I knew that now. Slowly, I unclenched my fists.

"I must find a way to fix this," I murmured. "To make us whole again, no matter how long it takes."

The *world* whole again.

A voice played in the breeze coming through the window. A voice I knew only too well—the voice of the wind goddess. The words eased my fear, and suddenly peace settled over me like a warm mantle.

Without love we are nothing, she said.

But I did have love. I fingered my locket tenderly, and then peered toward the open doorway of my bedroom. Though I could see little in the ascending gloom, I knew that Henry loved me, as well as the Bookbinders, and the heroic women I had met and fostered. Now, I just had to figure out how to push back the darkness. For us, for our children, and for future generations to come. Furthermore, we must find a way to survive. To beat back the terror. To hunker down to await a new day. One far better than the evil that swirled around us here. Until then, we could only wait, hope, and pray that a new day would dawn for *all* of us.

ACKNOWLEDGEMENTS

Writing is never done in a vacuum. Fortunately, writers have much to draw from, especially in today's ever-changing world. I have been fortunate to count friends and family, as my readers, as well as many authors, agents and clients who have taught me much about the writing process over the past twenty-plus years. They have shared their joys, their challenges and their friendship. I appreciate each and every one of them.

People who have helped me in untold ways are Darrin Brenner, whose book covers always give me a thrill and whose poster art is first rate. Thanks go to Sara Rolat, editor and interior designer. I love the addition of the butterflies! Jenna and Koda the Fluff, whose video of my book brings a smile to my face and whose nonprofit agency provides training videos for teenage drivers as well as aid to police officers and firemen in the greater Florida area. Danish from Fiverr who created a video that gave my previous book star power. My thanks go to Amanda from Fiverr who helped to promote my books through NetGalley, and NetGalley.uk.

I would be remiss if I didn't mention author Carmen Peone, who has a long list of wonderful books, including her new one, *Captured Secrets,* and who kindly offered a review of my novel, *Dancing the Loom.* To Karen Weaver, who read my books and gave me really heart-felt reviews and who is a writer in her own right. Jane Kirkpatrick, whose historical novels fill my shelves and who gave my previous novel a wonderful review. To Valerie Brooks who always offers great advice and writes super atmospheric crime noir novels. Thanks to Evan Howard who read and reviewed my book and whose own book, *The Galilean Secret,* came on the heels of the Dan Brown novels. Also on his docket is a new project to end gun violence in schools by creating a musical that he will take to the schools in an effort to get kids and parents talking about how to resolve this very important issue in our time. Please go to his GoFundMe site if you find it in your heart to help him with his cause.

Thanks also go to medical thriller author, Candy Calvert, who kindly read and reviewed my previous novel. To Nikki Arana, a gifted writer and friend. Her books are not to be missed. Grace Castle, whose book brought to life the theft of ancient Indian burial grounds. Danuta Pfeiffer whose stunning memoir laid bare the life of a broadcast journalist who co-hosted *The 700 Club* along with Pat Robertson and who now, along with her husband Robin, owns Pfeiffer Winery.

And of course to my family. My husband, Les, my rock, who helps me find time to work on my own projects. To Sara, who makes me laugh and brings her dad and me countless hours of joy. Plus she reads my books! To Kaylee, who lights up a room any time she walks into it. And to their significant others, James and Owen. Thanks and love.

Threading the Loom:
Reading Group Guide

In this reading group guide for Threading the Loom, I have included an introduction, questions for discussion, concepts for enhancing your reading experience, and a Q & A with the author, Carol Craig. Hopefully, the questions will help spur new ideas for your reading group so that your book club will evolve to more in-depth discussions. We also hope that the ideas that flow will provide a more meaningful and enriching experience. Enjoy!

Introduction

In this captivating novel filled with magic and intrigue, nineteen-year-old Brigid Anne Dunsmore has lost everything: her home, her family, and any sense of security she ever possessed. Her family has been thrown to the winds, and now Brigid is little more than a scullery maid holed up in a stuffy attic of a large manor. She has no hope of ever changing her circumstances until one day, she discovers a loom, and not just any loom. A loom from her childhood. A magical loom that foretells the future. Whoever owns it, owns the kingdom. But one man wants it and will stop at nothing to get it.

The loom warns Brigid that the kingdom is in peril, and that only she and a man she has yet to meet can save it. Thus begins her journey to put together an all women's army to save her kingdom and the people she has come to love.

Threading the Loom is a story of love, friendship, and sisterhood in a time of deep strife. It reminds us what it means to be human, under the worst of circumstances.

Discussion Questions
and Topics

1.   This novel contains both elements of History and Fantasy. Why did Carol Craig choose to mix the two? She also opted for a more stylized form of writing used near the turn of the previous century. Was this a conscious choice and if so, why? What does it add to the story at its emotional core?

2.   What does the loom represent in terms of society and our current means of connecting to each other? And why "dancing" the loom? The loom can foretell the future, but the future can also be changed. Can our future really ever be changed, or do certain cosmic laws clearly define our lives ahead of time? In other words, are we coded at birth by genetics to follow only one path or are we totally independent of it? Or are we a combination of both genetics and world experience?

3.   Why does Brigid find the traditions so loathsome? How can Brigid feel such a deep connection to the people around her and the country she's fighting for, and yet hate the traditions of her people and want to end those traditions? Do we as citizens have a right to work for change, or by

385

countering the narrative, are we being unpatriotic?

4.   Why does Carol Craig use nature as magic? How does nature play a part in our own lives, and what happens when we become disconnected to nature?

5.   Brigid could easily leave it up to other people to take on the fight. Why does she choose to take up the mantle to protect her people? And why does she decide on an army of women rather than men, or an army of both men and women in equal measure?

6.   How does Brigid's style of leadership affect the women in her group? Why are some women, like Winnifred, arch supporters of Brigid, whereas Beatrice and a few others are not?

7.   Alaric represents those despots in history who rule through iron-clad decree without any input from his people. In effect, a totalitarian dictatorship. What happens when a country no longer has the right to free speech or open dissent? Can there be too much free speech? Where is the balance?

8.   Birsha is both similar in ways to his father, and quite different in other ways. Compare the two men and what that represents for the kingdom going forward.

9.   Through no fault of her own, Brigid makes a terrible mistake at the end of the second novel in the series and weaves the beautiful thread into the loom.

How do we unwittingly feed the dark side, and can we fight the darkness and ever hope to win in these times when divisions have been amplified?

10.   At the end of the story, the wind comes to Brigid and reminds her that "Without love, we are nothing." How can we as people fight hate in a time when it is so freely disseminated? Can we ever restore the light, or do light and darkness go hand in hand? Most importantly, can humans ever evolve in time to save our planet?

Boost Your Book Club Experience

1.   Try your hand at a loom. It's amazingly therapeutic and is a great reminder that we are all part of the fabric of life. Design your own book club flag. Then post it on my Editing Gallery, LLC Facebook page.

2.   The hologram locket filled with family memories was important to Brigid. Share your family photos of events that were important in your life and tell the others in your book club why they were so meaningful.

3.   Nature plays an important role in The Tapestry Series. Design a terrarium, a microcosm of the world you would like to see. What is unique about your design? What message would you like to convey with your design? Then take a picture of your creation and post it on my Editing Gallery, LLC Facebook page.

4.   If your book club were like the women in
Brigid's army, what would your armor look like? Draw
a picture, creating your own unique design, and if
there are sewers in the group, you could even try your
hand at creating a prototype. Then let's post it on my
website!

A Conversation with Carol Craig

Why did you choose the title Dancing the Loom for your first book of the series?

In almost all of my books, I come up with a tantalizing title and then sleep on it for days. Then suddenly I wake up one morning and an idea is sparked while I was sleeping. The same was true for *Dancing the Loom*. I watched a PBS show about a family from Central America who came from a long line of weavers. Their feet danced the pedals. I loved that imagery and with it, the title Dancing the Loom was born.

You use the loom as a magical element in this story. What sparked the idea and what does the loom represent?

As a child, my family owned a loom, and like my protagonist, I don't recall where it came from or why we no longer owned it. It simply was gone one day. There's a certain magical element to childhood. I realized quickly that the loom represented not only our past, but the future. It also symbolizes our connection to each other as a society, that we are all part of the fabric that makes up a community. To take that even further, it represents the future. Computers, like looms, weave together people from many disparate nations. Our fingers dance "the loom" if you will. Computers both unite us and divide us. Our future is written in that loom. It can be one of great strength, or something that destroys the very fabric of society through the use of misinformation, racism, misogyny, bullying, and outright criminality. If we don't pay attention to that, we may end up like Brigid does at the end of Threading the Loom, unwittingly feeding the darkness.

Why did you choose Fantasy as your genre of choice in this novel?
Fantasy allowed me to blend many threads of life, both from the past, from the present, and from the future. It allowed me to showcase the family, and how, during times of strife we often lose that very basic connection. Furthermore, totalitarian governments often divide the family as a means of controlling the individual. Fantasy also allowed me to expose how nature can be used as a weapon when we don't honor it and protect it. Or when we use the aftermath of nature's

destruction to exploit those who are affected by it. Our future relies on our connections to each other and our protection of nature. The more we become divided, the more easily we are manipulated by the darkness. So these books are basically an exploration into how we feed the light, while minimizing the darkness.

You introduce a wide variety of characters. Why did you choose to add Native Americans and former slaves into the story, as well as a half-elf, half-human?

I chose to add marginalized people to the women's army because for centuries, women have been marginalized. They could not own their own property, could not vote, could not get loans, and were only allowed menial jobs in the workforce. What better way to keep women in chains? In my lifetime, women had to ask permission from their husband to obtain a charge card, and then it came in the husband's name. This happened to me. Teachers were no longer allowed to teach once they were married. My mother-in-law was forced to give up her job as a teacher in a one-room schoolhouse in Nebraska when she married. Women were basically the chattel of their husbands. Fortunately, life has improved for many women, but

the clarion call to take us back into the past has been
raised. We are witnessing it firsthand in the many
misogynist policies taking place in our country. We
have only to look at the lack of leadership positions
by women or minorities in many areas of industry.
Other groups of people have suffered the same
marginalization. Our voices are stronger as a unit than
separately.

**How did Brigid's character change throughout the
book?**

In the beginning, Brigid could see no way out of her
life as a scullery maid in a great manor. Her options
were few. Until she discovered the magical loom,
her life was on a trajectory of living alone, doing
menial labor until the day she died, with little hope
of reconnecting with her family. Once she found the
loom, she still had the option of selling it or staying
in the comfort zone of the life she was living, though
there was little comfort to be had. She chose to see it
through. That led to an adventure, and to her learning
about "the traditions" that plagued those in the manor.
It also led to her discovering that dark forces were out
to destroy her people. For the first time in her life, she
became aware of the darkness. But instead of falling

in line, accepting the traditions and simply becoming a cog in the wheel of the machine that ran the manor, she chose to rise above it, to try to change things both at home and abroad, as it were. If she had accepted the traditions, she would forever remain subservient to men and forced into roles not of her choosing. Her options in life would be limited indeed. She would no more escape the traditions than she could escape that attic unless she did something to change it. So, she risks her life to make a difference. Fortunately, other women who feel as she does join her. One woman alone can't save a nation and change things for the better. But together, they stand a chance to improve the lives of their daughters and granddaughters for generations to come. That is Brigid's hope when she sets out on this journey.

What are you working on now?
I am revising a sequel to *A Thousand Bits of Wonderful* from my Mending Warriors Series. Its title is *A Walk in the Dark* and has a bit of a mystery and a ghostly element about it. Like *A Thousand Bits of Wonderful*, *A Walk in the Dark* deals with the real trauma vets face when they return from war-torn areas like Iraq or Afghanistan. It also deals with service dogs and the

perils they experience when putting their lives on the line for humans. It reflects on their disposability and our responsibility to these animals for all they have done for us and our country. At the same time, I am working on the third book in The Tapestry Series. Its working title is *Restoring the Loom*. In this novel, Alaric is restored to his place of power, pushing Birsha aside and making his position in the kingdom more tenuous. Alaric is angrier than ever that he has been shunted aside and is out for revenge. This time he's taking it to the manor. Brigid has her work cut out for her because she made the horrible mistake of threading the loom and unwittingly inviting the darkness into their kingdom. Now she must help to restore the light even as she endures a new onslaught from Alaric, a potentially much more dangerous one that will test her skills and wit.

Do you have an idea for the end of the series?
I do. It's one that has been lodged inside me for many years. It will take us into the future, but that's all I can divulge for now. It allows me to bring in the history of movements for change and how one person, along with many, can become the catalyst to make things better for all of us. So I leave my readers with this:

What one small thing can you do, right where you are, to create positive change that will help even one person today? My greatest hope is that we will stop this culture of bullying that now afflicts our nation, and which was the impetus for "the traditions." We do it in the name of helping to make people better by pointing out flaws from birth until death. It helps no one. And in fact, I guarantee that it is the main reason for the unprecedented rates of alcoholism, drug addiction, depression, suicide, and gun violence in our schools and elsewhere. Imagine a world where bullying is not only no longer encouraged, but not tolerated. What a better world we would leave to our children and grandchildren, and to future generations to come.

www.ingramcontent.com/pod-product-compliance
Lightning Source LLC
Chambersburg PA
CBHW011124190726
48289CB00012B/2900